Pearl Cosindas
#328

To Karen,
Best wishes +
I hope you enjoy
my book!
Ann Mullen

WHAT YOU SEE

A JESSE WATSON MYSTERY

Ann Mullen

This book is a work of fiction. Any characters portrayed, living or dead are imaginary. Any resemblance to actual persons is completely coincidental. Any places, business establishments, locales, events, or incidents in this book are the product of the author's imagination, or used fictitiously.

AFTON RIDGE PUBLISHING
P.O. 162
Stanardsville, Virginia 22973

ISBN: 0-9725327-2-2

This book was printed in the United States of America—
land of the free, home of the brave.

Book designed by Designer's Ink

Library of Congress Control Number: 2003090476

I LAID THERE FOR WHAT SEEMED LIKE AN ETERNITY. The air had become hot and humid from the late afternoon rain. My knee was throbbing and the cut on my forehead was still bleeding. I held my breath as I crouched down, hiding in the damp leaves and the tangled mass of underbrush. Coming here alone was a stupid mistake... possibly the last one I would ever make. There was a killer on the loose in the woods and he was searching for me.

Then I heard a twig snap...

This book is dedicated to Wendy, Tommy and Tom.

CHAPTER 1

O NCE IN AWHILE you come across something that really catches your eye. But, beware, what you see is not always what you get, and what you get is not always what you want. My mother taught me that when I was a kid. Bless her heart, to this day; she has a saying that applies to everything under the stars. As a matter of fact, she comes up with some stuff that just baffles my mind. It makes you wonder if parents sit around all day and think up things just to confuse you. Don't they have other things to do?

I'm getting ahead of myself. Let me start from the beginning. My name is Jessica Watson. My friends call me Jesse. My childhood was like any normal childhood, with the exception of being fortunate enough to have the same two parents. Nowadays, not many kids grow up with a mom and a dad, especially ones that are happy and create a good home life. I'm not saying everything was perfect, but it was about as good as it gets. I have an older brother, Jack, and a younger sister, Claire. Jack is a lawyer and Claire is married, with two kids, a house, and a new Mercedes. That says it all. They grew up and met all the expectations of our parents, while I just grew up. I think I did, however, sometimes I wonder. I'm thirty-one years old and have never been married. I've done my share of dating, but my luck with men is like my luck with jobs—pitiful. The right job hasn't come along and Mr. Right hasn't shown himself. I haven't given up; I've just quit looking.

Like my brother and sister, I was born and raised in Newport News, Virginia. We call it Tidewater because it is part of several cities located on a small peninsula on the east coast, that boast of great fishing and hunting. You either made a living doing one or the other, or you worked in the shipyard where boats were overhauled. I don't think any of those challenging careers alone was the lifeline of our city. We also have Langley Air Force Base, Fort Eustis, Fort Monroe, Camp Peary, and the Norfolk Naval Base, where my dad, Mack was last stationed until he retired a year ago. Upon his retirement, he decided it was time to leave what was now an overgrown city, and move to a quiet place a little less populated. My mom, Minnie, was ready to do anything that he wanted.

Somewhere along the way, Mom and Dad finally found the place they wanted to live. They bought a house in the mountains located in a little town called Stanardsville, Virginia, thirty miles the other side of Charlottesville. I never thought they would actually pack up and leave until I got the call from them saying they had found that perfect place they were looking for and wanted me to go with them to see it.

I found it hard to accept the fact that the home we had all shared was going to be sold and there would be nothing left except the memories. Claire and her family lived in Washington, D.C., Jack lived in Fairfax, and now, Mom and Dad would be living in a little cabin in the woods, leaving me to be the only one left in our hometown. It made me feel so alone. I tried to comfort myself by the knowledge that at least we all lived within a few hours of each other. I could see this was going to be a major adjustment.

Saturday, as I was sitting around the house indulging myself in self-pity and trying to get my laundry done, the phone rang.

"Hello," I said.

"Hi, honey. This is your mom. I just wanted to see if next weekend would be a good time for you to go with us to see the house. We're planning to stay overnight. Oh, I just know you're going to love it. As I've said before, if you want to, you could move in with us. There's plenty of room."

How many times is she going to tell me that? I thought, but didn't say. Instead, all I said was, "Sure, next weekend will be fine. When are you leaving?"

"We'll be leaving on Friday. Why don't you come over after work and we can leave right after you get here?"

"I'll be there," I said, and continued to listen as she went on and on about the house, the mountains, and how much I was going to love it. "Ok, Mom, I'll see you Friday."

I hung up the phone and went back to the task at hand—laundry. I hated doing laundry. I really hated doing laundry when I was depressed.

Friday came all too soon, and the next thing I knew, we were on our way. The closer we got to our destination, the more I understood how my folks felt. I had forgotten how beautiful the mountains of Virginia are. Dad had taken us camping on the Skyline Drive several times when we were kids, until Mom had finally had enough of tents and the great outdoors... putting an end to our frolicking in the woods.

The weekend turned out to be very interesting. Mom was right. I loved the house. It wasn't as big as the one in Tidewater, but it wasn't the little cabin in the woods I had expected. It was just like one of the country homes you see in magazines. The structure was a Cape Cod design featuring a wrap-around porch, and I couldn't believe how far off the ground the house stood.

"Well, I guess you don't have to worry about floods, huh?" I asked.

"Exactly," Dad replied. "That was the whole purpose."

The minute I stepped onto the front porch, a swarm of flying insects attacked me. "What in the world was that?" I screamed, as I swatted at the flying pests. "Oh, yuck... beetles."

"They're not beetles, they're ladybugs. They won't hurt you. Just knock them off," Mom replied.

Dad went on to explain, "It seems some years ago, the Dept. of Agriculture released millions of them to eat the Gypsy Moths that were killing off the Oak trees. As many as there are of them, it must be working."

"I hope so. However, I think they have reproduced to the point where you'll have to wear bee's netting to be able to be outside without having them land in your face and hair and who knows where else." This was just too much. I couldn't stand it any longer. "Let's go inside," I said, as I listened to them fly into the outside walls. "Do you have to put up with this all the time?"

Mom looked at me like I was such a child. Imagine this attitude coming from a woman who couldn't stand camping, sleeping on the ground, cooking meals over an open fire, and dealing with insects and animals that you only come across while you are in the woods. Yet, she was born and raised in North Carolina, the daughter of a tobacco farmer—a long line of tobacco farmers. We won't go there. There are some things in my past history that I don't want to get into. I will tell you that my grandfather was a major player as a *Tobacco Lord*. He paid his people twenty-five cents and hour, the going rate at the time, and treated them like they were dirt. They were his "niggers" and weren't worth a dime. I still get mad every time I remember hearing him say stuff like that. He's been dead for twelve years now, the unfortunate victim of something he ate—his shotgun. What does that tell you?

"Mr. James, the previous owner, said they only get bad like this in the early spring and late fall. By the way, Mr. James is a very interesting man," Mom said, as I knocked off the remaining ladybugs and went inside the house.

The inside was just as warm and cozy feeling as the outside. Fortunately, I didn't see any of those nasty creatures lurking around. The living room had shiny hardwood floors that led into a kitchen and dining room, which was one big open area with a pass-through bar separating the living room from the kitchen. Off to the right of the dining area was a utility room. In between the living area and master bedroom to the left was a spare bath. The master bedroom had a private bathroom, walk-in closet and the biggest floor space for a bedroom that I have ever seen, except, maybe in the movies. I was impressed. You could almost fit my two-bedroom duplex apartment into this room. It had a fireplace just like the one in the living room, constructed with some of the many mountain rocks I saw lying all over the place outside. Dad claims this land was a riverbed at one time. You could dig forever and still come up with nothing but rocks. That must be why piles and piles of rocks surround all the flowerbeds. I do notice some things. It was early spring. You couldn't miss all the flowers beginning to bloom.

As Mom was leading me upstairs to show me the rest of the house, she went into her usual mode of explaining everything in great detail. "As I was saying, the previous owner, Mr. Tobias James, Jr., was the son of Mr. Tobias James, Sr. and Anna James. Together all three of them built this house when Tobias, Jr. was a teenager. When Tobias, Sr. and Anna eventually passed away, Toby and his wife, Carol, who was expecting their first child, moved into the house. They lived happily ever after until a couple of years ago. It seems his wife couldn't live out here in the middle of nowhere any longer and packed up the three kids they had by then and left. I'm sure there's probably more to it, but that's all he said. Says he's moving to Florida. Anyway, here we are!"

"It is a fine place to be," I said, as I was checking out the rooms and making conversation. There were two large bedrooms and a full bathroom in between, with a hallway big enough to set up a table and eat dinner. This was not bad at all. If you were going to live in the mountains, this would be the perfect house.

"Well, Minnie," which is what I called her sometimes when I wanted to get one of those happy, yet confused looks on her face, "I think you and Dad will be very happy here. It's lovely. Now show me the kitchen, I'm starved and I know you must have something to eat because I saw a cooler in the back of the mini-van. By the way, are we going to sleep here tonight?"

"Yes, and we brought sleeping bags," she smiled and said.

I've been camping. I can handle this.

SATURDAY MORNING I AWOKE to the glorious smell of coffee, a stiff neck, and something crawling on my arm.

"Mom, I thought you said these things wouldn't come in the house!" I screamed as I brushed it off and started to crawl out of the bag. I looked down and saw a dozen more. "Oh, no," I said to myself.

Mom walked into the living room and handed me a cup of coffee.

"For someone as old as you are you sure can act like such a baby. Let's have our coffee on the porch. Your dad is sitting out in the swing."

As we walked onto the porch I expected to be attacked again by some of those things that seemed to have taken a liking to me, but instead, I was treated to a cool spring breeze and the sweet smell of flowers. I sat down on the steps and looked up at the sky.

"*What is that sound*? Is that water running I hear?"I asked.

"Yes," Dad replied. "That's the South River you hear. Across the road, on the front part of our property is a stream. After we finish our coffee we'll walk over and check it out and then I'll take you on a tour of the property."

Ten acres is a lot of property to check out. By the time we got back to the house I was exhausted, not to mention the creepy feeling I had that I might be taking a tick or some other creature back to Tidewater with me.

Since none of us were big on breakfast we had an early lunch of sandwiches and iced tea. As we sat on top of our sleeping bags and ate, I watched the two of them chat and carry on like two young lovers. I sure was going to miss not seeing them all the time. They have always been so happy together and so much fun to be around.

Once the kitchen was cleaned and our gear packed we headed back home. For most of the trip they talked about what they were going to do with all their extra furniture—store it, or give it away—and how they were going to decorate the new house. Somewhere in the middle of the conversation, I dozed off and didn't wake again until we were pulling into the driveway.

"Have a nice rest, dear?" Mom asked. "All that walking must have really worn you out. Look, Mack, isn't that Claire's car? What's she doing here? She knew we were going to be gone, and didn't know what time we would be back. Something must be wrong. She never comes for a visit without calling first."

Mom jumped out of the mini-van and ran to the house in search of Claire, as Dad and I crawled out and began the task of unloading our things.

"Let me put my bag in my car and I'll help with the rest," I told Dad, knowing full well that Mom was going to be tied up listening to whatever exciting things Claire would have to say. Claire always had something wonderful going on. I could almost imagine it word for word: *"I've been selected as the new President of the PTA; the kids are perfect as always; Carl got a promotion and a big, fat raise; we're buying an even bigger house; and we're going to have another baby. Isn't it all wonderful?"* My sister doesn't gloat, but she has a way of saying things that makes me want to crawl under a table and hide. She has it all, and I don't have squat. Am I jealous? Maybe just a little. Why do some people get it all and some never get anything? My green-eyed dragon reared its jealous head.

I put all my jealous rivalry and nasty thoughts aside and helped Dad unload the contents of the van. The house was already starting to look like the deserted shell it was going to be. Boxes were stacked along the walls; the Persian rug was rolled up; and newspapers and empty boxes were scattered everywhere. Where was the sofa and chairs?

Lucinda, the housekeeper, met me as I walked in and said, "You must go be with your sister." Her tone let me know things were not cozy in paradise. "She has bad news, and your mama and papa are going to be very sad. Oh, things are not well." Lacy, as I always called her, was Puerto Rican and most of the time I couldn't understand half of what she was saying especially when she was excited. She walked away speaking to herself and then turned to me and said, "Tell your mama the movers will be here first thing Monday morning instead of Tuesday."

I was thrown for a loop. I couldn't figure out why there were packing all this stuff so early. Then it dawned on me that they weren't wasting any time. This move was happening ASAP. They hadn't even sold the house and they were already out the door.

I followed the sound of voices to the den. Mom and Claire were seated on the couch, one of the few remaining pieces of furniture left in the room, and Claire was crying. Mom had her arm around her, trying to lend comfort, in a way that mothers do best.

Trying not to upset Claire further by jumping right in on the conversation, I looked at Mom and calmly whispered, "Lacy said to tell you the movers will be here Monday instead of Tuesday."

To my astonishment, Claire jumped up and screamed, "Who cares about movers? Don't you realize my whole life is falling apart and all you can think about are movers? Whatever happened to *'How are you? Gee, I missed you. How are the kids? How's Carl?'* I can tell you how Carl is. He's having an affair... that's how Carl is. It's probably that blond bitch that works in his office. Little witch, I'll kill her and him, too! Carl's having an affair and I'm pregnant."

I felt like someone had just punched me in the gut. I didn't know what to say. This news was definitely not what I had expected and I couldn't believe my sister was using that kind of language. I don't think Claire has ever uttered a curse word in her whole life, so this must be serious. And she was going to have another baby! Didn't she have enough? When is it going to be my turn?

"Calm down, honey. I'm sure you must be mistaken," Mom said in her usual, *Everything is going to be fine* voice.This could reassure even the saddest child, that even though it was broken, it could always be fixed or replaced. Moms... you've got to love them.

I sat down on the floor, looked up at Claire and said, "I hate to say this Claire, but if you think something is amiss it probably is. Have you come across any clues? He must be acting differently or doing something out of the ordinary or you wouldn't suspect him of cheating. Tell us the details and we'll try to put your mind at ease or at least help you figure out what you can do about it. Claire, where are the kids?"

"Oh, they're upstairs taking a nap. They were so tired from the trip, Lucinda fixed them a snack and sent them to bed," she said, losing herself in thought for a minute, and with the stamina of a race horse getting its second wind, she blurted out to Mom, "What about Lucinda? Is she going to stay on with you and Dad when you move to the mountains?"

"No," Mom replied. "She's going to go live with her daughter."

"Not to beat a dead horse, but what is the deal with you and Carl?" I asked Claire. "Mom could be right. Maybe you're mistaken. Maybe your hormones are way out there, somewhere in that all too familiar place we call the *OZONE*. You told me on several occasions that being pregnant make your hormones go into orbit. Why should it be any different this time? Come back to me with proof and I'll help you to nail the rat."

I laughed out loud. Mom and Claire looked at me as if I had lost my mind. What can I say? I'm not the most perfect person. I don't have all the answers. When something smells bad, I've learned that it most likely is bad. I didn't know what to do or say, but I did know that someone here had to get it together. Face it—people tell lies... people steal... and people cheat. That's life, unfortunately.

"Listen, Claire," I said in the best tone I could muster up, "I have to get going. I need to do some paperwork, check my roommate's dog to make sure she hasn't wet everything in sight and see if Becky is still my roommate. Maybe she's run off again to reconcile with that jerk of a boyfriend, Tim, like she has many times before—usually when the rent is due. Whatever I can do to help, let me know and I'll be there for you. I'm not trying to make light of what's happening to you. I'm sorry, but until you can tell me something concrete I'll have to agree with Mom. Perhaps you're just whacked out right now and you're not being rational."

"I found receipts. I mean, I wasn't snooping or anything. I was getting his suit and shirts together to go to the cleaners and when I went through the pockets I found a receipt from West Florist and one from Victoria's Secret. I haven't gotten any flowers or sexy underwear since I can't remember when," she stammered, tears spilling down her cheeks.

"Ah, sweetie, don't cry. Everything's going to be fine. I just know it is. Go home, take some time to think this over, and if you still feel this way in a couple of days, call me and we'll go from there. Ok?" I asked.

"Oh Jesse, you think I could be wrong? I mean, Carl is a good husband and father. He's never done anything before to make me think he was interested in anyone but me. He's always telling me how much he loves the kids and me, and how happy we make him. You are right. I'm going to do just that." She looked at Mom and asked, "Is it ok if the kids and I stay here tonight?"

"Of course it is, dear."

"Now that everything's under control, I really do have to get going. Claire, call me if you need me. Mom, thanks for the grand tour. I love your new home and can't wait to visit again. I guess I'll see you guys later." I gave both of them a hug and kiss and said my good-byes. I saw Dad on the way out. "Everything's going to be fine. I'm headed home. Thanks for everything." I gave him my usual peck on the cheek and yelled to Lacy, "Bye, Lacy." I didn't wait for a reply.

Backing out of the driveway, I had to chuckle to myself. Claire always had a way of blowing everything out of proportion or working her mind into a state of utter chaos. But that little voice inside me wasn't laughing.

On the way home it occurred to me that I hadn't asked Claire about her pregnancy. During her last two times, that was all she talked about. She drove me nuts. She was depressed and crying because she was fat and ugly or she was ecstatic because she had chosen a name for the baby. The ones I liked best were the midnight calls concerning her digestive track and her ever-enlarging breasts. I find it tacky to call in the middle of the night and complain about the discomfort of a B-cup becoming a C-cup. Give me a break. I made a mental note to call her before she returned home.

Ten minutes later, I parked in my tiny parking space in front of the duplex I shared with Becky. In actuality, Becky had shared the place with me for the last six years. I met her when I was doing clerical work for a moving and storage company. That was several jobs ago for both of us. We have much in common as you can see. As I said before, I haven't found my niche in life. My current job is your every-day-run-of-the-mill office girl for a company called Whitley Chimney, a small chimney sweep business operated by two brothers, Mark and George. They give a whole new meaning to the phrase—*Tall, dark, and handsome*. You know the kind— 6'3", olive skin, shoulder length, curly black hair, weighing in at 180 pounds each. Fortunately, they're both married, which keeps me from making the mistake of trying to mix business with pleasure.

As I retrieved my belongings out of my ten-year-old Chevy, my neighbor, Janet came storming out of her apartment. She had that determined look in her eyes that I had seen on many occasions. Either our trash was scattered all over the yard, or Becky and I had our music too loud and it had kept her and her live-in lover up all night. What now? I thought.

"What is going on in that house? You didn't come home last night and your roommate left for work Friday and hasn't been back since. You've got to do something about that dog. You know, I could turn you in to the landlord. We're not supposed to have pets," she spewed, spraying me with slobber. Gee, some people are so nasty.

Wiping the dampness from my face in a gesture that did not go unnoticed, I replied, "Calm down, Janet. I just got back from an overnight trip with my parents. Let me get inside the house and see what's going on." I brushed passed her in a manner that I hoped she found offensive.

I couldn't get the key in the door fast enough. My mind was racing with thoughts of torn clothing, half-eaten shoes, or worse, pee all over my bed. Oh, no, my CD's! I'll kill that dog. Better yet... I'll kill Becky!

I opened the door and couldn't believe my eyes. Everything appeared to be normal except for the smell. I dropped my bag on the floor, keys on the coffee table and called Athena's name. "Come here, girl. Athena, where are you?" I glanced around on the floor and knew instantly the source of the smell. Athena had done her business in at least four places that I could see. Immediately, Athena burst out of the kitchen and jumped on me. I could almost read her mind, "Feed me. Let me out... please!" I knew she was glad to see me. Bless her heart, she's so sweet. She's two years old, and can wreak havoc with the best of them, considering her puppy days are long gone. I tried to convince Becky to spend the money to have her pet fixed, assuring her it was best for the dog and us, but she complained she couldn't afford it. If it were my dog, that's the first thing I'd do. Or, do they have to have shots first? How many? I know she's had a couple. Hey, what am I thinking? That's not my concern. I can't get all hung up on a dog.

I gingerly walked to the kitchen, scooped out a bowl's worth of dog food from the bag we kept under the counter, and dumped it into her eating bowl. She gobbled the food down like I do when I sit down in front of a pile of steamed crabs. I filled her water bowl, grabbed a roll of paper towels, and went about cleaning up dog poop and checking for more damage. Amazingly, the first piles I encountered were the only ones I found. The smell of urine blasting out at me would have to be dealt with immediately. I figured if I stepped on wet carpet, I'd just throw a towel on it... one of Becky's. I cleaned up the poop, which was not an easy feat considering I'm the type of person who gags when I see someone spit on the sidewalk. Plus, I'm not an animal lover. When we were kids, we had a dog once.

Jack was allergic to dander, so that was our first and last pet. We never considered owning a cat because Mom thought they were scary animals. They have talons that lash out at you if you make the mistake of getting too close.

After spraying the house down with a can of room deodorizer, Athena was ready to go outside and do whatever it was she missed doing earlier. I let her out and by the time she was scratching at the door ready to come back in, I had begun to seriously worry about Becky. Was she all right? Where was she? I got out my address book and looked up the listings I had under her name for people that might know her whereabouts. I called her mom in Hampton, but she said the last time she had heard from Becky was two weeks ago. My mother would be banging down my door if she hadn't heard from me in three days, let alone two weeks. Next on the list was her dad. Her parents had been divorced for several years, but tried to be civilized to each other for the sake of Becky. Becky was an adult, but she was still their only child. That meant they were always going to be polite to me because I was Becky's roommate—regardless of the fact that her father told her once he thought I needed to get laid more often! What a macho pig! I dialed his number. After five rings, I hung up.

Athena walked over to me and tried to lick my face. I patted her on the head and rubbed behind her ears. For some reason, dogs seem to love that little show of affection. She started to get excited. I had to push her away; she must weigh eighty pounds. German Shepherds are big dogs and when they jump all over you, their paws can dig nasty places in your skin. She lay down on the floor as I propped my feet up on the coffee table, trying to decide what to do about this situation. I knew Becky was with Tim. I refuse to let him take over my apartment again. I will not tolerate him eating my food, controlling my stereo and my television, leaving his clothes everywhere, making long distant calls on my phone and not paying for them, and most importantly, I didn't want him in my house. All they ever do is fight. I would put my foot down this time! The minute she got home, we'd have a serious talk. But for now, I was not going to let this get me down. I was not going to worry about them.

I got up from the couch, grabbed my duffel bag and went to the kitchen.

I needed to do something to take my mind off what was obviously going to turn into another shitty situation. I gathered my dirty clothes from the trip and began loading them into the compact washing machine. I had purchased the washer at a yard sale two weeks earlier for thirty dollars. This brought a smile to my face. I no longer had to make the weekly trips to the Wash and Spin, or when it rained, go over to Mom's house and freeload off her. I hated feeling like such a user. We spent many a Sunday dinner together with me doing my laundry. Too bad our kitchen was too small to accommodate the matching compact dryer. It would have saved me from having to trudge out back to hang the clothes on the line.

I put a pot of coffee on to brew, and went to the living room with the intention of calling Mom, when the phone rang.

"Hello," I answered.

"Hey, you're home," Becky said, her voice sarcastic as she slurred her words. She sounded like someone who had been drunk for two days. That only meant one thing—she was back with him. First, she would be in denial... denying she was back with him. Then, I'd have a week or so of him dropping in for long visits. She'd move out again only to return a couple of months later, bags at her feet, cigarette hanging out of her mouth and elephant tears running down her face.

I was hot. I could tell this wasn't going to wait. I jumped in and said, "Why would you go off and leave your own dog locked up without food or water and no way of getting outside? Are you crazy? Or, is it that you have been too busy with Tim to think about your responsibilities to others?"

"What others? What do you mean?"

"What I mean is, I'm not going to deal with this again. You have one week left on the rent you paid this month. That should be enough time for you to get your things and your dog and move in with Tim. Besides, I've been thinking about moving to the mountains with Mom and Dad." Lord, what made me tell that lie? One minute I'm trying to lay a guilt trip on her and the next I'm telling lies.

"Can we still be friends?" she pleaded.

"Sure, we just can't live together anymore."

"You know you are the best friend I've ever had."

She was starting to get sappy and I could see this conversation was only going to go downhill.

"Becky, I need to get off the phone and call Mom." Plus, I need to think about the bad person I am for telling yet another lie.

We agreed she would come get her stuff, remain friends, and most laughable of all, keep in touch. I knew this was the end of the line for me. There was no more going back.

It was barely dark, but I was ready for bed. I promised myself I would get up early in the morning and call Claire before she left. I just didn't want to deal with another crisis today. I left the clothes in the machine, turned off the coffee pot, and let Athena out one last time. Five minutes later she was finished. She followed me to the bathroom and watched while I brushed my teeth. As I crawled into bed in my underwear and T-shirt, she laid down on the floor. I guess a dog wants some company, too.

Sunday morning started out to be a sunny day with just a sprinkling of white, fluffy clouds and the promise of more warm days to come. I love the spring. I threw out the old coffee, made a fresh pot, and called Claire. We talked our usual sister-talk and she couldn't tell me enough about her plans for the new baby. When I hung up, I felt much better. Things were starting to look up. I hung the clothes on the line to dry, took a shower, and started in on the paperwork I had promised Mark and George I'd have done by Monday morning. I needed to sort work orders, receipts and checks; get on my computer and download all this to the computer at work; and have the bank deposit ready to deposit on Monday. Once all that was finished, I spent the rest of the day kicked back, eating junk food, watching TV, and walking around the apartment thinking about all the lies and crap that flowed so easily out of my mouth yesterday. Is that what I'm down to now? Thirty-one... no life... no man... no babies... no career... a liar... a shitty duplex apartment... a piece-of-junk car... and breasts the size of plums. The worst part was, I couldn't even get drunk. I take Zoloft, the wonder drug of the year 2000. I don't want to go there right now. That's another one of those tales I don't want to re-live just yet.

I have to think positive. Isn't that what the therapists tell their patients? I wandered into the bedroom and looked into the mirror. "Well, on the bright side," I said to no one in particular, "I'm not bad looking. Ok, I might have one or two crow's feet, but who doesn't at thirty-one? I have good skin, my blue eyes sparkle, and on a good day, I only weigh 115 pounds, which is perfect for my 5'5" height. I have long, straight, bottled red hair. I don't have a big nose, or funky teeth. I have a great personality sometimes. What more could a man want?

Deciding I'd had enough for one day, I took Athena outside one last time to do her thing, took my clothes off the line, and retired for the night.

Like Scarlet would say, "Tomorrow is another day!"

I awoke Monday morning with a tight and heavy feeling in my chest. Anxiety attack... I know the feeling well. I opened my eyes and immediately realized the pressure source. Athena was lying on top of me.

"Wait a minute, girl. Since when have you and I become bed partners?" I asked her. She looked at me with those loving eyes, and started licking my face. "Look, we need to get something straight right now. You and I are roommates, and it's only temporary. Pretty soon, you will be moving to a new home. So don't get too cozy here." I don't normally like animals, so why was I talking to a dog? What's happening to me?

I hadn't heard from Becky since Saturday. It was Monday and I had to go to work. So, I did what I had to do. I fed Athena, and made sure she was set for the day before I left to go to work.

Work was in utter chaos. Over the weekend Mark had broken his arm, and George was irked about it because his brother was not going to be able to do his work. They fought most of the morning and by lunchtime they had pulled me into their battle.

I don't know if it was the relaxing time I had with Mom and Dad in the mountains, or if I was just fed up with my boring life, but I was ready to call it quits. So, I did.

On the way home, I stopped at a fast food joint and got my usual burger, fries, and a large Coke. As soon as I parked my car in the driveway, Janet came out to greet me. I was not in the mood to listen to her whine.

"Don't you have a job, girl?" I asked, as I brushed passed her.

"Oh, funny," she hissed. "I see your roommate has packed up and moved out. She left the dog."

"What do you mean, she left the dog?"

"She said she left a note. Did you two have a lover's quarrel?"

I ignored her and went inside. Sure enough, there was a note on the kitchen counter saying she'd come back for the dog when she got settled. At least this time Becky left me a note.

I let the dog out, sat down at the table and began to devour my food. Stress always makes me hungry and I was dealing with quite a bit ot it now. I called Mom. She answered on the first ring.

"Hello," she said.

"Hi, Mom, it's me. How is it going?"

"Busy, the movers are here. I'm glad you called. I was going to call and see if you wanted the piano. We're not going to take it and since we bought it for you, I thought you might like to have it. If not, Claire said she would take it for the kids to use when they get older."

"Let Claire have it. I don't have the room, and right now I don't know what's going to happen."

"What do you mean? What's going on? You don't sound too good."

"Never mind, I don't need to burden you with my problems. You've got enough going on as it is."

"Since when has that ever stopped you? Tell me what is wrong."

"Well, let's see. My roommate deserted me and left her dog, and then I quit my job."

"Perfect timing," she said, excited. "Now you can come with us to the mountains. I know your dad would be thrilled, and so would I. We love you. Think about it, honey and then give me a call. I've got to run."

I laid the receiver back in the cradle, and thought about what she said.

Wallowing in my usual *poor... poor... pitiful me* mood, I retreated to the bathroom to take a long, hot bath. I had to sit down and think about my life and what my next step was going to be. The hot water and bubbles made me feel relaxed, something I desperately needed. I was beginning to drift off when I heard Athena out back barking. Oh, I guess she's ready to come back in. I got out of the tub, pulled the plug, toweled myself and then let the dog inside. All the emotion I had been holding in came pour-ing out. I sat down on the couch and had a good cry. Athena came over to me and licked my hand. Her show of affection caused me to cry more. I spent the rest of the day curled up on the couch watching television, and talking to my new roommate. I guess it was at that very moment that I decided I needed to change my life. Anything would be better than this. Besides, I did not have a life... all I had was a dog.

I called Mom.

"You must be reading my mind," Mom said. "Your father and I were just talking about you."

"I know it's getting late and you and Dad are probably ready for bed, but I have something to tell you. I've been thinking over your offer to move to the mountains, but I have one problem. I have that damn dog. I can't leave her behind. She's been dumped on enough, and I just can't bring myself to take her to the animal shelter. Besides, she starts to grow on you after a while."

"Ok," Mom said.

"Ok? Is that all you're going to say? Aren't you even going to ask Dad? What about ground rules? What about..."

"I told you before, we would love it. No rules. You're an adult. You don't need me to tell you how to behave."

Within a blink of an eye, I had changed my life. I was going to live in a new place, meet new people, get a new job, and hopefully, meet a man. If all else failed, I still had the dog.

By mid-day Wednesday, I had notified my landlord that I was leaving. My car was packed with everything I owned except the washer, and with my dog in tow, we were headed for a new life.

Oh... *if I'd only known then..........*

CHAPTER 2

LEAVING TIDEWATER was an empty and sad experience. I expected to pick up and head out without having the least bit of reluctance. But as the miles flew by and the past was left behind, I began to feel like I was losing a little bit of myself. I guess I was. The closer I got to Stanardsville and a chance at a new life, the more I realized that what I thought I was losing was something that would be with me no matter what. I guess that is why they are called memories.

Athena didn't fare too well on the trip. I wish someone had told me it wasn't a good idea to feed a dog before you put one in a car, especially for three hours. An hour into the drive, she turned to me with a pitiful look on her face, leaned her head to one side and threw up. Bodily functions excreted from either man or beast will cause me to react in a most unpleasant way. Usually, I gag. I don't know what it is, but I just can't handle those awful sounds. It never bothered me before to change a diaper for one of Claire's kids, but once either one of them barfed; I was a goner.

Does that mean when I get married my husband will have to get up in the middle of the night with one of the kids when they get sick because their mother will throw up, too? There goes that biological clock, again. Tick... Tick...

Man, what a life. I'm thirty-one; on the road with a dog that is not really mine; going to live with my parents—*again*; in a town so small, I wondered if it was even on the map. The ride was pretty. In a couple of weeks we would be celebrating Memorial Day, the official start of the summer season, and as we turned onto Rt. 33, I noticed the forsythia was just beginning to sprout blooms. Back in Tidewater, the daffodils had already bloomed, died back, and the tulips and daylilies had started to blossom. Azaleas were at their peak. It's funny how you notice these things.

Almost to our destination, we made a right hand turn onto Rt. 230, drove for a couple of miles, made a left hand turn onto the South River Road, and within minutes, had reached our destination—home sweet home.

Athena couldn't get out of the car fast enough. My legs were stiff and I had to go to the bathroom. I got the strange sensation that the atmosphere here had changed. Or, was it my attitude about the place?

I got out, stood by my car, and looked around. This had to be God's country. It was beautiful. The house had at least an acre of cleared land surrounding it, with a few cedar trees left here and there, obviously for shade. Beyond the realm of the yard, blooming Dogwood trees were clustered everywhere you looked. They were nestled between endless amounts of huge Pine, Tulip Poplar, and Cedar trees. I spotted Redbud trees covered with small purple flowers; just enough to add color to a gap here and there. In the skyline of all this scenery, were the mountain peaks. I was truly mesmerized. Where have I been all my life? The freshness of the air and the clean feeling you got when you took a deep breath was like no other smell I've ever experienced. Oh, no! I've crossed over! I knew I had because I remembered hearing that statement somewhere. Was it in a movie perhaps? I was transforming!

I pulled myself from the stupor I had fallen into, and started gathering my belongings out of the car, trying not to inhale the gross, permeating smell coming from the front passenger seat and floorboard. I would have to clean up the remnants of Athena's lunch soon, or it was only going to get worse.

I followed Mom and Dad inside the house, as they carried the few items packed in the van that they didn't want the movers to haul.

"Your room is upstairs on the right, honey, unless you want the other one," Mom said. "The bedroom furniture you had at home is up there, except for the personal stuff you left behind. We packed all that in boxes and had the movers store them in the cubbyholes where you see the small doors. Remember those?"

"Yes, I remember. That's a lot of room for storage. Tell me again how or why that came about," I said, making conversation as I worked my way upstairs.

"Something about building the roof with such a steep pitch so the snow wouldn't accumulate and be too heavy. That way the snow would just slide down the roof. When you have a roof with that kind of pitch, you end up with a ship's cabin effect in the upstairs rooms. So, why not use it to your advantage? Mr. James enclosed that space and added access doors. Now, the space is not wasted."

"That was very astute of Mr. James. I would think you'd have to have an enormous amount of snow to justify constructing a roof like that. I sure would not want to have to climb on that roof to make repairs or do whatever people do when they climb up on roofs. Wait a minute, are you telling me they have a lot of snow here?"

"A neighbor fellow named Fred stopped by when we were here once before and said they had twenty-two inches of snow overnight last winter. The snowfall stopped by the time it was daylight and had already settled to the point where he couldn't get his car out of the driveway. He said it wasn't like that all the time."

That ought to be interesting, I thought to myself. The only snow we ever got in Tidewater was maybe a flurry or two in February, and we never got any around Christmas. Well, except the year we had the ice storm. It had started raining on December the 23rd, and by Christmas Eve, it had turned to ice. By Christmas Day, almost everybody's Christmas dinner was celebrated by candlelight. Every household in Tidewater lost electricity. Some residents lost power for only a couple of hours, but others lost it for as many as five days. The majority of the residents were in the latter category. However, I was fortunate to be in the category of the ones who lost it for just a few hours. That happened at a time when I did not own my own personal computer. I had friends that were on-line at the time and their computers crashed, forcing them to spend huge amounts of money to salvage their life. A life they had stored in one little box. How ridiculous, I thought. That is, until I finally joined the twenty-first century. That's when I purchased a surge protector for my computer.

The next two hours were spent hauling and unpacking. At five o'clock, Mom busied herself in the kitchen preparing what would be the best meal I had eaten in days. I guess that's why I'm so thin—food is not my first priority in life. I only eat when I get hungry. Of course, if I could just sit down to a gourmet feast without having to do anything in its preparation, I would probably weigh a hundred pounds more than I do. Cooking is not one of my attributes. However, microwave dinners are meals I know something about. Take-out is me at my best. Unfortunately, I think take-out would be taboo in this little corner of the world. Maybe it is because the nearest take-out is twenty minutes away, and delivery... you've got to be kidding! From what Mom has told me, we're out in the country and if we want anything other than the companionship of our neighbors, we have to go in town. In town, they have a grocery store, video rental place, gas station, and a Dollar General Store. Across the street is the school area. The school is housed in a little community environment, separated into three sections—elementary, middle, and high school. Down the road, in the middle of town, is a post office, library, police station, and a few odds and ends stores, along with a dental office, the courthouse, and a couple of law offices. That's it. Each one of those places of business or public service centers are so close together, you could put all of them in one mini-mall anywhere, any town, USA. Strangely, when we stopped in town to fill our gas tanks for our trip home, the first and only time I had been here until now, I noticed people in the store talked to each other like they were best friends, or at least knew each other in a more personal way than I did. Now, I had a feeling one day I would be among that select group of *Bubbas and Mamas*—country folk that were friendly and had no teeth. You know the drill. Later, I would come to realize what a jerk I had been for thinking that way. You're never too young or too old to learn something new about yourself. I always seem to learn the hard way.

"Dinner's ready," Mom yelled.

It was at that moment that I thought about Athena. I was so busy un-packing, I had forgotten about her. I hope she didn't run off, or worse, be lying in the road, dead. She's not used to having all this free space to run about. I ran downstairs and opened the front door.

"Where are you going?" Mom asked. "Dinner is ready. Take a break and come eat."

"I'm going to check on Athena. I forgot about her. She's..."

"She's right here in the kitchen. She came inside when Mack was bring-ing in the boxes. I put a bowl of water down for her. She looked thirsty."

"I guess she is. She's probably hungry, too. Whatever she had in her stomach before the trip is now on the seat and floor of my car."

I walked over to the table where Dad was sitting and sat down. Athena was curled up on the floor beside him. Mom had a smile on her face. "I think she's found a new home, and a couple of new friends. We've always liked animals, but with your brother's allergies we could never have any. Once he left home, we never thought about getting a pet. Now, well... she's just so lovable." I could tell Athena had found herself a permanent home, and the love of a good family.

We dined on a quickly thrown together meal of fried pork chops, mashed potatoes with gravy, and sweet peas. It was wonderful. It seems the movers also moved the food along with the furniture. For that, I was so thankful. I was starving. I allowed Athena to have some of the leftover pork chop bones, outside, of course—something I normally wouldn't do because I know that feeding a dog people food is not good for them. I heard that somewhere. Usually Becky and I dined on fast food most of the time, and the only thing we had to feed the dog was dog food. What can I say?

After dinner, dishes and small chitchat, I retreated to my room. I put clean sheets on the bed, hung up my clothes in the closet, stuffed boxes of junk I didn't want to deal with in my cubbyholes, and began the task of hooking up my computer. Fortunately, everything went well and in no time I was back on-line. I was beginning to get the hang of this computer business. One day, I'd like to be able to hack into something and not get caught. It is a bad idea... I know.

As the day ran into night, I lay in bed thinking. Well, now that I'm here, I've got to think about what I'm going to do about my life. First, I have to get a job. Tomorrow, I'll go into town and get a newspaper to check the help wanted ads. I'm sure I can find something to tide me over, or maybe I'll get lucky and find a decent job. I still have a nice little nest egg stashed away in my savings for a rainy day, but without a job, the clouds will start to move in real fast. Saving money has always been easy and something I made myself do. I avoided buying anything useless, like fancy clothes or a new car. The only jewelry I own are the two pairs of pierced earring sets that I got as gifts, and a watch I bought at the drug store. The last thing I thought about before I fell asleep was the ladybugs. I hadn't seen any! Wonder where they're hiding?

I slept with the windows open, allowing the cool, sweet smell of spring to flow through my room. I awoke to the sounds of birds chirping and other noises echoing from the woods. A cow mooed from somewhere off in the distance. Was I living on a farm? I half expected to see a rooster perched on the roof.

I went to the bathroom that separated the two bedrooms upstairs, and took a shower. The water was refreshing and I was ready to start the day.

Downstairs, Mom was fixing breakfast.

"Where's Dad?" I asked.

"He's outside, sitting in the swing, drinking his coffee and reading the paper," she answered. "Are you ready for some breakfast? I'm making bacon, eggs, and grits."

"It's been a long, long time since I've had grits. I think the last time I had grits was when I was living at home." I poured a cup of coffee and sat down at the table. "Where did Dad get a newspaper?"

"We had that arranged before we moved here. *The Daily Report* has been delivering us a paper since Monday; so if you want to read one, go see your dad. He's got four day's worth."

"I'll wait until after breakfast. What can I do to help?"

"I don't know. What can you do to help?"

"You know what I mean, for an old country girl you're pretty smart. You know I can't cook," I said, as I winked at her. Mom had dropped out of school in the ninth grade to help on the farm, but when she met Dad, he insisted she go back to school to finish her education. She had been the oldest in her class to graduate, but she took pride in her accomplishment. I always liked to remind her of how smart I thought she was.

After breakfast, Mom insisted I leave her to cleaning the kitchen. I got another cup of coffee and went out on the porch to read the paper.

"Come over here and sit on the swing with me. We can read our papers together," Dad said. "It's been sometime since you and I had the time to sit down like this. Remember the weekend we all spent at Grandma and Grandpa Watson's house at the lake? You were the only one I could get to go fishing with me. We sat out on that pier for so long, your knees got badly sunburned and your mom gave me the dickens over it. Boy, did she ever get mad! She wouldn't talk to me for two days."

"That was a long time ago," I said. For just a minute, I could see a sadness come over him. "I know you must miss Gramps and Granny. I know I do. I think about them sometimes, especially when I smell home made pies cooking in the oven. Granny use to make the best pies, and Gramps used to tell the worse jokes." That got a laugh out of Dad. A few years back, Gramps died of a heart attack and a year later, Granny died. Dad says it was from a broken heart, because she missed Gramps so much.

"Let's talk about something else. This is too sad to think about on such a beautiful day," I whispered.

"You're right. We need to start our first day here on a happy note. How about you and I go over to the pond later and do some fishing?"

"You have a pond?"

"No, but the man next door does. He said we could fish there anytime we want. He owns the house and the land, but he doesn't live there all the time. He comes for a stay once or twice a year. His name is Burt Crampton. He lives in Louisa County. He doesn't come here as much as he used to since he and his wife got divorced. He seems like a real nice fellow. He's got about thirty acres. He has some man down the road look after the place for him."

"I would love to go fishing. First, I need to look through the paper and see if I can find a job."

"What's the hurry? You've got plenty of time. You need to take a few days and relax, enjoy this country life. You'll find it's very agreeable. Have you noticed the ladybugs are gone?" He laughed.

We were reading the paper, enjoying the warmth of the sun and the sounds around us, when Mom walked out, coffee cup in hand, and sat down in one of the wicker chairs. "Are you two enjoying yourselves?"

"Very much so," I said. "Dad and I are going fishing later. Want to come?"

"No, I don't think so! I can tell you right now, I'm not cleaning any fish, and we're not cooking any nasty smelling fish in the house. Y'all can cook those stinky things on that fancy new grill your dad bought last summer," Mom blurted out. Dad and I looked at each other and laughed. Mom couldn't stand the smell of fish.

In the distance, I heard the rumblings of what sounded like a motor-cycle. Seconds later, two ATV's with a man and woman on each, pulled up into the yard.

"Hey, there's that fellow, Fred, from down the road," Dad said, as he stood up and walked to the steps to greet them. Fred and the rest of the group got off their bikes and approached the porch.

"Howdy, folks," Fred said. "This is my wife, Dolores." Pointing to the other couple he announced, "And this here is Ralph, and his wife, Carol Mitchell. We thought we'd drop by and say hello. See if there was anything we could do to help you get settled in."

Dad introduced us to our new neighbors. All greetings aside, I couldn't help but notice their appearances. Fred, dressed in camouflage pants and a green, ragged T-shirt, was a short, rugged looking man with dark curly hair and a deep scar on his right cheek, that led me to believe he might have taken a nasty tumble off that bike of his at some point in time. Both men had a gun strapped to their hips, and small coolers strapped to their bikes, obviously packed with beer, since both of them simultaneously pulled one out and after offering us one, began to drink. Dolores was short, a little plump, had a pretty face, and a head full of the most beautiful red hair I'd ever seen. I was instantly envious. Carol and Ralph were a head taller than their two friends and much more slender. Carol had short, black hair, legs that never stopped, and an attitude to match. She knew she was pretty. Ralph was at least 6'3", slim, and had brown hair, tied back in a short ponytail. His mannerisms were charming and I got the impression he was a womanizer. He had blue eyes that appeared to bore right through you. At least they all had their teeth, which killed my theory about mountain people not having a full set. Live and learn.

After an hour of conversation, I learned that Fred and Dolores had two teenage girls, 14 and 16 years old, while Ralph and Carol remained childless—by choice. Both couples had moved to the mountains around ten years ago from different states and have been friends ever since. What a crew. After talking to them, I was convinced they were honest, easy going, and interesting people. I'm going to have to stop going by my first impressions. Looks can be deceiving. That's what Mom always said.

As they got on their bikes to leave, Fred yelled out to us, "We're going target shooting up at Ralph's place. Why don't you guys come with us?"

Not wanting to tell Mom and Dad I had purchased a gun a few months ago when someone tried to break into my apartment, I just said, "I'm afraid I don't know how to use a gun properly."

"Well, come on and we'll teach you," he offered.

I glanced over at Mom, and to my surprise she said, "Go ahead, Jesse. It wouldn't hurt for you to learn how to shoot a gun." She then smiled at Fred. "I think Mack and I'll stay here. We've still got some un-packing to do." She looked back at me. "Your dad and I purchased a gun last year and had been taking lessons at the shooting gallery in Hampton, until we moved here." I was speechless. My Mom owning a gun was a shock. She never said a word to me about buying a gun. All of a sudden, I had this picture of her and my dad with two cowboy guns strapped to their hips, like something out of a Roy Rogers and Dale Evans movie. I hadn't been in the mountains two full days and I was already getting an education. What next?

"Let me get my purse and I'll follow you in my car," I said, figuring I could hide my little Saturday night special in the bag, and slip away.

Ten minutes later, we were at Ralph's range, each of us with a gun in our hand. Ralph strutted over to me with a smile on his face and said, "First off, you need to get yourself a real gun. These things are nothing but trash. If you ever find yourself in a situation where you need protection, this thing is only going to piss off the bad guy. Or, you'll shoot yourself in the foot with it. Seriously, take mine, for instance. Here you have a Glock 9MM, semi-automatic, with all the stopping power you'll ever need. It has a magazine that holds eighteen rounds, and one in the chamber. Try it out."

At first, I was insulted, but then I realized he wasn't trying to hurt my feelings. He was just trying to be helpful. So, I took the gun. It was a heavy chunk of steel in my hands, and after a few instructions, I fired a round. "Wow! That was intense," I screamed so he could hear me through the hearing protection.

Fred walked up to me and said, "Here, try mine. It's a Rossi .357. If you liked Ralph's gun, I think you'll like mine. Even though they're different types, they still have a lot of power. This one has a cylinder that holds six rounds." He went on to show me how to open the cylinder to remove and replace the rounds, and the minute I fired, I felt a powerful punch. I loved the way it stung my finger.

"Now, try yours."

I handed the gun back to Fred, picked up mine, and fired. The small handgun felt like nothing. "What a big difference." I was amazed. Both of them were right. My gun was like a fly swatter compared to a cast iron skillet. "I'm convinced. I'll have to trade mine in on something with more guts. What's the use of owning a gun like mine when I can have a real gun like yours? Like you said, if you ever have to use it, make sure it will do the job."

"If you're interested, I'll sell you mine, and for a fair price," Fred offered. "I've been planning on buying one like Ralph's. I'm tired of a revolver."

"How much do you want for it?" I asked.

"I'll take two hundred dollars."

Two hundred dollars was a lot of money considering I bought mine from a pawnshop for fifty bucks. Without hesitation, and feeling that I had formed a trust with these folks, I said, "Okay, I'll take it. Will you take a check?" The deal was sealed. I now owned a powerful gun, and had made four new friends.

After shooting a few more rounds, I was ready to take a break. I sat down on a tree stump talking to my four new friends, and tried to get to know them better. I was curious about what these people did for a living, since it was a weekday and none of them were at work.

"The county fair is in town and everybody takes a few days off from work. We set up booths and sell crafts, T-shirts, food, or games for the public. It's kind of like a pre-Memorial Day celebration. Sunday, the fire station in town will have their buffet breakfast. All you can eat for five bucks. The money collected goes to the up-keep of the fire engines, or whatever is needed to run the fire station. You might want to check it out. The food's pretty good," Dolores said.

We sat and talked for so long, my butt was beginning to get sore. I realized the day was starting to slip away. I gave Fred a check for two hundred dollars, stuffed my new *toy,* as they called it, into my purse, and said goodbye. I can't imagine anyone calling a gun a toy. Hey, what do I know?

I didn't mention anything about the gun to Mom or Dad when I returned home, fearing they might be skeptical of the transaction that just occurred. Dad was in the detached garage, straightening things up so they could park the van in it. Mom was in the house getting the spare bedroom ready to become her sewing room, which would eventually become a catch-all for whatever they decided to put in it.

I asked Dad, "Where's Athena?"

"Oh, she went inside with your mom the minute she heard the shooting. Don't think she likes the sound of gunfire. She 'bout tore the door down. You ready to go fishing?"

"Sure, just let me put my purse in the house and check on Mom. When I come back, I'll help you get the fishing gear together."

Mom was busy getting everything put just where she wanted it. "I'm sure your dad will come in here and rearrange everything so he can have a place to put his junk. He had the movers put that loveseat in here and he said he wanted a place to put the small television set. I hope he doesn't think this is going to be his hide-out."

"Dad needs a place where he can go to and watch football games and all the other shows you don't want to watch. I think it might be a good idea. Think about it. You can always run him out if you want to sew. We're going fishing now, unless you want us to help you do something."

"No, you two go on. I'll be fine. Just be back in time for dinner. How about six o'clock?"

"It sounds good to me. But don't you want to wait in case we catch some fish? You know if we catch some fish, Dad is going to want to have them for dinner."

She gave me one of her looks that let me know we were not going to have fish tonight.

"By the way, Dolores said the county fair was in town and I thought we might check it out if you and Dad want to," I said, knowing how much Mom liked stuff like that.

"Oh, that sounds wonderful, Honey. I love fairs. Have you said anything to your dad?"

"Not yet, but I will," I replied, as I turned to leave. "We'll be back in a little bit, Mom." I looked at Athena, who was now running around my feet, jumping and trying to get my attention.

"Come on, girl. You can go fishing, too."

I don't know who had more fun fishing. Dad and I laughed at Athena when one of us would catch a fish. She would bark and prance around as she tried to sniff our slippery friends. We caught several fish, but didn't keep them because they had some kind of fungus on their skin. I think throwing the fish back into the water was a concept that confused Athena.

"Minnie is going to be so disappointed that we will not be having fish for supper," I told Dad, as we were walking back to the house.

"Yeah, right." He rolled his eyes, as he stopped and turned to me. "I've been meaning to talk to you about the lack of men in your life. It just so happens, while you were gone, the deputy from up the road stopped by to welcome us to the neighborhood, and we invited him to dinner. Now, don't get mad. It's just a dinner."

Whoa! I thought to myself. I've barely been here two days and they're already trying to fix me up with somebody. Oh well, what could it hurt? They mean well. I couldn't help but have visions of Barney Fife from Mayberry, RFD. The things we do for our parents!

As Dad and I were coming around the bend, I noticed a black motorcycle the size of a Volkswagen, sitting in the front yard. What now?

I looked at Dad and said, "Have I moved to Mayberry? Every time I turn around somebody's dropping by. This is the friendliest place I've ever seen."

"Kind of makes you wonder if anybody around here works," he commented.

"Oh, I meant to tell you. The reason everybody is not working is because the county fair is in town. Seems the whole town takes off work and gets involved. It's some big thing they do. Also, they have a buffet breakfast at the fire station on Sunday. Mom and I thought we might all go. What do you think? Do you want to go?"

"Whatever," he said. I knew Mom loved this kind of thing, but Dad couldn't care less. He'd do whatever made Mom happy.

The long walk up the driveway gave me plenty of time to examine the man and woman I saw talking to Mom. Both were clad in black leather pants and jackets. What kind of people dress like that when the temperature was almost seventy degrees? They had to be the bikers from hell.

"Come on Dad, pick up the pace," I whispered. "Let's see who these folks are."

Much to my amazement, Sharon and Joe Downey turned out to be beautiful people. Joe was so handsome it almost took my breath away and she was a stunning brunette with hair down to her waist, and a healthy looking, slim figure. Of course, she had the same large breasts I noticed on all the women I had met so far. What is it about these women here? They all have large breasts. Was God standing in the middle of a watermelon patch when he gave them boobs and under a fig tree when he did the rest of us?

Sharon and Joe were the All-American Most Beautiful Couple out for an afternoon ride and decided to stop by to greet their new neighbors. They were from Texas and who knows how they ended up here, but they loved it. I was shocked to learn that he was a doctor and she was a pediatric nurse at the UVa Hospital. They didn't have any children; instead, they have a dog—named Harry. Mom invited them to Sunday dinner.

After they left, I told Mom, "Gee, Mom, if you're not careful you're going to spend all your time cooking."

"I can't help it. I love this place. I love how these people are so friendly. I've always wanted to live around people like this, and you know in the city it's just not that way. Someone is always trying to hurt you, break into your home, or steal from you. These people here are different, and I'm going to enjoy my new friends." She looked at Athena and said, "Come on, girl, let's get dinner started. It appears we're not going to have fish tonight after all." She laughed and walked inside. Dad and I just stared at each other in amazement.

"Do you think she's making fun of us?" he asked.

I went upstairs to shower and get the smell of fish off me. I heard the doorbell ring as I was putting on a pair of clean jeans. Oh, no, my date was here. I'm going to have to talk to Mack and Minnie about their little matchmaking shenanigans. First, I dug out a chambray shirt that wasn't in too much need of ironing, put it on, and rolled up the sleeves. My hair was still damp, but there wasn't anything I could do about it. The blow dryer I normally used belonged to Becky, but she took it with her when she moved. When I go into town I'll have to buy a new one. I dried my hair the best I could with a towel and went down to meet my mystery man. This was the ultimate blind date from hell. Why? Because my parents had set it up! What do you do? Break their hearts?

Those fifteen steps down the stairs were the longest and most mind-deadening steps I've taken since Dad took us to the Washington Monument. You keep on going even though you know there's not going to be much excitement at the end. I couldn't erase the thought from my head that my blind date would be a geek, or a serial killer who had an uncanny resemblance to one of Santa's elves, with a bad attitude. Or, maybe he would be drop-dead gorgeous, and think I was a loser with bad hair. But, persevere, I did.

Downstairs, Mom and Dad were standing in the living room talking to a man that had his back to me. When I walked into the room, he was introduced as Cole James.

"Hello," he said. His smile was charming and my heart skipped a beat. "It's nice to meet you. I was just telling your folks that I wouldn't be able to have dinner with them this afternoon. Unfortunately, two of the deputies called in sick with the flu; so another deputy and I have been asked to pull part of their shift, along with our regular duty. I'm sorry. I hope I can have a rain check."

The room began to fill with the aroma of flowers blowing in the wind, and thoughts of a lazy summer afternoon lying in a hammock between two trees. Where was I? Lost in the mist of clouds my mind lapsed into when I started daydreaming or wandering off into another part of the world? I couldn't help but find this man intoxicating. He was a head taller than me and out weighed me by fifty pounds. Obviously he exercised regularly, because his body was firm and muscular. His brown hair was short and curly, and his eyes were the shade of sapphires. He wore the uniform of a tan shirt and brown pants. Each time he moved, I could hear the creak of his leather belt that held a gun and police radio. The only thing missing was a nightstick. Through the living room window, I noticed a brown and yellow police cruiser parked underneath the large Poplar tree in the middle of the yard. The tree stood along the semi-circular driveway, which I thought was the best thing since parking garages.

"I'm sorry you can't stay for dinner," I said. "Maybe you can come some other time." I was utterly disappointed and wanted to detain him just a little while longer. "Did you say your last name is James? Are you any relation to Mr. James that lived here?"

"As a matter of fact, I am. Toby is my cousin. His father and my dad were brothers. Sad to say, they both have passed away. But my mom is alive and kicking, and lives in Ruckersville." He smiled an even more seductive smile. I don't think he realized how sexy he was at that very moment. "I live up South River Road about a mile and a half from here. I'm sorry, but I really have to be going. I have to be at work in half an hour. It sure was nice to meet you folks, and I hope we can get together for dinner real soon."

Dad walked him to the door; with me following behind like a little puppy.

"How about coming to dinner Saturday night? Say, maybe six o'clock? That is, if you don't have to work," Dad asked. "Here, let me give you our phone number. If something happens and you can't make it, just give us a call. If you can make it, we'll see you Saturday."

Cole turned to Dad, as they walked down the front porch steps, and replied, "It sounds good to me. I'll be here. I'm off every other weekend and this just so happens to be my weekend off, unless one of the guys calls in sick. There's a bug going around. It must be that pre-summer thing." He removed a small pad and pen from his shirt pocked and began writing. "This is my home phone, cell, and pager numbers, and the number of the police station. If you ever need to reach me, you'll find me at one of these numbers." He tore the piece of paper from his notepad and handed it to Dad. I stood there looking at him. I felt like one of those mannequins you see in a store window with my hands all stretched out, trying to look like I had style and grace, while pleading, "Hey, over here, look at me!"

Why is it, you spend your entire life, subconsciously, or maybe in your dreams, wondering what it is going to be like when you meet Mr. Right, and when you do, you're so dumb struck, you don't even realize it? Or, maybe you do, and it's too scary to think about. I felt as if I had just peed on myself and everybody was watching.

I waved good-bye to Cole and walked in the house.

Suddenly, I felt twinges in parts of my body that I didn't even know existed. It'd been a good while since I've had sex, or even thought about it. Do you forget how, if you don't practice? The last time I had sex or even entertained ideas of a romantic relationship was four months ago when I was dating Matt Whitefield. The sex was rapturously exotic, but the romance was missing. At first, our relationship was filled with romance. He wined and dined me and said things to boost my ego, but after just a few short weeks, the romance was replaced with nothing but sex. He stopped taking me out, and eventually, only came over when he wanted to sleep with me. It didn't take long to figure that one out. I hated giving up the good sex, but I wanted more out of a relationship. I wasn't looking for a husband—just someone who would be good company.

This was my chance to make a fresh start. My brief encounter with Cole was enough for me to know that I wanted to get to know him better. I told myself this time things would be different. I would not jump into something before thinking long and hard about it, especially someone's bed.

I couldn't get Cole out of my mind. All through dinner I fantasized about going out with him. Every time my folks tried to have a conversation with me, I had to jolt myself back to reality. Maybe it was my hormones or endorphins kicking into overdrive, but whatever the case, I was swimming in a sea of lust, romance, and dreams, planning my next move. I had to be careful. I didn't want to blow my first relationship, if that's what it was going to be.

Friday morning, I was startled out of a restful sleep, full of sexual and emotional dreams about Cole, by Athena jumping on the bed and licking my face. This had become her usual morning ritual. I think dogs have this thing about their tongues. They have to put it everywhere and touch everything with it. I find it difficult to deal with them licking their butts and then trying to lick my face. It's too nasty to think about.

I got out of bed and went downstairs with the intention of putting food in Athena's bowl, but someone had beaten me to it. A note was lying on the bar from Mom, saying she and Dad went to the grocery store in town.

I fixed a cup of coffee and walked over to the bay window in the dining area. The sky was gray against the green trees and a yard bursting with the color of spring. Small raindrops had begun to fall, as I sat down at the table. I began to read the newspaper, scanning the want ads. I needed a job. If I couldn't find one in the paper, I would have to go to the unemployment office for help. I had a good feeling about this place and the opportunities it offered. Was this because I had a different outlook on things since I had met Cole? It's amazing how your attitude can change so suddenly. This time last week, I thought my life was going to shit, and it probably was, but now, I had found myself a man, lived in a great house, and would eventually find a good job. I was so happy.

I searched the want ads until I had decided it was hopeless. Every job I came across was either something I couldn't do, or wouldn't do. I guess Athena could sense my frustration, because she came over and lay down under the table beside my feet. I reached down and patted her head.

"Not to worry, girl. We're going to do fine. We have each other and a good home. How lucky can we get?" She started that licking thing again, as I slipped back to the spot in my fantasies where Cole and I were relishing each other. Our first embrace was followed by our first kiss, and right then and there, I knew I was hooked. My mind had shifted into a realm of confusion and emotional make-believe, brought on by a lifelong need to have someone to love. I gathered my wits and continued my job search, trying to put Cole out of my head. I was just about to give up, when an ad caught my eye.

Help Wanted. Office girl. Billy Blackhawk Investigations.
200 Greenbriar Road, Charlottesville. No phone calls.

The ad was appealing. I can do this, I told myself. I hope the job hasn't been taken. I bet working for a private eye could be exciting. Yet, deep in the back of my mind, I kept remembering that old saying... *Be careful of what you wish for...*

CHAPTER 3

I TORE THE AD OUT OF THE PAPER and hurried upstairs to shower. I didn't want to waste any time, however, choosing something to wear might take awhile. My selection of clothes was pitiful. I had a jeans skirt and jacket outfit, one black skirt I could wear with different blouses, and two dresses that should have gone into the trash years ago. I had one pair of black high heels and the Reeboks that I wore most of the time. Damn, I definitely needed to buy some new clothes. I gave up and pulled my newest pair of jeans out of the dresser, and went back to the closet and to get my white silk blouse. The blouse was tapered and short to the waist, with short sleeves. Maybe it would dress up the jeans a little.

I had just finished taking a shower when I heard the beep-beep of the door alarm. It sounds when someone opens either one of the three different entrance doors to the house. Good, Mom and Dad must be back from the store. I was wondering whether I was going to have to leave Athena in the house, or put her outside when I left, but now I wouldn't have to worry about her. If I left her outside and she took off into the hills and never came back, I'd feel terrible. Dressed in a towel, I went to the hallway and called out, "Is that you guys?"

"Yes," Mom replied. "We went to the IGA to get some groceries."

I heard them downstairs rustling paper bags and talking to each other, and the familiar click, click of Athena's toenails scrapping the hardwood floors. An occasional bark echoed up the stairwell. Mom must have bought her a treat, and she wanted it now!

"I found a job in the paper I want to check out," I shouted. "I'll be down as soon as I get dressed, and tell you all about it."

I got dressed and applied a little mascara and blush. I'm not much for wearing a whole lot of make up because I can't stand the feel of all that junk on my face. I'd rather be plain than have to take a putty knife to my face to get the layers of crusted foundation removed. I don't wear lipstick because it makes my lips look like a prune covered with paint.

After quickly checking my computer to see if I was still connected, or if I had fallen into a dark hole somewhere in the bowels of hillbilly hell, I grabbed my purse and car keys and went downstairs.

Mom and Dad were putting away groceries. Athena was laid up in a corner chewing on one of those fake bones made out of rawhide. Somebody loved that dog besides me.

Not wanting to go into any long, drawn out conversation, I said, "I found a secretarial job in Charlottesville, but I need to find out how to get there. Do you have any idea how to get to Greenbriar Road?"

Dad walked over to a kitchen drawer, retrieved a telephone book and said, "The telephone directory has maps of the city. I'm sure we can find the street you're looking for."

We scanned the pages until we found Greenbriar Road. It was off Route 29, which meant I had to take a right at the stoplight in Ruckersville and go down for about five or six miles. That didn't concern me. What did concern me was trying to figure out how to get to the main road to Ruckersville. I'm not the best when it comes to following directions, and I would be dealing with small, curvy back roads that lead into different crevices and dead ends. The one thing I remember from my association with my new beer-drinking, gun-totting friends was to stay away from a place called Bacon Hollow. That was good enough for me.

Assured of my ability to find what I was looking for, I said good-bye and headed out. It was still raining outside. I grabbed a piece of the newspaper to cover my still damp hair and ran to my car. The minute I slid into the seat, I crumbled the newspaper and threw it down on the floorboard. Crap. I was going to look like a drowned puppy when I got there. The minute I started the car, the windows fogged up. Give me a break! It was warm in the car and it was raining outside... does that equal fog? Needless to say, that didn't last long. I turned on my defroster and the cloudiness cleared. However, once the car had been running for a few seconds, I heard a weird, thumping noise. On our drive here for the big move, I had passed a car on the interstate to keep up with Mom and Dad, and that was the first time I noticed the engine making a noise. It was the same now, only louder.

"Car... don't freak out on me now!" I whispered to myself. I didn't know what was wrong, but I knew that noise wasn't a good sign.

I put the car in drive and headed to the end of the driveway. I made the right hand turn and followed the road to the concrete bridge. By then, my old Chevy sounded like it was beating the drums to some tribal dance ritual. Actually, it wasn't that bad, but the noise was getting louder, and to me, that was a sure sign something was not right.

Should I turn around and go get my folks' van, or should I take my chances in a place I wasn't familiar? As soon as I crossed the bridge, I made a U-turn and went back home.

Back on the road again, I managed to make it all the way to Charlottesville without a hitch. I memorized all the landmarks, and checked out the scenery for future references. I wanted to see all the beautiful trees and mountains. I was finally getting a chance to soak up the magic this place held for my parents. There must be something special about this area. People come from all over the United States to visit the Luray Caverns, Skyline Drive, Blue Ridge Parkway, and to ski at the Massanutten and Wintergreen Ski Resorts. Also, Charlottesville is the home of the University of Virginia Cavaliers, which is one of the finest basketball teams in the country, as far as I'm concerned. I try not to miss one of their games on television. But baseball is my true passion. I love the Atlanta Braves. I even have a Braves' jersey—one of the few expensive purchases I allowed of myself. I do have my little idiosyncrasies.

Forty minutes after I left the house, I reached Greenbriar Road. I wasn't sure whether to take a left or a right at the light, so I flipped a coin in my head, and since I was in the right hand lane, right won out. Shortly, on the right side of the street, I saw the number 214—a Quick Stop gas station mini-mart, and next to it was 212—a McDonald's. This led me to believe I was going in the right direction. After passing several business establishments, I came to a two-story, brick building with the number 200 on the front. The parking lot was big enough to hold six or seven cars, but there was only one there and it looked pretty rough. The car was a faded green Mercury sedan that had to be at least twenty years old. I hoped this wasn't any indication of the boss' clientele, or worse, belong to the boss. I guess I'm just the pot calling the kettle black. Even so, I was out to make a living. On the left side of the building was a driveway.

It was still raining. I scanned the inside of the van hoping to find an umbrella, but no such luck. Contemplating how I was going to get inside the building without getting soaked, I sat there and looked around. Maybe, I should take some time and look this place over before I get out of the van. The building itself reminded me of a warehouse because of the size, but the red brick on it was clean and looked new. There weren't any windows in front, just two glass doors with *Billy Blackhawk Investigations* written in three-inch, cursive letters on the left door. From what I could see through the doors, the office looked like one big open space with a desk in the middle. Behind the desk were two offices, separated by a hallway down the middle. Straining to see through the rain, I could tell the desk was a large, heavily carved mahogany piece of furniture. I appreciate real furniture... not the junk you put together in ten-easy-steps, and then turns into a sponge, if you get the least bit of water on it.

With my spirits lifted a little, I jumped out of the van and ran to the door. Once inside, I shook the water off onto a slate foyer the size of a small bedroom, and was immediately and pleasantly surprised. The *beep-beep* of the alarm system sounded. The desk was indeed a fine piece of furniture, uncluttered with the usual paperwork normally scattered everywhere. On top of the desk sat a computer, telephone, and various office supplies. To my right was a set of double windows with a pair of burgundy leather, Queen Anne chairs. A large rubber tree plant separated the two chairs. To the left of the room was the same set-up of chairs and plant, but instead of a rubber tree, the large plant was a schefflera. Both of the plants were so healthy looking; I was beginning to wonder if they were real. The carpet was a dark gray Berber pile with specks of burgundy. The walls were painted a light shade of gray and all the wood trim and doors were stained a deep, walnut shade. Someone had impeccable taste. I wished I had been a bit more selective in the clothes I had chosen to wear for this job hunt. I felt like a waif going to dine at the Captain's table on a luxury liner. I thought about turning around and heading to the nearest clothing store, when the door on the left opened, and a man appeared. He was not just an ordinary man, either.

Now I understood where the name Blackhawk originated. This man was obviously of Native American descent. He was huge—six-three possibly, and at least two hundred and ten pounds. Are all the men around here that big? He had long shiny black hair, pulled back in a ponytail that went down the middle of his back. His skin was dark, and under his reading glasses, a pair of brown eyes focused on me. He was dressed in a well-tailored, black suit with a gray and red-stripped tie. I thought the ponytail and suit were a strange combination. I guessed him to be about forty, or forty-five years old.

"Hello, may I help you?" his husky voice greeted me.

I held out my hand to him and said, "Hello, my name is Jesse Watson. I'm here to see about the job you had advertised in the paper. I hope I'm not too late. I just moved here a few days ago, and I didn't know how long the ad had been running. I'd like to apologize for the way I'm dressed, but I still haven't finished unpacking..." I lied, and continued to ramble, "This is the type of work I usually do. I don't mean work for a private eye... but the office part of it." I was falling all over myself. Later, I would realize my reason for acting like this was because he was such a big man, and the fact that he was Indian intimidated me. I don't think I have known but one Indian, and I did not know her that well. He did not scare me—I just felt tiny and limp. Maybe it had something to do with the lie I had just told.

He reached out his hand, and took mine in his, shaking it firmly, but not hard. Looking me directly in the eyes, he stated matter-of-factly, "Take a deep breath, Miss Watson. The job is still open. My name is Billy Blackhawk, and I own this agency. I've talked to a few people so far, but I haven't found the right one yet."

All the anxiety and nervousness I had amassed in the last hour or so, seemed to slip away. He was a large man, but he also was gentle. He made me feel calm and safe, and I felt bad about telling him a lie. I had to clear that up immediately.

"I lied about the clothes thing. I have finished unpacking and the truth is, I don't have many clothes. I have enough to get by, but I can tell from my surroundings, I did a poor job of dressing for this interview. I mean this isn't Taco Bell. Please don't hold that against me. Next time I promise I won't be an embarrassment to you because of the way I dress."

He released my hand and replied, "I like that in a person. I like someone who will feel guilt when they have told a lie. But, one must learn how to control that guilt. You must be strong and firm about your beliefs and learn how to channel them for your own good. You must never follow the paths that others will try to send you." He motioned for me to sit in the chair behind the lobby desk. I did not know if he was preaching the word of God to me, or if this was some Indian thing, but I did as he instructed. I sat in the chair.

It felt nice. The chair was one of those computer chairs with armrests, only the cushioning was thicker, and the fabric was the same color of burgundy as the rest of the furnishings. There was a heavy, clear plastic mat underneath. I rolled the chair around on the mat and decided I could get used to this. God, I hope this guy isn't some weirdo.

Looking up at a man the size of a bear made me feel small. I think he sensed it, too. He walked into his office, returned with a small chair, and sat down at the corner of the desk.

"I'm looking for someone to run the front desk, take calls, do all the paperwork that needs to be done, make coffee when the pot is empty, and help me keep things cleaned up when it gets dirty. We do not have a cleaning service. I can not seem to justify paying someone a hundred dollars a week to come in two times and vacuum. Also,you have to know how to use a computer," he stated. "You tell me how much of this you can do."

"I can do all of the above, and I'll even dust. I know my fair share of computer, but I can't go in there and draw a butterfly, not yet anyway."

"Suppose I asked you to sit in a car one night and listen to people talking, what would you say to that?"

"How much do I get paid, and would I get to carry a gun?" I wasn't sure what he meant, but it didn't matter. At least, I didn't think so at the time. I was only joking about the gun.

He leaned back and laughed the laugh of a good-natured man.

"Ok, tell me about yourself, and not that enhanced junk you put on applications, but the real stuff."

"I'm thirty-one years old, single, and I do not have any children. I just moved here from Newport News, Virginia. I live with my folks in Stanardsville. I have a dog. Her name is Athena. I inherited her from my roommate back in Newport News. My life has been average and duller than dirt, so, why not make a change? Now I need a job. I have some money saved, which is good because I think my car just died. I borrowed the family van. There's always Mom and Dad if I get desperate. I figured it was time I got a life. I want to do something different, and I think this job would definitely qualify as different. I've worked for quite a few companies doing various types of work, but never for someone who carries a gun." I noticed the weapon in his shoulder holster earlier when he walked out of his office. "Do you always wear a suit to the office?"

"No, I don't. I have an appointment with a client in an hour. Why don't you run over to Belk and find a skirt and a pair of shoes to go with that pretty blouse and be back here in time to greet them?" He reached into his pocket and pulled out his wallet. "Here, take my credit card and ask for Robert. He's the manager. I'll give him a call."

I couldn't believe he was going to trust me—a stranger—with his credit card. Was he that desperate?

"Does this mean I have the job?"

"Yes, but only temporarily. If it doesn't work out, I'll have to let you go, and I'll send you a bill for the clothes. How's that?"

"It sounds like a deal to me. Where is Belk?" I asked, as I took the card from his hands.

"Go out to Rt.29 and take a left. The store is two blocks down on the right. Please hurry back. My appointment will be here soon."

I left him standing in the middle of the floor and ran to the van. It was still raining outside, but rain was the last thing on my mind. I had a strange feeling Billy Blackhawk and I were going to become good friends.

CHAPTER 4

A S SOON AS I WALKED INTO THE STORE, a young man with the appearance of someone fresh out of high school, politely greeted me. "Hello, Miss Watson. Mr. Blackhawk called and asked me to help you find a nice outfit for the office. He said you were having a little problem with your wardrobe due to a recent fire. I'm sorry for your misfortune. I understand time is of the essence. A size six?" he asked, as he rushed me into a room where two ladies were busying themselves with clothes and shoes for my benefit. Wow, talk about feeling special.

Twenty minutes later, I was on my way, dressed in a lightweight, black linen skirt and fitted jacket to go with my blouse, a pair of black leather heels, and black sheer panty hose. I hadn't worn hose in a long time. My jeans and tennis shoes were placed in a plastic shopping bag for easy carrying. I was a new person. The rain had let up, which was good because I had forgotten about the umbrella I was going to buy.

I walked into the office, feeling like I was right at home. This is where I was meant to be. I could feel it. Now, all I had to do was fit in. I was going to do my best to make Billy glad he hired me. Speaking of which, we never did get around to discussing money. We barely knew each other and already he was giving me a chance to... *what*... help him out? He needed me to be his office girl when his clients arrived. This was to be a test. It was either going to make, or break my chances of a permanent job with Mr. Blackhawk. I had to impress him, if I wanted this job.

I walked over to my desk and stuffed my ragged-ass excuse for a purse in one of the drawers, just about the time Billy walked out of his office. He had a serious look on his face.

"We don't have much time to get to know each other before my clients get here, but we will when they leave. For now, just follow my lead. Act like you know what you're doing. If I ask for a file, they're in the back conference room through that door." He pointed to the closed door at the end of the hall. "Everything is filed under last names. The toilet is on the left, down the hall, and the coffee pot is on the right. The office across from mine is vacant, and I'll tell you about that later. Do you have any questions? Oh, always refer to me as Mr. Blackhawk when others are around. Otherwise you call me Billy. I will address you as Miss Watson in the company of clients. P.S. That's a nice outfit."

I handed him back his credit card and said, "After what you just paid, it should be nice." Getting off the subject, I asked, "May I make a suggestion?" He nodded his head. "Why don't we open some of the office doors? It seems so impersonal when everything is closed up."

"Good idea," he replied. "Do you have any other suggestions?"

"You might want to do something with that funky looking car out front. It's an eyesore."

"I forgot all about that thing. It's my surveillance car. I usually park it in the garage out back along with my truck, but I got busy. Let me take care of that right now."

So, that is where that driveway leads.

"Billy, I need to call my parents and let them know what's going on. I have their van. They might need it."

"Go ahead, and while you're doing that, I'll move my car," he replied, as he was walking out the door.

I got on the phone and called the house. Mom answered on the first ring. I could hear Athena barking in the background the minute she picked up the receiver.

"Mom, I got the job, so I won't be home until later. I hope you don't need the van." Then I thought about my car. "Has Dad had a chance to look at my car yet?"

"He has it in the garage now. Do you want me to go get him, Jesse? Oh, about the van... don't worry, we don't have plans to go anywhere."

"If he's not too busy, ask him to come to the phone, and if he is, ask him what he thinks is wrong with my car."

"Hold on, and I'll be right back," Mom replied, as she laid down the phone.

Instantly, I heard loud barking through the receiver and a grating noise as if someone was chewing on the phone. In the background I heard Mom say, "Don't chew on the phone cord." She must have taken the phone from Athena because I heard the bang of it being laid down again, and what must have been Mom slapping her hand against her leg as she said, "Come on, girl, Let's go outside. That's a good girl."

Dad picked up the phone, caught his breath, and said, "Hi, honey."

"Hello, Dad. Have you been running?"

"Well, I didn't want to keep you waiting. Your mom said you got the job. You can tell me all about it when you get home. Right now, I hate to tell you this, but I think your car is shot. I'm pretty sure the noise you heard was a rod knocking. It's pretty much a goner. The cost to fix it is way more than the car is worth. Your best bet is to get it to a car lot now, and trade it in on a new one. Otherwise, you might as well junk it. A used car dealer isn't going to give you a dime for it."

"Can't you just replace the old rod?" I questioned. I had no idea what he was talking about, but I knew if it could be fixed, my dad could do it. Maybe it's more than he wants to tackle, I thought.

"You don't understand, Jesse. When a rod starts knocking, that means you have to tear the engine down and rebuild it. When you take apart an engine, you can't put it back together with worn out parts. Trust me."

Trust me was what Dad always said when he was sure you could.

"If you say that's what I should do, then that's what I'll do." I didn't want to tell him I was down to my last couple of thousand dollars in my savings account, plus, the money I have in my IRA is not enough to justify a withdrawal—since the government would want half. They always do. My checking account, minus the check I wrote to Fred for the gun, was at a little less than $800.00. "I'll worry about this later," I added.

Things were moving fast. Now, I could add to the list of changes in my life, a new car that I can not afford. I've had two used cars altogether. Both of which, as they say, served me well. Now it was time to make a change. Mom always says—*"Things happen for a reason."*

As I was hanging up the phone, Billy walked in the front door with a man and a woman. They both were probably in their late fifties. The man was almost bald, heavy set, with a potbelly, and was wearing a leisure suit. The woman was petite, with brown hair that appeared to have been styled at the beauty salon. She wore a bracelet loaded with charms, a pair of small diamond earrings, and her diamond wedding rings were big enough to weigh down a small boat. I envisioned the woman to be the one with the money and the class, married to a man that she loved, but couldn't get him properly attired, regardless of how long they had been married. I could not help but go by my first impressions. They looked like midgets compared to Billy.

"Miss Watson, this is Jack and Myra Carrolton. Mr. and Mrs. Carrolton, this is my assistant, Miss Watson," Billy said, as he introduced us.

"Nice to meet you," I said. "May I get you some coffee?"

"Coffee would be nice," Myra Carrolton responded. She was nervous, and I could tell she was not a happy person. She was carrying a heavy load on her shoulders and it showed on her face.

I didn't know what kind of problem brought them here, but it was obvious to me from their appearance, and the way their eyes revealed a sadness I've never known, that they were intense people with burdens that most of us hope we never have to endure. I wasn't quiet sure how involved I was going to be with Billy's clients, but I was about to find out.

Billy looked at the Carroltons and said, "If you don't mind, I'd like Miss Watson to sit in on this meeting." After getting their approval, he turned to me and said, "We'll take our coffee in here, please." He led them to his office.

I stood there for a minute thinking, what now? They didn't say what they wanted in their coffee, and I didn't get a chance to ask. So, I put my brain back in gear and walked down the hall to the coffee room. I found a fresh pot of coffee and a well-stocked cabinet of cups, saucers, and the usual sugar and powdered cream. On the counter was a small refrigerator. I opened the door and sure enough, there were several small cartons of 2% milk. After checking the date on one of the cartons, I searched the top cabinet for something to pour it into. I found a creamer, sugar bowl, and a set of matching mugs. In the bottom cabinet, I found a tray.

I was busy pouring coffee and arranging everything on the tray, when all of a sudden, my stomach growled. I looked up to find a clock, and realized it was way past noon. I hadn't eaten all day. I decided I'd better fix myself a cup of coffee so that I would have something in my stomach. What I'd give for a piece of bread right now.

I took the tray to Billy's office and sat it on a small table to the right of his huge desk. I went about serving coffee, while I listened to their conversation. I waited for a cue from Billy as to what I was supposed to do next. When he didn't say anything, I sat down next to the table and remained silent.

Billy was taking notes, as he listened carefully to every word Myra and Jack were saying. I noticed he had a tape recorder sitting in the middle of his desk, with the green light flashing. Pretty smart, I thought. This man thinks of everything.

Myra looked at Billy, then turned to me and said, "We're at the end of our rope. The police still don't have anything, and I don't think they're even trying anymore. Every time I call that police detective... oh, what's his name, Jack? Oh, yes... *Detective Hargrove*, I can almost see him rolling his eyes back in his head. It's been almost six months and they don't know anymore now than they did then. I know my daughter's out there somewhere and she needs our help. I can just feel it." She burst into tears.

I jumped up, grabbed the box of tissues from Billy's desk, and handed them to her. This was heartbreaking. She was in so much pain.

"Mr. and Mrs. Carrolton's daughter left Poquoson the day after Christmas to stay a few days with a friend in Charlottesville, but never got there. Nobody has seen, or heard from her since," Billy explained to me.

I sat dumbfounded, while Billy fired off questions to the Carroltons.

"What is your daughter's full name and social security number?" he asked, waiting for her to regain control of her emotions.

Jack Carrolton sat stiff and upright, staring straight ahead as if he was in another world, while Myra dried her eyes and said, "*Helen Sue Carrolton*" and then rattled off the number. "She just turned nineteen in December. We bought her a new car for a birthday and Christmas present. She's such a sweet girl. She never gave us a moment's trouble. Made straight A's almost all the way through school. She's in her first year at Christopher Newport University. They were on Christmas break when she left to visit her friend Emma Lee. Emma attends the college in Charlottesville. They were... are best friends. They grew up together." She dabbed at her eyes and continued. "Jack is Helen's stepfather. Her real father died when she was six. But Jack has been like a father to her since day one. He loves her as much as I do."

That last statement sounded like she was letting us know there was no reason to suspect her husband of anything. Maybe the police had questioned Jack's possible involvement in his stepdaughter's disappearance.

Jack must have been reading my thoughts. "*Yes*, to the question you are about to ask. Since I'm only her stepfather, at the very beginning they grilled me up and down. If that wasn't ridiculous enough, they started giving Myra a raking over. Once they established we didn't do harm to our own child, or have anything to do with her disappearance, they went down the list of her friends and everybody she knew... or *knows*."

Jack and Myra desperately wanted to believe their daughter was alive. However, after six months of trying to find her, I think they were beginning to accept the possibility that maybe Helen was not alive, and if that was true, they had to know. They were both wound so tight; I was expecting one of them to go off any minute.

Billy eased himself back into the conversation. "I'm going to do my best to find out what happened to your daughter. I'm going to need every bit of information I can get on her—everything."

Then the worst thing happened. My stomach growled. What an icebreaker. The room lit up with laughter.

"Why don't I take us all out to lunch?" Billy asked. "We can talk more about your daughter, and Miss Watson can make up for not having breakfast this morning. It sounds as if she needs to eat."

More chuckles echoed off the walls, but at least it made Myra stop crying. Her tears were breaking my heart.

Even though I was terribly embarrassed, I was glad it happened. Now we could take a break, and get some food. Billy was treating. Does he do this kind of thing often? I wondered.

Billy picked up his tape recorder and said, "My brother, Robert, owns a nice family restaurant a mile down the road called the Rising Sun. He has a couple booths he keeps available for anyone in the family who comes in to eat, so we won't have to wait for a table. The food is excellent and the atmosphere is soothing. We can discuss everything as we eat."

As the Carroltons were walking out the front door, Billy pulled me aside and asked if we could take my van. He said his truck wouldn't hold all of us and he sure didn't want to take his junky car.

"Sure," I whispered, as I grabbed my purse and turned on the answering machine. I assumed it had a recorded message on it to take care of missed calls, but I didn't have time to make sure.

Robert Blackhawk greeted us with a smile and led us to a booth in the back, talking to Billy the whole time. Occasionally I picked up on a few words of English, but most of their conversation was spoken in their native language. Robert left and a waitress appeared at our table with menus. I discovered the menu was made up of foods I had never heard of until now.

"What do you recommend?" Billy asked the waitress, as we all sat down and he placed his tape recorder in the middle of the table.

"Our special today is pan fried buffalo steak, twice baked potatoes, black beans, and the house salad," she answered in a tone all too personal. She must know Billy, I thought. Her smile was almost sickening.

"Sounds good to me," Billy replied.

"Sure, why not? I've never had buffalo steak." I added.

"Well, I'm afraid I'll just stick with something less exciting. How about the baked chicken platter? I have to watch what I eat at my age. The digestive system is the first to go," Jack said to the waitress.

"I think I'll have the same," Myra replied.

By the time the food arrived, I was seeing another side of Billy. He was all business at first and then the caring side of him appeared. He told the Carroltons his fee was two hundred dollars a day, plus expenses, with a fifteen hundred dollar retainer, from which fees would be deducted until the retainer was used up. After that, he would bill weekly. If, for some reason, they wanted to terminate his services, any money left would be returned to them, and if any money was due, it was payable upon termination. Then his demeanor became softer, " I'm sorry to have to tell you this, but once a person has been missing for several days, unless they just ran off, the outlook is not too good. I'm sure the police must have told you the same thing. It's been almost six months, and I can't promise to bring your daughter back to you alive, but I will do my best to find her."

Myra started crying again, as Jack pulled out his checkbook, ripped out a check, and handed it to Billy.

"Whatever it takes," Jack Carrolton said. "Money is no problem."

The buffalo steak turned out to be delicious. It tasted like a T-bone steak. By the time we finished eating, I knew more about the awful disappearance of Helen Carrolton than I wanted to know. She was young, pretty, and had it all. She left her home in Poquoson the day after Christmas, but never arrived at her destination in Charlottesville, and she never returned home. That was six months ago.

Once our late-lunch-early-dinner was finished, we returned to the office. It was starting to rain again, and I couldn't help picturing an ominous dark cloud hanging over all of us. For some strange reason, I had a bad, nagging feeling of doom. It was so depressing. Did I take my Zoloft this morning? I couldn't remember.

Myra and Jack retreated to Billy's office. I watched them sign the required contract. Jack withdrew a bulky envelope from the breast pocket of his leisure suit and handed it to Billy.

"This is a copy of all the information we have on Helen's disappearance. Myra and I own a landscaping business in Newport News. You can reach us anytime, either there, or at home. We don't socialize a whole lot. We're going to spend the night at the Ramada Inn, so if you need to talk to us, we'll be there until checkout time tomorrow. It's too long of a drive for us to make in one day. But if you need us to, we will come back at any time. That is, if you come up with anything."

By the time the Carroltons left, it was pouring outside. Billy explained to me that when it rains in the mountains, like it's been doing, it could go away anytime. When it drizzles all day, it is usually set in—steady and non-stop. That was something to keep in mind for future reference.

"I'm so glad you're going to find Helen," I said to Billy, as he was settling into his chair, going over the papers in the envelope Jack Carrolton had given him. "This is so sad. Is this the type of cases you handle all the time? I mean, I've never worked for a private investigator before, and I have no idea what is involved. Can you really find her? How? Where do you start looking?"

"I never said I would find her. I told the Carroltons I'd try, and that's what I'm going to do. I'm pretty good at my job, and if anybody can find her, I can. The truth is, Jesse, when it's been this long, they usually turn up dead, if they turn up at all. Believe me, we'll earn our money, but it might not be so pleasant an outcome."

I was surprised. I thought it was in the bag. I guess I just don't know how these things go. I pictured a scene where Billy and I found the girl and saved the day, but now, that didn't seem likely. It was a no-win situation. If we did find the girl, chances are, she would not be alive.

"What do you mean? Are you telling me you think she's dead and you didn't tell the Carrolton's?"

"I told them the outlook wasn't promising. You heard me tell them. Look, here's a detail you need to know right from the start—when people come to me it is usually their last resort. They have done everything else. They're been everywhere, and there's nothing left. They come to me because I'm their last hope of finding an answer to whatever it is they need to ask. I'm their last chance. Sometimes I find that answer, and sometimes I don't. I don't cheat them as far as money goes. I only charge for what I do, and I give them the best service I can."

"I guess there's a lot of things I need to learn about investigating," I replied, as I began collecting the cups and left over dishes from earlier.

"Don't worry about it. You'll learn as you go along." He reached into his jacket and retrieved the check from the Carroltons. "Take this check and log it in on the computer and also write it in the black book that you'll find in the top right hand drawer of your desk. If you have any problems with the computer just yell. When you're done, bring me the check. I have a zip bag in my desk drawer where I keep money and checks. Oh, and print out a receipt for the check and mail it to the Carroltons. I forgot to give them a receipt. Here's their address." He wrote the information down on a notepad and handed it to me. "By the way, you did pretty well today. I didn't know what to expect considering this is all new to you."

"I didn't know what to expect either," I said.

"Well, you did fine. I saw something in you when we first met. I don't know what it is yet, but I think we're going to make a good team."

"Fear and embarrassment for the way I was dressed," I replied.

"Speaking of which, when you're in the office I want you to dress nicely. You know, dresses or skirts, or whatever, as long as it's conserva-tive. If you need an advance on your salary to buy some more new clothes..."

"I think I have got it covered, but thanks anyway."

"All right then, about your salary. Your salary, after taxes, will be two hundred and fifty dollars a week to start. The more you are involved with the day-to-day operations, the more you can make. I'll pay you bonuses on jobs when you do more than just office work."

"What do you mean, more than office work?"

"For example: going out in the middle of the night and staking out the target of an investigation, or, if you take pictures for me—just the general stuff that a trainee in this line of work would do. If you're not interested in doing anything like this, it's ok. Just tell me now and I won't hold it against you. This line of work is not for everyone."

"I would love to do something like that. I could learn and earn at the same time," I joked.

"All right then, we have work to do."

As I was walking out of Billy's office with the coffee tray, he called out to me, "When I'm out in the field, I wear casual clothes; jeans or whatever. Sometimes it can get right rough out there. You might want to keep a change of clothing in a duffel bag in your car. You never know when you might need them."

I let this sink in, as I went to the coffee room and washed out the cups. After putting everything away, I went to my desk to continue the task at hand. I didn't have any problems with the computer system, and I found everything I needed to do what Billy had asked of me. I laid the envelope with the Carrolton's receipt in the outgoing mail basket and took the check back to Billy.

After listening to the messages and taking notes at the same time, Billy handed me a piece of paper from one of those *While You Were Out* pads, and said, "Get Mrs. Miller on the line for me, and then call Mr. Dempsey and set up an appointment for Monday morning. When you're finished, maybe we can talk."

Fifteen minutes later, I was back in Billy's office.

"Mrs. Miller wants me to find out if her husband is cheating on her—two to three days at the most. A few pictures and several hours of surveillance, and we'll be done. She'll be here in twenty minutes," he said.

"You say that so nonchalant. How do you feel when you get the dirt on a guy and then have to tell his wife, 'Yes, your husband is having an affair'? I mean, don't you feel bad for the injured party?"

"I sure do. I hate it, but that's life. Shit happens, and I just shovel it around. It's a dirty job, but someone has to do it." Then he made one of those head-rolling, eye-crossing gestures that just cracked me up.

In the best Scarlet voice I could muster, I said, "Why, Mr. Billy, I do believe you are filled with more clichés than Savannah has plantations." I should have never said that. We both started laughing so hard, I had to give Billy a tissue to wipe away his tears.

Once we both settled down, Billy was the first to open up. "I'm a Cherokee Indian. Actually, I'm half-Indian. My father is an Indian Chief and my mother is white. To you this probably means nothing, but to me this is a lifetime of trying to endure the pain and suffering of being different. Our people frown on marrying outside of our own kind, and when you do, you suffer the wrath that goes along with the sin. The Indian doesn't marry the white man, or in this case, the white woman. When my father married my mother, they were shunned by other leaders, and dealt with very much like one of your Catholics that have been excommunicated from their church. It has only been in the past twenty years that our family has mended the scars left by the tribe's old-fashioned ways. Through all of this, we managed to hold onto our pride."

"I don't know much about your culture, but I can understand the reason why your people would feel the way they do. Right from the beginning the white man has shit all over the Indians. Even I know that," I responded.

"I don't dwell on the past. I try to learn from it," Billy said. "Tell me something about your life, Jesse."

"There's not much to tell. I'm thirty-one and I've spent most of my life doing nothing impressive. I have a sister named Claire, and a brother named Jackson... but we call him Jack. Claire's married to a man she now thinks is cheating on her, and they have two kids, with another one on the way. Jack is a lawyer, and single. My father retired from the Navy and my mother doesn't work. She's always been a housewife. They just moved to Stanardsville a couple of days ago, and I moved with them. And believe me, I didn't leave much behind. What about you? I guess that picture on your desk must be your two boys. What about your wife?"

"Ruth and I got a divorce five years ago, but she's still in my thoughts. She found someone else to give her the time and attention she deserves. I don't blame her. I was always so busy trying to make a good life for my family that I forgot the most important thing—sharing that life with the ones you love." He cleared his throat and continued, "I'm 47 years old and I've been doing this kind of work forever. I have two sons. Will is twenty-two and in his senior year at the University of Virginia. John is twenty years old and goes to Virginia Tech. I can't tell you how proud I am of my boys." He picked up the picture of his sons and handed it to me.

"Good-looking boys," I observed, as I handed back the picture. "Do you date? I mean, is there someone you're romantically involved with?"

"You do get right to the point, don't you?"

"Well, I figure the more we know about each other, the better. It looks as if we're going to be spending a good deal of time together, so it would help to know which side of the fence we're standing on, and where to draw the line. If I'm getting too personal, just say so. I can handle it. I don't bruise too easily."

"I can tell. You're strong, yet a little insecure, which usually comes from a long line of letdowns and disappointments. You need a man to make you happy. One that will give you the fulfillment you are missing. It will happen," he announced. "As for me, I date sometimes."

"It will happen," I joked.

Changing the subject, he continued, "What's this about your car? You're going to need a car. Is there something I can do? I'm pretty good with fixing cars, and I'm great with motorcycles. I have a 1955, K-Model, Harley Sportster parked in my garage. I used to ride it all the time, but now I just take it out on cruises when the weather is nice. I'm getting too old to ride it in the dead of winter, and I wouldn't want to around here. I want to keep the bike's body in good shape and the harsh winter snow and muddy rains are killers on metal."

"Maybe some time you will drive it to work so I can check it out. I can ride bikes. I went through a phase at one time when I actually owned one. It was a 360cc Honda. I forget the year, but it had roll bars, and a king and queen seat, with a sissy stick. That was a long time ago and the phase didn't last long. Every time I got out onto Denbigh Boulevard, everybody on the road wanted to see if that was a girl or a guy, with all that long hair, riding a motorcycle. I had too many close calls. I said forget it, and sold the bike to a friend. As far as my car goes, my dad said it was a goner. He said something about a rod knocking. It's an old car—real old. It's about time for..."

I was interrupted by the *beep-beep* of the front door. I stood and walked out of Billy's office to greet our visitor. "May I help you?"

"I'm here to talk to Billy Blackhawk. I'm Mrs. Miller."

Billy came out of his office. "Hello, I'm Billy Blackhawk, and this is my assistant, Miss Watson. Come right in," he gestured toward his office. "Miss Watson, hold my calls, please."

The digital clock on my desk read 4:45. Good, I'm ready to call it a day.

At ten minutes after five, Billy led Mrs. Miller out of his office and to the front door, assuring her the whole time he would get what she wanted and be in touch. Then he came over to me and handed me a file and a key.

"This is the key to the front door. All the doors are keyed to this one key. If, at any time, that far door over there on the left is locked, don't go in. It's the entrance stairway to my place. I live upstairs. The garage out back is where I normally keep my car, my truck, and my Harley. If you want to see my bike sometime, all you have to do is go through the second door on the left, down the main hallway," he motioned. "Here's the file on the Carrolton girl. Make a copy and look it over this weekend, please. Keep it to yourself. Don't let anyone see it. When you're done, you can leave and I'll see you at eight, Monday morning." He handed me a business card. "This card has my home phone number in case you need to talk to me after work hours. Write down your phone number on a piece of paper and leave it on your desk for me before you leave, please."

Once I finished the last few things I had to do, I dug out my purse and headed for the door. The rain was coming down harder than it had been all day. It figures. I had to stop somewhere and pick up dog food for Athena, and I wanted to shop for some new clothes.

I yelled good-bye to Billy and made a run for the van. I made a stop at Wal-Mart and purchased dog food, two skirts and two blouses, a pair of navy heels, and a black leather shoulder bag. Luckily, by the time I left the store the rain had stopped.

The drive home was pleasant, although my mind kept drifting off to Cole, my new job, and Billy.

When I made the left turn onto Rt.33 at Ruckersville and drove down the road a bit, I noticed a sight to behold. "Wow," I said out loud. I couldn't believe what I saw. How could I have missed this? Where was my mind? There on the top of a hill to my left, sat a brown and yellow police car with a sign on top that read, *Law Enforcement-Out of Control*. I almost ran off the road. Never in my wildest imagination could I believe someone would have the courage to do something so bold. Back in Tidewater, you'd never get away with a form of expression such as this. At best, they're probably put you in jail. Whoever was responsible, has more guts than I do. America! Land of the free. Home of the brave! I love this country!

I drug my old tired butt into the house, along with the stuff I had purchased at Wal-Mart. The house was empty, but, true to form, Mom had left a note saying they had taken Athena for a walk. When I took the bag of Purina Dog Chow to the utility room, I noticed someone had already bought her a bag. It brought a smile to my lips. What wonderful parents I have. I made my way upstairs and after hanging up my new clothes, I flopped down on the bed.

I must have dozed off, because the next sounds I heard were Athena barking, and voices downstairs. After washing my face, I went down to talk to my folks. I couldn't wait to tell them about Billy and my new job, and about that police car. I wondered if they had seen it.

I stopped when I noticed Cole sitting at the kitchen table with Dad.

"H-hello," I stammered.

"Hi, honey," said Dad. "Come on over here and tell us about your new job. We're dying to hear about it."

Mom was in the kitchen preparing dinner.

"Well, I got a job working for a private investigator named Billy Blackhawk," I answered, waiting for Cole to make some kind of comment, considering he was a cop and probably had some contact with men in this line of work. But he said nothing. "I like him. He seems to be honest and he knows what he is doing."

"Good," Mom offered. "We want you to be happy."

Her comment embarrassed me. I felt as though she was implying I was not happy, which might have been true in the past, but I didn't want Cole to hear about my distress. I didn't want him to think I was some poor, old, lonely woman with a rotten life. Things were different now. For the first time in a long time, I felt happy. I liked my new life.

CHAPTER 5

COLE HAD STOPPED BY on his way home from work to tell us he couldn't make dinner tomorrow night. He was scheduled to work the fair that was in town, and suggested we go check it out.

"It's something the whole community looks forward to every year. There is going to be games, food, animals, and live entertainment. I think you folks would enjoy it."

He was so good-looking; I couldn't help but stare. I hoped I wasn't drooling when I replied, "I'd love to check it out. What do you think, Mom and Dad? Shall we go?"

"We said we would probably go, remember?" Dad replied.

Parents can be so blunt sometimes, and being candid is not always their strong suit. Sticking my tail between my legs like a dog, I decided I'd keep my mouth shut. This is getting all fouled up. I wanted Cole to see me as a lady and not some dumb bimbo trying to grab onto the first person that came along. I felt like a child being admonished for acting silly. It must have been the guilt I was feeling for wanting to climb all over him. I had to put those thoughts out of my head.

"You say you were on your way home? Why don't you stay and eat with us. There's going to be plenty of food," Mom offered Cole.

"Actually, I need to go let my dog outside. River gets kind of crazy after being shut up for so long."

"You have a dog named *River*? That's a strange name for a dog," Mom questioned him.

"Yeah, I guess it is. I named him River because I found him when he was just a puppy, wet and all beat up, down by the river. It was raining hard just like it has been doing today, and I heard a whimpering, sad bark coming from that direction. So, I went over to the river, and there he was all curled up. I brought him home and we've been together ever since. That was three years ago."

"Why don't you go home and let River out and come back for dinner? It should be ready by then," Mom suggested, as she continued to take food out of the refrigerator.

Cole smiled, as he got up to leave. "Do you think I might have time to grab a quick shower? I've been chasing bad guys all day, and a shower would hit the spot."

Was he kidding? I let out a giggle; quickly becoming the idiot teenager I had reverted back to. Maybe I should just be sent to my room. Isn't that what a parent does when a kid gets out of control?

After Cole left, I ran upstairs to take a shower. I needed to get fixed up and try not to make an ass out of myself later.

Cole returned at 7:31 on the dot. I remember because I was already dressed and watching the clock. I would never admit it, but the truth was, I couldn't stand the anticipation. I had fantasies of what the evening would be like. After dinner, Mom and Dad would retire for the evening and Cole and I would have an intimate conversation, sitting in the swing on the porch. It didn't turn out quite like that, but the evening was interesting.

After a dinner of Mom's wonderful fried chicken, Cole got up and started to help clear away the dishes. That surprised me. From my experience, most men usually get up from the table and hit the couch. And as far as a dishwasher is concerned, forget it. I think men believe there's a monster living in there, because they won't go near one. I wiped down the table, as Cole continued to help Mom. Dad retreated to the couch, and turned on the television set.

"Mrs. Watson, that was the best fried chicken I've had since I had dinner at my mom's house," Cole admitted.

It was obvious Mom was charmed by him. "Thank you," she giggled. "Why don't you just call me Minnie? All my friends do."

A few minutes later, we managed to pull Dad away from the TV. We had our after-dinner coffee on the front porch. Mom and Dad conveniently sat in the chairs, which left the swing for Cole and me. I'm sure she planned it that way. She knew I was interested in Cole, and she was going to do everything she could to help it along. Cole must have sensed what she was up to. He stretched his arm out behind me and laid it on top of the swing. I looked around in time to catch him wink at her. Those rats, something was going on here that I did not know about.

Shortly, Mom jumped up and proclaimed, "Mack, I almost forgot. We were supposed to call Claire tonight. Remember, I told you she said to call her Friday night before we went to bed? Let's do it before it gets too late. I want to be able to talk to the grandkids."

Dad was taken by surprise. "What? Oh, yeah. Now I remember."

"Would you excuse us for a minute, Cole? We need to call Claire. She's our other daughter, and we promised her we would call tonight."

In a flash, they were gone, and I was left with egg on my face.

"I'm sorry, Cole. Mom's always trying to fix me up with someone."

"Don't worry about it. I understand how mothers can be. My mom does the same thing to me. She will invite me over for dinner, and I find out when I get there, she's also invited a friends' daughter, or someone she met at the grocery store. I've had my share of dinner dates, thanks to her."

"That's bad. I'd die if my mom did something like that. It makes you appear so *needy*. Mom wants me to be happy like my sister Claire, and I think she would do anything she could to help it along. I bet the first thing she asked was if you were married. At least, she didn't flag you down and force you to come to dinner. Did she?"

He laughed.

"Oh, God," I murmured, as my head dropped down. I wanted to throw up. Please don't let this be happening. Here's a man I am truly attracted to, and Mom goes and does this. It was embarrassing.

"No, she didn't do anything like that. She did, however, tell me it was such a shame that a girl as pretty and sweet as you are, couldn't find a man. You deserve to be happy. She's right, except for the part about not being able to find a man. I told her one day the right man would come along and you'd find the happiness you deserve."

This was getting worse by the minute. Did she also tell him that I dyed my hair? I know she must have mentioned something about the size of my breasts. What else? I had to get out of here. The tone of his voice felt patronizing—something I couldn't handle.

I stood and was about to excuse myself, when he gently reached out his hand, touched my arm and said, "Please, don't go. I wouldn't be here if I didn't want to be. Don't worry about your mom. She's like every mother that loves her child. She wants to help."

"Promise me you won't let her manipulate you," I begged, as I sat back down in the swing. "She has a way of getting people to do things they might not otherwise want to do."

"Hey, I'm a cop, remember? I'm used to dealing with people. I've met up with some pretty bad guys in the line of duty and you think some little old, sweet mother is going to strong-arm me? No way. Why, I think I'll just go inside right now and slap the cuffs on her. I'll put her in jail for feeding me a good dinner. She'll probably get five to ten for such a heinous crime."

I laughed. "Bull, you like my mother. I can tell."

"Now that we've come to the conclusion that mothers always have the upper hand, tell me about your new job. How did you come to meet Billy Blackhawk?"

"I read his ad in the paper for an office assistant. I knew I could do the job. I can't tell you how many office jobs I've had. However, this was different. The job seemed interesting. I mean, working for a private investigator sounded like fun. I can learn something new, and perhaps have a little bit of excitement at the same time. Billy is a nice guy. He's intelligent, and he seems to really have it together. I've been with him for one day and already I feel like we are old friends."

"Billy's a good man, but this is serious business. Do you realize what you're getting into? He comes in contact with some pretty rough people. Promise me you'll be careful. Watch your back, and don't take any unnecessary chances. It's a hard world out there."

"Billy and I had a long talk. The only thing I will be doing is the usual office stuff. Things like answering the phone, filing, making coffee, and spying on clients."

"I caught that remark," he said. "Detective work is serious business. It's dangerous, and you could get hurt."

"Why, Rhett, I do think thou dost protest too much."

Cole turned to me and looked deep into my eyes. "I like you, Jesse. I don't want anything to happen to you. This isn't a joke. I meant it when I said things could get dangerous. Did Billy tell you about the time he got shot?"

"What? Billy got shot? When? What happened?"

"Five years ago Billy was on a stakeout tailing a cheating husband. The guy came out of the motel and caught Billy with a camera. The guy went crazy and shot Billy in the gut with a .22 pistol. Good thing it was only a .22. If it had been a 9MM or a .38, Billy would be dead. It broke him up when Ruth left, and I don't think he had his mind on his job. He was lucky, and I told him so. Billy and I are old friends. We go back a long way. After the shooting, I made him promise he'd start wearing a vest."

"You're starting to scare me," I whispered.

"Good, you need to have a bit of fear in you. Besides, if something happens to you, whom will I marry and have a house full of kids with? Plus, it would break your mother's heart."

He was joking, but the way he said it with such a warm smile on his face, touched my heart. I sat there with my eyes glued to his, mesmerized. I actually thought he was going to kiss me, and he might have, if Mom hadn't appeared at the front door. Talk about bad timing.

"I'm sorry to bother you kids. You look like you're having such a good time, but we didn't want to go to bed without saying good night. Claire says to tell you hi, Jesse." She turned to Cole. "I hope you'll come have dinner with us again real soon. Maybe we'll see you tomorrow at the fair. I'm sure Jesse would like that. Wouldn't you, honey?"

"I live for the moment," I replied, causing Cole to chuckle.

She looked at the two of us as if we'd lost our minds. "Well, good night." She was shaking her head as she went back inside.

Cole looked at his watch and exclaimed, "I had no idea it was so late! It's almost 10:30. Where did the time go? I need to get home. I've got a long day ahead of me tomorrow. I hope you'll come out to the fair, but if you don't, how about I take you sight-seeing Sunday? We could go up on the Skyline Drive. It's beautiful this time of year."

"Oh, you can bet I'll be at the fair. Mom will see to it. I would still like to take you up on the offer to go sight seeing."

He leaned over and kissed me on the cheek. Then he was gone, and I was smitten.

I stood on the porch and listened to the sounds of the night, and took in the clean fresh smell of the air. Crickets made their funny sounds and birds chirped in the background. Somewhere in the distance, the lone cry of a bobcat echoed. Or maybe it was the cry of somebody's house cat. I didn't know, and it didn't matter.

I went to bed with one thought on my mind. Tomorrow I would see Cole. I felt like a teenager again. This was getting crazy. I knew I had to get myself together, or I would be heading for a full-blown crash. Things were just moving way too fast, and I knew it. I lay in bed and reminisced about the past men in my life, and decided I would take a step backwards. The few times I had overwhelming feelings for someone, it usually resulted in heartbreak. I've learned that when a man comes into your life with a big bang, he usually goes out like a fizzled-out sparkler on the fourth of July. I fell asleep determined to not let that happen this time.

Saturday morning, while Mom and Dad were still sleeping, I showered, got dressed, made a pot of coffee, and then took Athena for a walk. The morning air was cool and crisp, yet the sun was bright and warm. Off in the distance, dark, puffy clouds appeared on the horizon. Was it going to rain today and ruin our plans to go to the fair? I prayed not.

Athena and I scouted the area, ending up at the stream. The water was cold, but that didn't stop her from jumping in and digging for rocks. She stuck her head under the water and didn't come up until she had a rock in her mouth, which she promptly brought over and laid at my feet.

"Athena, get out of there, girl. It's too cold."

She climbed out, ran to me, and shook the water from her coat. "Whoa, girl," I said, trying to dodge the spray. "Let's get back on the road, away from this cold water."

We walked until we came upon a house set back behind a row of tall Pines. Two dogs were sunning themselves in the front yard. The minute they saw us, they jumped up, started barking, and ran towards us.

"It is time to go home, Athena," I whispered, and in one quick step, we turned and headed back home.

When the dogs finally caught up with us, I thought there was going to be one hell of a fight. Oddly enough, all three of them sniffed each other a few times and began a playful romp before settling down.

"Hey, even the dogs are friendly, Athena."

As we got closer to the house, I turned and said to our new companions, "All right, you two dogs go on back home." Much to my surprise, they turned and headed back in the other direction. Cool, dogs that obey your command. What will I discover next?

Dad was reading the paper at the table and Mom was cooking breakfast, humming a familiar song.

"I remember that song. You used to sing it to us when we were kids," I said. "I just can't remember the name of it."

Ignoring my statement, Mom replied, "So, what do you think of Cole? Y'all stayed up pretty late last night."

Remembering what Cole had said about Moms, I softly answered, "I like him. He's nice. We hit it off, so you can stop playing matchmaker. We're going for a ride on the Skyline Drive tomorrow."

Dad snickered under his breath, as Mom said, "I knew you two were perfect for each other. I told Mack you were meant for each other."

"What gives you that idea? Is it one of those feelings you get?"

"Maybe it was the way you drooled all over yourself the first time you met him," Dad laughed, turning his back to me.

"I did not drool all over myself," I promptly replied, as I sat at the table with a fresh cup of coffee. "I admit that I was taken with Cole when I first met him, and I may have reacted strongly, but I did not drool."

"Oh, don't be silly, Mack. She was doing what most women do when they meet a handsome man like Cole. She was examining him," Mom came to my defense. I love it when women stick up for each other.

I heard the rumble of thunder and went to look out the window. The dark clouds I saw off in the distance earlier had moved overhead.

"Please, tell me that's not what I think it is. I was hoping those gray clouds were going to move on out. Is it supposed to rain today, Dad?"

"According to the weather forecast in the paper it says—*Early scattered thunderstorms tapering off to light rain in the afternoon*—but it looks like rain all day to me. I guess we'll have to miss the county fair. I was *so* looking forward to playing games, riding rides, and following you two around ."

"Oh, don't fret Dad, you still have tomorrow. Of course, I'll have to pass on all the fun. I have a date with Cole."

I was disappointed we weren't going to the county fair. I would miss out on seeing Cole, but at least I still had a chance to be with him tomorrow. Mom must have sensed my frustration. She came over and put her arm around my shoulder, and gave me one of her motherly hugs. She has an uncanny way of knowing how I feel, without me saying a word. I can never hide anything from her.

By the time we finished eating breakfast, the storm had moved in. I've always had a thing about thunderstorms. Maybe I was traumatized as a child. Now when I see lightning and hear thunder, all I want to do is close the curtains, and crawl into bed. However, on the other hand, I love the rain. I don't want to stand out in it, but there's nothing like curling up on the couch with a good book, while the rain beats down on the roof. Rain makes things grow, and when it's over, the air smells so clean. I could never figure out why people get depressed when it rains.

Since the day was going to be a wash out, I decided I'd spend time going over the file Billy had asked me to read. I offered to help Mom with the dishes, but she said she'd take care of them, when the storm passed. I went up to my room with Athena hot on my heels—maybe she was afraid of storms, too. I closed the curtains on the front dormer window and the big double window on the side, and sat down on the bed, file in hand.

The file contained a copy of the newspaper article published two days after the disappearance of Helen Carrolton; a copy of her birth certificate; and three pages of handwritten notes concerning the case. I assumed the notes were written by one of her parents because there were bits of information added here and there in the margins. The last page of the notes had stain spots on it, as if someone had been crying while writing, and their tears had spilled onto the paper. It was all so sad. I could sense the agony with each stroke of the pen. Their only child had been missing for six months—vanished without leaving a trace. Unless Helen Carrolton was found, dead or alive, there would be no closure for Myra and Jack Carrolton.

From the information contained in the file, it appeared that Helen Carrolton, age 19, had left her home on Wythe Creek Road in Poquoson the 26th of December, around four o'clock in the afternoon. She should have arrived at her friend, Emma Lawrence's home in Gordonsville around seven or eight o'clock, depending on the traffic on I-64 and the I-295 Richmond by-pass. Emma was going to use her Christmas vacation to move to her new apartment closer to the university in Charlottesville, and Helen was going to help her with the move. At ten o'clock, Emma's parents, Wayne and Donna Lawrence called Jack and Myra looking for Helen. From that moment on, there were a frenzy of phone calls placed to various local and state police departments and hospitals. Eventually, calls were made to Helen's other friends, obviously a last ditch effort. There were no reports of accidents involving a red '99 Chevy Geo, driven by a 19 year old female, 110 pounds, short blond hair, blue eyes, and wearing glasses. There was nobody admitted to area hospitals that fitted that description either. She wasn't in an automobile accident, or in the hospital, and she wasn't in jail... so, where was she? An official missing person's report was filed with the Poquoson Police Department twenty four hours later. The Carroltons had driven to Gordonsville to the Lawrence's house, checking out every little nook and cranny on their way, looking for Helen's car. They stopped at the rest area on I-64 westbound, near the weigh station, checked every hill, pasture and building in the background of I-295, and then stopped at the rest area on the second leg of I-64. Finally, they had taken the Zion Crossroads exit, and ended their drive at the

Lawrence's farm. Neither Helen, nor her car was anywhere to be found.

That was the complete file. There was no official police report. Yet, from what I had read, there were so many questions left to be answered—questions that could only be answered by a police report. Billy and I had to get that report, or we were dead in the water. We had nothing to go on. Somewhere along the way, somebody must have seen her. Did she stop to get gas? Did she stop to eat? Where were the eyewitness reports? It was a three-hour drive. Who drives for three hours without stopping to get gas, or at least stopping to pee?

In the middle of my reading, the phone rang.

"It's for you, Jesse," Mom yelled up the stairs.

"I got it," I replied, as I picked up the receiver thinking, I've got to get a private line.

"Hello," I said.

"Jesse, this is Billy. How are you doing?"

"I'm fine. How are you doing?"

"I'm good, thanks. I called because I have some work to do tonight, and I'd like you to be with me. It's surveillance work, so all you have to do is sit in the car. If you don't want to do it, I will understand. I just thought it would give you some insight as to what kind of work I do. Surveillance work is a big part of a private investigator's job. Unfortunately, it's a lot of sitting and not much excitement."

"Sure! I would love it," I answered, without hesitation. "I have a slight problem with transportation at the moment. My car has turned into a vegetable. Let me ask my folks if I can use the van."

"Forget the van. I'll pick you up."

"Ok, what time?"

"Don't you want to know anything about the job first?"

"No, not now. I'm sure you will fill me in on it later, right?"

"You got it! I'll be there around five o'clock."

"Do you know how to get here?"

"Yes, I do. I'm a private detective. Don't you remember? I have your address. That is all I need. I will see you at five."

"Whatever you say..." I mumbled, as I heard the dial tone in my ear.

Wow! I was getting my first chance to go out on a real stakeout, and I couldn't help but feel excited, until I remembered Cole's warning. What was going to happen tonight? Were we going to be in danger like Cole said? Or, am I going to see what the life of a real private eye is really like? What if it turns out to be boring?

I hung up the phone. I had been so busy studying the file I didn't realize it was past noon until Mom called out, "Lunch is ready, Jesse."

The thunderstorms had passed by the time Billy arrived, but the rain was still coming down, slow and steady. The weather forecaster had been right on target.

Billy was driving a blue, Dodge pick up truck. It looked new, and was a sight better than the ragged Mercury I had seen parked in front of the office on Friday. After a quick introduction, and a question and answer session with my parents, Billy and I left for our night of spying.

"Your parents are nice people, Jesse. They kind of remind me of mine. They have to know everything," Billy said, a smile forming.

"Yes, they do have a tendency to dig right in," I agreed. "I appreciate your candidness with them. I don't think they realize how dangerous this job can be. It can be dangerous, can't it? I mean, I met this man who knows you, and he told me you got shot doing the same thing we're getting ready to do tonight. That's not going to happen, right?"

He looked at me with a reassuring smile and said, "I sure hope not. I can't promise anything, but I can tell you, I've learned a lot since that happened. I didn't have my mind on my work and I paid for it dearly. I won't let that happen again." He was silent as we crossed the South River Bridge. Then he asked, "Who is this man you're talking about?"

"Cole James," I replied. "I met him a few days ago when he stopped by the house to introduce himself. He lives up the road a couple of miles. He's a cop here in Greene County."

"Actually, he's a deputy."

"There's a difference?"

"Yes, and no. A deputy can act in place of the sheriff, and a policeman acts for the department."

"I don't see the difference."

"Oh, you will."

"Now that you've completely explained that one to me, tell me about the job." It was obvious Billy was going to let me find out for myself the dealings of a small town sheriff's department. "Does this have anything to do with that Mrs. Miller woman?"

"That was a good guess," he replied.

"Well, it wasn't very hard, considering she's the only client I've met since the Carroltons. However, you could have other clients that I haven't met," I said, trying to pry a little deeper into his business.

"I've got two other cases, but I'm about ready to tie those up real soon. I've got this one case involving employee theft at Walker Hardware Store in Albemarle County. That's an easy one. I went in last night with Mr. Walker after the store closed and set up a video camera."

"Who is going to turn it on?"

After a good little bellylaugh, Billy replied, "I can see I'm going to have to teach you a few things about modern technology. They have equipment out there that allows you to listen to someone without being in the room, and cameras that operate by motion detectors."

I could tell he was making fun of me. He probably thought I was dumber than dirt. I sure felt like it.

"Anyway," he went on, "Mr. Walker won't be at work until noon, so that just leaves our boy, Bobby Weaver, all by himself. The minute he steps behind the service counter... gotcha! The camera is activated, and we'll have it all on tape."

"What is he stealing? How does he get it out of the store? Or, is he just taking money?"

"Oh, he steals money, but mostly, it is tools and equipment. It seems he has someone come into the store and pretends to be buying something. A few minutes later, the person leaves, with goods in hand."

"How can you be sure you are going to catch him today?"

"Because of all the money and stuff this boy has been stealing, he's got to be doing it on a regular basis. Why stop now? He's actually stupid enough to think he's going to continue to get away with it. Mr. Walker said his inventory girl keeps good records. She keeps track of all the deliveries to the store, and all sales. Nothing gets passed her. Oh, we'll get him today. I'm sure of it," Billy said; confident that he would prevail.

"How much money would a job like this pay?" I asked, as I cut my eyes sideways to him, and smiled that sheepish smile I conjure up every so often.

"Nosy, aren't we?"

"Hey, that's my job, remember?"

As we pulled into the office parking lot, I asked, "What are we doing here, instead of going to the hotel?"

"I want to go over the details of the case before we venture out on surveillance, and I want to explain a few things to you."

Billy unlocked the front door, stepped inside, and began punching in numbers on a wall alarm pad, as he explained, "I forgot to tell you about the alarm. There's one here by the front door and one inside the garage door that leads to apartment. The code is 2525. Like the song says—*In the year 2525, if man is still alive...*"

"You are as bad as Mom," I said, laughing at his silliness, as I followed him to his office.

After several minutes of rummaging through paperwork, he turned and said, "Ah, here's one of my weird, off-the-wall cases." Then he mumbled something in his native tongue I didn't quite understand.

"Wait a minute. I don't understand *Indian*. Could you please explain it to me in plain English?" I wasn't trying to be a grouch, but I wasn't ready to learn a new language just yet.

"Crazy, this whole thing is crazy," Billy answered. "Barbara Jenkins asked me to follow her husband, Darin. She says he is having an affair with her sister, Caroline Webster. Mrs. Jenkins wants proof. Well, it turns out that Mr. Jenkins is a very wealthy man, and he is having an affair with Caroline. I know this because he came into my office about twenty minutes after she left, and told me he was. He said not only was he having an affair with Barbara's sister, but Barbara was also screwing her training coach. He didn't care. Their marriage had been nothing more than a marriage of convenience. The love has been long gone. This is typical shit that goes on when you deal with people who have money.

They have two kids in college, so they both pretty much come and go as they please. Only now, she's getting greedy. She wants money, property and freedom. He's not going to let that happen. He is willing to give her a settlement in cash and let her go, but that's all. He says she has enough money to keep me going for about a month, and when that ran out, there was not going to be any more. He was going to make sure. So, why not work for him and make some serious money. The end result was going to be the same. She would run out of money, and I would never get anything on him—he assured me. I believe him. It's a waste of my time, and her money.

"So, what are you going to do?"

"I called her and told her exactly what was happening. I told her about her husband's visit, and assured her she was in a no-win situation. She should accept his offer. He knew about her affair, and the best thing for her to do was to settle. I told her what he offered and convinced her that the only person to gain anything from this was going to be me. They could fight back and forth until the end of time, but it wasn't going to get either one of them anywhere. They were both cheating. I also explained that a portion of his money would be better than nothing.He has a lot of money. So, why not put an end to it right now, before things got really ugly? She said she would think it over. In the meantime, I have her deposit check for two thousand dollars, and five thousand dollars in cash from Mr. Jenkins."

"It doesn't seem right that you would take money from both of them," I said, stunned. "Isn't that illegal?"

"Oh, don't worry. I have the money, but somewhere along the line, one of them will get their money back. I'm just giving them time to think it over. I am not going to cheat anybody. About the Miller job..."

I just didn't seem to understand his logic. Billy took money from two people that are investigating each other, plus were married to each other. Wasn't that a conflict of interest? I had questions about the situation, but I trusted Billy, and I had a feeling he wasn't going to do anybody wrong. I sure hoped not. I don't think I could work for a man that wasn't honest.

Something's not right in the kitchen... as my mother would say.

CHAPTER 6

B Y THE TIME IT GOT DARK, Billy and I had his spying gear (as he so laughingly called it) packed in the ragged Mercury. We stopped at Walker's Hardware Store to retrieve the surveillance camera and tape for future viewing. In the process, he explained some of the rules of being a private eye.

"The main thing you have to remember is to be discrete, and most of all, stay alert."

As we reached the Red Mountain Inn, located on an isolated strip of Rt. 29, and parked in the back of the parking lot, he went on to explain the uses of his surveillance equipment. He had the camcorder we picked up from Walker's; a Nikon camera with a telephoto lens the size of Milwaukee; and a gadget that resembled a small satellite dish used to listen in on conversations. We were hot. We were ready to go.

"What good is all this stuff if you don't have a recorder in place," I asked.

"Watch this," he replied. After taking out the tape from the Walker job, and replacing it with a new one, Billy connected a wire to the camcorder and then plugged it into the car lighter. Then he plugged in another wire from the camcorder to a small laptop computer. He sat the camcorder (which was the size of a small shoe box) on top of the dash. After a few adjustments, a clear picture of a section of the hotel, appeared on the screen. Several pecks to the small laptop keyboard, and the camera lens moved, zooming in on the target.

I was impressed. This was the coolest thing since man had created the microwave oven.

"Impressed, huh?" Billy boasted. "If you think this is great, wait until you see the new fiber-optic set up I've ordered. It's got a camera in a box the size of a cigarette pack, and all you have to do is put it in place, hit the remote control, and go."

I was still marveling at all the hi-tech stuff when Billy said, "I know you think this car is an eye-sore, but let me tell you, I've got this thing set up so that it does what I need it to do. I can turn the ignition on ACC, hit a switch, and the dash lights go out. That way, I can still have power without lights. You don't want the interior lights on when you're on a stakeout. Somebody could see you. That's just the tip of the ice burg. It guzzles gas, but it's got an engine in it with enough horsepower to out run almost anything on the road—even Charlottesville's finest," he gleamed. "Nobody pays attention to a piece of junk that looks like this. Now, if I were going into a high dollar hotel parking lot, I'd drive my truck. It's got pizzazz, and it looks nice."

Billy continued to tell me all about his car, until I finally butted in and asked, "So, what's the deal with Mrs. Miller and her husband? Why are we sitting here, instead of following him from his house? How do you know this is his destination?" I must have missed something along the way.

"Simple," he answered. "Rebecca Miller called me around three o'clock and said her hubby, Jeff, was going to play poker tonight—something he usually does on Thursday nights. Earlier, he had said something about the two of them going out to dinner, but she told him she was coming down with a bug. Once she got the kids in bed, all she wanted to do was to lay down. So, he decided to go ahead with the poker game."

"What's that got to do with this place?" I asked.

"A while back, Mrs. Miller got suspicious about her husband's Thursday night poker games. Seems he came home one night and she smelled a woman's perfume on him. She said it 'bout took her breath away. But she didn't say anything to him. After that, she started going through credit card bills, looking for anything out of the ordinary. He normally takes care of the bills, but she explained to him that she was looking for a charge she made for a new dress. She wanted to take the dress back, but couldn't find the receipt and couldn't remember which card she used. He got pissed, but eventually let it go. What she didn't tell him was that she found a charge on the Master Card for the Red Mountain Inn. The date of the charge was on a Thursday. So she started going through his files in his study and came up with other charges on various credit cards. The point is, she followed him two weeks in a row, and this is where he went."

"If he's having an affair, why would he be so stupid as to charge stuff on his credit card so his wife could find it? I mean, even I know better. If I were screwing around, I sure wouldn't leave a paper trail. Maybe he wants her to find out," I suggested.

Billy said, as he looked at me strangely, "Now, that's a thought." He handed me a picture. "This is Jeff Miller. Rebecca said he would probably be driving his silver, 1999 BMW convertible. Nice, huh? He doesn't usually drive her Saturn station wagon. I wonder why."

I rolled the window down in the Mercury. It was almost June. The days were warm, but the nights were still chilly. Yet, I couldn't resist the clean, fresh smell of the great outdoors. In Newport News, the days would be hot and the nights would be warm and humid. The contrast was amazing.

I laid my head back on the headrest and tried to soak in all the information Billy had given me.

"Jeff Miller is a handsome man," I said, holding the picture. "What about Rebecca? Would you classify her as good-looking?"

"Who cares what she looks like? She's paying me to do a job, not critique her beauty."

"Yes, but I thought maybe..." I stopped in mid-sentence. "Hey, isn't that him?"

I watched the BMW drive through the parking lot and stop in front of room 108. The inn had ten rooms downstairs, numbered left to right, with number 100 on the far left, and number 110 on the far right. The lobby was situated in the center. This was your typical small time motel, but from what Billy had said, it was decent. The rooms were nice; the service was good; and the confidentiality of the guests was impeccable... almost.

"Ok, look alive," he demanded.

"Look alive? I don't know what to do."

Billy put his arm over the back of my seat, looked into my eyes and said, "Just sit here and keep looking at me. Now, wiggle your head... slowly, like you're flirting with me."

I did exactly as he said.

"Now take your hand and rub my face... that's it... kiss the side of my face. Don't freak out. Slide backwards and act like you're laughing... not crazy... just smooth and simple. You're doing very well."

We sat there acting like we were making out, as Billy's fingers clicked away on the keyboard. This was weird. Billy didn't actually kiss me, but he got close enough so that I could smell the scent of Old Spice. Compared to other men's cologne, Old Spice was my favorite. It was the kind my dad always wore and I loved it. I was beginning to drift off into fantasyland when Billy reached into the back seat and grabbed the Nikon. Click... Click...

Jeff Miller walked up to room 108, knocked on the door, and then walked in. We couldn't see the woman he was meeting, but the bottle of liquor in his hand, was an obvious give-a-way. What a scumbag! I hate men that do this kind of thing. His wife is probably a good woman, just like my sister, Claire.

The whole time I was fawning all over Billy, he was steadily doing something else, while pretending he was having a romantic interlude with me. Boy, he is good.

Once Jeff was inside the room, Billy slid back to his side of the car and said,"Well, now we have a video and pictures of him entering the room. All we need is one of him coming out. Maybe we'll get one of her, too."

It was seven o'clock, according to my Timex. Sitting here, I couldn't help but go over in my mind the strange feelings I had when Billy got close to me. What's the matter with me? He's sixteen years older than I am! He's my boss! I kept telling myself to get a grip, don't even go there.

Boy, I really need a man in my life! Those thoughts brought me back to Cole James. I couldn't wait to see him tomorrow.

I sat there in my own little world until Billy interrupted my thoughts.

"Might as well relax, we're going to be here for awhile." He rolled down his window and pulled out a pack of Marlboros.

"I didn't know you smoked," I growled.

"I know it's a bad habit. It probably will kill me. What can I say?"

"It's been almost four years for me. I've had a few here and there, but I try to stay away from them. Every once in a while, when I get really whacked out in the head, I might have one."

Billy looked at me in amazement.

"Oops, I'm sorry. I didn't mean to imply that you were whacked out. It just came out that way."

"Before too long, you and I will see all kinds of sides to each other," he said, ignoring my remark.

You have got that right, I thought to myself. All I was doing was looking for a job, and now I'm sitting here in a hotel parking lot with my boss, snooping on people, and thinking all kinds of *nasty* thoughts. I needed to have a sex life. It's been far too long.

Two hours later, after we had finally exhausted every area of our life we could talk about, the door to room 108 opened. Their voices sounded through the laptop.

"Hey, that's pretty cool," I squealed in delight.

"Oops, here he comes, Mr. Jeff Miller, I do believe," Billy said, as he hit a few keys on the computer, then picked up his Nikon again. Click... Click... "We've got you, pal."

"Holy Moses," I screamed. "He was meeting a man! Yuck, look at him kiss... oh, man, how gross." I was stunned. This was not at all what I had expected.

A quick kiss and then both men walked out of the room. Jeff walked over to his BMW as the other guy got into a white Ford Explorer.

"I don't believe it!" I screamed. "Good ole Jeff boy is not only screwing around, but he's doing it with a guy. Wow!"

"This could be really bad," Billy mumbled.

"What do you mean, really bad?"

"I mean, when you tell a woman her husband is cheating, they get upset and cry, but when you tell them he's cheating with a man, they go nuts. I know, I've been here before. They do all kinds of crazy things."

"Well, then don't tell her."

"I can't do that. I have an obligation. I have to tell her, and I have to tell her the truth."

Trying to put myself in her place, I said, "Yes, I guess you are right. If I paid you good money to do a job, I would expect you to be honest with me. You're right, this is nasty."

A few minutes after nine, we were leaving the hotel parking lot, heading towards the office.

"I'm going to let you take my truck home," Billy said. "I know your car is history, and you probably haven't given much thought to it, but you need something to drive. You can take my truck, while I see what I can do about your transportation problem."

What did he mean? Was he going to provide me with a company car? This was great. Benefits are an important part of any job.

Once we got back to the office, Billy started putting his gear away. I stood and watched him work as he talked.

"I'm going to look over the tapes from the hardware store and the one on our pal, Jeff. Why don't you go on home?" he asked. "Come on, let's go out to the garage and get the truck."

"Ok," I said.

Billy's truck was a monster. He had to lift me up to get in to it.

"It's all automatic, so you can't go wrong," he assured me.

"I can't believe you are going to trust me with your truck."

"I know where you live," he chuckled. His smile was so warm, it made me feel special. "If you get stopped, the registration and proof of insurance is in the glove box." He walked over to the other side of the truck and opened the glove box. "I guess I'd better take this gun. I don't want a cop to see you with a concealed weapon. I'd have to bail you out of jail."

"This is really nice of you to lend me your truck, Billy." I said, looking around the garage. On the left was a small workbench with a red

Craftsman toolbox sitting on top. A washer and dryer sat next to the box. Then I saw it. Billy's *Harley* was sitting to the right. I hadn't noticed it when we first came in because it was covered with a black plastic cover like you'd see on a grill.

"I've got to have a look at your bike. Do you mind?" I asked.

"Please help yourself," Billy said, obviously proud. He walked over and removed the cover. "Voila!"

"It's beautiful. Someday, I want to go for a ride on it," I demanded. I had never seen so much chrome on a bike. Forget it, I don't want to get that fever again, I told myself.

"Boy, this has been a long day," I added. "I was supposed to go to the county fair with my folks, but because the storms rolled in, I ended up spending the afternoon with you in a motel parking lot. Things can sure change fast around here."

"We have only just begun..."

"You're a hoot," I laughed. "I can't wait to meet your family," I said. "Are all the men in your family as big as you are?"

"Yes, and so are some of the women."

I started the truck, and asked, "What are you going to do now?"

"Well, once you leave, I'll look through the video tape of our buddy Jeff and the one from the hardware store, write up a report, calculate the bill, take a shower, eat something, and then go to bed. After that, who knows? Tomorrow, I will go be with my family. The rest can wait until Monday. I need a break."

"I'd better head out," I replied. "My folks will probably be wondering what happened to me."

As I was leaving, Billy yelled, "Don't be afraid to use the car phone. Just remember, any long-distant calls come out of your check."

On the road, I fell into a state of euphoria. Things were good, and I was happy. I didn't like what went down with that asshole Jeff, but that was beyond my control. I hated to think what was going to happen when Rebecca found out her husband wasn't seeing another woman... he was seeing a man. That had to be the worst. All that aside, things were good. I can't remember the last time I felt so at peace with myself.

When I drove down Rt. 33 a ways, I saw that police car on the hill again. I'm sure somebody is really up in arms about it, but it brought a smile to my face. I wonder what Cole thinks about it.

It was close to eleven o'clock when I got home. I figured Mom and Dad were probably in bed. All the lights were off, except the one on the front porch. The minute I got inside, Athena came barreling out of the downstairs bedroom, barking like crazy.

"It's just me, girl," I said, as I patted her head. "I know, I know. I've been neglecting you, haven't I? I'm sorry, I've... hey, what are you doing coming out of Mom and Dad's bedroom?"

"She's been sleeping on the floor beside the bed. She's lonely. Besides, your mom likes her," Dad mumbled, running his hand through his hair, as he came out of their bedroom.

"I'm sorry I woke you."

"Would you like a sandwich or something? You hungry?" he asked.

"That would be great. I forgot all about eating. Billy and I had a strange night. It is amazing what people will do to each other."

Dad went into the kitchen and started taking food out of the refrigerator, as I turned on the TV, and sat down on the couch. I was tired. Just about the time I was dozing off, Dad walked in with a plate of fried chicken and French fries. I came to life. I didn't realize how hungry I was, until I had finished eating everything on my plate.

"That hit the spot," I said, as I finished the last bite. Athena stared at my chicken bone. I was about ready to give it to her when Dad looked at me and shook his head.

"Sorry, girl, but Dad knows more about dogs than I do," I said.

I scraped my plate into the trash, put it in the dishwasher, and headed upstairs for some much needed rest. I said good night to Dad, and blew a kiss to both of them.

The phone on the dining room wall rang. Dad jumped to answer it, mumbling something about not waking up Mom.

"Hello… It's for you, Jesse," Dad whispered, as he stretched out the cord, and handed me the phone.

"Hello," I said.

"Jesse, this is Billy. I'm glad you're still awake."

"I just finished eating left-over dinner and was headed for bed. It is almost midnight. Is everything ok?"

"No, it is not. Things could not be any worse. Our Mrs. Miller... that serene, mild-mannered, patrician woman I had the pleasure of working for, turned out to be a murderer."

"What are you talking about, Billy?"

"Look, I'm on my cell phone, ten minutes from your house. We need to talk. Meet me out front in ten minutes."

"Ten minutes," I repeated, and hung up the phone. I turned to Dad and said, "I'm going to meet Billy out front. Something has happened. I don't know what, but I'll let you know as soon as I find out. It probably isn't anything to worry about. Why don't you go on back to bed?"

Not wanting to question my rationale, Dad kissed me on the cheek and replied, "If you need me, come get me, ok?" He turned to Athena and said, "Come on girl, let's go to bed."

It almost brought tears to my eyes to see the love between a man and his dog.

CHAPTER 7

BILLY WAS RIGHT. Things were not good. According to him, Rebecca Miller called shortly after I left his house. She was frantic and wanted to know everything. So, he told her all the details. He had to tell her the truth. By the time he hung up the phone, she had seemed calm and appeared to have taken it pretty well.

"Then she goes into the bathroom while he's taking a shower, and promptly blows his brains all over the shower wall with his .45 caliber Smith and Wesson. You can bet the cops are going to be all over our butts about this one. I will be the bad guy here."

"What are we going to do?" I asked. "I mean, she killed her husband after you told her he was having sex with a man. It wasn't your fault, but she has to lay the blame somewhere. This isn't good."

We sat in his old Mercury, not saying a word, trying to sort out the mess. Billy rolled his window down and lit a cigarette. The air was warm. There was a half-moon high in the sky, casting shadows across the yard.

I could feel my anxiety rising. That's when it occurred to me that I hadn't taken my Zoloft since I had moved here. Well, if I can make it through this, I guess I don't need it anymore. That was a comforting thought.

"How did you find out so fast about Mrs. Miller shooting her husband?" I asked, as I noticed a light go on in the living room. I hoped we hadn't disturbed Mom.

"When you left, I went into the office and started going through all the information we had accumulated. I was in the process of tallying up the bill and calculating man-hours. I didn't need to watch the video. I already knew the outcome. I was going to take a shower, have a bite to eat, and then watch the video from the hardware store. Then the phone rang. It was Rebecca Miller," Billy said. He was obviously distressed. He put out the cigarette and went to wringing his hands. "I never should have told her over the phone. I know better." He leaned over the steering wheel and put his face in his hands.

"It's not your fault, Billy. She must have just snapped. She probably would have anyway, no matter how you told her. It was a no-win situation. Go on, tell me the rest." I reached over and patted his back.

"I went up to my apartment. The first thing I did was turn on the police scanner, and jump in the shower. I usually turn on the scanner instead of the television. I was in the kitchen making a sandwich when I heard the report of a shooting at 1569 Barn Yard Road in Greene County. I knew the address sounded familiar, so I ran down to the office and checked the address in her file. Sure enough, it was the same."

The front door opened, and Dad walked out of the house.

"Oh, no," I murmured, looking at Billy. "Something must be wrong."

Billy and I got out of the car and met Dad in the middle of the yard.

"What's wrong?" I asked him.

"You just got a call from Cole James. He said he hated to call this late, but he wanted to know if you were home. I told him you were outside talking to Billy Blackhawk. He said to tell you both to stay right where you are. He is coming over. He said it was a police matter. What is going on, Jesse?" I knew Dad wasn't mad. He was worried.

"Something bad has happened," Billy jumped in. "One of my clients went and shot her husband after I gave her the report that her husband was seeing another man. It had nothing to do with Jesse or me, but since we were working for her, I'm sure the police will want to question us both. They probably know everything by now."

"Dad, why don't you go inside? It's late and you don't need to get in the middle of this. We'll take care of everything. Plus, I don't want Mom to wake up and see a police car in the yard at this time of night. If I need your help, believe me, I'll come get you."

"You take care of my girl, you hear?" Dad said to Billy.

I turned to Billy and asked, "Are we in trouble? I mean, they don't shoot the messenger, but will they put the messenger in jail?" I was beginning to get scared. I was just as much a part of this as Billy. I have never had much dealings with the law and I did not want to start now. I didn't want any trouble.

"If you could only see your face," Billy replied. "Relax, Jesse. We only worked for her. We didn't kill her husband, she did." The tables were turned. Earlier I was trying to comfort him, and now he was trying to comfort me.

"I guess you are right. All we did was what she paid us to do, but I still feel bad. I sure don't want to go to jail over it."

"Jesse, in this line of work, this is what you're going to be exposed to. If you can't handle it, now is the time to get out. I'll understand. If you decide to stay, you're going to have to get tough."

"I can handle it. Don't you worry about me. I'm stronger than you think," I assured him. Who was I trying to convince here? I was scared shitless.

I heard Athena barking inside the house the minute the police car pulled into the driveway. I was about to go let her out when the door opened and she came running outside. I could see Dad on the porch with his hands in the air, as if to say he was sorry.

"It's ok, Dad," I yelled, as he retreated back inside, leaving us to clean up our own mess.

Athena ran up to the car and barked. Cole got out, reached down, and patted her on the head. He looked straight at Billy.

"The minute I got to the crime scene, I heard your name mentioned. Why is it you're always into something?"

"I thought you were working the fair. What happened? You get fired from community service detail?" Billy asked, sarcastically.

"You know the fair was cancelled when the storm hit this morning," he said, and then turned to me. "I came by your house around five to talk to you, but you had made the unfortunate mistake of being hooked up with this joker. When this is over, don't say I didn't warn you."

Now I was getting mad. Who was he to choose my friends, or stick his nose into my business?

"I can see you're angry. I guess that means our date is off for tomorrow." I know I shouldn't have been so snotty, but I was not happy either.

"I didn't say that," Cole replied. "What I'm trying to tell you is, if you get involved with this guy, you are headed for trouble."

Billy jumped right in his face. "You're just jealous."

"Wait a minute!" I got in between both of them. "What's going on here? I thought you two were friends. You sound like a bunch of kids. Am I missing something?"

Billy backed off. "Yeah, we are friends all right."

I stood there waiting for an explanation.

Cole stepped closer to me. "Billy is much older than I am, so he's spent most of his adult life trying to run mine."

"Oh, bull, that's not true and you know it. You just can't get passed the fact that I tried to warn you about that *a-tsa-s-gi-li* you married," Billy yelled at him.

"I didn't know you were married," I said, looking at Cole in disbelief.

"It lasted three months, that's all. It was a mistake," he responded.

"Just long enough for her to get pregnant," Billy added.

"It wasn't my baby," Cole shouted.

"The two of you just stop it. Get a grip," I demanded. "You'll wake the whole neighborhood."

Billy tried to explain. "A few years ago when he was about to marry Rachel, I tried to tell him what she was like. He was in love, and he didn't want to listen to me. When things went sour, he shifted the blame to me. I tried to warn him, and he got mad. He's been mad for a long time."

"That's a lie. I did not blame you," Cole said, and hung his head. "Well, maybe just a little."

"See, you guys are friends," I said. "I think you both have some issues to work out. I'll tell you like my mom tells me, if someone is a true friend, you can always work it out. I think the two of you need to sit down and have a long talk."

I noticed they both were hard at work trying to get passed this uncomfortable moment, and I sure didn't want it to drag on any longer. I changed the subject by asking, "What's going on with this killing? Do you actually think Billy and I had something to do with Rebecca killing her husband? You must be joking."

"Do the two of you know something?" He stared at Billy, and asked. "How did you learn about this so quickly? She just killed the man a couple of hours ago. The M.E. just arrived on the scene. When I was called to the crime scene, there was a boatload of cops and technicians everywhere. Sheriff Meatball was even there. He filled me in, told me to find you, and haul your hind parts off to jail. You stepped in it this time, buddy."

"Sheriff Meatball? You can't be serious?" I giggled.

Billy and Cole turned to each other and started laughing.

Cole replied, "His name is Sheriff Josh Mealphall. Billy called him Sheriff Meatball the first time he met the man. Of course, he didn't do it on purpose, but the sheriff has disliked him ever since." They were still snickering. "The name just kind of stuck. Now, everybody in the department calls him Sheriff Meatball. Not to his face, of course."

"Of course," I mimicked.

"Here's the deal, Cole," Billy said. "I heard a report of a shooting on the police scanner, and I knew right away what had happened. I came to tell Jesse so she wouldn't hear it on the news. By tomorrow, it will be on every channel and in every newspaper. She's smart. She would have put two and two together, and blast me for not telling her."

"You are right about that," I announced.

"Tell me what happened," Cole demanded.

Billy began explaining everything in great detail. He didn't leave anything out—even the bit about us pretending to be lovers in the motel parking lot. I was embarrassed. I didn't want Cole to envision a romantic interlude between Billy and me, real or imagined.

"Enough about our sex life," I joked.

That statement woke up both of them.

When Billy finished, Cole shook his head and said, "I'm telling you, this woman dropped a dime on you, pal. She claims you told her he was having an affair with a man, and he ought to be shot. So, she did what you told her to do. She shot him."

"No way, she's crazy. You know me, Cole. You know I have more ethics than to even suggest something like that to a client. She's distraught. She doesn't know what she's saying. She got some disturbing news, and then went off the deep end. That's it in a nutshell."

"I'm going to need a statement from both of you," Cole replied. "Off the record, I think she knows exactly what she's doing."

"What do you mean?" I questioned.

"She is one smart cookie," he glanced at Billy. "We're talking about the insanity defense. *Someone made me do it*."

"This is crazy," I hissed.

"It doesn't matter whether it is crazy, or not. I will still need your statements. Shall we go?" Cole motioned to his car.

"Wait a minute. I need to tell Dad what is happening."

Billy and I rode in his truck as we followed Cole to the police station. I guess one of the advantages of having friends on the force, is you don't have to be dragged away in handcuffs... sometimes.

We gave our statements to the police. By the time the inquisition was over, I felt as if I had been run over by a train. I was asked questions I couldn't possibly answer. Did I know anything about the victim's past indiscretions? Was I aware that the wife had been hospitalized for manic-depression? Had I ever had any social contact with the victim, or his wife? I was asked the same questions over and over, until I was ready to scream. Not only was I given the third degree, but I also had to sit and listen to the graphic details of the crime. It was awful. By the time Billy drove me home around three in the morning, I was a wreck.

I fell into bed, without bothering to change clothes. After a long and restless night, I awoke Sunday morning with a pounding headache.

Athena jumped on the bed, licked my face, and tried to nuzzle my neck. I rubbed her head, which only incited a loud bark.

I got out of bed and hit the shower. The water was hot and refreshing, as thoughts of the previous evening played through my head. What a nightmare! What was going to happen? The police let us go, so they must not think we did anything wrong. Then I thought about Cole. Was he coming over today? Did we still have a date? He implied we did last night. I guess I'll just have to wait and see. Men—I can never figure them out.

I dressed and went downstairs to the kitchen where Mom and Dad were having their morning coffee.

"Cole called this morning," Mom said. "He wanted to know if you were all right."

"Oh, yeah," I replied. My head ached and I needed an aspirin, if I was going to make it through the day.

Dad answered my un-asked question, "I haven't had a chance to talk to your mom about last night," he whispered.

"What are you two whispering about over there?" Mom asked.

I got my coffee and sat down. I felt it was my place to tell her about last night. I gathered my nerve and began the task of explaining. She just sat there, taking it all in.

"Things must not be too bad. Cole's coming over at ten. We're all going out to the breakfast buffet at the fire station in town, unless, of course, you don't want to go."

"He is?" I asked. Maybe things weren't so bad after all.

CHAPTER 8

BREAKFAST WAS PLEASANT. The food was good, the price was fair, and the company was excellent. I didn't know what to expect from Cole after the fiasco last night, but he didn't say a word about it in front of Mom or Dad. Was he waiting until we were alone?

We rode to breakfast in the mini-van. When we got back to the house, Cole and I switched to his Jeep Wrangler. Mom asked me to try to make it home for dinner since our neighbors, Sharon and Joe were coming to dine with us. She made it a point to invite Cole.

"I think my mom's trying to make sure you get a home cooked meal," I stated, as we were pulling out of the driveway. "What with you being single and all."

He turned his head and laughed. "I was wondering when you would get around to asking me about Rachel. Listen, I didn't tell you because I don't like to talk about her. It was a mistake. I don't like to even think about her." He gave me a forlorn look as he shifted gears. "I guess Billy filled you in on the details last night, huh?"

"Actually, the only thing we talked about was that crazy woman who killed her husband." I hesitated a moment, then slyly asked, "Can you and I talk about Mrs. Miller, or is that off-limits?"

"We can talk about certain things concerning the case, but there are privileged areas we can't go into. You can ask me, but if I say I can't tell you, you're going to have to let it go at that. Ok?" he replied, smiling. "Now what do you want to know?"

"First, are you going to try to pry stuff out of me that I shouldn't answer without an attorney present?" I laughed, but I was being serious.

"I see you learn fast," he interjected. "Did Billy warn you to watch what you say in front of me?"

"To be honest, he told me if I was going to be friends with you, I had to always remember that you are a cop. He said cops could be tricky. So, why don't we lay down some ground rules right now? I promise never to lie to you, if you promise never to try and trick, or use me. What do you say? Have we got a deal?"

"You play a tough game," he answered, as he made the turn onto Rt. 33, heading in the direction of Skyline Drive.

The ride in his Jeep was bumpy, but it was also masculine, just like him. I kept stealing glances, sizing him up. He was a good-looking man. His body was firm, yet he had an air about him that conveyed a gentle side. I kept wondering what kind of lover he would be. Would he be soft and gentle like his personality, or would he be tough and brutish? Are big men rough lovers?

"Did you hear me?" he asked.

"I'm sorry. I was thinking about something else," I replied, bringing myself out of the trance I had slipped into. "What did you say?"

"I said it was a deal. If we're going to have any kind of relationship, it has to be based on honesty and trust."

"Are we going to have a relationship?" I asked, as my heart fluttered.

He looked at me with a huge grin on his face and continued, "That's one of the things I admire about you, Jesse. You don't pull any punches."

"Oh, you just don't know me that well. Wait until you get to know me better before you make up your mind."

We spent the next couple of hours enjoying the ride and talking about ourselves; what we wanted out of life; what was important to us; family; all the things people talk about when they are trying to get to know each other.

The subject of last night didn't come up until we were on our way home.

"I know you like Billy, but I'm worried about you, Jesse. I don't think you have any idea as to what you're getting into. This detective stuff is a dangerous business." He reached over, picked up my hand and kissed it. "I like you and I don't want you to get hurt."

My heart skipped a beat. His intense blue eyes made my body turn to mush. I knew I was falling for him and there was no turning back. Unfortunately, I always fall in love with the men I date. That was my weakness, but not any more. This time it was going to be different. I would not let myself be sucked into the same game I've played so many times.

I pulled my hand back and said, "Billy is a good man. I trust him."

"You don't even know him!" Cole growled. "You've known him for what... two, three days?"

"It doesn't take me long to size up a person. A couple of minutes, and I know if I can trust them, or not," I shot back.

"You are right. I'm sorry. Billy is a good man. You can trust him, probably more so than anybody you'll ever meet. I'm not attacking his character, just his line of work."

"You've made your point. I'll be careful, and if I ever have any doubts about something, I'll call you. How is that?"

"Do you promise?"

"Sure," I swore.

When we pulled up in the yard, the first thing I noticed was Billy's aqua blue truck. Cole hadn't said a word to me about why Billy's truck was still here, so I offered an explanation.

"Billy's letting me use his truck for a couple of days, until I decide what to do about my car. Dad says I need a new one because mine's shot. It's not worth fixing... something about a rod knocking."

"I know, Mack told me. I told him I could probably help you find another car, one you can afford and rely on to get you through our harsh winters. That's important when you live in the mountains."

"What did he say?"

"He agreed."

FORTUNATELY, our dinner table was big enough to hold eight people. Besides our invited guests, we had an added addition. Ralph just happened to drop by right at dinnertime. I had the feeling that his explanation about his wife being gone for the weekend and leaving him to fend for himself, was an excuse to be invited for supper. In the course of the meal, I learned that he was in business for himself. He offered services in land excavation and almost anything you needed done with a bulldozer. His wife, Carol, didn't work. Fortunately for her, he does such a thriving business... blah... blah... blah.

Joe and Sharon didn't talk much about themselves, but what they did say, I found delightful. It was obvious they were happy together. They found their jobs fulfilling, and they adored their dog, Harry.

"In a couple more years, we plan to start having children," Sharon stated, with a gleam in her eyes as she glanced over at Joe. That brought a round of cheers from everyone, except Joe. I think it was news to him.

After dinner, Dad served mixed drinks to the men, and wine to the ladies. Since I had forgotten to take my drugs for many days, I figured it wouldn't hurt, and it might help me to relax.

Amazingly, the first one went down so smoothly, I had a second one. By eight o'clock, I had turned into the idiot from *Hell*. I was giggling and snorkeling like a crazy fool. I was going to regret this tomorrow, but tonight I was intensely uninhibited, and having a good time.

I caught Mom giving Cole the eye, as he stood up and announced that he had to leave.

"Jesse, why don't you walk our guest to his car?" Mom asked.

Cole said good-night, while I followed behind him the way a child does when their parents suggest they do something that they don't have enough sense to think of themselves. Who cares? I wasn't embarrassed. I was having fun, and wanted it to continue.

The radiant glow of the full moon, combined with the cool, gentle breezes made everything seem so summery. Next weekend was Memorial Day. I love Memorial Day. It was the official beginning of the summer season. All the stores at the beaches, from Nags Head to Buckroe Beach, would be coming to life. Soon, people would be out in full force, having picnics or cookouts, lounging by the pool, hanging out at the beaches, and enjoying the summer sun. But, I was in the mountains. What would we be doing? Taking a dip in the stream? Cutting down trees to have firewood for the winter? Those thoughts ran through my mind as I followed Cole to his Jeep.

I knew it was the wine. I had not had a drink of alcohol in so long, I forgot what it tasted like. But I never forgot the feeling it gave me. It made me want to do things that I wouldn't normally do, and say things I wouldn't normally say. Maybe that is why I don't miss drinking. I can screw up enough on my own without having alcohol to help me along.

Standing by Cole's Jeep, he turned to me and put his hands on my shoulders. "I would love nothing better than to take you in my arms and kiss you, but I won't. Not now. I know there's something between us. I feel it, and I know you do, too," he murmured, as her ran his fingers through the hair hanging down around my face. His hands slid down my arms and back up to my face. "I've spent too much of my life in meaningless relationships. I'm tired of it. I want something real. I think you and I can have something together, and I want you to be in control of your emotions when I take the first step." He leaned over and kissed me softly on the lips. He got into his Jeep and pulled out of the driveway, leaving me standing there with my lips still puckered out.

What happened here? That's it, no more wine for me. Something just went down, and I missed it. I walked back into the house.

"Is Cole gone?" Mama asked.

"Yes," I whispered, as I started upstairs. "I'm going to bed," was all I could manage to say. Suddenly I felt sick. I made it to the bathroom, turned on the fan to muffle the noise, and threw up. The wine didn't taste as good coming up, as it did going down.

I set my alarm, stripped down to my underwear, and crawled into bed. Monday morning was going to be a rough day.

The alarm went off at 6 a.m.

Athena, who now slept at the foot of my bed, and not on the floor, started dancing on top of me.

"I'm up!" I rasped out. My head was pounding. I fumbled for my purse and fished out a bottle of aspirin. I successfully made it downstairs without falling down, went to the kitchen, and gulped down two aspirins. Ah, relief was on the way! I scrounged around and found the fixings for a pot of coffee. Once the coffee was on, I trudged back upstairs to take a shower, wondering what new and exciting thing was going to happen to me today.

I left a note on the bar, listing my number at work and Billy's car phone number. I gave Athena a pat on the head, and headed off to work. I was looking forward to another day of intrigue and suspense. Hopefully, none of Billy's clients would kill anyone today.

Billy was already at the office when I walked in. I smelled the aroma of fresh coffee. The cup I had earlier, was sitting in the pit of my stomach, gnawing away. I dropped my purse on the desk and headed to the coffee room, while the *beep-beep* of the door alarm was still going off in my head. I opened the refrigerator door and grabbed a coke, popped the top, and guzzled the cold liquid.

Billy walked into the room with a big smile on his face. "*O-s-da sunalei!*" he said, with a cheerful smile on his face.

"Yeah, *o-tis sunny* to you, too," I sneered.

"Did we have a bad night?" he asked. "Your date with Cole yesterday turned out to be a rough one, huh?"

"What are you talking about? How did you know about our date?"

"I seem to remember you mentioning it Saturday night."

"The date was fine. The wine after dinner was a little more than I could handle."

"Don't tell me he tried to get you drunk on the first date? *I' -na-dv!*"

"What does that mean?" I scoffed. "If you're going to talk to me in that funny Indian talk, you're going to have to tell me what it means." I was getting indignant. I hated it when someone said things I didn't understand. I made up my mind, right then and there, that I would learn some of his language. If we were going to work together for any length of time, I wanted to know what he was saying. As a matter of fact, I thought, this could help us in our work. If we ever got into a situation where we needed to communicate without anyone knowing what we were saying, a second language would be a big plus. Maybe I could learn just enough to get by.

"*I'-na-dv* means snake," he replied.

"He's not a snake!" I assured him. "He's nice... sweet... charming... sexy... good-looking..." I drifted off again, remembering Cole's gentle kiss.

"You are crazy about him, aren't you?" Not waiting for a reply, he continued, "You have only known him for two days and you are already hooked. I don't get it."

"It has been five days, if you must know," I hissed. "Funny, he said something similar about you."

"Jesse, forget it. He's a cop. He will use you and then break your heart. That is all a cop knows how to do. They live and breathe their job."

"It won't be the first time some guy used me. Isn't that what you all do? You use us, and then dump on us."

"My, aren't we bitter?" he fussed. "Why don't I drag out the old peace-pipe, and see if we can't get you in a better mood?"

"Do your people really smoke the peace-pipe?"

He ignored my question. "Alright, no more fighting. I'll let it go for now, but beware; I'll be keeping my eyes on that fellow. You can bet on it."

"Great! Now, I have two fathers."

"Come on, Grouchy, we've got work to do."

Billy went to his office, while I went to my desk.

The phone rang.

"Billy Blackhawk Investigations," I answered. "This is Jesse. May I help you?"

"Yes, this is Robert Blackhawk. May I speak to Billy?"

"Sure, just a minute, please." I hit the hold button and called out, "It's your brother, Billy. Want me to put him through?"

Billy walked out of his office, picked up my phone, and hit the hold button. "Hey, brother, what can I do for you? Sure... I'll be there... ok.... see you Sunday." He hung up the phone and looked in my direction, but not directly in my face. "Sunday, we celebrate the coming of the warm months. I would like it if you joined us."

"Sure, I'd love to," I answered. "Memorial Day is usually a pretty big day for us, too. Now, that we live here, I don't know what's going to happen. Normally, we all get together for a cookout at Mom and Dad's, but it is different now."

"So be it. I could pick you up, and we could spend a little time with your folks before we leave. Or, they could go with us."

"I don't know," I shuttered. "I love my parents, but I don't know if I want them to be a part of this crazy lifestyle. Besides, they pretty much stay at home. They don't socialize very often." I skirted the truth.

"Whatever you want," he said, not trying to pressure me.

The phone rang, again.

"Hi, honey," said Mom. "I just got a call from Claire. They will be here for our Memorial Day celebration."

"That's great, Mom," I muttered, rolling my eyes at Billy.

"Something's wrong, honey. Claire seemed awfully upset. She didn't say why, but she said she needed to talk to us both when she gets here. I think it is Carl. I'm afraid their marriage is on the rocks."

"Don't worry, Mom. I'm sure everything is fine. Remember, she's pregnant. She's not rational."

"Do you think that is it?" Mom asked, obviously looking for comfort.

"Sure," I lied. "Don't worry, we'll work it out." I didn't want to tell Mom about my plans for Sunday. She was too worked up right now. I was sure everything would be fine by then.

Hours passed into days. Billy had solved the case of the stealing clerk, and the cheating husband—even though the husband paid dearly for his indiscretions. He dumped Darin Jenkins and had returned his five thousand dollars, after deducting $200 for his time. He sent a check for $1800 to Barbara Jenkins—telling her it was a waste of time and money to pursue the matter. What they needed was a lawyer and a therapist. And last, but not least, Rebecca Miller recanted her statement, thus relieving Billy of any possible charges of wrongdoing. Is it true that all good things come to those who wait, or all things work out in the end?

Billy and I spent most of our time working on the Helen Carrolton case, going over and over every piece of information. Finally, after days of endless brainstorming, phone calls, and dead ends, I'd had about enough. We just weren't getting anywhere.

"Billy," I said, dropping the folder on the desk. "You haven't taken on any of the new clients. You have devoted all your time to this case, and we're just pissing in the wind. Don't you think we should... ah... you should take on another case?"

"This is going to be the only case we work on for awhile," he told me, frankly. "When I take on a case of this magnitude, I don't do anything else. I can't. Missing persons is usually a pretty involved case, and it takes up a lot of time. We'll give it one month. If we don't come up with something by then, we never will."

I guess money wasn't an issue. As long as I got paid, what could I say?

After an entire week, we still didn't know any more than the cops did. I don't know where Billy got his information—and I didn't want to know—but he had all the details concerning the case of Helen Sue Carrolton, right down to the last newspaper clipping. We dissected every piece of information carefully. We pried into the private life of Helen Carrolton, until I felt like she was laid out on a table naked for the whole world to see. We knew everything about her, from what she had to eat before she left Poquoson, to the prescription in her eyeglasses. We knew she had a fight with her ex-boyfriend before she left home, but he had an alibi. Her parents were solid people, and Helen's welfare was all they ever cared about in life. You could see it in their eyes. Nobody would have any reason to harm Helen Carrolton, yet, somebody had. I felt it in my heart. It seems we knew all there was to know, except... where was Helen Carrolton? Was she missing, or was she dead? Or, was she missing and dead?

"I work for you, Billy. I'll do whatever you want, as long as it's legal, and I get paid. If you can afford to spend all your time on one case, I'm with you. I just felt it was my responsibility to make a few suggestions."

"That is one of the things that I found so up-front about you when I first met you—your ability to not hold back, and to say what is on your mind. I welcome your input."

I was still trying to discover the realm of our working relationship. I wasn't quite sure how close I could get to Billy. Was I supposed to do my job, and keep my mouth shut, or was it ok for me to become his pal and confidant? I took a chance. I stuck my nose into his business.

"Where did you get all this stuff?" I asked, wondering if I really wanted to know. I was new to this business, and I wasn't sure what to expect.

"Connections," was all he would say.

Friday afternoon, I went home for the weekend with a briefcase—an inner-departmental gift from Billy—full of notes, pictures, and reports to read over for the hundredth time. Billy and I had brainstormed so hard all week, I could actually feel the clouds rolling in. A storm was on the way.

I hadn't heard from, or seen Cole all week long. Either we were done for, or he really had been busy. He is a cop I tried to tell myself, surpressing the feeling that I had really messed up my chance with him. Yet, even cops have lives, don't they?

My car was dead meat, but thanks to Billy, I still had something to drive. He told me not to worry. His brother, Daniel owned a car lot and would fix me up real soon. Billy didn't mind driving his ragged old Mercury for a few days. We could work out the details later... just give him a week. This was too good to be true, I told myself, pulling into the driveway.

Athena came running out to greet me. Her hair was all fluffed up and her tail was wagging. What a great dog! She was always there when I needed a warm greeting, or a loving lick. She never asked for anything, except affection and food. How could you not love her?

Then I noticed Claire's new, gray-blue Mercedes SUV. What is she doing here? I wondered. Knowing Claire doesn't like to travel at night, I assumed she would not be here until Saturday morning.

Sucking in my breath, I went inside. The house was quiet as a tomb. Nobody was home. What was happening? I walked to the mudroom, then out the back door, heading for the garage. My car was still sitting there, but the mini-van was gone. Maybe they had gone out to eat, I told myself. They probably went to the Burger King in Ruckersville. No way... Claire wouldn't eat anywhere unless it was a nice restaurant where she would be pampered, and cleaned up after.

Thinking everything was all right, I went in and showered. I grabbed a Coke, sat on my bed, and became deeply immersed in Helen Carrolton's life. Thirty minutes later, I heard car doors slam, and Athena's outrageous bark. I got up and went to the window to have a look. Mom and Claire got out of the van, while Athena ran around in circles. Dad crawled out of a little black Toyota pick up truck. Where did he get that?

I ran downstairs and out into the front yard to greet them. After giving Claire a big hug and kiss, I watched Dad walk around the truck, mumbling about something.

"Hey, what's going on here? Whose truck?" I asked.

Mom was the first to answer. "Your dad and I decided we needed another car. You should never be in the mountains without a backup. That's what Cole told us. He said the winters can get real bad. What would we do if one of us got stuck? How would the one at home come and help out if we didn't have a way to get there? Of course, I told him we always go places together. He said it didn't matter. You just never know what can happen. We need to be prepared. So, we took his advice."

"I think he is right. It sounds like the smart thing to do." I was just talking out of my head. My real thoughts were about Claire. Why was she here without the kids? Where was Carl?

We all stood there for a minute, looking at each other.

"All right, what is the deal?" I finally asked, aiming my question at Claire. "Where is Carl and the kids?"

As usual, Mom was the one with all the answers. "Claire is here by herself. She needed some time alone to relax."

"Bullshit!" I growled, as Mom looked at me as if she couldn't believe one of her daughters could spew such vile language out of her mouth. "Claire doesn't breathe without the kids, or Carl."

"Come on into the house," Claire said, as she guided me inside. "We need to have a talk. The news might be a little disturbing, so I think we should be sitting down."

Mom fixed dinner, while Claire and I sat on the couch, discussing her husband's infidelities. Dad was outside, tinkering with his new/used Toyota pick-up. Athena lay in the yard, soaking in the last rays of the day's sun, without a care in the world.

"I did what you said, Jesse," Claire admitted. "I looked for clues. I tried not to over-react. Once I calmed down, I started looking for things. I found receipts for a diamond bracelet and a pair of pieced earrings. He purchased them at Beyer's for twenty-two hundred dollars. I also found receipts for dinners and hotel rooms at the Regency. I found it all. He wasn't even smart enough to hide them. He is such a damn jerk. It is over between us. I can't take it anymore."

I had never seen this side of my sister. She has never been one to curse, and she always gave everybody the benefit of the doubt. Now she was waking up to a whole new side of herself, and I was her witness.

"What do you propose we do about the situation?" I said in jest, knowing she wasn't going to do anything, but cry and whine, and eventually go back to her husband.

"I'm going to divorce him," she announced. "I've been the best wife and mother any man could ever hope for, so as far as I'm concerned, he's the one who fucked up. Let him pay the price. He betrayed me."

Mom and I looked at each other, stunned.

'*Fucked up?*'—Is that what she actually said? I knew trouble was surely in the air, if Claire had used the *F* word. *Never—ever,* in a million years would any of Minnie's kids use that kind of language—at least, not while she was around to hear. It's just something we wouldn't do. Claire was obviously losing her mind. Was she using drugs?

"Don't you think you should reconsider?" Mom said, totally ignoring Claire's outrageous vocabulary. "It could be a mistake."

"I don't think so! Get over it, Mom. He's a jerk," she spat. "It's time I got myself together and dumped him. Like you always said... enough is enough. I have reached the end of my limits."

My little sister had grown up right before my very eyes. Not only could she recognize a no-win situation, but she also became stronger in the process. I was glad to hear it. I loved my sister, and I knew what it meant to have someone you love let you down. I knew exactly how she felt. Life could be hard sometimes. I understood her frustration.

"What about the kids?" I asked.

"They're at home with Carl. I packed a few things and told him to enjoy it while it lasted. Right now, he's got his head so far up his butt that he doesn't know what time of day it is. I told him to pack his stuff while I was gone, and be ready to move out when I got back."

"Is everything out in the open?"

"Yes, we had a nice long talk. I yelled and cried, while he begged and lied. He denied everything. He's a man. When confronted, most men will always lie. He must think I'm pretty stupid."

I hugged her and told her not to worry. We would get through this.

"Have you seen a lawyer?"

"Yes, I went to one before I confronted him. I wanted to know what to do."

I pointed to her stomach and asked, "What about this baby?"

"I guess Carl will have to support it, too. He is the father, and I am not getting rid of it."

"Did he suggest you get rid of the baby?" I asked, shocked at the idea of terminating a pregnancy. Under certain circumstances, I might have felt differently, but I have never been put in the position of having to choose.

"He said I might be more appealing, if I wasn't pregnant all the time." She began to sob.

"What a rat!" I yelled. "Why do men say such horrible things? Do you still love him?"

"Yes," she whimpered.

"This isn't going to be easy, Claire. We will be here for you. You can count on us, right Mom?"

Mom came over to the couch, and said, "Don't worry, honey. We'll be with you every step of the way, no matter what you decide to do. Why don't I go home with you? Your dad will not mind."

Claire started crying again. Next thing I knew, we were all crying when Dad walked in.

Our emotional behavior must have upset Athena. She started howling and whimpering, and rubbing her nose on us. It was her behavior that caused us to start laughing. One minute we were crying, and the next we were laughing. Poor girl, she must have thought we were nuts.

After dinner, I retreated to my room. I wanted Mom and Claire to have a chance to talk alone, and I needed a break from all the emotion. I hated to see Claire go through this, but it was a part of life. I also knew a man would dump on you, and you would just have to get passed it. I've been there a few times, myself.

CHAPTER 9

I POURED OVER THE CASE OF HELEN CARROLTON. I couldn't understand why Billy wanted me to spend so much time going over the same information we had already burnt our brains out over. What was I going to find that the two of us had missed?

I followed her trip from the time she left home until the young man working at the gas station on Rt. 15 last saw her. The police report filed with the Charlottesville Police Department that we now had a copy of, along with other info I didn't think we were supposed to be privy to, stated she left her house between two and three o'clock on December 26th. It was assumed she took I-64 to the I-295 Richmond by-pass, and picked up I-64 again, because she exited at Zion Crossroads. Taking a right at the crossroads onto Rt. 15, she stopped at the Piney Mountain Grill, two miles down the road.

Piney Mountain Grill, situated between a mini-mart gas station and a used car lot, was owned and operated by a man named Bubba Johnson. One of his waitresses, Rose Hudgins, age 22, reported serving someone fitting Helen's description. When shown a picture of Helen Carrolton, she positively identified her. She confirmed seeing the woman leave in a red, jeep-like automobile. She said she remembered her because they had a conversation about ex-boyfriends. Rose said it had been a slow day, and she had plenty of time to talk. According to her statement, Helen Carrolton had just had a nasty break-up with her boy-friend. He drank too much and had a violent temper. She told police the girl in question stated that her ex-boyfriend was jealous and pos-sessive. Helen feared he might become dangerous. He had hit her sev-eral times in the past. She was scared of him.

I found it odd that there was very little information on Rose Hudgins in the report. I guess once Bubba Johnson confirmed that Rose had talked to Helen only briefly, the police didn't need to dig any deeper. Maybe, that is why they are cops, and I'm not.

Five miles down the road was the Stoney Point Gas station. The atten-dant on duty, Tom Dorey, could not positively identify Helen. He recalled a red Geo driven by a cute, young blonde. He also reported seeing a male in the passenger seat. She got ten dollars worth of gas, and left.

Again, there was no personal information on Tom Dorey.

I couldn't figure it out. The three people who had last seen Helen alive, had nothing in their file, except a short statement confirming they had seen her. Where did she pick up the male passenger? In a stretch of five minutes, Helen Carrolton had obviously picked up her killer. Oops, did I just think, *'her killer'?* All of a sudden, I had a real bad feeling. I sensed doom. I knew she was dead, and I couldn't shake the feeling. I almost felt sick to my stomach. I tried to put the bad thoughts out of my head, as I continued reading the statements from Helen's parents and her ex-boyfriend. The statements were a biography of Helen. It contained gen-eral information concerning their life, and what they were doing at the time of her disappearance. The twenty-year old ex-boyfriend, Greg Allen, was employed by T.W. Moving and Storage in Grafton. He was on an airplane with his parents on their way to visit his grandparents. They took a flight out of Newport News International Airport on December 26th, at 6:15 a.m. His alibi had been confirmed. He was off the hook.

The rest of the file contained useless data from the State Police and various local police departments. It basically stated that after a thorough investigation... Helen Carrolton was missing.

Did it seem like there was something missing, other than Helen Carrolton? I had a stack of paperwork, and none of it was worth a dime. I got more out of the newspaper clippings than I did out of the police reports, and that wasn't much. Was this all there was, or was this all that Billy could get? I needed to know.

I reached over to pick up the telephone and call Billy, when it rang.

"Hello," I answered.

"Hello, Jesse?"

I recognized the voice immediately. It was Carl. As of late, he was not one of my favorite people. I was about ready to chop up his body, and feed his parts to the wildlife roaming the woods around my new home. Yes, I could do that. I would cut him into little pieces, and feed him one chunk at a time to the animals. I may get lucky. A bear might come along at just the right time, and eat him for dinner. Even though the idea of a bear gnawing Carl to the bone was extremely tantalizing, I had to remember one fact: he was my sister's husband—rat that he is.

"Yes, *Carl*. What can I do for you?"

"I need to talk to Claire. Is she there?" he whined.

I wanted to slap him. Where did he think she would be? I was losing my patience. The emotions I had been through for the last several days, had begun to form a knot in the pit my stomach, the size of a grapefruit.

"Carl, you're such an idiot. Have you lost your mind?" I sneered. "Don't you have enough sense to separate your real life from your fantasy life?"

"I know I messed up..."

Before he could go on, I growled, "Save it, Carl. I don't even want to go there with you. You're such a low-life. If you're going to play around, don't get caught!"

"I'm..." he tried to say.

"Shut up. I don't want to hear it. I'll put Claire on the phone," I said. "Just remember Carl, you've got me in on it now. When it comes to my sister, you're just a fly on the wall."

I went to the hall and yelled downstairs for Claire to pick up the phone. The minute she picked up, I hung up. I didn't want to listen to Carl whine, cry, and sing the blues. My call to Billy was going to have to wait, or, maybe not. I remembered Billy's phone in the truck. I grabbed the card with all his numbers on it, and went outside.

The sun was just beginning to set, as I sat in his truck, waiting for him to answer his phone.

"Hello," he said, out of breath. "This had better be good. You got me out of the shower."

"I'm sorry, Billy. I'll call you back later," I apologized.

"Jesse! No, forget it. It's ok. Actually, I was drying off," he softened. "What can I do for you?"

"I was going over the file, and there seems to be something missing. I know we worked on this all week, and it didn't come to me until now, but I was wondering if there was any more information about Rose Hudgins' or Tom Dorey's personal life. What about the grill owner, Bubba Johnson?"

"You have got all there is. Besides, what good is that going to do us? They are minor players in the scenario."

"They might be minor," I added, "but they're the last three people to see her alive. I think there is more to it. Don't you think it would be worth it to check these people out more closely? I mean, what could it hurt?"

"You might be right. We will pay them a visit on Monday. What are you doing? Other than going over the file, are you busy?"

"I was just studying this file, why?"

"Well, I got a call from my brother just before I got in the shower. He wants me to check out this car he has for you. I was just thinking about giving you a call. Do you want to go with me?"

"Robert's looking for a car for me?" I asked, confused.

"No, silly," he laughed. "Daniel is the one who has the car lot. I told you about him."

"How many brothers do you have?"

"Three brothers, and two sisters," he boasted.

Chuckling, I replied, "Now I know why they are called tribes. Are all Indian families this large?"

"Yes, they are. How about it? Do you want to go? It would save me from having to take you to look at it later."

"Sure, give me an hour to change clothes and get there."

BILLY TOOK ME TO REDMAN'S AUTO CENTER. It was a huge car lot filled with an array of new automobiles. I wondered what Billy must have been thinking. I could not afford a new car.

"Does Daniel own this car lot?"

"He sure does," he answered, as we pulled up to the front entrance. "Daniel owns a car lot; Robert owns a restaurant; Jonathan is a bounty hunter; Elizabeth is a financial advisor; and Jenny is a lawyer."

"What, no doctors in your family?" I snickered.

"My father is a doctor, but he's retired."

"What does your mother do?"

"She's the grease that keeps the gears lubed."

Daniel came out to greet us. He was a younger version of Billy. He was handsome, dark skinned, had long black hair, and was tall, with a muscular build. I soon discovered he was a smooth talker, with charm and wit. He quickly changed my mind about sleazy car salesmen.

Billy introduced us.

""What a pretty young lady you are, Jesse," Daniel said. "My brother was right. But you are awful small, and not much for child-bearing."

They both laughed.

Did he just insult me, or was he making a joke?

"Don't listen to him, Jesse. He is always looking for wife material. He's been married three times, and has five children. He wants his own personal tribe," Billy said, as he slapped Daniel on the back.

We followed Daniel until we came to a red Jeep. He handed me the keys and said, "Here she is. It's a 1997 Jeep Grand Cherokee, with all the bells and whistles. It's got power windows and door locks, a separate jack for a car phone, and it is equipped with a Lo Jack tracking system. If you like it, all we have to do is sign some papers, and it's yours. Why don't you take it for a test drive?"

"What's the price?" I asked, knowing full well whatever it was, I couldn't afford it.

Daniel stared at Billy. "Didn't you discuss the details of this deal with her?"

"I didn't have time. She called shortly after you did, and we came straight here."

Daniel opened the car door, and said, "Take it for a test drive. Billy can discuss the details with you, while you are driving. I will go get the paperwork started."

I loved the Jeep the minute I sat down. It still had the smell of a new car, and the leather seats were wonderfully comfortable. I was impressed with the compass overhead.

"What is this deal that Daniel keeps talking about, Billy? Why all the secrecy? Is something illegal going down?"

"Ah, you break my heart, `ge ya," he cried, as he placed his hand over his heart. "You know I'm not into that kind of stuff." He smiled. "I told you I would take care of you, didn't I?"

Before I had a chance to say anything, he went on, "The agency is going to purchase this car as a tax write-off. That is, if you decide you want it. It will be licensed and insured through the agency. When you get it paid for, I will give you the title. Then you are on your own."

He waited for me to respond, but I was too flabbergasted. Why was he doing this for me? He hardly knew me. We have only been together for a little over a week, and already he has bought me clothes, let me use his new truck, and now he's going to buy me a car. This was scary. Nobody has ever looked after me, except my parents, who didn't expect something in return. What did he want? What did I have to do to get this car? My mind was spinning in all different directions.

"Jesse, you've got that suspicious look on your face!"

"What look? What are you talking about? I don't have any look on my face! You are seeing things."

"Yes, you do. It is that look you get when you think something is fishy. Nothing fishy is going on, so stop worrying. You're getting a fairly new car, and I'm getting a tax write-off. No big deal."

I pulled out of the car lot and made a U-turn onto Rt. 29..

"First off, it is a big deal," I scowled. "I can't afford a car like this. It probably cost twenty thousand dollars. And secondly, how do you figure I'm going to pay for it? Hell, the payments alone are probably more than my rent used to be."

"Payroll deduction," he said. "We're getting the car at cost—fifteen-five."

"Who gets the car if I quit?"

Billy looked hurt. "Well, I'm hoping you'll stick around. But if you do decide to leave, you can get a loan and pay it off, or you can leave it with me, and walk away. How does that sound?" He reached into his back pocket and removed his wallet. "Here's your paycheck. I forgot to give it to you before you left today. I'm sorry."

I was trying to drive and concentrate on Billy at the same time. I reached over, took the check without looking at it, and said, "I wasn't expecting to get paid until next week."

"I'll pay you at the end of the week. Besides, I don't know how long you're going to hang around," he said, as he laughed.

"Why are you so good to me? You hardly know me."

"Whether or not you know it, we're going to be partners for a long... long... long... long time, so get used to it. Partners look after each other."

"You're assuming a lot, Billy Boy," I joked, as I parked the Jeep at the front door.

"No, I'm not. I'm just a good judge of character."

Fifteen minutes later, we left Redman's Auto Center in separate automobiles. Billy had his truck back, and I was driving a sweet ride. He had lived up to his promise, and asked for nothing in return except what was expected. It made me realize he was a good man, someone I could trust. I had been shit on and treated like dirt from every man in my life, except for my dad and brother. It was it hard for me to trust any man.

I honked and waved at Billy as he made his turn off Rt. 29. As I drove, my mind began to wander—which it does quite often. It amazed me how quickly our lives can change. Thinking back to my past life before the mountains, I realized just how lucky I was now. I had such a boring life before, and now I have a good one. I was happy. I have a home, family, friends, job, and a great boss. Now, all I needed to do was work on my relationship with Cole, if there still was a relationship.

Pulling into the driveway, and still thinking about how much I liked my new car, I saw Claire walking down the steps. Dad was behind her carrying luggage, while Mom walked along side of him.

"Where are you going?" I asked, getting out of my car.

"Claire is going home," Mom reluctantly announced. "She's going to try and work it out with Carl."

"What do you mean, work it out?" I cried, running up to my sister. "Claire, don't go. You need some time to think this over. Besides, you just got here. Take a couple of days and see what develops. Who knows, maybe you will find the answer. If you go back to him now, you won't be giving yourself a chance to find out your true feelings. I know you are lonely without him, but can you really tolerate him cheating on you? Once they cheat, they never stop. Please, think it over." I was desperately trying to get her to listen to reason.

Claire began to cry. "I can't help it, I love him, Jesse. We have two kids and another one on the way. I have to think of them!"

Claire has always been the weak one in the family. You could talk her into anything. I knew she would go back to that creep and be miserable for the rest of her life, for the sake of the kids. It was a lost cause. That is just the way she was. I backed off and let her go. I watched her leave, with a sinking feeling in my heart.

Mom cried, while Dad tried to console her. "Come on back inside, Minnie. She'll be fine."

"Dad is right, Mom. Claire can handle it. She will be ok," I lied.

That sorry bastard! He better get his shit together, or he would have me to deal with. He was not going to hurt my sister and get away with it! I would hurt him so bad that he wouldn't know what time of day it was. I could get Billy to help me. We would make his life miserable. I knew we could do it. Once again, I had visions of a bear eating him for dinner. It could happen!

I tried to change the subject by asking Dad what he thought of my new car.

"Is that your car?" he asked.

"It will be mine when I make the last payment. Billy, more or less, financed it for me."

"More or less... what does that mean?" he asked, giving me the eye.

"It means he's going to use it as a tax write-off for the agency, deduct the payments from my paycheck, and when it's paid for, it's mine. He gets something, and I get something,"

"Is that legal?" asked Mom.

"Yes, according to Billy, and he would know," I said, in my best know-it-all tone.

"Let's have a look at it," Dad replied. "Start it up, and pop the hood. I want to see what it has under there."

Dad was impressed with what he saw, and was even more impressed when he drove it. He had good things to say. "This is nice. It handles well, and has a smooth ride. It will be perfect when it snows."

Mom loved my car, and kept talking about how nice it was.

"Maybe you'll let me drive it to the store sometime. You can be with me. It's new, and I wouldn't expect you to let me drive it by myself."

"You can drive it all you want. You don't need me with you. You can take Dad. I used your car a many a time. So, now, you can use mine."

Athena had been riding in the cargo area, and was damn glad when we let her out. Poor dog, I guess I'll have to get her some Dramamine for dogs... if they make it. One day we might have to take a trip, and I didn't want her to puke in my new car. Dogs are so much like kids...

Later, as I crawled into bed, I thought about my paycheck. I dug for my purse and discovered that even after taxes were taken out, I had a check for $400.00. I thought Billy said the job paid $250.00 a week. Had I heard him wrong? There was so much going on in my life right now that money was the last thing on my mind. Yet, I knew this had to be wrong. Billy must have made a mistake. I dialed his number at home.

When he answered, I said, "Billy, this check is for $400.00. You must have made a mistake."

"I pride myself in not making mistakes," he assured me. "It's correct. You earned every bit of it. It's your share of the last couple of jobs."

"But I didn't do anything."

"Oh, yes you did," he rebutted. "You did more than you think."

"I'm not going to argue. I'll take your money and be glad to get it."

I hung up the phone, my trusty dog by my side, and went to bed. What a great life!

CHAPTER 10

S ATURDAY, I spent the morning doing laundry and organizing my room. I helped Mom around the house a little, and by the afternoon, we decided to take a ride to the IGA in my new car. Mom was nervous driving, and Dad kept telling her to pick up the speed.

"You're driving too damn slow, Minnie," he said to her.

"Oh, hush up, Mack," she scolded. "I drive at a speed I'm comfortable with. These roads are so curvy. Besides, we're not on the main roads, yet. So, what's the problem?"

Parents, are they all the same? Haven't I seen this same scenaro played out in a movie somewhere?

As we parked in the IGA parking lot, to the left of us, we noticed four police cars with their lights flashing, surrounding the Amoco gas station.

"Wow!" I exclaimed. "I wonder what happened over there? Maybe somebody robbed the gas station. What do you think, Dad?"

Hesitantly, Dad proclaimed, "I don't know, but I think we'd better sit here until we see what's going on. Lock the doors."

"Mom, hit the button to your left on the armrest that says *Door Lock*. It locks them all," I commanded.

I heard the door locks click. We sat there for a minute, looking around.

"Isn't that Cole standing over there by the gas pumps with that other officer?" Mom asked.

"It sure is," Dad mumbled.

"It must be over," I said. "Two of the cop cars are leaving."

"Let's go and talk to Cole," Mom insisted.

Dad saved the day by saying, "No, Minnie. He's on duty. We can't bother him. We will just be in his way."

"Yeah, Dad's right, Mom. He's on duty."

As we got out of the car, I glanced over in the direction of Cole. He turned just in time to make eye contact, and I felt like a school kid again. My knees got rubbery, and my heart started to flutter. I'm such a dork.

All of us waved at him. He leaned over and put something in his car, and then motioned for us to come over. He made a thumb's up signal to let us know everything was safe.

"Hello," he said. "I've been so busy I haven't had time to stop by."

I thought he was talking to all of us, but he looked directly at me and said, "I get off at four o'clock today. God willing that nobody else decides to rob the gas station before then, I would like it very much if you'd come to dinner at my house tonight. I'm cooking."

Mom stepped up and said, "Oh, I'm so sorry, but Mack and I have plans for the evening. Thank you anyway. Maybe Jesse could make it. What do you say, honey?"

Oh, lord, there she goes again. "I would like that very much," I politely responded, trying to avoid the obvious. "What time and how do I get there?"

"Say, around seven?" he replied. "Take a left out of your driveway and go until you reach a dead end, and then take another left. You can't miss it. I'm the only house on the road."

I was floating on a cloud when I replied, "I'll be there."

I grabbed Mom by the arm and led her away. "Don't we have some grocery shopping to do?"

LET ME CATCH MY BREATH. I tried to figure out what to wear. If a man invites you to dinner at his house, what do you wear? Should I wear

jeans, a skirt, a dress, or sexy underwear? I was freaking out. I didn't
know what to expect. Should I go casual, or try to fancy myself up some?
He wouldn't ask me to dinner at his house unless he was still interested. I
could feel my anxiety getting out of control. Calm down, and get it together, I kept telling myself.

Finally, considering the type of man I thought Cole to be, I decided to
wear a pair of Levi's and a T-shirt. This was the real me. I'm not going to try
to be someone else for the sake of others. I have a life. I'm going to be me.

I threw myself together, and drove up to Cole's house. I was doing
those breathing exercises that they teach you to control anxiety, the whole
way. My heart was pounding so hard, I thought I would choke to death.

I kept hearing Mom's voice telling me how to behave in the company
of a man. Over and over, her instructions on how to get a man's attention
and keep it, were roaring through my head. She had fussed over me the
entire time I was trying to get ready for my date, until I thought I would go
crazy. Why was I listening to her anyway? Times had changed. Women
chased men. They asked them on dates, and they were the ones who decided when and where they were going to have sex. Sometimes they even
paid for the movie or dinner. It wasn't like it used to be when she was
dating. But, then again, she had been happily married to the same man for
a hundred years! I wish I could be so lucky.

I followed Cole's directions. When I parked in his driveway, I was surprised at how neat and clean the place looked. For a cop/single man with a
dog, living alone, I had pictured a small cabin in need of repair; a place littered
with several work-in-progress jobs; and a pile of trash somewhere, waiting to
go to the dump. I don't know what made me see those images in my mind, but
I was totally shocked to see how wrong I had been. It would not have been the
first time. Assumptions can be a waste of time.

Cole's house was a two-story, A-frame. It had a porch that appeared to
go all the way around the house, and come out in the front, with a wide set
of steps down the middle. To the right and left of the house were clusters
of trees that blended in with the rest of the forest behind it. Mountain
peaks lined the horizon. His small parking area in the front was graveled,
and the only automobile parked there was his Jeep.

As I got out of my car, I saw what looked like a dirt road to the left of his house. I walked about ten feet passed his Jeep and looked down. The dirt road sloped down to a cleared field the size of a tennis court. To the right, facing the mountain was his police cruiser.

I walked up to his front door and knocked. It was almost seven o'clock and the sun was beginning to sink behind the mountains. The early evening sky was a mix of royal blue, streaked with orange and shades of yellow. The temperature hovered around sixty-five. What a beautiful night it was going to be.

Tonight was the deal breaker, and I knew it. If Cole and I were going to have any kind of a relationship, tonight was the night. Sometimes you just have that feeling, and I was having one now.

Cole answered the door wearing jeans and a T-shirt. His dog was by his side, barking and howling just like Athena.

"This must be River." I leaned down and patted his head. He nuzzled my leg, licked my hand, then rolled over and made funny noises.

"Ah, he likes you," Cole said. "Normally, he bares his teeth at most strangers. Come on in the house. I'm glad you could make it."

"You invited me to dinner," I replied. "After the last time we were together, I'm surprised you asked me. I wasn't exactly the best company. Drinking and I do not mix."

"I could tell you weren't much of a drinker. I thought you were cute. At least you weren't driving. You know we frown on that here, being a deputy and all. I'd have to take you to jail."

"You are really trying to impress me, aren't you?" I joked, as I tagged behind him to the living room. "Hey, this is nice."

"Thank you," he replied. "I built this house myself, with the help of my family and some friends."

"You did a great job. I love the way the room seems to go on forever. It's like one big open space, yet it has a cozy feeling. The cathedral ceiling is breath taking. What is upstairs?"

"My bedroom," he replied. "Beneath us is a basement that's divided into a recreation room and a bedroom. There's also a half bath down there. Here's the guest bathroom," he gestured to a room to my left. "Upstairs, I have a full bath off my bedroom. I also have a pantry off the kitchen, down here," he pointed. "But don't go near it. River seems to think it is his room. It's a disaster area."

He laughed as he guided me into the kitchen. "I thought I'd grill us a steak for dinner. I put a couple of potatoes in the microwave, and I fixed a salad earlier. I hope you like Italian dressing because that's all I have. Sorry, but shopping is usually the last thing on my mind at the end of the day."

"I understand," I said. "As long as I'm not cooking, anything is fine with me." I wanted him to know that cooking was not one of my fields of expertise. "I'm not much of a cook."

"That's alright. You don't cook well and I don't clean well. We ought to get along fine. How about a glass of wine, or maybe a shot of Tequila?" he joked.

"I'm afraid I'd better pass on the wine. It makes me crazy. Tequila would probably kill me. What else do you have?"

"I have beer, tea, milk, or water... you choose."

"I'll take a beer. I haven't had one in a long time," I said, knowing I would need something if I were going to survive this night. My stomach was doing flip-flops, and my heart was trying to set a world speed record.

We settled into an evening on the back porch. The night was warm, with a slight breeze blowing in through the trees. As Cole grilled our steaks, I couldn't help but notice how nice he looked in jeans.

"Is there anything I can do to help?" I asked.

"Nope, everything is under control."

The food was good; the atmosphere pleasant; and the promise of what was to come, was even better. I could feel the attraction between us begin to intensify.

Towards the end of the meal, Cole went inside and turned on some music. Oldies were his favorite, he told me. "Real music, the kind you can understand." We listened to Diana Ross, the Temptations, and even a little John Denver. I had to admit, I liked this music, especially Percy Sledge's— *When a Man Loves a Woman.*

"So, what happened at the gas station today?" I asked. "Can you talk to me about it?"

"Sure," he replied. "Two punks from upstate New York managed to make a pit stop in our fair town. It seems they were headed back home to Texas. They made a mistake by stopping here."

"They probably didn't realize the police station was two blocks down the road, huh? Criminals can be so stupid."

"The gas station attendant claims one of the guys jumped the counter, demanded money, and then hit him in the face with a gun. The crook's partner was to be the lookout, while he pumped gas. Fortunately, Deputy Briggs was making his routine check of the shopping center, when he noticed a suspicious looking character at the pumps. He says the guy was looking around like he was covering for someone. So, he called for backup, then entered through the back door, and subdued the guy inside. Two units pulled up to the front and got the one at the pump. Bam! It was over." Cole got up to clear the table.

"I am glad that nobody got killed," I stated. "Here, let me help with the dishes. It is the least I can do."

If I had been by myself, the dishes would still be on the table in the morning. However, I didn't want Cole to see that side of me, yet. That was one of my bad habits I have been trying to change. When I moved here, I made up my mind to change some of my old habits. I'm still working on it.

All the appliances in Cole's kitchen were white, except the double stainless steel sink. I didn't see a spot of grease anywhere. The knotty-pine cabinets looked new.

"The kitchen looks pretty good for someone who does not clean," I remarked. "You must have a tidy person."

"I said I didn't clean *well*, not that I didn't clean at all. That could get pretty nasty," he responded, as he laughed out loud. "Mama did the best she could with me."

"Didn't I just hear that phrase a minute ago in a song?" I toyed, as I sat the dishes on the counter. "Shall I wash and you dry—since you know where everything goes?"

"Why don't we take the lazy way out, and put them in the dishwasher instead? I hate to wash dishes."

Duh... he must think I'm backwards as hell. Recovering from being such an idiot, I replied, "That is a good idea." What he didn't realize was that I was having a hard time being so close to him. His aftershave lotion was permeating that soft spot I have for sensual smells, and the warmth of his body was about to overcome me. One more step, and I'd probably fall into his arms.

"Hand the dishes to me, and I'll put them in the dishwasher," he said, as he leaned over and opened the door.

"Don't you want me to rinse them first?" I asked. "We would not want the drainhose to get clogged."

"No," he said, as he reached out and took the dishes. He stood there for a second, pondering something, then sat the dishes back down. He slid his arms around me, pulling me close to him. His lips were on mine before I had time to catch my breath. I could feel the room spinning, as I got lost in his kisses. Our soft kisses turned into passionate longing—picking up momentum. I wanted his lips all over my body. I wanted his body all over my body.

He scooped me up in his arms, and carried me upstairs. It all happened so fast. One minute we were standing at the sink, and the next we were in his bed. I barely remember how we got there, but that night of passion will be with me forever. Cole was intoxicating. His gentle caresses and his manliness sent shivers throughout ever fiber of my body. I realized I had never experienced a real orgasm until that night. I thought I had, but Cole proved me wrong. I lay in his arms, fulfilled, and totally exhausted.

He looked at me and said, "I can see you're going to break my heart."

CHAPTER 11

THE PHONE RANG and startled us both. The digital clock beside the bed read 2:00 AM. "Please tell me it isn't my mother," I begged, as Cole reached across me and picked up the receiver.

"Hello," he muttered, half asleep. "Yes, she's right here." He looked at me and smiled, "It's your mom." He buried his head under the covers and chuckled.

"Hello, Mother," I said, as Cole's hands explored parts of my body. It soon became difficult to concentrate on the conversation.

"Honey, it's late. We were worried. I'm so sorry to bother you. I know this must be embarrassing," she rambled. "Tell Cole, I'm sorry." There was a lull in the conversation and finally she said, "What with all the weird cases you and Billy have been working on, we were scared. We thought you were in a ditch somewhere."

"I'm glad you called. Cole has me tied up to the railroad tracks, and I can't get loose," I joked, sensing a sigh of relief on the other end of the line. Her fears of me lying dead in the road somewhere were only in her imagination. I was alive and well.

"May I talk to Cole so I can apologize?"

"Yes, you may."

I handed the phone to Cole, and replied, "My mom wants to talk to you." Now, it was my turn to giggle.

"Yes, ma'am," he answered. "That's perfectly all right. Call anytime you feel the need... Yes, I'll tell her... As soon as she's finished cleaning and doing the laundry, I'll let her go home... I'll tell her you said that... Good night, Mom." He hung up the phone.

"Your mom said to tell you to please call if you are not coming home tomorrow. She seems to think you will never get your housework done here in time to make it home for dinner."

"Oh, crap! I'm not going to be home for dinner tomorrow. I forgot to tell her," I said, remembering the invitation I had for Billy's parents' get-together... or whatever it was.

Cole stared at me with a strange look in his eyes. "Do you have a date tomorrow? Have I lost you already?"

"Well, sort of," I said. "Billy is taking me to his family's celebration. He says they celebrate various holidays several times a year. It's supposed to be some kind of big shindig."

"But, is it a date?"

"Not in terms of a date like I would have with you, if that is what you mean," I whispered. "Billy is my boss, and my friend. But my heart will always belong to you. Did I just say that? What a corny thing to say."

I could have slapped myself at that very moment.

"I don't think it is corny," he spoke, as his face met mine. I think it is kind of nice. You stole my heart the first day that I met you. It is about time that I stole yours."

He made love to me again, and I was in heaven.

It was still dark outside when I awoke Sunday morning. I heard noises downstairs. It took me a few minutes to remember where I was, as the night before flashed through my head. I never wanted to crawl out of this bed, or Cole's arms. I could lay here forever.

Grabbing the sheet, I found my way to Cole's bathroom. I didn't get a chance to check out his bedroom to any great lengths last night, but I knew there was a bathroom up here somewhere. I showered quickly and threw on the bathrobe I found on the back of the door. It smelled like him. Hum...

I noticed the phone had rung a couple of times while I was in the shower, and it was ringing again when I went downstairs to the kitchen. Cole had the dishwasher running, and was talking to someone on the phone. He didn't sound very happy.

"I'm afraid you are just going to have to deal with it, pal," he told the other person, as he leaned over and gave me a quick kiss on the lips. Thank God, I thought to smear toothpaste on my teeth, and rinse out my mouth.

The clock on the kitchen wall beside the refrigerator read 6:10. Through the sliding glass doors in the living room, I could see the light of a new day breaking. Life was beautiful.

I needed some coffee. He pointed to the coffee pot, and continued to give the person on the phone a hard time. I was taking my first sip, when he hung up the receiver.

"The fur is flying, as they say."

"What do you mean? What happened?" I asked.

"Let's see," he responded, as he counted on his fingers. "Deputy Briggs called to tell me the perpetrators from the gas station have a rap sheet the length of my arm. It seems the gunman Tyree Wallace got released from Attica a week ago after doing a nickel for boosting cars. While he was in the joint, he met up with his pal, Randy Blains, who was doing two to five for robbery. Blains got released the day after Wallace. Seemed they had another connection besides prison—they're both from Texas. Once they got out, they headed back to Texas. On the way, they met us!"

"So, what's going to happen to them now?"

"They've been charged with six felony counts. They're on their way back to prison. You can count on it."

River moseyed into the kitchen and wanted to play. I think he liked the idea of having me around.

"Would you like some breakfast?" he asked, as he retrieved a frying pan from the cabinet. "I thought I would fix us something to eat." He went to the refrigerator and took out a package of bacon and a carton of eggs.

"Who else called? I heard the phone ring a few times." I didn't want to sound nosy, so I added, "My mom didn't call again, did she?"

"As a matter of fact, she did," he replied. "Billy called your house to say he would be picking you up around noon, and your mother told him you were here. She is upset because she did not know that you would not be home for the cookout they are going to have. Billy was mad because you spent the night with me."

"Oh, boy," I mumbled.

Cole put his arms around me and whispered, "Just tell me last night meant something, and I will be happy."

"It did," I softly said.

After breakfast, Cole and I went upstairs with the intention of getting dressed. A blissful hour later, we crawled out of bed. He went to the bathroom to shave, while I dressed. River lay by the bed, taking everything in.

I decided to push the boundaries of our relationship. I asked Cole if he would go with us today. Of course, I would have to talk to Billy about it, but I did not think it would be a problem. I wanted to spend my time with him, and hoped he wanted the same.

I was surprised when he replied, "One of the calls that I got this morning was from my mother. I grew up with the Blackhawk family. We always go to their family gatherings. Ever since my dad died, I am the one who takes Mom. She just wanted to make sure that I remembered. Yet, she always calls to remind me."

My heart sank. Was this a rejection? Was he trying to tell me that his mother comes first? Why not? I know mine does.

He walked out of the bathroom with shaving cream all over his face. He smiled and kissed me, leaving traces of the foamy stuff on my lips.

"I told her all about you. She said she can't wait to meet you."

"I am glad to hear it."

After thinking about it for a while, I said, "Maybe we could meet up when we get there. If Billy is as angry as you say, I might need some time to talk to him. I definitely have to fix things with my mom. Why don't we just play it by ear?"

"Hey, I'm not going anywhere. I'll be here when the dust settles," he answered. "I'm going to the police station for a couple of hours to check on our two prisoners. I'll follow you out, and call you when I get back."

"I'll let you know if the dust has settled," I repeated his words.

He kissed me good-bye, as I got into my car. He walked over to his Jeep, turned and said, "I see that you bought a new car."

"Yes," I answered. "My other one had just about seen its last day. It was time. I did not have much of a choice."

I put the key in the ignition and started the car. I didn't want to leave. I was afraid that if I left now, Cole would forget all about me, or maybe decide he didn't like me as much as he thought he did. There I go... just another one of my insecurities... *abandonment*—being cast aside, and forgotten. I'm sure somewhere in this world there's a psychologist I haven't talk to yet, that could probably help me with that problem. Unfortunately, I have not found him.

In the rearview mirror, I watched Cole drive behind me. He was headed to police headquarters, while I was going home to face Mom and Dad. What a nightmare! How would I explain what happened last night? Gee, folks, I haven't had sex in six—maybe eight months—I had to have it. No, I would tell them the truth. The truth is... I spent the night with a man who makes me feel wonderful. He makes me feel like a real person. He does things for me that nobody has ever been able to do. Well, maybe I will not tell them that last part.

Oddly, no one had anything to say about last night. Mom did not bring it up, and Dad was not home. Athena wasn't even interested. She was curled up in a corner. Good, I didn't want to answer any questions. Mom and I did discuss our plans for today. It seems Billy had invited them to go, and since none of the grandchildren were going to be here for the weekend, they decided to join us.

"I hope you don't mind, Jesse," she said.

"I think it would be nice. That way, you and Dad could get to know Billy a little better. You will like him, Mom."

"We already like him, honey. It's just that your dad is concerned about the kind of work he does. I think your dad might be right."

I knew she was talking about that crazy Mrs. Miller, and I had to agree with her. Yet, I did not want her to worry every time that I walked out of the door. We would both go insane.

"Sometimes things happen that have nothing to do with the work," I tried to reassure her. "That woman was probably unstable, and would have killed her husband eventually. She went off the deep end."

"It seems a little dangerous to be dealing with people like that."

"Mom, you could encounter someone like that at the grocery store. You just never know. Besides, every time you get out on the road, you face danger. You put your life on the line."

Changing the subject, Mom said, "Your Dad walked down to the mailbox. We forgot to check the mail yesterday. He should be back any minute. I'm going to fix us a sandwich. Do you want one?"

"That sounds good to me," I replied. "I'm going to change clothes. If Billy is coming at noon, I need to find a clean pair of jeans now."

"Are you wearing jeans?" she called to me, as I reached the top of the stairs. "Don't you think you should dress up a little?"

"Mom, it's a cookout. We don't need to get fancy. Billy said it was definitely a casual affair."

I went to the bathroom to brush my teeth, and comb my hair. I looked in the mirror. My waist length, dyed-red hair, was starting to look ragged. It was boring. I wore my hair in a ponytail most of the time. Now, even that was starting to get old. Maybe, it was time for a change. I found myself examining every aspect of my physical being. Perhaps, I should start exercising. I am thirty-one years old. Soon, everything is going to start falling apart.

I've got to stop thinking like that. Every time a new man comes into my life, I start analyzing myself to death. It's self-destructive... something I don't need. I can change the way I look, but I can't change who I am.

Keeping that in mind, I put on a little make-up, and went to my closet to see what I had to wear. After choosing a clean pair of jeans and a T-shirt, I dressed, and headed downstairs. I was following the smell of bacon frying, and realized I was hungry. Food had not been important. All I could think about was Cole. He was the one. I knew it!

"Where is Dad?" I asked. "Shouldn't he be back by now? It is only a ten minute walk."

"Oh, he's probably met up with one of the neighbors," she said, while she sliced a tomato.

"Mom, I have been home almost an hour. Maybe I should walk down and see if he is ok."

"I didn't realize it had been that long."

"Come on, Athena," I said. "Why don't you and I go find Dad? Do you want to come along, Mom?"

"No, honey, you and Athena go. I will finish the sandwiches. I'm sure everything is fine. Tell your dad to get back here. I have a snack almost ready," she said, trying to hide the fear I saw in her eyes.

The closer I got to the mailbox, the more concerned I became. It does not take anybody this long to walk a tenth of a mile. Hopefully, Dad had met up with one of the neighbors. All of that went out the window when I came around the bend. Just across the little concrete bridge sat Cole's Jeep, and a police car with its lights flashing. Cole was standing in the middle of the road talking to an officer.

What was wrong? Where was my dad?

Instantly, Athena went nuts. She started howling like someone in pain. I knew something bad had happened.

Cole walked up to me and said, "I'm sorry, Jesse. I was just getting ready to come up to your house. We think your Dad has had a heart attack. They took him to UVA. Fortunately, Mr. Lawson, who lives in the house over there," he pointed to the house in the bend of the road, "went to let his dog out, and saw someone lying in the road. He called 911 right away. The ambulance just left."

"How is my Dad? Is he all right?

"We don't know anything, yet. When they took him away, they were giving him CPR. That is all I can tell you."

Athena sniffed around our mailbox, whimpered and lay down in front of it. Her eyes told me everything I needed to know. Something really bad had happened here.

"Oh, God," I whispered, tears finding their way down my cheeks. "Dad, please be ok. We need you. God, please let my dad be all right," I prayed. Finally, I was racked with uncontrollable sobs.

Cole put his arms around me and hugged me tight. "Go ahead, Honey, let it all out."

I felt like part of my heart had just been ripped out. I could not lose Dad. He was the one man in my life who would love me no matter what. He was my rock. I wasn not ready to let him go, and I never would be. Life without him would be unbearable.

Wiping the tears away with the back of my hands, I cried, "I have got to go tell Mom. We need to get to the hospital. Dad needs us to be there for him. I do not want him to be alone."

"I'll take you and Athena home," he said. He called Athena's name, and motioned for her to get in the Jeep, as I crawled in the front seat.

Suddenly, Athena bared her teeth and snarled as if she was going to tear Cole apart. Her back was haunched, and her hair was standing up.

"Leave her," I said. "She hates cars. She will come home when she is ready." How I knew this was beyond me, but after looking into those sad eyes, I saw a pain that nobody could help with, until she was ready.

Giving it one last shot, I leaned out of the Jeep and called to her. "Girl, we need to go home and be with Grandma. She needs us."

To my surprise, Athena stood up, ran to the Jeep and jumped up on my lap. This was no easy feat, considering Athena was almost as big as me and probably weighed close to the same. I laughed and closed the door. For one split second, the pain of what was happening had left me.

The instant I walked in the front door, everything came back to me in a blinding wave of sadness. I was so overcome with grief. I could not speak. How could I tell Mom? This is the man she has been with for most of her life. They lived for each other. If anything happened to my dad, what would happen to my mom? She would not be able to go on without him.

Cole went to Mom. "Minnie, we need to get to the hospital." He didn't mince words. "We think Mack's had a heart attack. We need to go right now."

Mom stopped what she was doing and walked over to the pie-safe, where she kept her purse. Grabbing it, she quietly said, "Let's go."

I couldn't believe how calm she was. She must have been in shock.

Cole put his arm around Mom and we walked out the door. Athena was sitting on the porch. Her whine was heart-wrenching.

Stifling a tear, Mom reached down and rubbed Athena's head. "You stay here and take care of everything. Grandpa and I will be back soon."

I broke down. The agony was too much for me to handle. I cried all the way to the hospital, while Mom sat in the back seat of Cole's Jeep, not saying a word. Her silence was eerie.

The hospital ER was a madhouse. Nurses were running here and there, while doctors screamed orders to everyone in sight. Aides, assistants, and interns were busy helping other patients. Cole led us to the emergency room desk. The receptionist had her hands full.

"Hello, Deputy James. May I help you?" the lady asked.

It struck me odd that she knew Cole's name. I thought it over for a second and figured they probably knew all the police officers. I was sure they had seen everyone of them at some point in time.

"Yes," he answered. "Do you have a listing for Mackenzie Aaron Watson, age 65? He was just brought into ER. His wife is here."

"Mackenzie Aaron Watson," she repeated, as she clicked on her computer. "Yes, he is still in OR." She motioned to one of the women behind the counter. "Miss Olson will take you to the OR waiting room. Dr. Bryant and his team are with him now. The doctor will be right with you as soon as possible. We are real busy."

This did not sound good. Dad was already in surgery and none of his family was here to sign papers. You always have to sign papers, don't you?

It seemed like an eternity, sitting around, waiting to hear about Dad. I cried, as Mom paced the floor. She was too calm about all of this. What was wrong with her? She must be in shock, I thought.

As I was trying to figure this out, Billy walked into the room.

"Oh, Billy," I cried. "My dad's had a heart attack!"

"I know, I know." He tried to comfort me. "Cole called me."

"He did?" I asked, looking at Cole.

"Yes, he did. I am here for you," Billy said. He looked over at Mom and took her hands in his. "What can I do for you, Mrs. Watson?"

"Please find out if my husband is all right," she cried.

"I'll see what I can do," he assured her, and then left the room.

When Billy walked back into the room with the doctor, I knew Dad had died. The look on his face said it all. Mack was gone.

"Mrs. Watson," Dr. Bryant said, as he walked up to Mom, "I'm sorry, but we did everything we could. Mr. Watson had a heart condition, and his heart just gave out. I'm so sorry... but we lost him."

"That's not true!" I screamed. "My dad did not have a heart condition. He was healthy as a horse! Tell him, Mom."

She turned to me, and calmly replied, "Yes he did, Jesse. Your dad had a family history of heart disease. We've known for a long time this could happen. He started having trouble about a year ago. After all these years, why do you think we left Tidewater? Your dad needed some peace and quiet in his life. That's why!"

"No, this can't be true. I would have known if something was wrong with Dad. There would have been signs."

While I was trying to come to terms with this startling discovery, Mom tried to comfort me. "Your dad decided a long time ago that this was something you kids did not need to know. Anyway, what could you all do about it, except worry? It was the way your dad wanted it."

My dad was sick, and I did not know a thing about it. I wished I had known. Maybe if I had, I would not have been such a worry to him. I could have tried to be better. I could have made him proud of me... if I just had a little more time.

It was too late now. I had been to my father, all that I was ever going to be. All I had left were our memories, and the hope that one day I would do something to make him proud.

Chapter 12

"**I** WANT TO SEE MY HUSBAND," Mom cried. "I want a chance to say good-bye."

I wanted to tell her I did not think that was such a good idea, but when I looked at her and saw the determination in her eyes, I knew this was something she had to do. And, if she was going to do it, so was I. As much as I loved my father, I did not want my last memory of him to be on his deathbed in a hospital. But, I could not let Mom do this alone.

Cole walked over to where we were standing. He edged in between us and put his arms around our shoulders. He kissed Mom on the cheek and said to the doctor, "I think that can be arranged, right doctor?"

Dr. Bryant looked at Mom and me, searching for signs of stability. I had seen that look a few times. He was wondering if we could handle the sight of death.

"I'll need to sign some papers first," he replied. "Have a seat and I'll have the nurse come take you in when I'm finished. It should only take about ten minutes." The expression on his face turned from one of dread— having to tell someone the person they love had died—to one of comfort. "I'd like for you to talk with our trauma counselor while you're waiting," he suggested, looking from one of us to the other. "If it's ok, I'll send in

Dr. Joyce Vince." He quietly turned and left. As soon as Dr. Bryant walked out of the room, Dr. Vince walked in. They must do this so much; they had their procedure down pat. If a person dies, the doctor comes in and tells the family, while the counselor stands outside the room, ready to come in and pick up the pieces. This gives him enough time to go back and clean up the smell of death.

The talk with Dr. Vince helped us gain a little more strength than we had when we first got the news. An hour later, Mom and I walked into a small alcove where Dad lay. He looked peaceful. He had been a big man in his day, but now the years had made him look smaller. Is that what death does to you?

BILLY MISSED HIS FAMILY GATHERING. He stayed at the hospital and took care of Dad. He handled everything, right down to the details of the funeral. He even made sure there was an obituary run in the local paper, as well as the Denbigh Press in Tidewater.

Cole had the chore of taking us home from the hospital. I am sure that must have been a nightmare for him. I cried all the way, and Mom sat in the back seat mumbling to herself. When we reached the house, both of us had gotten worse. Mom walked around in circles, talking to no one in particular. At first she was calm, and then she became this other person. She started talking loud and fast, her words running together. I sat on the couch crying. Athena lay in front of the fireplace stretched out with her front paws over her eyes, howling a sad cry.

This went on for most of the night. Mom ranted and raved, while I cried my face into a limp, two-month old, dried-up pumpkin. Claire would be here in a couple of hours, and Jack was flying in from Fairfax. He had been in court when Billy tried to reach him. He would arrive at the Charlottesville Airport at 3:45 A.M. Robert Blackhawk was going to meet him, and bring him home to us.

For the next few days everything was kind of a blur. Claire and her asshole husband, Carl had arrived safely, and Jack was here when I woke up the next day. By the time of the funeral, we had all been exhausted by the grief we shared. Cole and Billy kept us all together... kept us from falling apart.

Dad had a proper military burial in Arlington Cemetery. I wanted him buried in the Stanardsville Cemetery on the other side of town, so he would be close to us, but Mom insisted he be laid to rest in a place of honor. He had earned it.

The trip to the cemetery was long and exhausting. The funeral was overwhelming. When they played *Taps*, it brought tears to my eyes, but when they handed Mom the folded flag, it broke my heart. I am surprised we all managed to endure the pain, but we did.

Several days after Dad's funeral, once everybody had gone home, Mom and I tried to put our lives back together. I silently swore to my father that I would take care of Mom, but the truth is, she was taking care of me. She talked about Dad and all the wonderful times we had shared. She said we should hold onto those thoughts, and put aside the unpleasant ones.

I don't think I will ever look at Memorial Day in the same light again. Now, it would hold only sad memories for me.

Dad had been buried a week. During that time, Mom and I spent hours upon hours, crying and reminiscing. We burned out every bit of pain, agony, and energy we had in us. Cole and Billy came by to bring food, and give us as much support as possible. They helped when they could, and stayed away when they thought they should.

Wednesday morning around ten o'clock, Billy stopped by. Even though Dad had been dead for ten days, Mom and I still could not get our act together. I was beginning to wonder if we ever would. I think Billy knew we were having a hard time, and that is why he came over. He said I needed to go back to work.

"I don't know, Billy," I said. "I am scared to leave Mom alone so soon. What will she do all day by herself? It is ten o'clock, and she is still in bed. That is not like her."

"Of course, it's not. Her husband died," he replied. "It's going to be a long time before she'll even want to go out of the house." He looked around the living room. "This place is a mess." He walked into the kitchen and started going through the cabinets. "Where is the jar of coffee? You look like you could use some."

I searched the cabinets until I found the coffee. I did not tell Billy that I had just gotten out of bed, when he rang the doorbell. Here I was worried about Mom still being in bed, yet I had just gotten up myself.

"I know you are not going to forget that your father just died, or get over the pain anytime soon, but you need to start taking a little time to do something different. You can not think about this for twenty-four hours a day, or you will go nuts." His voice was soothing, "I am going to make some coffee and I want you to go wake up your mom. Then, I want you to go upstairs, take a shower, and put on some clean clothes. I want to talk to both of you. I will tell you why, when you get finished."

"But..." I started.

"Just trust me."

"How many times have I heard that?" I asked, as I walked away from the kitchen. I could see a lecture was on the way.

The door to Mom's room was opened. I peeked inside. She was lying on top of the bedspread, still dressed in the same clothes she had been wearing yesterday. This is bad, I thought to myself. Billy is right. We have to go on with our lives. Dad would not want Mom and me to spend the rest of ours lives like this. I could hear him now, "Snap out of it! Get a grip!" That *get a grip* was a phrase he had picked up from me. He got a big kick out of it, the first time I had said it to him. He thought it was cool.

I went into Mom's bedroom, gently shook her, and said, "It is time to get up. Billy is making coffee, and he wants to talk to us. I am going to take a shower. I will be back down in a few minutes."

"What time is it?"

"It is a little past ten," I replied, as I walked out of the room. I wanted to give her time to wake up, and realize it was another day. I resisted the urge to sit on her bed and talk. I did not want us to start our day crying, and feeling depressed.

By the time I got back downstairs, Billy and Mom were in the kitchen... laughing. That lifted my spirits. I had not heard Mom laugh since before Dad died. It was good to have her back.

"What is so funny?" I asked.

"Billy was telling me about some of the cases he has worked," she answered. She still had the pain in her eyes, but she seemed relieved to be able to laugh again. "I can't believe how dumb some people can be." She hesitated for a moment. "Billy was also telling me that you and I should try to start living again... without Mack. I know that sounds harsh honey, but it is true. Mack would not want us to sit around all day   and turn into vegetables. He would want us to go on with our lives."

"*Turn into vegetables*... where did you learn that?" I asked, looking in Billy's direction and pointing my finger, "You've been around him too long."

We were not going to get over this overnight, but I think the two of us realized that we had to go on without Dad. We were still alive, and it was up to us to make the best of it. This was a start. We laughed, and for just a minute, I did not think about the sadness I felt from Dad's death. For just a minute, I did not see grief in Mom's eyes.

Billy had made coffee and between the three of us, we managed to throw together a pretty good breakfast.

"I did not realize how starved I was until now," Mom said, as we sat down at the table. "Poor Athena, when was the last time somebody fed her? Look, she is famished."

"She seems to be pretty happy to me," I said, as Billy placed a plate of eggs and bacon down in front of her.

We ate breakfast in silence, trying to come to grips with reality. Mom seemed to be doing a little better now that Billy was here. He had a way of doing that—making the best of a bad situation, and getting you to do the same. I guess there was still a lot I had to learn about him.

As we cleared the table, Mom faced Billy and said, "Why don't you tell Jesse what you have asked me to do?"

"What?" I looked at him.

"I know it is a bad time, but I need you Jesse," Billy assured me. "I have been making background checks on all the people involved in the Carrolton case, and you were correct. There might be more we need to investigate. The police report does not have zilch on any of them, other than their prior statements."

I had forgotten all about work. My mind had been on trying to get through the funeral, and looking after Mom. Besides, what did work have to do with Mom?

Billy must have sensed my concern. "I've asked your Mom to help us for a couple of days. I want to go talk to the waitress and the gas station attendant. We can check out where they live, and who their friends are. I am going to need your help, plus, I need someone to run the office while we are working. It will only be until we get caught up. I've got a back-log of phone messages to go through and someone needs to man... or should I say... woman the phone." Billy said, smiling that silly smile of his.

"What do you think about this, Mom?" I asked.

Hesitating a minute, Mom turned to me and said, "Billy has been here for us since your father died, and now he needs our help." She glanced at Billy and smiled, "There is no way I could turn him down."

Oh, boy, what a load of crap. Billy is such a persuasive person. He actually had Mom believing he needed her help. But not me, I could see right through him. Billy does not need anybody... it is the *anybodies* that need him. He knew it, and so did I.

"Give me a few minutes to get myself together and I will be ready to go," she said to Billy, and glanced in my direction. "I think it would be best if I drove my own vehicle, since Athena will be coming." Then she hurried out of the room, not giving me a chance to say anything.

Still not being able to call my mom by her first name, Billy replied, "I think that is a good idea Mrs. Watson."

"Are you nuts?" I asked, pouncing on him the minute she got out of sight. "She is not ready. It is too soon."

"You do not give her enough credit. She is stronger than you think. She is a very brave woman. You might be surprised."

"I know what you are doing."

Billy's attempt at distracting us from our misery was working. Within an hour's time, he had brought the color back into Mom's cheeks. After watching her turn into a shell of a person, in a span of less than two weeks, it was good to see her come back to life, however short lived. I would take what I could get.

"I almost forgot Athena's bowl," Mom said. "I think we ought to stop at Wal-Mart and get her one of those dog beds. You don't want her stretched out all over the place. This is a place of business." She scurried around, looking for anything she might have missed.

I ran upstairs to get my handbag. I found my briefcase and shoved the scattered paperwork off the computer table into it. My head was spinning, and I had the feeling I had slipped into an episode of the Twilight Zone. It is funny how things flash through your mind. Something was constantly happening, and information was bombarding me from everywhere. I could not seem to process it all at one time. I have had more stuff going on in the past month than I have had in my whole thirty-one years. It was not sur- prising that I felt so confused.

After making sure the alarm had been set and the house was locked, Billy ushered us out to our cars. He was ready to get moving, and did his best to make sure we were safely packed and ready to go, before we pulled out of the driveway. Mom and Athena were in the mini-van behind Billy, and I followed her in my Jeep. I could have gone with either one of them, but I liked driving my new car.

Athena got her new dogbed, and Mom got comfortably set into her new role as office manager. She fell for Billy's charm just as I had. He seemed to have a special way of making you feel right at home, and at the same time, he is trying to guide you in the direction he thinks you need to go. He is always babbling about something in his native tongue, which Mom finds delightful.

A few days later, Mom had found her niche. She loved answering the phone, making coffee, and at the same time, taking care of Athena, Billy and me. She had her freedom to run things as she saw fit. To her it was like taking care of her household, which was something she knew how to do pretty well. Most importantly, I think it helped to ease some of the pain she was trying so desperately to deal with. It was going to be a long road to recovery, for all of us.

At the end of each day, we would have dinner together at Billy's apart- ment, or at our house. We were soon becoming a family of another sorts— me... my orphaned dog... my mother... and an Indian private detective. What a life!

During the several days that my mother was being indoctrinated into the private eye business, Billy and I were out running down every piece of information that we had. We went to the Piney Mountain Grill and talked to Rose Hudgins, but she did not tell us anything we did not already know. However, we got a chance to observe her reactions to certain questions. To me, she seemed a little bit uncomfortable at times, especially when we asked questions about her family. This was obviously a subject the police had not explored aggressively.

Finally, she hissed, "What has my family got to do with anything? They had nothing to do with that girl's disappearance, and neither did I."

"We are just trying to cover all the bases," I assured her, as I sipped coffee that was fast becoming lukewarm. "Do you think I could get some more coffee? Mine seems to be getting cold."

"Sure," she replied, as she got up and went to fetch the coffee.

"I am beginning to think this is a waste of time. She does not know anything. We are just beating a dead horse," Billy said.

I leaned across the table and whispered, glancing back and forth to see if she was coming, "No way, Billy. Did you see the way she flinched when I said *family*? She almost wet her pants. I noticed her hands started trembling when she said she also has a brother. What is the deal?"

"Perhaps, they do not get along," he answered. "Maybe she comes from a dysfunctional family. Doesn't everybody these days? I mean, look at us: an Indian; a skinny little white girl; and a grandma, trying to run a PI business. How odd is that?"

Ignoring his reference about our newly formed family, I said, "I am telling you Billy, something smells funny."

"It is probably the grease from the kitchen," he joked. "These places are famous for greasy food."

Rose returned before I could convince Billy to ask more questions about her family. Her hands were trembling when she poured the coffee. Instead of sitting in the booth with us again, she stood, holding the half-filled coffee pot. Obviously, this was her way of telling us she'd had enough. This conversation was done.

Billy ignored her seemingly uncomfortable attitude. "One more question, if you don't mind," he asked, not waiting for her to refuse. "Can you tell us anything you remember about your conversation with Helen Carrolton the day she was here? I know you have been through all this with the police—probably more times than you want to remember. Yet, you never know what might turn out to be that one piece of information that could lead to solving this mystery. We need your help." Billy was playing her. I have seen him do this to other people, and it usually worked.

Rose seemed to relax a little. She was probably glad she didn't have to answer anymore of my questions about her family.

"We talked about half an hour. She said she had just broken up with her boyfriend. I could tell she was sad. Maybe she still loved him. But the one thing I do remember was that she was scared of him. He hit her a few times. Once a man hits a woman, nothing is the same anymore."

"Did she mention anything about him trying to reconcile with her after they broke up?" I asked. "Did he come by, or make harrassing phone calls to her?"

"Yeah," Rose replied. "She said he called her all the time. Finally, she refused to talk to him. The day before she left, he came to her house and they had a big fight. Her parents called the police on him, and once the police arrived, he was forced to leave. Story over."

Shift the blame. That always works.

"How old is your brother?" I asked. I knew this was going to make Billy hot under the collar, but frankly, at the time, I did not care.

She glared at me in the most undignified manner. "Eighteen, if it is any of your business," she answered. "If you will excuse me, I have a job to do." She spun around and huffed off to the kitchen.

"Well, I hope you're satisfied!" Billy moaned.

CHAPTER 13

W E ARGUED ALL THE WAY BACK TO THE OFFICE.
"I had her eating out of my hands," Billy swore. "Then you go and rile her up by talking about one thing that has nothing to do with the other. It is a dead end. Drop it. Helen was at the diner, and they spent thirty minutes together. That is not enough time to get to know someone. Rose Hudgins does not know squat."

"I think you are wrong, Billy. I think she knows a lot more than she is saying. She is keeping a tight lip about something."

"What gives you that idea?"

"I do not know. It is just a feeling I have."

We were still arguing when we walked in the front door.

Mom greeted us with a smile, and a warning. "You two need to chill out. Let's go home and cook some steaks. We might as well get some use out of that grill your dad bought."

The instant she said *dad*, Billy and I froze and stopped arguing.

"It sounds like a good idea," Billy replied. "I am as hungry as a bear."

When he said, *bear*, I cracked up. Again, I had visions of my brother-in-law being chased by a killer bear, viciously clawing at him. Yes, that would make my day!

THE NEXT DAY, Billy and I talked with the gas station attendant. He was much more cooperative than our waitress. He told us he pumped ten dollars' worth of gas for her, she paid in cash, and then left.

"I recognized her by the picture the police showed me. She's pretty, you know," he rambled. He talked as if he was trying to remember it all. "It had just started to snow, and by the time I had pumped her gas, it was coming down pretty hard. Normally, I would offer to clean the windshield and check the oil, but with the snow and all..."

"Mr. Dorey, you reported to the police that there was a man in the car with her," I butted in. "Can you tell us anything about him? What he looked like? What was the color of his hair?"

"I didn't pay much attention to him. I was too busy looking at her. All I can tell you is that he was white, and had dark hair."

"Was he fat, or skinny?" I asked.

"He was average. He wasn't fat, or skinny."

Now, it was my turn to throw in the towel. I looked at Billy and rolled my eyes, signaling a sign of defeat. "He had his eyes glued to the girl," I whispered. "He doesn't remember squat about the guy. Let's call it a day."

Taking the lead, I said, "I think that's all for now. If we have any more questions, we'll be in touch, or if you remember anything... anything at all, give us a call, please." I handed him one of Billy's business cards, and grabbed Billy by the arm, dragging him out of the gas station.

Billy was slightly dumbfounded by my abruptness and ability to control the situation. "Why are you brushing him off like that? He might be able to identify the guy, and you cut him off. What's the matter with you?"

"Come on," I said, taking the keys from his hand. "Let me drive, and I will see if I can explain the meaning of raging hormones to you."

By the end of the week, Billy and I were at each other's throats. At noon on Friday, Billy and I returned to the office. We had spent most of the morning doing surveillance on the waitress, the gas station attendant, and even Bubba Johnson, the burly guy that owned the restaurant. I thought there was something fishy about the waitress, and Billy thought the gas station attendant knew more than he was telling us. Needless to say, we could not see eye-to-eye on anything.

Mom was sitting at what used to be my desk, talking on the phone. "Yes, Mrs. Jordan, I'll see that he gets the message." Without looking up, Mom pushed her chair back and stood up, saying, "I'm done for the day. Athena and I are going home." Then she walked over to Billy and handed him a pink while-you-were-out piece of paper. "I was just on the phone with Mrs. Louise Jordan. She wants to talk to you about her daughter. I told her you would call as soon as you got back. So, you need to call her." Mom took a deep breath and stepped backwards, looking directly at Billy and me. "I love you both, but you two have got to stop fighting. All my kids are grown now, and I'm not going to bring up any more. So get yourself together." She stood there just long enough to give us the evil eye. Without saying another word, she hissed as she walked out of the office with Athena.

"She's getting rather pushy, isn't she?" Billy whispered.

"Yeah, well... that's my mama!"

That night, the three stooges and their dog were having dinner, when Cole rang the doorbell. I had not seen him this last week because he had been tied up in a police training class. I missed him, but at the same time, I was carrying a considerable amount of guilt about our last night together. I did not come home. Mom and Dad had been frantic; she called me in the middle of the night. Dad had a heart attack the next day. Did this have anything to do with it? Was that what pushed his heart to the limit? They say stress can kill a person. Did I contribute to Dad's heart attack? Sadly, the guilt would be another downfall in my emotional stability. I would carry this in the back of my mind always, even though, I knew it wasn't my fault. Maybe, beating myself up was my way of dealing with the pain. I was saddled with sadness and guilt.

That all changed when Cole arrived.

"Hello, everybody," he shouted, walking into he kitchen. I noticed he looked tired.

Mom pounced out of her chair like I had seen Athena do when she saw something move in the woods.

"Come and sit over here," she said to him. "Just because it is getting warm outside now, doesn't mean we can't have a good old bowl of beef stew. Does it?" She went to the stove and dished him up a bowl. "I took off work early today, and fixed a big pot," she continued, not taking a pause for a breath of air. "I guess you know I am running Billy's office while they go out and catch the bad guys?"

Billy and I just about fell out of our chairs.

What has happened to this woman in the last few days? She was acting like she was in a different world. She reminded me of a butterfly, fluttering from flower to flower. One minute she was bossing us around, clearly the one in charge, and the next, she would turn into another person. Was my mother having a nervous breakdown?

"Don't worry about her," Billy whispered, leaning across the table. "Just let her do her thing. She needs to get it out."

I was not sure what he was talking about, but I have learned that Billy pretty much knows about people. I have seen him handle enough situations to figure out he has got the right idea. So, I put it out of my mind. If Mom needed to be in charge, then so be it. If she wants to cater to our every need, who was I to question it? I just can not help but feel a little bit concerned when she acts like a yo-yo. She was definitely bouncing back and forth. I was waiting for the string to break.

"This looks good," Cole replied. "I have not had a decent meal for a week. I have been in re-certification class, and by the time it was over at the end of the day, the best I could muster up was a pit stop at the Burger King." He smiled at Billy and me, as he dug into his bowl of stew.

"Well, you go on and help yourself," Mom buzzed. "I have got plenty more." Then she burst into tears.

Billy was the first one out of his seat. Giving her a shoulder to cry on, he led her over to the table and said, "You sit down, Mom, and finish your stew." He ripped a paper towel off the roll and handed it to her. "You've been mighty brave, and I know how hard it has been." His compassion for her was touching. He was such a gentle, caring man.

Athena jumped up, put her front paws on Mom's lap, and whimpered.

"You are such a silly girl," Mom said, half-laughing, as she rubbed Athena's head. A few spoonfuls of soup later, Mom put the bowl on the floor for Athena.

"I do not believe it! You are letting her eat out of your bowl!" I said, shocked. "I remember once when we were little, Claire and I wanted to feed a stray dog out of one of our dinner bowls, and you had a fit. You said no animal was going to eat out of a plate that we used. You said it was not sanitary, and you gave us a long lecture."

"I can change my mind," she said, smiling at Athena.

I could tell Mom was tired. After dinner I told her to go on to bed and we would take care of the kitchen mess. I put the leftover stew in the refrigerator, while Cole and Billy cleared the table. It was funny watching the two of them trying to load soup bowls into the dishwasher.

The phone rang, and I jumped to answer it.

"Hello," I whispered.

"J-J-Jesse," Claire stammered. "It's me, Claire." She barely got my name out, before she started bawling.

"Claire, what's wrong?" I asked. By the tone in her voice, I was sure the world had come to an end. My sister was in dire distress.

"I-I-It's Carl. He's in the hospital," she cried.

"Ok, calm down. Tell me what happened." I tried to soothe her, but the image of the man-eating bear flashed before my eyes, and it was all I could do to keep from clapping, and laughing out loud.

Claire proceeded to tell me the events of the last couple of weeks. "Just before Dad died, Carl and I had a big fight. Some woman called here and said they were having an affair. So, naturally when he got home from work, I confronted him."

"What did he say?" I asked, rolling my eyes at Billy and Cole as they sat down at the table, intent on listening in on my conversation.

"H-He said it was a lie," she sniffled. "Anyway, I was so mad at him, I couldn't see straight. I ran up the stairs and slammed the bedroom door. He followed me. One thing led to another, and I fell down the stairs." She started to cry again. "Jesse, I lost the baby."

I freaked out. "That b... I'll kill him myself!" I screamed, trying to recover from the shock. "But I thought you said Carl was in the hospital. I'm confused. He knocked you down the stairs and killed your baby, yet he's the one in the hospital? Am I missing something?" Then it struck me—maybe she retaliated for what he did to her, by shooting him. Now that was a pleasant thought. I could live with that. At, least she did not kill him, did she? Did Carl even own a gun?

She continued, pulling me from my thoughts about Carl being hooked up to a string of hospital monitors... gasping for air. "When I lost the baby, Carl was so supportive."

"I guess he was," I hissed.

"Jesse, it was just as much my fault as it was his. We should not have been fighting. I was just so angry with him, I could not stop myself. I forgot all about the baby." She broke down in tears again.

"So, how did he wind up being the one who is in the hospital?"

"Well, I am getting to that," she muttered. "A few days after I lost the baby, Dad died. I told Carl he had better get his shit together and be the perfect husband throughout the funeral. What was happening with us could wait until later. I did not want Mom to have to deal with this, on top of losing Daddy."

Did Claire just say shit? Claire is cussing now, and Mom let a *dog* eat out of her bowl. What could I expect to happen next?

Meanwhile, I noticed Billy and Cole were getting into a deep and hushed conversation. I tried to listen to what they were saying, but Claire kept distracting me.

"All I can say is, you better make sure," I heard one of them say. I watched Billy shake his finger at Cole.

Claire interrupted my loss of concentration. "Once we got home from Daddy's funeral, I told Carl I wanted a divorce. He begged and pleaded. But, I'll be honest, Jesse, I'm tired of his bullshit. He's a liar and a cheat."

Now, I knew this was a dream. My sister never used to curse. I did not think she knew how until, a few months ago. I tried to pull myself together. This was a revelation. My sister was actually developing a mind of her own. I was at a loss for words.

"... So he moved out of the house the night we got home from Daddy's funeral," she ranted. "He rented the Penthouse at the Hyatt. The Penthouse... for God's sake! What a louse! Several days later, the husband of the woman that called me, showed up at Carl's suite, and shot him in the leg with a gun. At least, that is what the police said."

"Well, that is what you usually shoot someone with... a gun." I was not trying to be curt, but that is how it came out. "Can I assume that means Carl is still alive? He's not dead, yet?"

"No, he's not dead, yet," she fumed.

Cole and Billy stopped fussing among themselves, and glared at me as if I had been the one to pull the trigger.

"Jesse, give the girl a break," Billy fussed.

"So," I said, ignoring him, "are you going to file for a divorce?"

"Not now! Not while he is still in the hospital. I can't do that to him."

I could feel my anger building. I knew she was going to say something I did not want to hear. Claire would take him back and try to make the marriage work, because that is her way. She is always the one to forgive and forget. She got that trait from our mother. Sometimes, it drives me insane. For someone so smart, she sure was naive.

"I'm sorry, Claire," I groaned, trying to end the conversation. "We have had a pretty hard time here, too. Mom is just beginning to come around and I don't want anything to upset her."

"I understand," she replied.

"I know this might sound horrible, but unless Carl dies, I'm not going to say anything to Mama about it right now. Is that alright with you? Claire, I'm really sorry about the baby."

"Thanks, Jesse," she whispered, and then raised her voice a decimal. "That is fine with me. I just wanted to let you know the situation."

"I knew something was wrong at the funeral," I suggested. "You were so quiet, and Carl was so nice."

"Yeah, well, I'm sorry about that. I did the best I could."

"If you need me for anything, call me at this number, it's my cell phone. You can reach me anytime. It's 555-1963."

"1963—that is the year Mom and Dad got married," Claire recalled.

"You are right!" I exclaimed. "I knew that number sounded familiar."

I hung up the phone, feeling sad that I couldn't help Claire. All I could do was talk to her, and hope for the best. I would be there if she needed

me, but I was not going to forsake my mother's well-bring to help her deal
with him. Mom would not hear about this for a long time, unless the shit
head managed to die. Then we would deal with it.

"I need to get home," Cole stood up and said. "Poor River has been
neglected far too long. I need to give him a little attention."

Billy pushed his chair back, and said, "Yeah, I better go, too."

A lonely feeling crept over me. I did not want them to leave, but I
refused to be selfish, by asking them to stay.

As Cole and Billy walked out the front door, Cole turned to me, and
whispered, "I'll be back in an hour if that is alright with you."

That was more than ok with me! Regardless of all the sadness and
guilt I had been through in the last two weeks, I still had that burning
desire to be close to him again. But, I made myself do the right thing.

"I would love it," I whispered. "But I do not think tonight would be a
good night." I looked over at the bedroom window. "I think Mom is going
to need me tonight. She is having a hard time."

He brought his face close to mine, looked deep into my eyes, and
touched my soul. How could I not love this man? He is everything a girl
could possibly want—he is a nice person *and* good-looking.

"I understand," Cole said. "I will come by in the morning to see if you
need anything." He bent down and gave me a quick kiss.

My legs began to quiver and my insides felt like mush, until Billy
spoke and broke the spell.

Halfway down the porch steps, he blurted out, "Yeah, and I'll come
by early in the morning and see if we can't do something about this grass.
It needs to be cut. This time of year, you've got to watch out for snakes."

"What do you mean, snakes?" I shrieked.

"I mean, the kind you want to avoid," he snickered. "There are two
things you need to remember about snakes: if the snake is black, you are
safe; if it is red like me, run real fast!" He turned, and walked out to his
truck, laughing the whole way. Like my mother would say... This man is
going to be the death of me, yet.

Cole tried to calm me. "As much as I hate to admit it, he has a point.
The minute it gets warm around here, the snakes come out. As long as you

are cautious and be aware of them, you will be fine. You need to watch where you walk. Do you know how to use your dad's shotgun?"

"I did not know he had one," I replied. "I know he has a bunch of rifles and stuff, but I never paid much attention." I had been too busy trying to conceal that shiny little piece of steel that I kept in my handbag, I thought to myself. If I told Cole I was carrying a concealed weapon in my purse, without a permit, would he arrest me? My paranoia was out of control, and running wild, again.

"Tomorrow, I will show you how to use your dad's shotgun. It is easy. You can handle it," he assured me.

That night turned out to be uneventful. Mom and Athena were sleeping on Mom's bed when I went upstairs. I did not realize how burnt-out I was, until I crawled into bed. My whole body ached and my brain felt like cheese. Is this the way life is in the mountains? When we moved here, I thought it would be peaceful and quiet—not intense and emotional. I thought we were going to slow down... relax... enjoy life. What happened?

CHAPTER 14

S ATURDAY MORNING I AWOKE to the sound of a lawnmower. I rolled over and looked at the clock on the nightstand beside my bed. Seven o'clock! Don't these people ever sleep late? I forced myself out of bed and walked over to the window. Billy's truck was parked on the side of the house along with Cole's Jeep. Cole was wrestling a riding lawnmower off a trailer attached to his Jeep, and Billy was cutting grass with another one. I slipped on a pair of jeans and a T-shirt, and followed the noise I heard coming from the kitchen. Mom was rustling around in the cabinet, the aroma of coffee permeating the air.

"Good morning," she said. "They are hard at it first thing this morning."

"I heard," motioning to the sound of the lawnmower. I walked to the utility room and opened the door. I stood there marveling at how lucky we were to have such nice fellows as our new friends. Cole caught sight of me and waved. My heart did a flip-flop. This was the first time that I had a relationship with a guy that was also a friend. It was a good feeling.

I poured myself a cup of coffee, kissed Mom on the cheek, and said I was going upstairs to do some work. I thought I would use this time to read over the Carrolton file again. Once the guys finished cutting grass, Mom assured me she would have breakfast ready for us. By then, I might come up with more questions for Billy. I needed to contribute something. He had been there for me since the day I met him, and I had not done anything for him. He had done so much for me, and never asked anything in return. All I did was take. It was time for me to do my share. I needed to return the friendship and support.

I drank my coffee and tried to wash down another guilt attack. Sitting on the bed, I thumbed through what had become a briefcase stuffed with a collection of police reports, photos, notes, and various pieces of paper that one of us had scribbled some tidbit. I had also began keeping what I would call, an activities book—a small composition book in which I had recorded times and dates of things we did and the people we had talked to. I started doing this the day Billy called me into his office to take notes during his interview with the Carroltons. After Rebecca Miller killed her husband, I got serious about recording every specific detail of our actions. I felt it was imperative to be able to account for our whereabouts at any given time. As long as we were together, we could verify each other's word, something I have found to be important in this line of work. The minute the police learned that there was a private detective involved, their hair stood on end, and they started to foam at the mouth. Immediately, they assume the P.I. is the one at fault. They are like rabid dogs. Except for Cole—he is only semi-rabid.

Among the piles of paperwork, I found two new manila file folders. One was labeled *Rose Hudgins/waitress*, and the other labeled *Tom Dorey/ gas station attendant*. This must have been what he was doing on his computer before we left work Friday—gathering more information on them. I was curious to know if he had stumbled onto anything new. Any additional detail could spark my imagination. Also, I wanted to see if he had made any notations about my silly ideas. I know he thought I was way off base, but I just had this strange feeling.

Most of the information in Rose's file were reports that I had already seen. Then I came across a copy of a birth certificate stapled to a lone sheet of paper. The sheet of paper listed general data about Rose: address; where she went to school, etc., and the birth certificate was in the name of Patrick Jason Teale. Who was this guy? Why would a birth certificate be attached to her file, unless they were related? Could that be the answer? I needed to ask Billy about this.

I went downstairs and out into the front yard. The air had the smell of fresh cut grass. Even though it was barely eight o'clock, the sun was out in all its glory. Next weekend was the 4th of July: a holiday that my family always celebrated together. Claire would bring the kids and that man to whom she was married. Most of the time, Jack would show up alone. I wondered about Jack sometimes. He seldom had a girl with him, and never the same one twice. What about this 4th of July? Normally, a cookout at Mom and Dad's on Memorial Day, the 4th of July, and Labor Day was pretty much a set thing. Thanksgiving and Christmas were a must. You didn't dare miss either one of those. But, things were different now.

The guys had just finished cutting the grass, as I walked down the steps. They came head-to-head in front of me, and shut down their mowers. Beads of sweat lined the foreheads on both of them. It must have been from the heat. How much sweat could you work up on a riding lawnmower?

"Working up a sweat over me?" I joked.

"Ha… ha," Billy sneered.

"Mom is cooking some breakfast," I yelled.

"Great!" Cole shouted. "I could use some food."

I walked up to Billy and said, "I was going over the Carrolton file, and came across a birth certificate for Patrick Jason Teale. Who is he, and what has he got to do with Rose Hudgins?"

Billy climbed off of his lawnmower, pulled me aside and said, "Have you forgotten that your boyfriend is a cop?" The look in his eyes convinced me he was serious. "Never talk about our investigations in front of him. Ok? It is his duty to ask questions. What we do is none of his business, unless it becomes his business. Do you get my drift?"

Yes, I think I do. My new career choice had been to take up with a man who snoops into people's private lives for a living, and at the same time, I fell for his childhood buddy, who just so happens to be a cop. I thought it was going to be a bumpy ride.

Cole instantly knew what we were talking about. "Billy, I told you the CPD was handling this case. Why are you getting in the middle of it?"

Billy and I looked at each other. I did not say a word.

"Well, obviously they have not gotten any closer to finding the girl, otherwise, why would the parents hire me?" he stared at Cole. "From the looks of things, it was a smart move on their part. The CPD has not come up with anything, and it has been six months."

"Back down on this one, Billy," Cole warned. "There is stuff going on here you do not know about."

"Well, why don't you enlighten me?"

"I can not do that, and you know it."

"Yeah... right. You can do anything you want."

"It is not our case. It belongs to Charlottesville. They do not seem to have a need for our services. But if they do, I will give you anything I *can*. Until then, just leave it alone."

"I am not going to do that. Why do you even suggest it?"

Trying to spearhead what was developing into another argument between the two of them, I stepped in the middle. "Cool it, guys. Mom's got breakfast ready so let's go eat. I do not want her to hear the two of you at it again." I needed to talk to Billy, but not in front of Cole. "Cole, would you give us a few minutes? I have something to discuss with Billy, and under the circumstances, I think it would be best if you were not here."

"Fine," he retorted. "I will tell Ma you will be right in." He took out his bandanna and wiped his face, as he walked into the house.

I flashed Billy one of my mean looks and said, "Why can't you guys get along and work together? Why do you always have to be fighting?"

"*O-si-yo*, is anyone home?" he asked, as he tapped my head. "You just do not understand, do you?"

"Understand what?"

"Cops hate us. Not me in particular, but us in general. When all else fails, we come in and clean up their mess, and it really sets their blood on fire."

"Whatever you say," I rolled my eyes at Billy. "Listen," I huddled up to him, "I wanted to talk to you about this birth certificate. What is the deal here? Who is this guy Patrick Jason Teale?"

"He is Rose Hudgins' adopted brother. It seems after Rose was born, the mama couldn't, or wouldn't have any more babies. A couple of years later they adopted him. He was two at the time. His father was a psycho—high on drugs all the time. He beat his wife to death with a hammer, and then killed himself with a Colt 45. One shot to the head. It was not pretty. And you know Patrick Jason must have seen it, because when the police arrived, he was sitting in the middle of the floor between them."

"How do you know all this stuff?" I asked.

"I did some research. It is amazing what you can find out on the Internet. It is a bed of information."

"Where did you get a copy of his birth certificate?"

"It was simple. Once I uncovered the fact that he was adopted, it was just a matter of search and find. Then, just for shits and grins, I went back to the year of his adoption and searched the newspapers. Sure enough, there was a write-up on his parent's death, and a small picture of him in the article—poor kid."

"What made you decide to check him out?"

"It is my job to check everything out. Plus, if I remember correctly, you are the one who wanted me to dig deeper into Rose Hudgins' past. It is interesting, don't you think?"

"I think we should go pay her a visit, and have a talk with her."

"Do you want to go right now?"

"Yes, I do, unless you have other plans," I replied. "We have ridden by her house, but we have not gone up to her door."

"That is because it did not look like anyone was home."

"Yeah, but it is Saturday. Somebody is probably there now. What could it hurt? If we could just get inside, I am sure we could nose around and come up with something."

"Like what? A bloody hammer?" he joked.

"You have two choices: Rose Hudgins; or Tom Dorey. They are the only two people that had any contact with Helen, except the man in her car. If she is dead, he is the killer. If that is the case, I believe our man is a local. Who else would be on foot in an area, miles apart from any house or store?"

"Who says he was on foot? Maybe, he had a car parked somewhere. Or, she could have picked him up outside the grill. Who knows?"

"If she picked him up outside of the grill, don't you think it would seem strange to him if she stopped five miles down the road to get gas? She could have done that at the gas station next to the diner. How else could she explain it? This leads me to believe she picked him up en-route to the next gas station. Stopping for gas was probably a ploy on her part to get him to let her stop. She was hoping that she could get somebody's attention... someone that could help her. What about the used car lot? Was anyone working the afternoon Helen stopped at the Piney Mountain Grill? Maybe, someone saw something. Perhaps, the bad guy worked there. What about the mini-mart? It sits right in the middle of everything, and people are constantly going in and out of that place. Who was on duty the..."

"Hold on a minute, `ge ya. You sure have a wild imagination."

"You know, I'm getting pretty tired of your voodoo language. If you have something to say to me, say it in English. I have enough to deal with as it is," I demanded.

I was stressed out, and did not need to play footsies with Billy. I think I was just a little bit jealous that he could speak a language that I did not understand. It also made our communication more difficult.

"Forget it. It is not important," Billy said. "Let's go in and have breakfast with your mom, and your boyfriend—then we will go out and conquer the world."

CHAPTER 15

D URING BREAKFAST we discussed the up-coming holiday. Billy insisted we join his family for their 4th of July party. He assured Cole that he was invited as usual, which made me happy because I wanted the two of them to recapture their friendship. I sensed they had grown apart over the years, and I felt it was important that they mend fences if I was going to be a part of their lives. Mom was delighted to be invited, but insisted we all behave ourselves and not *show our butts*. What was that all about? Had we begun to act like children? Not me.

Billy and I made plans to go visit Rose Hudgins after breakfast. My curiosity was peaked by the birth certificate I had found, and I wanted to get inside her house. I already had my suspicions about her. I never suspected she had anything to do with Helen's disappearance, but I had a feeling she was hiding something. Her strange reaction to the mention of her family sent up red flags. What was it about them that made her so uncomfortable? Did it have anything to do with her adopted brother? Maybe he didn't know he was adopted and she was afraid if we did any more digging, he would somehow learn about it. Whatever it was, I was determined to find out.

When I mentioned that Billy and I needed to ride out to Gordonsville after breakfast, Cole glanced over at Mom, then back to me.

"If you are not going to be gone all day, maybe you and I could get together this evening."

I saw a smile come across Mom's face. Oh no, she has something up her sleeve, I thought. She always gets that silly grin on her face when she is up to one of her shenanigans. Well, at least she was smiling again.

"I'd like that very much," I gushed. I tried not to be overly zealous, but ever time I got close to this man, I found myself turning into mush. I was drawn to his firm, masculine body... his tanned skin. He was kind, gentle, loving, and perfect in so many ways.

Mom got up and started clearing the table, while the rest of us followed her lead.

"Mack was a good man," she started. "He loved his family and me for many years. He was the center of our universe. However, now he is gone." One lone tear rolled down her cheek. She wiped it away with the back of her hand, pausing just long enough to regain her composure. "Now it is just me—and I am going to do what Mack would have wanted me to do. I am going to see that our family stays together and continues to be a family." She pushed her shoulders back, and continued with the determination of a general commanding his troops. "So, from now on, I am going to run this house the way I should. I want to know what is going on with everyone in this family, and that includes our friends." She bounced glances back and forth amongst the three of us. "Cole, you and Billy have become a part of our family and I want you to feel at home. At the same time, I want you to keep in mind that I am a mother, and it is my job to worry."

I could not imagine what the guys thought about Mom's revelation, but I knew my mom. This was her way of getting her life back in order—taking control, and laying down the law. She was in charge of our home.

"When Mack was alive we always had dinner around seven every night. Anyone that can not make it at dinnertime, can heat up his, or her own leftovers," she said, matter-of-factly.

This was an open invitation for Billy and Cole to join our family, and was gladly accepted by both.

"Well, you can count on me," Billy said. "We will be home for dinner. Won't we, Jesse?"

"Hell, yeah," I exclaimed, as Mom shot me one of her dirty looks. She hated it when I cussed. She would sometimes tell me that cursing was for sinners and ignorant people; people who can not find an intelligent word to say instead.

Cole explained that he had to cut his grass and work in the yard. He would be back for dinner as long as he could bring something, and help Mom in the kitchen. Her eyes lit up. She even suggested that he bring River back with him.

"He is your dog, so I guess he is part of our family, too," she said. "Athena needs a playmate."

I could not believe this was my mother talking. She actually told Cole to bring his dog! Mom was just starting a new life and adapting a whole new outlook.

Billy and I loaded my Jeep with his surveillance equipment,which he carried everywhere. He said it was like his American Express. He never leaves home without it, along with his cell phone and his gun.

"Always be prepared is my motto," he explained.

Adhering to his words of wisdom, I collected my purse, briefcase, cell phone, and gun, which I named Rossi after the maker. I've been told when you name your gun, it becomes your friend. That's a scary thought.

It was almost an hour's drive to Gordonsville. Billy said it should have taken only forty-five minutes. That was just one of the things he complained about. I drove too close to the middle line. I rode my brakes too much...blah... blah... blah. I think he was just nervous. He was afraid of how I would act in front of the people we were going to interrogate. I could see why he would be reluctant about what was about to go down. This was my first time in a confrontational situation. Would I mess up? What did I know about investigating?

Rose Hudgins and her family lived in a large, white Cape Cod house. I guessed it to be about 2,000 square feet.

One of the things I had learned from my brother Jack, was how to assess the size of a house. He also taught me how to read blueprints, and to calculate the building materials for a job. He loved to build things, and there was nothing he could not build. Unfortunately, Dad had wanted him to get into a career that was not seasonal. So, in between being a teenager and a lawyer, he did carpentry work. Needless to say, with his help, I learned a few things about home construction. Not a lot, but enough to know the difference between a slab and a crawl space.

The Hudgins' house sat on two acres of well-manicured lawn. Surrounding the house and in some stage of blooming, were azalea, lilac, and rose bushes. Off in the background, close to where the woods began, sat a barn on the left and stables to the right. A fenced-in area large enough to exercise a whole herd of horses, surrounded the stables. I counted six horses grazing, or doing whatever they do in a corral. Parked in front of the barn was a backhoe, a John Deere tractor, with one of those things you cut big areas of grass, and a riding lawn mower the size of my car. You could probably buy ten of my Jeeps for the price of their equipment. From the looks of things, Mom and Dad had some serious money. So, why was Rose working in some dinky little diner, making barely enough money to put gas in her car? Was she trying to make a statement? What else could it be?

As I parked the Jeep and got out, Billy broke my train of thought.

"Listen Jesse, when we go in, just play along with me. Let me run the show. We will consider this a learning experience."

"Sure, whatever you say. This is all new to me," I answered. In the back of my mind, I was already coming up with questions I wanted to ask.

Billy rang the doorbell while I stood beside him, admiring the wicker furniture that had been neatly arranged on the porch. Out of the corner of my eye I caught a glimpse of something. Across the blacktop road, through a small gap in the forest of trees, I saw a mound of dirt. It was covered with lush green grass. It was set so far back into the woods that if you weren't standing in just the right spot, you would miss it. Maybe someone had cleared the trees, planning to build something, and never got around to it, I thought to myself.

An older, heavy-set woman, wearing an apron and holding a wooden spoon, answered the door. "Hello, may I help you?" she asked, opening the door just enough to stick her head out.

"Yes," Billy replied, as he removed his wallet from his jeans pocket and flipped it open. "I am Detective Blackhawk, and this is Detective Watson. We are here to speak with Rose Hudgins. Is she home?"

The woman barely glanced at his I.D. before opening the door and said, "Please wait in the sitting room." She pointed to our left. "I will go see if Miss Hudgins is awake. She usually sleeps late on Saturday."

I looked at Billy after she left the room, and said, "That was a lot easier than I expected."

"It is not over yet," he whispered. "I think she might be the house-keeper, and once our presence is made known, we might be out of here just as fast as we were let in."

We were standing at the entrance of a room most likely designed to entertain guests. The room looked like if was fresh out of a Traditional Home Magazine. All the tables were made out of a deep rich Cherry, and none of them had a speck of dust anywhere. In front of a huge fireplace, two Queen Anne chairs were situated opposite each other, divided by a sofa of the same style. Along the walls of the room were various pieces of furniture. I noticed a magnificent buffet table.

Pointing to the buffet table, I whispered, "I bet that piece set them back a few thousand dollars."

"There is no doubt in my mind that these people have a few bucks," he whispered. "I noticed it the minute we got out of the car."

Trying to trigger his curiosity, I added, "Why do you think Rose Hudgins would be working a greasy, nasty job for almost nothing, when she has folks with plenty of money?"

He surprised me when he said, "Maybe she just wants to make her own money." He walked around the room, examining the many fine pieces. He was holding a small vase in his hands, when a man walked in the room.

It happened so fast. I hardly had time to catch my breath.

"That vase is almost priceless," the man growled. "Most of the pieces in this room are. So, I would appreciate it if you would not touch anything. I am Lawrence Hudgins. I am afraid you can not talk to my daughter. She is in bed, sick with the flu. May I help you?" From the tone of his voice, help was the last thing he was going to do.

He wore dark dress pants, a white shirt, and a tie loosened at the collar. He was almost as tall as Billy, but did not weigh nearly as much. It was obvious to me that he was a businessman. Why else would he have on a tie, at home, on a Saturday morning?

Billy gingerly replaced the vase, walked up to Mr. Hudgins, and said, "I am sorry but I could not help but admire some of the beautiful things you have." He held out his hand. "I am Detective Blackhawk, and this is Detective Watson."

"I know who you are. My housekeeper told me," he said, ignoring Billy's offer of a handshake. "I think it would be best if you leave. Like I said before, my daughter is ill and can't see you." He was brushing us off in a big way, and I was not going to let that happen.

"What about your son, Patrick Jason? May we speak with him?" I was determined to get something out of this trip.

"He is not here."

"When do you expect him back?" I demanded.

"It does not matter," he insisted. "You have harassed my family enough. Get out of here, and do not come back without a warrant." Apparently, he was about ready to throw us out.

"Look," I said, as congenially as I could. "We are not trying to cause trouble. We are new to the case and we are at a dead end. Some of the paperwork handed down to us has a few holes in it. Perhaps, some of it was lost. We are just trying to put the pieces together."

He was not buying any of what I was saying. "I do not give a damn about your *lost* paperwork. As many times as the cops came by here, they ought to know everything there is to know. Just because you are new to the case, does not mean we have to go through all this again. Forget it."

Mr. Hudgins ushered us to the front door, slamming it the minute we stepped outside. A lock clicked behind us.

"Whew, he sure was hot," I replied.

Billy and I were almost to the car when a young man came around the corner of the house. We both stopped in mid-step, and stared at him.

"I bet that is the son," I whispered.

"You folks looking for my sister, huh?" he asked, walking up to us. He was holding a dead rabbit.

He had the strangest eyes I had ever seen. They were black! Or, was that just his pupils? I looked closer, and determined that his eyes were not black. His pupils were so enlarged you could barely see the blue. What drug was this kid using?

Shoving the dead rabbit close to my face, he laughed and said, "I killed him with my bare hands! Pretty cool, huh?"

Sick, is more like it, I thought.

His demeanor changed. "My dad is going to get real mad if you keep bothering us. You don't want to make him mad, trust me."

"Why?" I asked. "Does he have a violent temper? Is he a dangerous man?" I must have hit a nerve.

"Get out of here, and don't come back," he hissed.

"Did you see Helen Carrolton the day she disappeared?" I yelled at him, as he was walking away.

He stopped for a minute, laughed, and then kept walking.

"Let's get out of here," I said to Billy.

I backed out of the driveway, almost ran into the ditch across the road, and muttered a few choice words under my breath. I had enough of these crazies, and was more than glad to get away from them. They might have money, but they were just too weird for me.

"We have caught the crow," Billy said.

"What do you mean by that?"

"Either, they have been questioned more than we have been led to believe, or they have something to hide."

Ah! Now he was seeing things my way. I knew there was something going on all along. I could feel it. My mind started to drift as I stopped at the end of the road, ready to make the turn on to Rt. 15.

"Did the police question the boy?" I asked Billy. "I did not see anything in the report that would indicate that they had."

"There was not anything in the report about him, except that he is Rose's brother. She told them he was at home with Mom and Dad at the time."

"But, they never talked to him?"

"If they did, they did not put anything in the file."

As I was waiting for a chance to pull out into traffic, an idea came to me. Now would be the perfect time to use some of Billy's equipment. I was sure we had stirred up a fuss at the Hudgins household with our visit. They were probably discussing us right now.

"Billy, I have an idea," I said, turning to face him. "Why don't we park the car on one of those dirt paths, and sneak back up to the house. We can take that gismo you have, and listen to what they are saying. I bet we got them all riled up. There is no telling what is happening in that house. And we do not have to worry about anyone seeing us because they have the only house on this road."

On one of our earlier fact-finding missions, we had discovered that Rose and her family were the only people who lived on this dead end road. According to the information Billy got from the tax assessor's office, Lawrence and Rita Hudgins not only owned that grand house, but the fifty-two acres of land surrounding it. We had plenty of room to snoop without being seen.

"Did you hear me?" I snapped, thinking that Billy was not paying attention to what I was saying.

"Yes, I heard you," he replied. "Sorry, I was thinking about that kid."

"He is a strange fellow," I added. "He sure seems awful immature for an eighteen year old. Don't you think?"

"Not only that, but did you see the look in his eyes when he said he killed that rabbit with his bare hands? He was proud of what he did."

"It is the shock value, Billy. He was trying to get a rise out of us. Did you know that most serial killers start out torturing small animals? They torture them until they die. Eventually, they move onto something else... like people."

"Turn around and let's go back," he ordered.

I found a little dirt path just big enough to drive the Jeep down, and parked between two trees. We were far enough from the house not to be noticed, yet close enough so we would not have to trudge through a lot of woods. I thought about what Billy had said about the snakes as soon as we started making our way through the tangled mess of downed trees and underbrush. Summer was here, and I did not like the idea of exploring what could be snake-infested territory.

Fortunately, the edge of the woods had plenty of large trees that were just right for hiding. Crouching down, Billy went about connecting his audio equipment. He had a satellite dish the size of a plate, with a cable that plugged into a jack on the side of a small black box. He opened the box, pushed a button to turn it on, and then pulled out a set of headphones. He plugged them into the side of the box.

"Whatever we pick up will be recorded on the mini-cassette recorder inside," he explained. "If I plug in the headphones you will not be able to hear. I will not do that, unless someone comes out of the house. We do not want to take a chance they might hear us. It is awfully quiet out here, and sound carries through these woods."

He aimed the dish towards the house, scanning for sound waves. Up-stairs, several of the windows were open, and I could hear voices. I could barely make out what they were saying, until their conversation blared through the receiver. Billy adjusted the sound level. The reception was so clear, I could have sworn we were in the room with them.

"I told you. I don't know what they want! I didn't have anything to do with that girl's disappearance. I don't even know her. All I did was talk to her when she came into Bubba's."

"Why do the cops keep coming back if you don't know anything? They must suspect you of something or they wouldn't keep bothering us."

"I don't know, Daddy."

The girl began to cry. After what seemed like an eternity the man spoke.

"Alright, sugar. Here's what we're going to do. I don't want you to talk to anybody that comes to the house unless I'm with you. Don't say a word to them. Don't even let them in the house. I'll talk to Betty and make sure she understands the situation. I'll also talk to your mom and Jay. I don't want anyone talking to the cops without me around. Do you under-stand what I'm saying?"

"Yes, Daddy."

We heard a door slam, and the room fell silent. The door opened again, and we heard the voice of the teenage boy.

"You didn't tell him anything about me did you?"

Billy and I looked at each other.

"No, I didn't," the female voice replied. *"But I have to know where you were that afternoon you were supposed to be home with Mama. I can't keep covering for you if I don't know the truth. You have to tell me!"*

"What I do is not your concern. Just keep your mouth shut, or you're going to be real sorry. You hear me?"

A door slammed. Muffled sobs echoed in the room.

"I told you, Billy. She is hiding something. She is covering for her brother. He probably killed Helen, and buried her body on his parent's property. That kid is crazy!"

"*`Ge ya*, you sure have a wild imagination."

"There you go, again. What does that word mean?"

"*Woman*," he said, and smiled.

"Well, this `*ge ya* might have a wild imagination, but at least we found out there is more to this than we thought. I will bet money the boy had something to do with Helen's disappearance. I will even go as far as to say he either killed her, or knows what happened to her."

"Jesse, he is just a kid."

"Don't you read the papers? Kids kill people. It happens all the time. They pick up a gun, go into a school and shoot other kids... teachers... anything that moves. They play with guns, and wind up shooting each other. Just because they are young, does not mean they do not get involved in crime. I am telling you..."

Before I could finish, voices echoed through the dish.

"Betty, I don't want you to let any cops in this house again when I'm not here, unless they show you a warrant. Then you get in touch with me immediately. Ok?"

"Sure, Mr. Hudgins," the woman said.

"I've got to go to the office for awhile. Keep an eye on the kids, and the minute Rita drags her butt out of bed, tell her to call me. I need to talk to her. You got it?"

Everything went silent, except for the banging of pots and pans. Shortly, Lawrence Hudgins came out of the house, got into the little red sports car parked in the driveway, and sped off.

"What a creep!" I hissed.

CHAPTER 16

B ILLY AND I SAT ON THE GROUND for two hours listening to what appeared to be a typical Saturday at the Hudgins' household. Rita, the mother, had finally gotten out of bed and made it to the kitchen for her morning dose of caffeine. Betty, the housekeeper promptly informed her about the morning happenings. Instantly, she went into a tirade. She cried, shouted obscenities, and eventually got on the phone to her husband.

"No, I don't know where the kids are. I assume they're upstairs... Don't shout at me, damn it. I just got out of bed and I have a headache... Ok... Ok... I'll take care of it. Betty, get the kids down here now!"

Within ten minutes, the kitchen became chaotic. Rita and Rose were shouting at each other and in the background we could still hear pots and pans being banged around. We didn't hear Jay anywhere in the house. The last time we had seen him was earlier when we had encountered him in the front yard.

I was just about to ask Billy where the boy was, when I heard a noise behind us. We looked at each other and turned around at the same time. Jay was standing behind us with a double-barrel shotgun hanging from the crook of his arm.

Billy was the first to react. "Son, you do not want to do this. Put the gun down and let's talk about it."

"You're trespassing on private property," he raved. "I could shoot you right now and nobody would say a word about it." He raised the gun.

In two quick steps, Billy lurched forward and grabbed the shotgun. Instantly, I heard a blast. I fell to the ground with a burning sensation in my shoulder. I had been shot. The pain was ungodly, and I felt like I was going to be sick.

"You are a maniac! You shot me!" I screamed. "Billy! Help me!"

Blood was running down my arm. I grabbed my shoulder and looked up at the two of them. I don't know which one was more frightened—Billy, me, or the kid who shot me.

Billy came to my aid. He jerked off his shirt, balled it up and pressed it to my shoulder. "You are going to be fine. It is just a flesh wound," he tried to comfort me.

"You're lying!" I screamed. "That's what they always say! I'm dying here, and you are telling me it is only a flesh wound! Are you crazy?" I was quickly becoming hysterical. I was in agony.

Once I finally calmed down enough to assess the situation, I realized the boy was gone.

Billy glanced over into the woods and then said to me, "Oh, he's gone. Don't worry. He took off the minute you got hit."

I sat up. I had never been shot and I had no idea the pain could be so intense. "Billy, it hurts something awful. Am I going to die?"

Billy laughed.

"I can't believe you're laughing at me. Have you lost your mind?"

"I'm sorry," Billy said, as he snickered. "Trust me. It might hurt for a while, but you're going to be ok. It is only a flesh wound. However, we do need to get you to a doctor." He helped me up off the ground and we ambled our way back to my Jeep.

"I can't believe this," I whined. "One minute I've finally gotten myself a decent boyfriend, which is something I have wanted for a long, long time, and then I go and get hooked up with you and find myself almost getting killed. Tell me, what's wrong with me? Am I crazy? Maybe I need a shrink. Oh, that's right, I've already been there."

"Calm down, Jesse. Everything's going to be ok. You're just a little upset." He opened the passenger's door and gently shoved me inside. He jumped into the driver's seat.

"Where are the keys?"

I fumbled through my jeans' pocket with my good arm and came up with them. "Here," I hissed as I threw the keys in his lap.

"Well, you don't have to be mad at me. It was an accident."

I was steadily ranting at him as he drove out of the woods. "Aren't we going to the police first?"

"No, I'm taking you to the hospital."

"Are we going to the police after we leave the hospital?"

"Why?"

"To have that kid arrested. He shot me. He belongs in jail."

"Maybe we ought to think about that for a minute," his said. "It might not be such a good idea."

I sat in silence until we got close to Charlottesville, thinking about what he had just said.

"We can't do anything, can we?" I asked Billy. "We were trespassing on private property, and the gun did go off accidentally. If I have the kid arrested for trying to kill me, he will turn around and bring charges against us for trespassing... which we know is a bullshit charge. But it would still get our name on a report with the police department. Am I right? In the end it will all be for nothing. It's a Catch-22—a no-win situation."

"Exactly," he responded.

"What about my arm?" I asked. "Will the hospital have to report my gunshot wound to the police? I thought that was standard procedure, some-thing they were required by law to do."

"They are..."

"Oh, me, I'm going to jail. I can see it now." I was on the verge of hysteria. The pain in my shoulder immediately intensified. "I'm going to spend the next five years of my life in some rat-hole prison with a stinky, fat-ass woman named Big Mama, just dying to be my next boyfriend... or worse... girlfriend." I started crying. I hated for him to see me cry, but I was scared. The thought of what had just happened and the prospect of what was going to happen was too overwhelming.

"Chill out," he said. "I'm going to take care of everything."

"What about this pain in my shoulder?" I whimpered. "What are you going to do about that? Are you going to get rid of it for me?" Lowering my voice, I needled him. He deserved it. "Actually, it's getting better, I think. It doesn't hurt as much now... now that it's *going numb*!"

"You will survive."

It was almost five o'clock when Billy pulled into the parking lot of the hospital. The name on the small building was Community Veterinary Clinic.

I came to life. "Whoa! Wait a minute! This is not the hospital. It is a Vet! Have you gone crazy?"

"Trust me," Billy said. "I want the best for you and the best is right here. Chief Blackhawk is the best medicine man there is on Earth. Plus, he is my father and he will help us take care of our little problem," he motioned to my shoulder.

"I don't know, Billy," I said, hesitating to get out of the car. "Don't you think we should go to a real hospital? You know—a place where they have machines and gadgets that keep people from dying?"

"I'm telling you, we have everything we need right here. So please stop worrying. I will take care of you."

"Yeah, right, it's not you that has to have a bullet dug out of your shoulder by a doctor that probably just castrated a dog, or delivered a pony, or did whatever the hell it is they do," I fumed.

"First of all," he said, as he led me through the front door, "it is not a bullet in your shoulder. It is birdshot. You were lucky. I think you only got the edge of the blast. You did not get a direct hit."

"It's birdshot?" I questioned, my anxiety easing up a little.

A small woman dressed in a bright pink housedress greeted us. Her graying, black hair was pinned up in a bun on the back of her head. Her skin was pale, and from the shape of her face I could tell she was Billy's mother. He had her chin and nose.

"Mom, this is Jesse Watson," Billy said, as he leaned over to kiss her on the cheek. "Jesse, this is my mom, Sarah Blackhawk—the wife of our great chief, and the mother of the Blackhawk tribe. Plus, she is the backbone of this clinic, among other things." He smiled.

"I see you are hurt," she said, as she wrapped her arm around my waist and led me down the hallway.

I was glad to leave the reception area. It smelled like pet supplies and wet dog hair. Well, it was a doggie doctor's office. And once your dog was made all better you could buy an array of supplies to keep him that way. What a racket, I thought to myself, as Billy's mom instructed me to lie down on the table. I am such a nerd. I am always expecting the worst of people. I just can not help myself.

Billy wandered off, as Sarah asked me to lay down on the table. She carefully removed Billy's balled-up shirt from my shoulder.

"This might hurt a little, but I have to see what your injury looks like. Just hold on for a minute. It will be over before you know it. Can you tell me what happened?"

"I don't know what I am supposed to tell you."

"The truth usually works," she replied, as she took a pair of scissors and split the sleeve of my T-shirt. Dabbing at my shoulder with a clean, white cloth, she added, "It looks like birdshot to me. We are going to have to x-ray this to make sure there are not any pellets lodged in the tissue."

"And what if there is?" I cried.

"It will not be a problem. We can handle it," she assured me.

I did have a problem. Billy was nowhere in sight and I was laying on a doggie table waiting to be cut up like a watermelon being sliced down the middle with a machete. My arm was throbbing, and my mind was going off the deep end. I had to get it together. I tried to relax while Billy's mother attended to my wounds.

"Billy and I were trespassing on private land, spying on people, and the teenage son came from out of nowhere with a shotgun. Billy grabbed the gun and it went off. And as they say, the rest is history."

"Ah, I see," she replied. I could tell she was getting the gist of the situation. "Please do not worry. Everything is going to be fine."

I laid on the table, while she scurried around me, cleaning up my bloody wound. She lowered the overhead x-ray apparatus and situating it over my upper body.

"Most Vets have only one large operating room just like ours," she explained as she looked around. "We have everything we need right here. Whatever we have to do, we can do it in this room. So, you can relax. You will not have to get off this table until we are done. I am going to give you something for the pain. Are you allergic to any medication?"

"No, I don't think so."

"I'm going to give you an antibiotic for infection and some Demerol to deaden the pain." She produced a syringe and withdrew a clear liquid from a small vile. I hated needles and this one was the size of a spear. She rolled me over on my side and injected the liquid into my butt.

"Hey, I hardly felt a thing. You are good."

"That was the Demerol. It was the easy one," she said. "This next one is Penicillin and it is going to sting a little. Powder burns have a tendency to get infected in an open wound. And we do not want to take any chances." She disposed of the first syringe and filled a new one.

"Ouch," I whined. I thought I was going to pass out.

"Lay back and relax," she said, her soothing voice almost putting me to sleep. She removed the wad of padding and began to take x-rays. "It will take me about ten minutes to develope these. I will be right back."

I was beginning to feel pretty good. I was in and out of a fog, until I finally dozed off. I knew what was going on, but I tried not to think about it. What on earth would I tell Mom? She would absolutely throw a fit. What about Cole? The thought of telling him made me shutter. No, I could not tell them the truth. I would have to lie about this one and it was going to have to be good.

Mom had told me more than one time that lies always catch up with you in the end. Too bad—I planned to take my chances.

Billy entered the examination room followed by a man who had the same physical presence and facial features. His face was tanned and wrinkled, and he had the same long pony-tail that I had seen on the other Blackhawk men. However, his was totally gray. This man had to be Billy's father. They looked so much alike.

"How is she doing?" Billy asked. "She isn't going to die, is she?" He was trying to cheer me up by making jokes, but I did not think it was the least bit funny.

"Oh, she will live. But she is going to be in considerable pain for the next few days," Sarah answered.

I drifted off into never-never land again, listening to the three of them banter back and forth in their native languages. One day, I told myself, I am going to take the time and learn that language even if it kills me. What a thought—me speaking Cherokee.

"Jesse," I heard someone say. "Wake up dear. We are finished."

"Wow, I was really out of it," I said, forcing myself to sit up.

"This is Billy's dad, Chief Standing Deer, but everyone calls him the chief, or Sam. He dug two pellets out of your shoulder. You were very lucky. They were not deep."

"As I explained to my son, this is not a good situation," the chief said, as he helped me down from the table. "By law, gunshot wounds are supposed to be reported to the police. Fortunately, I am retired."

Billy and Sarah laughed.

"Like I was saying, I am retired. I do not practice anymore, so I am not concerned with their law. I own this clinic and I see to its operation, well actually Sarah keeps everything in order. The point is, my nephew, Dr. Adam Nesbitt is the Vet and his office is closed on Saturday. Your visit did not occur." He pressed two bottles of pills into my hand. "Take these according to the directions on the label. One is for pain and the other one is for infection. If you see any signs of infection, get Billy to call me right away. You do know the signs of infection, don't you?"

"Yes, I do," I answered.

"Ok, I think you're finished," he replied. He turned to Billy as we were walking out of the door, "Make sure she goes home and gets some rest. That shot of Demerol is going to make her groggy and incoherent for a few hours. Do not let her drive a car. Remember what I told you, Son."

"Thanks for the help. I am sorry we had to meet like this," I said, walking out of the door on wobbly legs.

Sarah guided me to the Jeep, while the chief and Billy continued a conversation that I could not hear.

"So... *son*," I mocked, as Billy backed out of the parking space. "What did your dad want you to remember? Did it have anything to do with me?"

"You know it did," he growled. "He chastised me for getting you into this mess. He raked me over the coals."

"I am sorry he fussed you out, Billy. I do not blame you anymore. Oh, I did at first, but now that I have had time to think about it, you did the same thing I would have done if I had been more alert. Next time I will be."

"Next time?" he asked.

"Yeah, you do not think a little thing like getting shot is going to stop me, do you?" I laughed.

"You are a tough `*ge ya*," he said.

"That is right. I am a tough woman, and don't you ever forget it!"

CHAPTER 17

I T WAS ALMOST SEVEN O'CLOCK when we pulled into the driveway of
my house. Billy and I had practiced the story we were going to tell
Mom and Cole. He assured me that Sarah and the chief would not
breathe a word about the shooting to anyone, and we didn't have to
worry about one of the Hudgins turning us in for trespassing. They
wanted to forget the whole ordeal. Billy had talked to Larry Hudgins
while I was being fixed up and Larry agreed that it would be in
everyone's best interest to drop the entire matter. He hoped I was ok,
and he was real sorry for the unfortunate accident. However, he wanted
his shotgun back.

"He is such a loser!" I wailed. "I get shot and the only thing he is
concerned about is his shotgun!"

"It's evidence. Of course, he is worried. Not to worry," Billy said. "I
told him the only way I would return the shotgun and forget about the
attempted murder charge you could file, was if he agreed to let us come
back and question Rose and Jay."

"Did he agree?"

"Yes, he did. What else could he do? He's scared. He doesn't want the
police involved anymore than we do. Of course, I didn't say that to him."

"So, when do we go back?"

"Tomorrow afternoon. They have church first thing in the morning."

THE HOUSE WAS FILLED WITH THE AROMA OF FOOD COOKING. Mom was in the kitchen with Cole, laughing and carrying on when Billy and I walked in.

"Something smells good," Billy remarked, walking towards the kitchen. I followed him as far as the kitchen table and sat down. I was beginning to get dizzy and I didn't want to fall out the minute I walked in.

Mom instantly knew something was wrong. She hurried over to where I was sitting and cried, "What is the matter, Jesse? What happened to your shoulder? There is blood all over your shirt."

"Oh, it is nothing," I lied. "Just a little hunting accident, I guess you could call it." I winked at Billy, making sure Mom saw me.

Billy's eyes grew to the size of quarters. I thought he was going to faint. This was not what we had planned on telling her, but after seeing the look in Mom's eyes, I knew she would never believe a bullshit story about me falling on a pile of rocks, unless I embellished it a little. So, at the last minute, I made up a story I thought she would believe.

"We had a lead we wanted to run down," I said. "On the way home we passed a beautiful patch of Trillium growing by a stream just this side of Afton Mountain. I conned Billy into stopping. He did not want to, but I told him it was for you. I know how you love wildflowers. Anyway—against his better judgment—Billy pulled over to the side of the road and we went hunting for that perfect clump of flowers. As I was digging, I saw something move in the grass. I freaked, lost my footing, and fell on a jagged rock. We spent the rest of the afternoon at the hospital."

"Did you have to get stitches?" Mom asked.

"No, I did not get cut, just scratched up a little," I explained. "The hospital cleaned me up and sent me on my way." I had a terrible pang of guilt, but if I had told her the truth, she would probably never let me out of the house with Billy again. Moms have a way of controlling you like that—no matter how old you are.

Ann Mullen

Mom was so sympathetic. "Honey, why don't you come on over here and lie down," she said, as she helped me out of the chair and led me to the sofa. "We will have dinner soon. Cole and I have been fixing deer meat. I have not had deer meat since I lived on the farm. I was just a kid then."

I glanced over at Cole and Billy. They were in their own little hushed conversation and from the looks of things, Cole was not a happy camper. Billy looked like a deer at night, caught in the headlights of a car.

I did not want to deal with either one of them. Their constant bickering was beginning to make me crazy. Ignoring them, I did like Mom said. I stretched out on the sofa and fell asleep.

Dinner was uneventful and delicious. Whatever Cole and Billy had been discussing earlier was now water under the bridge, or it appeared to be. Mom gave no indication that she did not believe what I had told her about my accident. Athena sat by my feet. Everybody was happy.

Later, when Cole and I were alone—Billy had gone home, and Mom had gone to bed—we sat in the swing on the porch and talked. With his arm around me, and my head resting on his chest, I told him I did not feel like going anywhere, I hoped he did not mind.

"I understand," he said. "You've had a pretty exciting day." He smiled. "Billy and I talked about it."

"You did?"

"Yeah," he whispered. "Don't worry, your secret is safe with me. You did the right thing. I don't think your mom needed to hear all the gory details. She is just beginning to come around, and I think this would have caused a set-back if she knew the truth."

I trusted Cole, but at the same time I wondered if he really knew the truth, or if he was playing me. Was this the sneaky cop side of him that Billy had warned me about? I wanted to know.

"What did Billy tell you?"

"Just that you were someplace you were not supposed to be, and there was an accident," he answered.

"Is that all he said?"

"That is all I needed to hear, so we agreed to let it go," he said. "Some things are better left unsaid, if you know what I mean."

"Yes, I think I do."

It was almost the end of June. The evening was cool, and the sky was filled with stars. I could smell honeysuckle in the air. I was content just to sit with Cole, and swing in the swing. Nowadays it seems as if I could be happy with the simple things in life—as long as I had him.

"Hey," I said, "I thought you were going to bring River with you tonight. Why didn't you?"

"He tangled with a skunk this morning. He will not be presentable to go anywhere for awhile." Cole laughed. "You should try to give a seventy-pound dog a bath in tomato juice. It was a nightmare."

"Does that really work? I have heard that it does."

"I don't know, yet. By the time I finished pouring tomato juice all over him, my sense of smell was useless. It was all I could do to get his scent off me when I was done."

I leaned over, sniffed his neck and said "Well, you smell fine to me. Actually, you smell more than fine. You smell terrific."

Old Spice… I love that smell. There must be a connection between your nose and your vagina, because every time I get a whiff of Old Spice, I get horny. What is that all about? And I don't think I am the only woman who reacts that way. Men know this. That is why they always smell so good.

"I must smell like a swamp rat after what I have been through today. Sitting in the hospital with blood all over me can be pretty nasty. I hope I do not smell awful."

"You smell fine," he said, as he kissed me.

"Ouch... ouch... my shoulder," I cried.

"Oh, I'm sorry. I forgot," he replied. "Maybe if I massaged your breasts you would forget about your shoulder." He chuckled out loud at his joke, but made no attempt.

"Ok," I said.

He had a surprised look on his face. He was joking, but I was not.

"Oh, you were not serious?" I whined.

"Well, I could be, but I'm not too sure about doing it here on the front porch with your mom barely twenty feet away. What if she walked out and caught us? I would be embarrassed."

"Oh, but you weren't embarrassed when she called in the middle of the night and we were in bed together," I said, teasing him.

"That was different. She didn't *see* us."

"It just so happens, I have a blanket in my Jeep," I said. "I also keep several other items in the back in case of an emergency: a change of clothes; first aid kit; and rocket launcher... all the basic necessities."

"You are cute."

"Just what I wanted to hear," I snarled. "A thirty-one year old woman lives for the moment when a man calls her cute."

"You are so pretty. I'm sure I'm not the first one to tell you that," he said. His eyes had a glow that melted my heart.

"No, you are not. But you are the first one to say it and have it mean anything to me. I care about you."

I made myself stop. I had to shut up. Next thing I would say is... I love you. I want to marry you and have a house full of baby cops . It was my idea of the perfect family. No, I could not let anything like that happen. I had to take it slow. I did not want to scare him.

"What about that blanket?" I asked. "Should I go get it? It's been a long time since I've laid on a blanket under a tree and gazed at the stars."

"Let's do it," he moaned.

We walked out to my Jeep and retrieved the blanket. As soon as I shut the Jeep's hatch, I heard Athena bark.

"She thinks there is someone out here," I told Cole. "I need to go let her outside."

"Give me the blanket and meet me in the back yard. There's a huge Ash tree out back with a great view," he said.

I opened the front door and Athena came barreling out, jumping all over me. I rubbed her head and listened for a sign that we had awaken Mom. When I didn't see a light come on, I closed the door and the two of us walked down the porch steps.

"I want you to behave yourself tonight," I whispered, lowering myself to Athena's level. "Don't be making a lot of noise and wake Grandma. Do you hear me?"

Gosh, I think that dog understood what I was saying. She looked at me sheepishly, arched her back, and trotted off into the back yard. Women! We are all alike in some ways, aren't we? You can dress us up but you can't take away our pride or our raging hormones. At the moment, Athena had the pride and I had the raging hormones.

Cole was stretched out on the blanket with Athena at his feet by the time I got to the back yard.

"Well, aren't we cozy?" I asked. "Now, all we need is River to make this a complete foursome."

"That's a great idea!" he said, leaning over to pet Athena. "*Athena and River*, what a fine pair you two would make. Just think of the beautiful puppies you could have... or *can* she?"

"We both can," I said, with a big grin on my face. Yes, as far as I knew, I could give him babies. Just the thought of having Cole's child made me feel like I was on a cloud.

My heart was pounding, as I lay down on the blanket next to Cole. His warm hands swept over me with a gentleness I had never known. His kisses were soft at first, then soon became rapid with desire. We made love under the Ash tree.

"I love you, Jesse," he whispered into my ear, as we both reached the fulfillment we were seeking.

I did not know what to say. Was he for real? Guys do this all the time. Right in the middle of a climatic moment, they whisper those three words all women want to hear... I love you.

"Don't say it unless you mean it," I commanded. "Save it for someone that is not as fragile as I am. My heart has been broken more times than I can count. I do not need more lies."

"Jesse, you are a hard woman!" he whispered. "I meant what I said. I love you. I want to be with you. I want us to have a life together."

Athena jumped up and started licking Cole on the face.

"See, even your dog knows I am serious. She believes me. Don't you, girl?" he asked, as he stroked her back and rubbed her ears.

The look he gave me said it all. He was in love with me and he wanted to be with me! He wanted us to have a life together.

"I love you, too," I replied, tears running down my cheeks. "I love you."

CHAPTER 18

C OLE LEFT WITH THE PROMISE to come over first thing Sunday morning. He wanted to make sure my wounds were healing properly. Not only was he a policeman, but he also had extensive training in first aid and CPR. He could set a broken bone or he could give mouth-to-mouth resuscitation... whatever I needed. I liked the mouth-to-mouth bit. As a matter-of-fact, I liked everything about him.

There was only one drawback... he was a cop. How could we cope with him being an officer of the law and me being the flunky of a private detective? I guess that is what you would call me. I sure as hell didn't know what I was doing. But I knew enough to know that if I continued to run with Billy Blackhawk, I was destined to wind up in jail. I could see it coming. I was headed for trouble.

It did not matter. I liked Billy. I wanted to be a part of his life. I wanted him to be a part of mine. Sometimes I wondered about some of the things he did and how he managed to do them, but I tried not to ask why. He was a good man and he had a good heart. That was enough for me. We had formed a bond. He knew it, and so did I.

I now had Cole and Billy in my life, but they were like oil and water. Still, I loved them both. What was I going to do about their continuous, nerve-racking arguing? If these two men were going to share my life, we had to come to an agreement. We had to reach a happy medium. Eventually, I decided I would have to sit them both down and have a serious talk with them. I would not let them be at each other's throats all the time. We needed to lay it all out on the table, and set some boundaries.

"Here's the deal, guys. Cole, you are a cop and Billy, you are a private investigator. You're both my friends. I realize it' is hard for you to see eye-to-eye, but you have got to get it together. I am done with your arguing. You're best friends—for God's sake! Get it together, now! Get over the pettiness. Please! Do it for my sake." This is what I would say to them, later.

It was Sunday morning, one week until the 4th of July. I had the blissful feeling of a woman in love. I got out of bed with a whole new outlook on life. Cole was in love with me, and I was in love with him.

I was in desperate need of a shower. I removed the bandage and examined my shoulder in the bathroom mirror. It didn't look nearly as bad as I had expected. The blood on the once sterile gauze had dried and there was no indication that the wound had bled during the night. The blast had caught me on the edge of my left shoulder and took out a sizable patch of skin. What was left was an ugly red, raw area. It was not infected. Good ole' Dr. Chief Standing Deer Blackhawk did a fine job of fixing me up. I guess I was not going to die after all.

I turned on the shower, stripped down, and jumped in. The first wave of burning pain from the water hitting my shoulder, almost brought me to my knees. Trying to withstand the pain, I forged ahead. I used soap to wash my body and hair, as I leaned to one side. I wanted to get this over with as fast as possible. The thought of getting soap in my wound was scary. However, I felt like a new person once I was done. My hair would be funky from using soap on it and not using cream rinse. But I could live with that for another day. Using a hand towel to dab at my raw shoulder, I noticed a speckling of blood.

"Huh... this is not so bad," I said out loud. "I have seen worse."

I put on a pair of jeans and a tank top, sat down at my computer, and tried to brush the rats out of my long hair. I left my shoulder bare so it could get some air. I figured it would heal faster that way. That is what my mama always said. Soon I would have to do something about my hair. The red was fading and the brown was shining through. Also, three inches of it from the bottom up was nothing but dead ends. And it was drab. I needed a new hairdo. I have always loved Dyan Cannon's hairstyle. She is a bit older than I am, but she has great looking hair. Yep, I thought, that is what I will do. I will get my hair cut and re-styled as soon as I had the time.

Having made all my new resolutions of how I could fix myself up—I did have Cole to think about now—I started pecking away at my computer. I had tons of e-mail to answer, but that could wait. I wanted to surf the net and find out anything I could on this case. As much information as there is today on the web, I knew I could find something. And bingo, I found a site where you could find out everything there is to know about a person, from their credit history to the name of their family doctor, for the low, low price of $39.99, which could be billed to your carrier, or your credit card. You decide.

I wondered if Billy knew about this site. I would have to tell him. But in the meantime, I decided to check it out. I will pay for it on my credit card and then submit it to Billy for reimbursement. There should not be any problem. It was work related.

I hesitated. Whose name did I want to type in? This was going to cost me forty dollars, so I had better go for the gold. My main suspect was Jay. I typed in Patrick Jason Teale, hoping the information on him would be listed under his birth name and not his adopted name. I hit pay dirt. There were three pages—everything about him from the time of his birth to three months ago when he was cited for speeding on I-64 in Henrico County. What was he doing in Henrico County? It was almost an hour from where he lived.

I printed out all the information and put it in my briefcase for Billy to read. I made another copy for myself and left the web. After scanning the printout, I determined that this boy had been one busy guy. He had one heck of a rap sheet. He'd been arrested four times in his short career as a juvenile delinquent: the first time at the age of twelve for shoplifting; at thirteen for participating in a public brawl; 15—vandalism; and last but not least, at 17—DUI, for which he spent four hours in lock-up until he was bailed out by his parents. Whew! It looked like Jay had a promising future as a career criminal.

Wait until I tell Billy! Boy, he be surprised! I am so smart. Sometimes I even amaze myself!

I patched up my shoulder the best that I could with a sterile pad and tape that I found in the first aid kit in the bathroom vanity. Knowing my mom like I do, I knew she probably stocked all the bathrooms in the house with such necessities. It was her thing.

"I have coffee brewing," she offered, as I walked in the kitchen. "Poor dear, how are you feeling today? Is that shoulder bothering you?"

"No, I am fine," I replied.

She poured me a cup of coffee and said, "I think you and I need to talk."

"Sure, Mom, what is on your mind?" I asked.

"It's about last night..."

"What about last night?" I asked, afraid to hear what she had to say, or worse, afraid of what she might have seen.

"It's about you and Cole," she replied. "Jesse, I realize you and Cole are crazy about each other. I can see it in your eyes. I am not a prude. If you want to spend the night with him, go ahead. It is none of my business. You are a grown woman."

"Let me get this straight. You're saying you don't mind if I sleep around?" I asked. "You surprise me. I thought you were a firm believer in marriage before sex. What happened to change your mind?"

"Nothing happened to change my mind. No, I don't want you to sleep around, but you and Cole are in love. That makes a difference."

Here it comes.

"Let's face it Jesse, you're not getting any younger. Grab Cole. He wants you. You two could date, then get married and have kids. You can do whatever you want, and I don't care in which order you do it. Just do it. Do not let this one get away."

Mom's intense stare gave me the creeps. This wasn't like her. My mom is about as Southern Baptist as you can get. They don't go for stuff like this.

"Don't look at me like that, Jesse," she said. "I'm not so dumb. I know what goes on with your generation. Remember, I have been there. You do not know the places I have been."

"I don't think we need to go there, Mom. I trust you."

"Honey, all I'm trying to say is I want this to be your home. I want you to be able to be yourself and have some say-so about what goes on here. And if that includes having a sex life, you should go for it. If it makes you uncomfortable talking to me about it then why don't you just think of me as your roommate?"

"Oh, yeah, right. I don't think so," I replied. "I get the idea, Mom. I'll tell you what I will do. If I decide to stay away from home for the night, I will call you. Just do not ask me a bunch of questions and I will not have to tell you any lies."

"Deal," she agreed. "Just one personal question before we close the deal. I will ask you one, and you can ask one. Ok?"

"Fire away!"

"What's the relationship between you and Billy?"

"He is my boss and my friend," I stated. "I care about him. I hope our friendship will last until death we will part. But that is all there is to it. There is no romance, if that's what you are wondering."

"So you're saying there's nothing romantic between the two of you?"

"That is exactly what I am saying."

"Ok, you answered my question, now ask me yours."

"No!" I replied. "I reserve the right to save this question for a time in the future that I may deem fit."

"One question," she hissed. "But after that, if you force me, you will be subject to my lies."

That is a joke—my mom does not know how to tell a lie. Who is she trying to fool?

Mom and I were immersed in a heavy conversation about sex and the corrupt moral fiber of our society when suddenly Athena started to bark. I walked to the front window and saw Cole pull up into the driveway. My heart skipped a beat. It was only nine o'clock and he was at my door. I love this man!

I tried not to fall all over myself as I went to the front door to greet him. I had visions of last night in the back yard, and my raging hormones started to kick in again.

"Good morning, ladies," Cole said, as he walked in and kissed me lightly on the lips. He kissed Mom on the cheek. "How is everything going, Ma? Has Jesse been a good girl?"

"As a matter-of-fact, we were just having a long conversation about sex."

Not again! I was doomed.

"Sex?" he asked. "What about it?"

"I just do not get enough of it!" Mom laughed like a crazy woman.

Oh, my God!

Once I recovered from her outburst of insanity, I took Cole off to the side and said, "Don't mind her. I think she's in another world. She's been acting weird ever since she got out of bed. I think it is menopause."

"Oh, don't be silly. She was only joking. Can't you tell?"

Twenty minutes later, Billy drove up in the driveway.

"What is he doing here?" Cole asked.

"We have an errand to run."

"Like the one you had yesterday?"

"Don't be silly," I said, teasing him.

The expression on Cole's face surprised me. I thought he would go off if I did not tell him everything, but I soon learned that he was going to give me my space. He was not going to push me. That is what all women look for in men, isn't it? Someone who will give you love, trust, and the freedom to be a real person?

"Good morning, folks," Billy cheerfully said. He bent over and patted Athena's head, and then looked up at Cole. "How is it going?"

"Just fine," Cole answered. "Jesse tells me you two have an errand to run today. Do you need any help?"

"Nah, I think we can handle it."

"Like you did yesterday?"

"What are you talking about?"

"I am talking about Jesse getting hurt."

Mom walked back into the living room. "Ok, guys. No fighting. I swear, you two are worse than my kids were when they were little. Would either one of you like something to eat?"

"No thanks," they both said, and went to their separate corners.

"Are you ready to go?" Billy asked.

"Give me a minute. I want to change clothes." I left the room, keeping my fingers crossed they wouldn't go at it again before I returned. I ran upstairs, removed the tank top and put on a clean T-shirt. I grabbed my cell phone from the charger and slipped it into my shoulder bag, along with *Rossi*. From now on, my gun was going everywhere with me.

When I got back downstairs, everyone was sitting at the kitchen table drinking coffee. I caught the end of the conversation.

"What is this about Bill and Edie?" I asked.

"I was just telling Billy that I didn't know about the 4th of July," Mom replied. "Your Uncle Bill and aunt Edie are coming for a visit next weekend. They called this morning. But that's not all. Claire called last night to say that she and the kids were coming for the weekend. So, I called and invited your brother. He is bringing a friend."

"But Mom, we all ready told Billy we were going to his family's party for the 4th. He will be disappointed if we do not show."

"He said all of us could go to his celebration. He says it is a big shindig; the more the merrier."

I glanced at Billy.

"That is what I said. My family would love it. Believe me, there will be more food than you can eat, and it is going to be outside so there is plenty of room for guests."

Cole chimed in, "It is true. You will have a great time."

"Where will everybody sleep?" I asked Mom.

"Cole has offered to let Jack and his friend stay with him. Claire and the kids can share my room, and Bill and Edie can have the spare room. Unless you want to let Jack have your room and you stay with Cole."

"Ok," I winked at Cole. "Jack can have my room."

"Now that the sleeping arrangements have been established, I will make a few phone calls," Mom stated.

As we were leaving, Cole walked us outside and said, "I'm going to change the oil in your mom's van and the pick-up truck. If you want me to do your Jeep, I will need your keys."

"It is fine," Billy said. "Daniel serviced it before she bought it."

"Would you mind giving us a moment alone, Billy? I need to have a word with Cole."

"Sure, I will wait for you in the truck," he answered. "I will see you later," he said to Cole.

I turned to Cole and said,"You don't have to do all the things you do for us. We appreciate it, but we need to learn how to take care of ourselves. I can change the oil in the cars, and I can cut the grass. Whatever else I need to know, I can find out. I do not want you spending your time off from work doing our chores."

"I want to do it," he said. "There is a lot of work to running a place like this and you are going to need help. Living in the mountains takes some effort. Not only do you have to maintain the cars and cut the grass, but you will also have to do things like cut up downed trees, keep the animals at bay, and make sure the up-keep on the house is done."

"I get the picture," I said. "Thank you for looking after my mom."

"I have to," he whispered. "I want to make a good impression on my future mother-in-law." He kissed me and gave me a little shove. "Now go on before Billy gets in an uproar."

Did I hear him right—future mother-in-law? I walked out to Billy's truck in a daze. I turned and threw Cole a kiss. I was still reeling from Cole's declaration when I got into the truck and slammed the door. I must have been mistaken.

"You look like the cat that swallowed the canary. What happened?"

"I'm not sure, but I think Cole just asked me to marry him."

"That is crazy. You have not known Cole long enough to even consider the idea of marriage," he yelled.

"Don't yell at me!" I cried. "Maybe I was wrong about what he said."

"No, you understood him perfectly. Let me tell you something. Cole has a tendency to fall in love with every girl he dates. And he has dated plenty. He even got married once and you see how that turned out. He can't help it. I don't know what is wrong with the guy."

"Oddly, I have a tendency to be the same way," I confessed, "except that I never married one of them. This time it is different, Billy. Cole is not like the other men I dated."

"Yeah, it's different all right."

Billy pulled out of the driveway with a skeptical look on his face. Or, was it jealousy? I tried not to notice. I would not entertain those thoughts. The idea of Billy and me being romantically involved was just not going to happen. He's old and I'm too young for him.

Billy drove at break-neck speed. I barely got a chance to glimpse at what had become one of my favorite scenes—the cop car on the hill with the sign on top—Law Enforcement—Out of Control. I love it. I know there must be a tale behind it, but I did not know what it was. It didn't matter. To me, it was a symbol of free speech—the right to say whatever you wanted to as long as you do not cross the line. Obviously, this did not cross the line because it was still there.

"Can we please slow down?" I asked, as we came to a stop at the intersection in Ruckersville. "You are going way too fast. I'm on the verge of a major panic attack."

"Sorry," he said. "My mind was somewhere else."

"Well, you had better get it together," I demanded. "Remember the last time we paid a visit to these crazy people? One of them shot at me. I do not want that to happen again."

"I made a mistake. It will not happen again. You can bet your butt on it." he said, staring dead into my eyes. "I will not let you get hurt. After you were shot, I made a promise to myself that I would take care of you and not put you in another dangerous situation."

"What a joke. Everything you do is risky. But I am not scared. Let's go get the bad guys!"

"Hell, yeah," he yelled.

Billy was silent for the rest of the ride until we reached Gordonsville. "I've got something to tell you." He hesitated long enough to get a second wind. "I got a call last night from Daniel. Greg, one of his sons, volunteers for the Adopt-A-Highway program. They were supposed to meet Satur-day morning and do what they normally do. Well, it seems Greg had something to do and could not make it, so he went out alone Friday afternoon to do his share. Daniel said it was not uncommon for them to make arrangements like that, as long as everyone does their part."

"Get to the point, Billy. You are driving me nuts."

"Anyway, he went into the woods to take a leak and found a woman's purse. He picked it up and looked inside. And you are never going to believe who it belongs to."

"Helen Carrolton," I mumbled.

"Bingo," Billy said, as he ran his hand across his forehead. "This does not look good, Jesse. I am afraid the girl is dead."

"How do you know it is her purse? Was there a wallet in it?"

"*Dah,*" he smacked the side of his head. "Of course there was a wallet in it. How else would we know that it belonged to Helen?"

"Who has the purse now?"

"Let's just say I have control of it for the time being."

"How did you manage to come into possession of it?"

"Greg took it to his dad, and Daniel called me. Coming from a family of such diverse occupations, Greg knew right away what he had. He knew about the investigation we were involved in."

"How did he know?"

"Jesse, you ought to know by now that my family works together. We help each other. We know what's going on in each other's lives. That's what a family is all about, right?"

"So, Daniel called and told you that Greg found Helen's purse. It sure is a coincidence that someone in your family found evidence relating to your case. What did you do with the purse?"

"I took it to a friend this morning at the Charlottesville Research Facility for DNA testing. She will run hair and fiber samples, and test for blood and semen, etc. We should hear something soon."

"It's Sunday, Billy," I reminded him. "How did you manage that? Also, I thought DNA testing took weeks."

"I have friends in high places and friends in the right places."

As Billy drove, I sat and tried to absorb what he had just told me. Helen was probably dead, and somebody would have to tell her parents.

"Helen's parents do not know, do they?"

"Not yet. So far, only a handful of people know. But the point is, they are going to have to be told, and the evidence is going to have to be turned over to the police. We can not wait too long. Withholding evidence is a felony, and I do not want to go to jail."

"What do we do?" I asked.

"Hold your breath."

CHAPTER 19

"EXACTLY WHERE DID GREG FIND HELEN'S PURSE?" I asked. "It was in the woods about a half a mile from the road where the Hudgins live. It was strange."

"I will tell you what is strange... the fact that your nephew was the one who found the purse. You must be the luckiest man on the planet. How is that Billy?"

"Just lucky, I guess," he offered. "Sometimes things just go my way."

I found that hard to believe.

"Right about here," Billy pointed. "This is where he found the purse. It was back in the trees over there."

"Hey, there's a dirt path," I motioned. "Pull off and let's go have a look. Maybe we will come across something else."

Billy quickly glanced around checking for traffic and then slammed on the brakes. He pulled onto the dirt path and we got out of the truck.

"Watch out for snakes," he said.

"Did you have to say that?"

"I'm just warning you. You need to be careful. Have you ever been bitten by a snake?"

"Are you kidding? Not in this lifetime!"

"I have and I can tell you it's no picnic."

"Is there anything that you have not done or had happen to you?"

"Don't be cute."

We searched the woods for thirty minutes looking for evidence. The underbrush was thick with vines and dead tree limbs.

"There is nothing here," I said. "Let's go. This place gives me the creeps." Litter was scattered about, and I'm sure I saw a used condom. It was starting to gross me out. "Looks to me like people just ride by and toss trash out of their cars."

"Yeah, and that's what I think happened with the purse. Somebody just tossed it out the window, maybe as a desperate attempt to get rid of evidence," Billy replied, as we trudged back to the truck.

I stood by the opened truck door, analyzing the situation. "Whoever tossed the purse did it on the opposite side of the road, unless they turned around at some point. Helen was headed north, not south. That would be a pretty long shot considering Helen wasn't much bigger than I am. "

"Yeah, that's what I figured," Billy agreed as he crawled into the truck.

I jumped in and said, "Here's how I see it," I ran through the scenario as Billy backed out onto the highway. "Somewhere between the diner and the gas station, Helen picks up her passenger. By the time they reach the gas station, it's already starting to snow pretty hard. They leave, heading in the same direction as before. They get down the road a little ways and he gets control of the situation. Maybe he has a gun and makes her pull over. He gets in the driver's side and heads back in the opposite direction. By this time, she is frantic. She is afraid he is going to kill her, She tosses her purse out of the window, hoping someone will find it eventually. By now it is snowing so bad, who is going to pay attention to what is going on in a little red car? People would be too busy dealing with the snow to worry about others."

"Or, maybe he has already killed her and dumped the body," Billy suggested. "And now he is on his way home and sees the purse. He slings it out of the window."

I thought for a minute. "No, it can't be," I deducted. "It is snowing like hell and he would have the windows up. He would have to reach over and roll down the window. I doubt he'd be able to get it that far into the woods from where he was sitting, unless..."

"Unless she tossed it out right after she had picked him up." Billy finished my sentence. "Maybe she suspected something was wrong right off the bat. She was scared and it was the only thing she could think to do at the time."

"What about paying for the gas?" I asked. "No purse... no money."

"The attendant said she paid with cash."

Now it was my turn. "Sure," I said, mocking his earlier snide remark. "I doubt very seriously she is going to take the time to pull a ten out of her wallet before she says, *'Excuse me, but I need to have gas money before I throw my purse out the window so someone will come along and find it after you kill me.'* Get real."

"Boy, you sure know how to burst my bubble!"

"It just does not add up. None of this makes any sense. The purse had to be dumped after the fact."

Billy was still pouting when he pulled up in front of the Hudgins' house. The automobiles that were parked in the parking spaces the last time we were here had dwindled down to two: an old Chevy, and an old Ford convertible.

"Well, I see the kids are home," I stated. "Mom's mini-van is gone, and so is Dad's little red sports car. Where is the housekeeper's station wagon?" I smiled at Billy. "How lucky can we get? That just leaves the old Chevy for Jay, and the Mustang for Rose."

"The station wagon is probably parked out back since it does belong to the housekeeper. You don't think they would let her leave it out front all the time, do you?" he hissed, making some kind of internal noise that reminded me of a frog about ready to throw-up.

"Do I detect a little bit of prejudice there, Billy?" I sneered. "Got some little hang-up about common laborers?"

He laughed at me and said, "You know what I am talking about. What makes you think the Chevy belongs to Jay and the Ford is Rose's? It could be the other way around."

Billy parked the truck. I looked down at the two cars as we walked passed them and said, "See, it's like this. Rose drives the Mustang because women like to ride in convertibles, and Jay drives the Chevy because guys like to drive high-performance cars. It is a logical deduction."

"Wow, I'm impressed, Sherlock," Billy chuckled. "And I am sure that you are absolutely right!"

As we walked up to the house, Billy and I turned to each other. All the bushes that had been lining the flowerbeds had been bulldozed off to the side into an ugly mound of dirt and tangled greenery. We could hear the roar of heavy equipment in the backyard.

"What happened here?" I asked.

"Don't you mean what is happening here? Do you hear that noise behind the house?"

We listened for a second and then heard someone scream. Billy and I took off running, following the sound.

It was like a madhouse. Rose was running around yelling at Jay. Jay was steadily dragging bushes out from the flowerbeds with a backhoe.

"What the hell is going on here?" Billy asked, shocked at the sight.

The minute Rose saw us she stopped yelling at her brother, put her face in her hands and started crying. I ran to comfort her. She was frightened and the situation was obviously out of control.

Jay shut down the backhoe, climbed down and started to walk away.

"Have you lost your mind?" I screamed at him. "You have gotten your sister all upset, and I don't think your parents are going to be too happy when they see what you have done to their flowerbeds."

"I tried to make him stop!" Rose whimpered. "But he is crazy. He will not listen to anybody. He did this to punish Mom. He knows how much she loves her flowerbeds."

"Why is he trying to punish your mother?" I coached. "What did she do to him to make him so angry?"

"It was not anything he did't deserve, as usual," she answered. "Mom took his car away because he didn't come home until early this morning. The second she leaves the house, he goes into a rampage."

"Does he behave like this often? I mean, lose his temper and destroy things? Is his temper always this bad?"

It didn't take her long to figure out where I was headed with this line of questioning. She squared her shoulders, stopped crying, and said, "He'll be fine. He was just a little angry." She brushed passed me.

Before I could stop her, she ran to the house. Billy walked over to me. Jay stopped in mid-step and turned his attention to us. The look on his face made my skin crawl.

"Nice piece of equipment isn't it?" Jay asked. "I love playing on that thing. Just makes me feel so tough."

"What a nut case," I whispered to Billy.

"Oh, you're tough all right," I shouted to Jay. "I guess you are proud of what you did. You're a big man. You like to scare women, don't you? Hurt them? Kill them? Huh? What do you say?" My temper was on the edge, and any minute I was going to fly into a rampage that would make his little tantrum seem like child's play.

Billy got in between us. "Hold on a minute," he said, as he pushed me back and faced Jay. He knew I was getting crazy. "Get a grip."

"Where is my shotgun? You bunch of thieves!" Jay screamed.

That did it for me. I went berserk. I jumped on him and we both went tumbling to the ground.

"Son of a bitch," I screamed. "You killed her didn't you? I know you did! I can see it in your eyes. You're a useless piece of garbage!"

"Jesse, get off of the kid," Billy said, tugging at my arms.

By the time Billy pulled me off the boy, I was livid. Jay scrambled his way into the house.

"What is the matter with you, Jesse?" Billy demanded, as he helped me up. "Don't you know you can go to jail for what you just did? Have you lost your mind?"

I brushed off my pants. A pain surged through my shoulder.

"Forgot about that shoulder, didn't you?" Billy asked. "Let's see if we can do some damage control."

"He's guilty, Billy," I insisted. "I see it in his eyes. He killed her."

"Sure... sure," he tried to humor me. "Not only are you the next Sherlock Holms, but you are also clairvoyant. How lucky can I get?"

"You are not funny."

We made our way up the front steps and rang the doorbell.

"You know that crazy kid has probably called the cops by now," I said. "We are trespassing again."

"Not this time, honey. Look at the mess around you. You think he wants the cops to see this?"

I glanced around surveying the damage. "It looks like a war zone. Why would he do something like this? It's just pure mean. If he is this destructive and remains so calm, can you imagine what he could do if he was really irked?"

Rose cracked the door just enough to say, "Please go away. Jay has finally calmed down a little and I do not want him to go off again. He can be so mean. Please go."

"Are you going to be ok?" I asked. I was concerned about her. I had seen her brother in a fit of anger. He was not a nice person.

"I will be fine. Now, just go away," she cried. "I will tell Mom and Dad you were here." She shut the door.

"Well, what now? *Sherlock*," Billy demanded.

"Don't call me that. It's not cute anymore," I spat. "Do you have your equipment with you?"

"I sure do," he said, as we walked to the truck. "Why?"

"Let's go for a ride," I said. "I think now would be a good time to find us a little surveillance spot in the woods again."

"Good idea," he added. "Except this time, we have the shotgun."

"*Tsk-Tsk*. You don't think that is the only one he has, do you?" I asked, lifting my eyebrows in jest.

The day was turning into a scorcher, and I didn't relish the idea of sitting in the woods with the snakes. The blast from the air conditioner in Billy's truck felt wonderful. I tried not to think about the stinging pain in my shoulder, but every pothole in the road was a testament to my agony.

"Sorry," Billy said. "Is your shoulder bothering?"

"I will live," I winched. "I was just going over in my mind what just went down back there."

"What is your take on the situation?"

"Given all the facts," I answered. "I think the *teenager from hell* is the guilty party. I think he killed Helen Carrolton. Whether it was the antics of a fun time gone wrong, or the actions of a killer, I just do not know. I just know something feels wrong." I glanced at Billy. I wanted a sign from him—something that would indicate he did not think I was stupid. "I know I am not a P.I., and I don't have all the training and experience you have. All I have to go on is my gut feeling."

"So, this gut feeling is telling you that Jay is guilty?" he asked.

"Yes, it is."

"What about the gas station attendant?"

Before I could answer, Billy stopped the truck and pointed to the path we had taken the last time. "You want to try the same spot again, or have you developed a phobia about the place? If you have, I'd understand."

"Sorry, pal. There is no more room in my life for phobias," I said, joking. "My card is *full-up.*"

"Then why don't we follow this path as far as it goes and see where we come out?"

"I guess we do not have anything to lose?" I stated.

The red flash came at us in the blink of an eye. It was Larry Hudgins in his sports car hauling ass down the road. He was headed home and he was in a big hurry. Our eyes followed him as he flew by.

"In a hurry, isn't he?" I asked, making my own share of grunting noises.

"Big hurry," Billy agreed, as he turned the truck around. "Change of plans. We're going to take this shotgun back to the rightful owner."

"I don't know if that is a good idea. I have a feeling the roof is going to come down in a few minutes."

"That is the whole idea, Jesse." Billy raised his eyebrows and said, "The element of surprise, my dear Watson."

"What next, for Pete's sake?" I sneered at him. "If you start quoting Shakespeare... I'm leaving."

I had the feeling I had done this before. What's that word—*déjà-vu?* Well, it was happening now. The dust had barely settled when I saw the front door close. Larry was definitely in a rush. We slid into a parking space and followed in his path to the front door just in time to hear the lock click. Billy jammed his finger on the doorbell and held it there.

"Enough!" I screamed. "Are you trying to get him pissed?"

"I'm just trying to get his attention."

Rose opened the door and whispered, "What are you doing back? I thought I asked you to leave. This is not a good time. Dad just got home and he is really, really mad."

"That's what you said the last time we were here. Is there ever a good time at this house? Where is your father?" I demanded.

"Ok, but don't say I did not try to warn you," she said. She back to let us enter and then closed the door.

Billy turned to me, pointed his finger and said, "I want you to behave yourself in here. No more craziness."

"You wish!" I teased.

What a fine team Billy and I were together. We were two adults acting like little kids. Mom would be so proud.

"I assume you are here to return my shotgun," Larry stated, as he reached out and took it from Billy. "Now get out of here before I call the cops. I know who you shit brains are, so don't mess with me." He slammed the door.

"What do we do next, Billy?"

"We go to Plan B," he replied.

Now we were the ones in a hurry. We both knew what we were going to do. We had to find a spot so we could listen to every detail of the next few minutes in the Hudgins' household. Daddy's wrath was going to emerge and we wanted to hear it all.

Confident that we had found the perfect spot to spy, Billy parked his truck at the end of the same path we had visited once before. Except this time, we were in the middle of a grove of cedar trees behind the barn.

"You don't think they will see the truck from here?" I asked. I was getting nervous. Memories of a not-so-long-ago nightmare bounced back into my head.

"Calm down," Billy said, as he started digging out his equipment. "Everything is going to be fine. You worry too much. Now grab that bag." He pointed to a black bag in the cab. "It is the dish, so be careful."

An hour later, I was ready to call it quits. "What's going on? They haven't said a word, not one word, just that stupid elevator music they have been playing. Something is not right, Billy." I was getting frustrated. This was not normal.

"I was hoping he would think we had given up and left," Billy said. "He knew we were here the whole time."

"Who knew?"

"The father knew. He is no dummy. Come on let's pack it in for the day. We are wasting our time." Billy said, as he disconnected his equipment. "We are finished. Let's go home."

"Why didn't you tell me he knew we were out there?" I asked, as we packed the equipment.

"I was going to tell you once, but you had dozed off."

"I did not," I joked. "I was just resting my eyes!"

He threw his head back, laughed and said, "Lesson number four: if you think someone's listening, turn on some music. If you talk low they will not hear a word you say."

"Number four? What happened to one, two and three?"

"Jesse, you haven't been paying attention," he admonished me, beginning his lecture. "One—you must always be prepared. Two—suspect and expect anything, and three—don't let anyone catch you with your pants down, whether you are being watched, or you are the watcher."

"Ah, words of wisdom by Billy Blackhawk," I said, taunting him. "You should write a book."

CHAPTER 20

"**Y**OU MIGHT BE COMPLETELY WRONG about Jay Hudgins," Billy said, as we crossed over the South River Bridge heading home. "What about Tom Dorey? Why don't you suspect him?"

"He just doesn't fit the profile."

"What do you know about profile? Why, Jesse, have you been studying behind my back?" He was mocking my southern accent.

"*Honey*," I said, dragging out my southern drawl. "*I'm no dummy. I watch T.V.*"

"So, tell me what you've learned from this great institution of higher learning. I am dying to hear every detail."

"I learned that gut feelings are worth more than words on paper," I summated. "What you see is not always what you get. The Hudgins look like upstanding people on the outside, but on the inside they have secrets. Secrets they want to keep covered up because they're dark and dirty."

"You don't think Tom Dorey is dark and dirty?"

"Look at his dossier. He's just an average Joe. He has never been arrested—not even a parking ticket; goes to college; works part-time pumping gas; and tends bar at the downtown mall in Charlottesville. His mind is on his life. He has better things to do than go around killing people."

"This is your gut feeling?"

"Yes it is," I said. "I might be wrong, but I don't think so."

"Supposed we eliminate Jay and Tom, where would you go from there?"

" I hadn't considered that possibility," I answered, as we pulled into the driveway. "I'll have to think about it for awhile."

My cell phone rang just as I was picking my handbag up off the truck floor. "Hello," I said, as I got out and walked towards the house.

"Jesse, I'm sorry to bother you, but I have an emergency," I heard my sister say. "I didn't want to call the house because of Mom. I just can't face her now."

"What's the matter, Claire?"

"I got arrested two days ago," she cried, "for drunk driving. I didn't mean to. I was at a club with some of my friends. I didn't realize that I had that much to drink. I've been so depressed lately."

"Where were the kids when you got arrested?"

"Oh, they were safe. They were with a sitter," she assured me. "But that's not the point. Carl is threatening to take away the kids. He says no judge is going to award custody to a drunk. What am I going to do?"

"Don't worry about him," I said. "He's full of crap. Don't let him intimidate you."

"But I'm scared, Jesse."

"Listen, Claire. He's just blowing smoke. Forget about him for now. Are you still planning to come next weekend?"

"Yes," she whimpered.

"Well, why don't you pack up the kids and come now. It will give us plenty of time to decide what we are going to do. Mom would love to have you guys here for a whole week." Without Carl, I thought to myself. "I will talk to Mom and break the news about everything before you arrive."

"Thanks, Jesse. I knew I could count on you. That is a great idea. I will get the kids ready. We will be there sometime tonight. Carl can just kiss my... well, you know."

I held my breath as I walked into the house. Mom was in for a real eye-opener. I just hoped she could handle it.

Athena greeted us as we went into the kitchen. I bent down and patted her head and said,"You smell good, girl. Did you get a bath?" I looked at Mom and saw a big smile on her face.

"She sure did," Mom said. "She got into something nasty, so Cole helped me give her a bath before he left. He put her on top of the picnic table in the backyard and hosed her down with the garden hose. She loved it! It was so funny. You should have seen her. Cole was covered with shampoo, and all of us got wet in the end."

"You love this dog, don't you, Mom?" Billy chimed in.

"Sure I do," she replied. "She's so sweet. How could you not love her?"

We stood there for a few minutes not saying anything. The silence became unbearable.

"Mom, I've got to talk to you," I said, dreading every moment. "Why don't you come over here and sit down on the couch?"

"What is wrong, dear," she asked, drying her hands on a dish towel as she walked over to the sofa. "You didn't get shot at again, did you?" She glanced away from me and looked straight at Billy, giving him a strange look.

My mouth dropped to my knees. "How did you find out?"

"I'm a mother. Not much gets by me," she proudly announced. "Furthernore, Cole is a lot smarter than you think. He got a call on his cell phone and I overheard every word. It was about you and Billy. The boy that shot you—his father's lawyer is a friend of someone Cole knows. Cole did some off-the-record snooping and found out all kinds of things. Now he knows everything."

"I'm sorry, Mom. I didn't want to lie to you, but I was afraid you couldn't handle the truth. Are you mad? Is Cole mad?" I asked.

"Well, he is not happy," she replied. "He wants you to call him."

"Shit."

"Jesse, watch your language!" she demanded.

Regaining my composure, I blurted out, "Mom, Claire has got a little problem." I went on to explain all the gory details of her relationship with Carl, his infidelities, the fight and subsequent miscarriage of the baby, right down to the drunk-driving charge that he was hanging over her head.

"Poor Claire," Mom cried. "I have to call her. She needs me."

"I just talked to her," I said. "I convinced her to come home and stay for awhile. She will be here tonight."

"Then I had better get moving," she insisted. "I need to get the spare room ready."

"What can we do to help?" Billy asked.

By dinnertime, everything in the spare room had been shoved up against the wall, leaving plenty of room for the sofa bed to be folded out. The kids could sleep with Claire. At their ages, they would probably love it.

Billy and I sat at the picnic table discussing the case while Mom fixed hamburgers on the grill.

"I've been thinking about what you said," I commented. "If you exclude Tom Dorey and Jay Hudgins, or anyone in the Hudgins family from the list of suspects, I'd have to go with a serial killer. Who else is left?"

"Exactly," he replied. "We need to consider every possibility. We now have her purse, so we can pretty much assume that she is dead. As soon as I get the report from my friend at the research center, we will go tell her parents what we have. They have a right to know."

"Are we going to drive to Poquoson?"

The cell phone that Billy kept hooked on his belt rang. "Uh-huh... ok... right... thanks a lot. I owe you big time," he said.

"What was that call about?" I asked. "Was that from your friend who works at the lab?"

"Yes, it was," he sighed. "That was Caroline. She says there is dried blood on the purse that matches the DNA sample of hair the Carroltons supplied to the police. She also said she picked up three separate fingerprints. One of the prints belong to Helen, and one was her mother's. The third one has yet to be determined. She is going to call me back when she comes up with an I.D. on the third one."

"Then we have got him!" I shouted.

"Relax," he said. "It might turn out to be a print that is not on file."

"What do you mean?" I asked. "Not on file? I thought everybody had a print on file somewhere."

"Maybe," he replied. "But with the advancements we have in the computer age, anything is possible to erase. All you need is a good hacker."

"Scary isn't it?"

I watched as Mom removed the cooked hamburgers from the grill. She placed them to the side, turned off the knobs and reached down and shut off the gas. I was amazed at how self-sufficient she had become.

"You are getting pretty good at that," I proudly said.

"Oh, this thing?" she pointed to the grill. "Cole showed me how to operate it. Once you learn how to use it, it's not so scary anymore." She walked over to the table and sat down. "Dig in everybody. Oh darn, I forgot the potato salad. Jesse, would you run inside and get it?"

"And bring the mustard," Billy added.

"Who eats mustard on hamburgers?" I asked. "That is gross!"

I heard the phone ring as soon as I opened the door.

"Hello," I answered, stretching the cord to the refrigerator. Carl's voice was barely audible amongst the static and hissing. "I can't hear you Carl," I screamed into the receiver. He was the last person I wanted to talk to and I sure didn't want him talking to Mom. "Call back later," I yelled and hung up the phone. "And go to hell."

I walked into the living room and picked up the portable phone. Carl would surely call back and I wanted to be ready. I took the phone, the potato salad, and the mustard out to the backyard.

"Was that the phone I heard ring?" Mom asked.

"Yes," I nodded. "It was Carl, your beloved son-in-law."

"What did he want?" she continued.

"I don't know. The line was full of static. I told him to call back." I sat down and started piling food onto my plate, pretending to be unaware of any possible dilemma that might be heading our way. "If it is important, he will call back. Isn't that what you always tell me?"

"Oh, you know what he wants. He's a scumbag."

"You called Carl a scumbag!" I was shocked at my mother's remark. "Since when did Carl become a scumbag?"

"Since he hurt my baby," she retorted. "Boy have I got a few things to say to him! I dare him to call back." She leaned across the table and grabbed the phone before I had a chance to stop her. "Give me that phone. I'll show him a thing or two."

This was getting nasty. I hadn't seen my mother this angry in a long time. Carl was in for a good chewing out, and I wanted to be around to hear it. I didn't want to miss a single word. At the same time, this would be the perfect chance to tell him about my fantasy concerning him and a bear. I had to snicker at the thought.

Billy leaned over to me and said, "Did we miss something?"

"No," I smiled. "It was just something I remembered."

The warm June afternoon was pleasant. The cool breeze in the air kept the day from being so hot. Normally, back home, by this time of the year the heat and humidity would drive you inside. By August, you would not want to go outside, and if you did it wouldn't be for long. But here in the mountains it was almost July and you could stay outside all day and not feel like you were going to suffocate.

"Does it get stifling hot late in the summer?" I asked Billy. This would be our first summer here. I wondered how it compared to our summers in Newport News. Living on a peninsula, you would think there would always be a breeze from the ocean, but that is not true. We lived inland and the afternoons could be dry and blistering.

"In late August it can get a little warm, but it's not bad. Most people don't even run the air-conditioning until then."

"That's..." I started to say when the phone rang.

Mom snatched it up and spoke. "Hello," she said, putting her hand over the phone to cover her voice. "If this is Carl, perhaps the two of you should leave."

"Not on your life," I said.

"No way are we leaving!" Billy joined in.

For the next ten minutes, Mom gave Carl the tongue-lashing he deserved. Billy sat there in amazement, occasionally making remarks about what a tough cookie Mom could be. Finally, she handed me the phone. "He wants to talk to you."

I buried the phone in my hand. "What did he say?" All I had gotten from her side of the conversation were yells and accusations. She had really let him have it. "What were his excuses?"

"The same bull all men use when they are caught being bad boys,"

she snapped. "She doesn't understand me. It's not my fault. I made a mistake... or the lie some of them have the nerve to use—It's not true." She
sounded like she had first-hand experience. Had my Dad been unfaithful
to my mom? The thought nagged at me as I put my ear to the receiver.

"What do you want, Carl?" I spit.

Mom got up and started clearing the table, making grunting and hissing noises the whole time. They were the same noises that Billy makes
when he talks to me. The two of them were alike in many ways. They
showed their displeasure with gestures or mumblings, and when they were
happy or excited, they always wanted to hug you. I was just the opposite.
When I was mad, I would yell. When I was happy, I became quiet.

Carl whined in my ear. "Jesse, you need to talk to your mom. I tried to
tell her that this was all a misunderstanding. We are just having a little
spat. Now she has gone and blown it all out of proportion."

"Who has, Mom, or Claire?" I asked.

"Why, Claire, of course!" he said. He sounded like a wounded dog. "I
have been working late a lot, and she feels like I have neglected her. She
has even accused me of having an affair. It's..."

I couldn't listen to anymore of his lies. "Carl, get over it! Save it for
your lawyer." The next words out of my mouth were blissful to my ears.
"Did I ever tell you about the dream I had of you and a bear? The bear eats
you for dinner." I laughed like a hyena, as I hit the off button.

"You are a bad, bad girl, Jesse Watson," Billy growled. "Do you feel
better now?"

"Much," I gleamed. "Thank you."

"So, what did he have to say for himself?"

"The same things you said he would say," I answered.

Trying to bring peace back to our afternoon, Billy announced, "Men,
they are such pigs."

Mom and I got a good laugh out of his statement. Billy was a unique
person. He was first to admit the mentality of men in general, yet last to
own up to any responsibility of said genre. In other words, he could be a
man but have the insights of a woman. He knew what to say or do at just
the right time. From the day I met him and found out that he was Indian, in

my mind, I kept seeing him sitting bare-chested on a horse wearing full-feathered headgear... dark skinned, with his long, braided ponytail hanging down his back. In my vision, his slightly aged skin on his belly hung over the suede loincloth that he wore. But those were my pictures and I liked them. He was strong and loving. And he had a good heart.

"All right, ladies," he said. "We need to discuss tomorrow."

"What about tomorrow?" Mom asked. She finished cleaning up the mess from dinner and scraped the leftover food onto a plate. "Here, girl," she laid the plate on the ground for Athena.

"Mom, aren't you the one who told me not to feed the dog leftovers?" I asked.

"Well, I thought about it and I don't think it will hurt her once in a while. Dog food is so blasé."

Not only could my mother operate a gas grill, but also could critique the K-9 diet with an open mind.

"Mom, you are amazing," I said.

"Attention, Ladies!" Billy interjected. "We need to talk about tomorrow."

Mom and I looked at Billy.

"We need to decide what to do," he said. "I suggest we have the office calls transferred here. That way you can be at home with Claire and the kids, and still run the office.

"That is a great idea," Mom said. "What about you and Jesse? What are y'all going to be doing?"

"We have to go out of town on a job," Billy replied. "It's a short trip. We will be back by dinnertime."

"Does this have something to do with Helen Carrolton?" she asked.

Billy and I stared at each other.

"Unfortunately, it does," he responded. Before he told her the details, he adamantly said, "You must remember that whatever I tell you has to be kept in the up-most confidence."

"I know that," she replied.

"No, I'm serious. You can't tell anybody, not even Cole."

"Sure, I understand."

"Ok," he repeated. "Jesse and I might be going to Poquoson in the morning. We're pretty sure Helen Carrolton is dead, and this isn't something you can tell someone over the phone."

"How do you know? What evidence do you have?" she asked.

"Enough," was all he said.

I guess Mom could tell from the tone of Billy's voice that he had something pretty incriminating. She did not pursue the subject.

"Then it is settled. But first, I want you to show me how you are going to re-route your phone calls. Ok?"

"Sure," Billy smiled. "It is easy." He grabbed the portable and began the process of explaining as I cleaned up the rest of our mess.

I had a lot going through my head and I needed time to think. What about Helen's purse? How were we going to get it to the police in time to be able to tell the Carroltons about our discovery? What about that third print? What was I going to tell Cole?

"Billy," I interrupted, "Why don't we go for a walk? We need to talk."

They both looked up. Mom had been engrossed in what he was saying. She seemed so eager to learn what Billy was trying to show her that I hated to butt in, but I needed to get some answers.

"Go ahead," she said. "I've got it now. Thanks, Billy."

The three of us walked to the side of the house. As Mom walked up the steps to the utility room, she called out, "Hey, I think I'll run up to the IGA and pick up a few groceries. Does anybody need anything?"

"Not me," I replied. "What about Athena? Does she need some dog food? Do you need some money, mama?"

"Heaven's no," she said. "Your dad made sure of that. Just watch Athena while I am gone."

Billy and I went for a walk. Athena ran ahead of us, wagging her tail as she sniffed along the ground.

"Why is it that dogs always sniff everything?" I asked. I really didn't care. After talking to Mom about money, I realized I hadn't been paid since Dad had died and I was trying to get up the nerve to broach the subject with Billy. He had been so good to me, I hated to ask him for my check, but I was getting to the point where I needed some money.

As if he read my mind, Billy reached into the back pocket of his jeans and pulled out his wallet and said, "I have been meaning to give this to you, but I kept forgetting. You never ask for your paycheck and the only reason I remembered now was because you said something to your mother about needing money." He handed me three deposit receipts. "I have been putting your paychecks into your bank account each week, minus your car loan, ever since your dad died. You had enough on your mind as it was. Besides, I knew you would say something eventually. You just never did, and I forgot. I am sorry."

"But how did you know my account number?"

He chuckled, raised his eyebrow and gave me one of those looks. "You forget what I do for a living. I can find out almost anything I need to know. Besides, I snooped in your purse a while back."

"You dirty dog," I joked. Athena stopped in mid-stride and looked at me. "I wasn't talking to you, girl. I was talking to Mr. Nosy here." I glanced at the deposit slips, totaling it up in my head. "Billy, there's over fifteen hundred dollars in deposits. That's more than we agreed upon."

"Are you going to argue about money with me all the time?" Billy shook his head. "You earned every bit of it. So, take the money."

"That's fine with me. I'll go along with whatever you think is right." I folded up the receipts and stuck them in my pocket. I learned from past experiences that when Billy made up his mind there was no changing it.

We walked across the road and sat down on the rocks by the riverbank. Athena jumped in the water and started digging up rocks. I was shocked when she stuck her head under the water and came up with a rock between her teeth. She pounced over to us and laid it down.

"Did you see that?" I screamed, as I patted her on the head.

Billy smiled.

"Athena, you are such a smart girl," I praised her.

"Now what do you want to talk about?" Billy asked.

"Well, for starters, what are we going to do about Helen's purse? The fact that you even have it scares the crap out of me. What will you do if you get caught? I guess I'm just being paranoid."

"As soon as we get an I.D. on that last fingerprint, we will get Daniel's son, Greg to turn it over to the CPD."

"How soon do you think we will hear something?"

"I'm hoping it will be today. But you never can tell. That's why I said we might be going to Poquoson tomorrow."

Athena ran back up to us and dropped another rock at our feet. After shaking the water off her coat and spraying us with a fine mist, she laid down at my feet. Dogs!

"You know, I've been thinking about what you said about taking the Hudgins and Tom Dorey out of the equation. My idea of a serial killer just doesn't wash. Don't serial killers usually keep something of their victims as mementos? What would be better than a purse with the wallet inside?"

"Please continue," Billy said.

"What about money and credit cards? You never told me what exactly was found in her wallet."

"It seemed to be intact," he stated. "She had a driver's license, a Visa and Texaco card, two hundred dollars in cash and a few pictures."

"There, you see!" I exclaimed. "A serial killer would have kept all that stuff. Don't you think? But..."

"How do you know so much about serial killers?" he asked. "Don't tell me, let me guess... television?"

"You can learn a lot from television."

"Ditch the television. If you want to really learn something, take a class at the university. They offer a good course in Criminology."

"I might just do that," I hissed. "Let's get back to my questions. If a young adult committed this crime, such as our boy Jay, he was probably scared at the time and didn't think to take the wallet out of the purse when he tossed it. His goal was to get rid of the evidence as fast as he could."

"That's assuming he's the killer."

"Right," I added. "What about the car and the body? Neither one has been found. Hiding a body would be easier than hiding a car."

"Look around, Jesse," he motioned. "You could dump a body anywhere and it might never be found. But a car is a different story. Why, you'd almost have to dig a hole and bury it to keep the police from finding it."

Something was nagging at me but I just couldn't put my finger on it. Where was that car?

Billy answered the ring of his cell phone. "Hello... Caroline, what have you got for me? ... I was afraid of that. Ok... I will be right there." He folded the phone up and hooked it back onto his belt.

"What is it? Did she get an I.D. on the print?"

"Yeah, it was Greg's. She pulled up his print from the I-dent-A-Kid file that the school system started some time ago," he muttered. "I suspected it might be his all along. I knew we couldn't get that lucky." Billy stood up and brushed the dirt off his pants. "Let's get back to the house."

"So, what's next?" I asked, as we walked up to the house. "Are we going to go get the purse?"

"I'm going," he said. "I don't want you with me when I have it in my possession. No need for both of us to go down if I get caught."

"But you won't get caught, will you?" I was worried.

"Not me!" he exclaimed. "But just to be on the safe side, I want you to stay here until I get it back to Daniel. He will take care of getting it to the authorities. Don't worry. I can handle it."

"Call me the minute you are finished."

I SPENT THE NEXT HOUR IN A TIZZY. Mom had gone to the grocery store and hadn't returned. My imagination was working overtime. How long could it take to buy a few groceries? Then I thought about Dad. What if something happened to Mom? I was about ready to get in my Jeep and go looking for her when she pulled up into the driveway. I met her at the door.

"Where have you been? I was worried sick," I cried.

She looked at me like I had lost my mind. "Calm down, Jesse. I'm fine. I ran into Cole at the grocery store. He asked about you." Her arms were full of bags. "Here, grab these and I'll get what's left out of the van." I took the bags and sat them down on the kitchen counter, then walked back out to the porch and down the steps to the van.

"What did you tell him?" I asked. Knowing my mom, there is no telling what she might have said.

She handed me one of the two remaining bags and shut the van door. "I didn't tell him anything you wouldn't want me to," she confirmed. "I told him about our cook-out today, and about Claire and the kids coming. What's the matter with you Jesse? You're a nervous wreck."

"I'm sorry, Mom. It's just that I was worried about you."

"It's because of what happened to your dad, isn't it?"

My eyes welled up with tears. I felt like a little kid again as Mom patted me on the back. "You've got to get over this worry honey. Your dad had a bad heart. Me? I'm healthy as a horse. I'll probably out-live all my kids," she joked. "Come on in the house and let me fix you a cup of tea, or better yet... maybe a shot of whiskey. You look like you could use one!"

"Are you offering me whiskey?" I groaned, as I wiped the tears away with the back of my hand. "What are you doing with whiskey?"

"Oh, your dad took a nip or two every once in a while," she commented. "I have all kinds of alcohol."

I helped her put the groceries away, and listened to her ramble on about how she and Dad would fuss over him taking a drink.

"I told him it was bad for his heart, but he wouldn't listen to me. He said his doctor said it was ok... so it must be ok. What do doctors know? Huh?" She reached down into the cabinet beside the refrigerator and pulled out a bottle, while I got two glasses out and sat them on the counter.

She put one back and said, "None for me honey. You know I never touch the stuff. I tried it once and it made me gag. It's the nastiest tasting liquid I have ever put in my mouth... and that includes the time your brother peed in my face when he was a baby." She giggled. "Now that was a trip!" She poured a small amount and handed it to me. "Your dad says to gulp it all down in one swallow. That's probably because it tastes so bad."

I did as she said, and she was right. It was awful. I thought I was going to choke to death as I said, "Whew! That's nasty! How about one more? My nerves are shot," I explained. The second one went down a lot smoother. "That's enough. I don't think I could get another one down."

She put the bottle away.

"Where's Billy? I was hoping he'd hang around until Claire got here."

"He had to leave," I said. "But he promised to call later." The alcohol was starting to kick in and my nerves were settling down. "I think I'll give Cole a call. Do you think he's home yet? I didn't see him go by."

"Perhaps he took Turkey Ridge Road to his house," she suggested. "He told me it led to a short cut."

I walked over to the wall phone in the dining area and dialed his phone number. I was really starting to feel pretty good. Maybe there's something to this drinking, I thought to myself.

"I guess he is not at home," I said. "He didn't answer the phone."

"Maybe he's outside," Mom replied.

"He might be," I said. "I think I will run up to his house and see if he is home. I would like to talk to him."

"Jesse, you can't do that!" she snapped. "You've been drinking."

"I'm just going up the road. I won't even be on the main roads," I retorted. "I'll even take my cell phone, if it makes you feel better."

"I don't like it!" she announced. "I don't like it one bit! Why don't I drive you? You should not be driving in your condition."

"No thank you!" I fussed. "If you're that determined, I won't go."

"Good!" she huffed.

In the middle of our discussion, the doorbell rang. Mom sashayed over to answer it.

"Cole! I'm so glad it's you!" she said, ushering him inside. "I was just telling Jesse she couldn't drive up to your house. She's been drinking! Perhaps you can explain to her the dangers of drinking and driving."

Oh, Lord. Here we go again.

"I said I wouldn't go! Didn't I?"

"Drinking and driving is dangerous and it's against the law," he agreed with Mom. "I can't tell you how many times I've helped scrape bodies off the road because someone had too much to drink. It's not a pretty sight."

"Ok... ok... I get the picture."

Mom walked over to me, gave me a hug and said,"Don't get mad, honey. We're concerned about your safety. Aren't we, Cole?"

"Absolutely!" he replied.

"Why don't I leave you two alone for a while?" she asked. She motioned for Athena to follow her. "Athena, let's go outside and play ball." She looked at us. "Athena loves for me to toss her the ball, don't you girl?"

Once they were outside, Cole walked up to me and planted a big kiss on my lips. "I've missed you so much," he said.

I started to melt. His sweet smell and the gentleness of his touch was intoxicating. "Whew, I'm already 'bout drunk," I stammered. "Now you come along and make me crazy."

"What am I going to do with you?" he asked, wrapping his arms around me. "I'm so crazy about you that I don't know what to do with myself, and you turn out to be nothing but trouble."

"What are you talking about?"

He drew back and looked at me with those bright blue eyes. "Oh, I think you know where I'm coming from. How long did you think you were going to keep me from finding out the truth?"

His tanned, muscular arms were still wrapped around my waist. I was afraid if he let go, he would walk away and not come back. That was the last thing I wanted. He reached up to swipe a lone, blond curl of hair out of his eye. In that instant, I placed both my hands on his shoulders and ran them down his arms—a gesture I hoped he would find seductive. We had developed a relationship that was both physically exciting and emotionally stimulating, and I was determined to do everything I could to hold onto it, even stretch the truth... lie... whatever... it didn't matter. When it came to Cole, I had lost all the moral up bringing my mother had ever tried to bestow on me. I could play dirty... I think.

"You want the truth?" I asked, shyly. "Cole, I never lie to you." Now, I had really sunk low.

"Maybe you don't out-right lie," he suggested, "but, you sure know how to skirt around the truth." He released his hold on me and walked over to the front window. He stood there, staring out into the yard as if he was in a trance. I walked over to him and pressed up against his back. My arms instantly went around his waist.

I knew Billy would probably kill me for what I was about to say, but I didn't care. I could not lose Cole.

"I'll tell you the truth about anything you want to know. All you have to do is ask. But remember, at the same time you have to be totally honest with me." I let that sink in.

His hands came up and folded over mine. "Jesse," he whispered, "I haven't felt like this in a long time and I'm scared to death. I'm afraid I'm going to fall in a black hole and never be able to crawl out." He turned and looked at me. "We could have such a good life together, but..."

"Go ahead and say it." I said, waiting for the other shoe to drop.

"But," his voice cracked, "we're on opposite sides of the fence." His eyebrows curled up and the expression on his face made me feel like a dog that had just been scolded for digging in the flowerbeds.

"Who cares?" I vehemently demanded. "So what if we're not perfect? You want to know the truth? All right I'll tell you the truth starting with this." I pointed to my shoulder. "We did pull over to the side of the road and at one point in time I think I might have looked at some flowers. I probably even thought of picking some for my mother. I didn't fall on a pile of rocks and scrape up my shoulder. The truth is, Billy and I were hunkered down in the woods next to the Hudgins' house and Jay surprised us with a gunshot blast to my shoulder. You know the Hudgins, don't you?" I let go of Cole and walked into the kitchen. This was territory I didn't want to go into, but we were beyond that. The alcohol had set my lips free and there was no stopping now. "Yes... I'm sure you do. I'm sure you know all about the Carrolton case. That's your job, right?"

"I'm not directly involved, but I am familiar with the case," he said, meandering over to where I was standing. "Why? What do you know?"

"Well, I know enough to know that we have her purse, and you can bet the bank on her being dead."

His face was indescribable. "You've been concealing evidence from the police?" he yelled. He slapped his forehead and began pacing the floor. "I don't believe it! I knew this was going to happen the minute you hooked up with Billy. How many times did I try to warn you about him? Huh?"

"You don't understand," I said. "It's not what you think." My stomach was tied in knots.

He stopped pacing and pointed his finger at me. "Do you have the slightest idea what is going to happen to you when the cops get wind of this? They're going to throw your butt in jail! And there's not a thing I can do about it."

"But, I didn't do anything!" I pleaded. "I didn't know anything about it until it was too late. Please, just let me explain."

I could see he was wrestling with his emotions as he came over to me and touched my face. "Ok, start from the beginning. I'll try to help as much as I can but I can tell you right now, don't lie to me, and don't leave anything out."

I had opened a can of worms and the only thing left for me to do was to come clean. I told him everything that happened, starting with our first visit to the Hudgins', right up to Billy leaving to go pick up the purse. I felt better afterwards, but I knew I would pay for it when Billy found out. I assured Cole the purse would be in the hands of the police soon and everything would be fine as long as everybody kept quiet.

CHAPTER 21

"YOU DID WHAT?" Billy screamed into my ear over the phone. "Jesse, I leave you alone for one minute and your brain takes a hike. What is the matter with you? Don't you realize he has no choice but to report us? He's a cop, for Christ's sake!"

"You don't have to get huffy with me," I whined. "Besides, he promised to take care of everything."

"You can bet he will." The line went silent for so long, I thought he had hung up. Finally, he said, "Does your mother know any of this?"

"Yes, she knows all of it."

"All right, here's what we're going to do. Pack a few things and I'll take you to my folks for a couple of days. That'll buy us some time."

"I can't do that, Billy. Claire is coming and Mom needs me to be here. I can't leave now."

He ranted and raved about being led away in handcuffs in front of my family, including the kids, but I finally won over. I convinced him that I wasn't going anywhere. If the police were going to arrest me, then so be it. I wasn't going to run away from anything anymore. I don't know if it was the alcohol talking, or if I was going over the edge, but I had to bring things to a halt. Life was getting too complicated.

"Jesse, are you all right? You don't sound too good."

"I don't feel so good." I dropped the phone and ran down the hall to the closest bathroom. I managed to get the toilet lid up just in time to puke my guts out. I felt awful. After I recover from this, I'm never going to drink again... ever, I told myself.

Ten minutes later, as I stood in front of the mirror washing my face Mom knocked on the door and said, "Honey, are you ok?"

"I'm fine, Mom. I'll be out in a minute," I could barely answer. A few minutes later, I thought I heard voices in the living room. God, please let that be Athena she's talking to, I prayed. Pulling myself together as much as possible, I opened the bathroom door and peeked out. "Aw, crap," I mumbled under my breath as I walked out to face the music.

"You look like shit," Billy said. "Oops, I'm sorry Mom."

"It's all right, son. She does look pretty awful."

"What is this?" I snapped. "I'm dying here, and you two turn into the Brady Bunch. What about me? I feel like I'm going to die. I'm going to jail, and the two of you stand there critiquing the way I look." My self-pity floated through the room as I broke down and cried.

"I'm sorry, dear," Mom said, as she and Billy engulfed me in hugs. "We didn't mean anything by it, did we, Billy?"

He had that puppy-dog look on his face. I half expected him to shake his head and wag his tail.

"We were just making an observation," he said. "You do look a little rough, Jesse."

I had to laugh at the silly way they were acting. They say laughter is an escape route and I desperately needed something to help me escape the scared feeling I was harboring. I didn't know what was going to happen next, but I was sure it wasn't going to be fun.

"We're going to jail, aren't we?" I cried.

"No, we are not," he replied. "Come over here and sit down. We need to talk, if you think you are up to it."

"Why don't I fix some coffee?" Mom asked, walking to the kitchen. "I think Jesse could use some."

"I think that's a good idea," he whispered.

"I had to tell Cole the truth," I turned to Billy and said. I tried to explain why I had betrayed his confidence. "I love him and I couldn't lie to him anymore. I don't want to lose him. You just don't understand what it is like to find someone you can truly love."

"Oh, I think I do. I know exactly how you feel," he sympathized. "I know how it feels to love someone so much that you would do anything to keep them. Love does weird things to you. But for now, we have to concentrate on getting out of this mess in one piece."

"What are we going to do?"

"First off, where is Cole?"

"He said something about damage control and went home. Said he was going to clean up your mess, again. What did he mean by that?"

"It's not important," he said, pulling out his cell phone. "Get yourself together and follow me. We are going for a visit." With that said, he got up and walked to the door. "I'll wait for you in the truck." His gaze flicked over to the kitchen where Mom was still fixing coffee. "Save the coffee for later, Mom. Jesse and I need to do some damage control of our own before things get totally out of hand."

Cole was sitting on the steps, drinking a beer when we parked in the driveway. It was almost dark and I could see the sun beginning its descent into the night. Shadows lined the haggard face of an otherwise handsome man. He was deep in thought.

Billy looked at me and said, "You still think he's taking care of things?"

I didn't reply. I got out of the truck and ran to Cole. I wanted to wrap my arms around him and make the last few days disappear. But it was too late now. The look in his eyes told me everything I needed to know. Things were bad and most likely were going to get worse.

Surprisingly, he hugged me and reached out his hand to Billy, shaking it repeatedly. "You lucky son-of-a-gun," he said. "Somebody loves you, and it sure isn't me." Cole gestured for us to sit down and offered us a beer as he opened the lid of the cooler next to him.

"Not me," I replied. "I've had enough to drink for one day." I sat down and waited for the bomb to explode.

"I'll take one," Billy said.

The three of us sat on the steps watching the sun go down.

"Ok, how much trouble are we in?" I finally asked.

"It's funny how things work. I called in to report what was obviously an erroneous tip made by a drunken female, and was told about the startling discovery of a vital piece of information. A worker picking up trash for the Adopt-A-Highway program turned in a purse to the CPD. And we all know who owns the purse. The CPD has been searching for this girl for months. Anyway, my information was moot at that point."

Whew! We were off the hook. I leaned over and kissed him. "Thank you," I whispered. "I love you."

"Don't thank me. I didn't do anything. The important thing is the police have their first real lead in months." He stared into Billy's eyes. "I made my report. I did my job. What happens now is anybody's guess."

Billy's cell phone rang. He got up and walked off to the side. "We'll be right there," he said, closing up his phone and returning to me. "Your sister is here. That was your mom on the phone. We need to get back." He reached out his hand again and said to Cole, "I won't forget this."

"Just take better care of my girl. I mean it."

Thanks to the man I love, I wasn't going to jail this time.

"I told you he would take care of everything," I bragged, as we pulled into my driveway. "He loves me. I knew he would not let me get into trouble over this little mishap."

"You're in another world, girl," Billy said. "It's not over till it's over."

"You sound like Mom."

Billy parked on the right side of the house next to Mom's van. In front of the detached, three-car garage, sat two automobiles. Billy got out and asked, "Who drives the new Camaro? What a great looking car. I want one of those."

"Then why don't you buy one? I know you have the money, and if you don't, you can always get Daniel to fix you up with a good deal. No money down, no interest, and no payments until 2010," I poked fun at him. "I'm sure he can work out a deal to fit your every need."

"Don't be cute, Jesse," he hissed, as he closed the utility room door behind us. We walked into the dining room and found Mom at the table with my brother Jack, and a man I can only describe as an Adonis—the youthful, gorgeous, perfect replica of what God designed men to be. Claire was asleep on the sofa, wrapped in a quilt, a book lying beside her.

The first words out of my mouth were, "Where are the kids?" It was the only thing I could think of to say after I looked around and evaluated the situation. Claire was stretched out on the sofa, while the kids were probably sleeping peacefully upstairs and hopefully not in my bed. Jack was sitting at the table with a man that I was sure was not just another pretty face. Mom had the weirdest expression on her face.

"Jesse... Billy," she stood up and motioned. "This is Dennis—Jack's partner," she introduced us.

After all the confusion and chaos that has over-taken my life since I moved here, why not a little more? My underlying suspicions of my brother being gay had just been confirmed, and my puritan sister was a drunk. As for me, I was still dealing with my own demons.

Billy walked passed me without showing the least bit of surprise. "Nice to see you again," he said to Jack, extending his hand to him, and then to Jack's friend. "Fortunately, this time it's under different circumstances. How have you been?"

"Just fine, thank you."

"You're here early," I said. "I thought you weren't coming until this weekend." I glanced in Dennis' direction and understood why Jack would want him as his partner. What a looker! At the same time, I wondered if Mom understood the meaning of the word partner, and how it applied to this situation. I had my doubts.

"They're going to stay all week!" Mom gladly said. "I hope you two don't mind sharing a room. Jesse has offered to let you stay in hers, but we had not planned on it being a whole week. But we will work it out."

"Don't worry about it, Mom," Jack announced. He looked over at his partner and smiled. "We needed a vacation, so we got us a room at a little bed and breakfast just outside of Stanardsville. We don't want to impose on anybody for that long."

"But that's so expensive," she replied. "I don't want you to spend all your money on a place to stay."

"It is not expensive," he said. "You'd be surprised."

I pulled up a chair and sat down. My head was pounding and my stomach was churning. Now I remembered why I did not drink alcohol anymore. I put that out of my mind and tried to carry on a decent conversation.

"So, what do you do for a living, Dennis?"

"He's a lawyer, silly," Mom said. "They're partners, remember?"

That answered my question. Mom didn't know. She had no clue.

"Mom, I think you misunderstood," I slowly tried to introduce the meaning of their relationship. "I think what Jack is trying to tell you is that they are in an intimate relationship like me and Cole."

Mom jumped and shouted, "That is not true! Tell her Jack!"

The room fell silent as Jack reached out to take Mom's hand and said, "Mom, I've been trying to tell you that for the last half-hour."

"You are not one of those queers, are you?"

"Mom, don't say that!" I yelled. "We don't use that word. It is a slur. Jack is gay, mama."

I saw the relief in Jack's face. He had obviously spent many confused years in his life coming to terms with his sexuality. Now it was all out on the table and we had to deal with it.

Mom stood there, rubbing her hands together while she studied something imaginary on the floor. A couple of minutes passed before she could bring herself to speak. Slowly, she lifted her head. "I apologize to both of you. I didn't mean anything ugly. I was just surprised, that's all. Please, give me some time to think about it." She whimpered, went to her room, and slammed the door. Athena jumped up from her crouching position by the window and ran after her.

Claire bounced off the couch, springing to life. "What's going on?" she asked. "I fell asleep." She looked haggard and in a daze, but still had the composure of a fine woman. "You'll have to excuse my appearance. I've been... Jack! When did you get here?" She walked into the dining room and gave him a hug.

"Jesse! I'm so glad to see you! How are you doing, Billy?" Claire had covered all the bases, except one. "Who's the handsome man?" she asked, pointing to Dennis.

I still had a headache and I was tired of pussyfooting around. "This is Dennis—Jack's boyfriend."

Claire didn't even flinch. "It is so nice to meet you, Dennis," she said, holding out her hand. "I'm glad you could come for a visit."

I decided right then and there that Claire was not only a drunk, but she must be taking some heavy medication. Her whole life had evolved around up-tight and moral standards that none of us could live up to. Yet, here she was being the picture of perfection. Nothing appeared to faze her. Did she already know about Jack being gay?

Claire was comfortable with the situation and I didn't have a problem with my newfound knowledge. So, why was I having this uncomfortable feeling in the pit of my stomach? I was worried because of Mom. How was she going to deal with having a son that was gay? Would she come around? So many changes had occurred in the last few months, nothing would surprise me. I was just about ready to call it a day when I heard a door open and Mom walked back into the room.

She spoke to us as a group. "You will have to excuse my earlier behavior. This is all new to me." Her gaze fell directly on Jack. "Maybe one day you can sit down and explain the meaning of a gay relationship to me. I just don't understand it all. In the meantime, I want you and Dennis to feel right at home."

What a day! Perhaps some things did surprise me.

"Well, you will have to excuse me," I said. "I've got to go to bed. It has been a long day and I am beat."

Billy had been sitting quietly at the table. "I think it's time for me to go home. It was nice to meet you Dennis. It has been a pleasure to see you all," he said, as he got up from his seat. "I'll call you in the morning, Jesse. Good night Mom." He leaned over and gave her a kiss.

I went to bed that night with the headache from hell. I tossed and turned for what seemed like forever. Dreams of my brother doing all kinds of immoral acts and my sister falling all over herself in a drunken stupor clouded my night. But I knew that wasn't true. My sister was not really a drunk and who cares if Jack is gay? That's life.

A flash of something awoke me. I rolled over and looked at the clock beside my bed. Two A.M.! What was that? I thought to myself. Then it came to me. I had been dreaming about the Hudgins' place. I was standing on the front porch looking at the small green mound through the trees off in the distance. It was a cozy place that would be great for a picnic. But something else was bothering me. Now I remember! I jumped out of bed and ran to the bathroom. Splashing water on my face to wake myself up, I realized what it was that was so eerie about our last visit. I couldn't put my finger on it at the time, considering the place was in such a mess from the antics of a pissed-off teenager, but something was nagging at me. Somewhere in the back of my head I kept hearing what Billy had said to me while we were at the river, *"A car is a different story. You'd almost have to dig a hole and bury it, to keep it hidden from the police."*

That was it! I could feel it. Jay Hudgins had killed Helen Carrolton and buried her car in the woods. That's why the car hasn't been found. But why hasn't the body surfaced? Did he dump her off in some remote area, hoping nobody would find the body until she had turned into nothing but bones? What about DNA. DNA tells you everything about a person, whether it comes from one single hair, or a drop of saliva. Bones are a dead give-away. But why would he kill her? What was his motive? Was I grabbing at straws?

The house was quiet, yet I was wide-awake. I didn't want to wake anybody, but I couldn't go back to sleep after what was going through my head. I tiptoed downstairs and went to the kitchen. I heard a thump in Mom's bedroom and then the click of toenails on the hardwood floor. Athena came around the corner , wagging her tail. I bent down and rubbed her coat. She responded by licking my hand.

"Did I wake you, girl?" I whispered. I walked over to her food and water bowl. "Yep, you have plenty of food and water. Ole' grandma takes pretty good care of you, doesn't she?" She looked up at me. Her legs slid out from under her as she plopped down in the middle of the floor, rolled over and threw them up in the air. "Oh, you want a belly rub, huh?" I rubbed her stomach and watched her legs twitch. Dogs—it doesn't take much to make them happy. Too bad people aren't that easy to please.

I searched the cabinet for the jar of instant coffee. I knew Mom kept it somewhere. I was hoping coffee would help clear my head. I got a cup down, filled it with water and put it in the microwave. The buzzer on the microwave blared through the downstairs like a sonic boom. "Darn!" I screeched, as I hit the off button as fast as I could. Unlike me, Mom had always been a sound sleeper, but it was so quiet here, I figured it wouldn't take much to wake her up. Or was it Dad that was a sound sleeper? I couldn't remember. My mind was totally off somewhere in left field and for some reason I just couldn't think straight. I had to talk to Billy.

Adding milk to my cup of coffee, I picked it up and went over to the table and sat down. I could sure use a cigarette right about now, I thought to myself. As usual, the lamp in the living room had been left on and cast a dim glow across the coffee table. Mom had always left a light burning at night ever since I could remember. Speak of the devil! There in plain sight was Claire's pack of cigarettes. The *only* flaw my sister had was that she smoked. I ran over and picked up the pack. Should I... or shouldn't I? I had quit smoking a long time ago, so one here and there wouldn't hurt. I lit up and took a deep drag. It was so nasty, I thought I was going to puke, but I didn't put it down. That would turn out to be a big mistake.

I sat at the table, drinking coffee and smoking cigarette after cigarette, trying to decide what to do. Should I call Billy and tell him I was having these revelations? He already thinks I am halfway crazy because I let my heart lead me around. What if I am completely wrong about Jay Hudgins? What if I am persecuting an innocent person? What am I doing in the middle of this mess, anyway? I'm no private investigator. I don't know what I'm doing. I couldn't put these questions out of my head, yet at the same time, I could not get over this nagging feeling that I was right. Who else could it be?

I picked up the phone and dialed Billy's number.

"This better be good," he ranted, coughing into my ear.

"Billy, this is Jesse. I need to talk to you. Are you awake?"

"Right," he said. "I'm always awake at... 2:30. What's the matter? Is something wrong? Is everyone all right?"

"Everybody is fine. I just need to talk to you."

"Can't it wait until the morning?"

"No, it can't. It is important, and I want to talk about it now."

He made a rumbling noise, and I heard the flick of a light switch. "Ok," he said. "I'm awake now. What is so important?"

"I think I know the location Helen Carrolton's car."

"Is this another one of your gut feelings, or do you actually have some evidence?"

"Don't make fun of me. Gut feelings are not without merit."

"Sure."

I lit another cigarette.

"Are you smoking?" he asked. "You are smoking! This must be good. Tell me what you are thinking."

"Remember when you told me you would almost have to bury a car to get rid of it?"

"What? Yeah, I remember saying something like that. So what? It didn't mean anything. People don't just go around digging holes in the ground and burying cars in them. What is your point?"

"I never told you, but one time I saw something that was a little odd. It was a mound of dirt covered with what looked like brand new grass. It was off in the woods. I saw it through a tiny slit in the trees. Anyway, it was just the right size."

"The right size for what?" he asked, obviously confused.

"Allowing for the size of the car and the displacement of dirt, it would be the right size for someone to have buried a car there."

"Where did you see this?"

"At the Hudgins' place, silly," I replied. "Someone buried Helen's car on the property and I am willing to bet she is in it."

"You are crazy. I'm going back to bed. We'll talk about it in the morning," he hissed, and hung up the phone.

Perhaps it wasn't a good idea to call Billy. I woke him and he was not the nicest person in the middle of the night.

"Ok, be that way," I growled, slamming down the phone.

I crawled back into bed and tried to get over my hurt feelings. What's the matter with him? Doesn't he realize I am onto something? Why can't he see that I am right?

I slept peacefully. As daylight filtered through my open bedroom window, I rolled over and felt the tiny hands of a child stroking my head.

"Let's play!" I heard a tiny voice say.

I opened my eyes and saw Claire walk into the room.

"I'm sorry," she said. "But Benny wanted to come see his Aunt Jesse." She gently took hold of his hand and started to lead him out.

"Hey, it's ok," I replied, sitting up in bed. "Come on over here, Benny. I haven't seen you in a long time. What you been up to?"

He jumped up on the bed and yelled, "Ant Jess, I missed you."

"You did?" I asked, hugging him. "You have gotten so big. Look at you. You're so handsome. How old are you, now? Ten?"

He giggled.

"He will be five in September, and Carrie will be three in August," Claire said as Carrie squiggled in her arms. "Come on, Benny. Grandma's cooking breakfast." She held out her hand. "Let's go down and get something to eat. I'm hungry, aren't you?"

Benny jumped off the bed and followed his mother. Their footsteps were quiet compared to the laughter they shared as they went down the stairs. I wanted that so badly... kids... family... and a good husband to love.

I glanced over at the clock. It was six o'clock. I did not have to get up for another hour. Don't these people ever sleep late? Mom was downstairs fixing breakfast, and Claire was running around being herself. I didn't need to get up for another hour. Then I thought about last night. I sprang out of bed and grabbed my robe. I had to get moving. I wanted to get to work as fast as I could so Billy and I could talk. I had to prove to him that my theory was right. I was sure I knew where to find Helen Carrolton!

I took a quick shower. My shoulder was scabbing over, so I didn't bother to put a dressing on it. I slipped into one of the cotton skirts and a silk blouse I had purchased when I first met Billy. Searching my closet for a pair of matching heels, I reminisced about the day I bought the new clothes. It seemed like a lifetime ago. I folded a pair of jeans and a T-shirt and stuffed them in a duffel bag, along with my tennis shoes. I wasn't sure if we were still going to see the Carroltons, but I wanted to be ready for anything. I found my handbag lying on the floor and checked to make sure my gun was still in it. Grabbing my briefcase and my cell phone from the charger, I headed downstairs.

"Would you like something to eat?" Mom asked.

Claire was sitting at the table drinking coffee and smoking a cigarette, while the kids were on the floor playing with Athena.

"Just some coffee, please," I replied. "I'm in a hurry." I walked over to Claire and asked for a cigarette.

"I thought you quit," she smirked, reaching into the pack and pulling one out. "You know these things will kill you."

"I did quit. And you are a fine one to talk. Look at you."

They both eyed me suspiciously, but didn't make any comments about me falling off the wagon... again.

"Tell Billy if he needs me today for anything other than answering the phone to give me a call," Mom yelled out to me, as I ran out the door.

Chapter 22

As usual, the traffic on Rt.29 was moving at a snail's pace. Up ahead, the police were working an accident at the Forest Lakes intersection. This reminded me of the traffic in Newport News—always congested. Perhaps I should find an alternate route to work, I thought. This was nerve racking. I stopped at a gas station and bought a pack of cigarettes, just in case my addiction had returned.

I pulled into the parking lot and noticed a white Buick laden with antennas parked beside Billy's old Mercury. It was too early in the morning for him to be seeing clients, so I could only assume the worst. I hesitated to enter, but knew I could not put off the inevitable. It was time to face the consequences of our deeds. I grabbed my handbag and briefcase, shut off my Jeep, and went inside. Billy was standing by my desk talking to two gentlemen. The familiar beep-beep of the alarm caught their attention.

"Good morning, Jesse," he said, walking over to help me with my briefcase. "This is Detective Hargrove and his partner, Detective Willis from the Charlottesville Police. They've been asking questions about the Helen Carrolton case." He led me over to my desk and sat my briefcase down. Looking at the two men, Billy introduced me as his secretary.

I could only imagine what this was all about as I searched for the right things to say. I looked at Billy, noticing the small beads of sweat on his forehead, and prayed I was doing the right thing.

"Is this about the purse your nephew found?" I asked.

Detective Hargrove was a tall, well-built black man with a shaved head and a pencil-thin mustache.

"So you know about the purse?" he asked.

"Well, not much, actually," I replied, sliding my handbag under my desk. The last thing I needed was for them to find a gun in my purse. "Billy's brother called and said his son found a purse in the woods while he was doing his volunteer work. He asked Billy what to do with it."

"What did Billy tell him?" the other detective asked. Detective Willis had short, red hair and freckles on his nose and cheeks. He was a foot shorter than his partner, and appeared to be twenty pounds lighter.

"First, he asked him if there was any identification in it."

"And was there?"

"Shockingly, there was," I said. "It belonged to Helen Carrolton. The Carroltons hired Mr. Blackhawk about a month ago. It seems they were unhappy with the progress of the police."

"That is a little convenient, don't you think, Miss Watson?" Detective Hargrove asked.

"Sir, I wouldn't know," I answered. "All I know is when Mr. Blackhawk found out who the purse belonged to, he immediately told his brother to turn it over to you guys."

"And did he?"

"I don't know, but I assume he did. It appears you have it. Why else would you be here?" I answered.

"Wouldn't it hinder your case if you were to turn the purse over to the police?" he asked.

"It's not my case. I'm sure that Mr. Blackhawk would agree that the most important thing is to find Helen Carrolton. Who finds her first is not important." I turned to Billy. "Isn't that right?"

Billy nodded his head in agreement.

The red-haired detective flipped through his pocket-sized notebook.

"I see according to my notes, Miss Watson, that you reported to Deputy James of the Greene County Sheriff's Department that Mr. Blackhawk had possession of the purse before it was turned over to the police. Is that correct?"

Trying to appear embarrassed by hanging my head and fiddling with the papers on my desk, I murmured, "Yes, I did." I looked at Billy. "I'm sorry." I turned my gaze to the two detectives. "You see, Deputy James and I date. We were having a conversation about the case, and when I told him about the find, I was kind of ... well, let's just say I had too much to drink. Normally, I'm not a drinker so it doesn't take much to get me a little tipsy. Anyway, I guess I led him to believe I knew more about what was going on than I really did. I wanted to impress him, so I embellished."

"So, what you're saying is, you filed a false report with the police?"

"What I'm saying is that I didn't file anything. All I did was talk to my boyfriend about it," I whined, looking in Billy's direction. "I'm sorry. I had too much to drink. I didn't realize everybody would take this so seriously. I made a mistake by shooting off my mouth." I turned back to the detectives. "All I know is, Mr. Blackhawk told his brother to go see you guys." I stared at Billy again. "Am I going to lose my job over this?"

Appearing patronizing, Billy put his hand on my shoulder and said, "No, Miss Watson, you are not fired. Everybody makes mistakes occassionally. I just hope you learned something."

Apparently, Detectives Hargrove and Willis believed my story. They mumbled something about confirming what Billy had already told them and if they had any more questions you could bet they would be back. They said good-bye, turned and left.

Once they got into their car, Billy grabbed me and gave me a bear hug.

"Damn, you were good! I thought for sure you'd lose it." He stepped back. "You made me proud. Are you always this good at telling stories?"

"The truth is I was scared to death," I answered. "All I could figure out to do was say what I thought you would say. I got lucky. It was obvious they had something. I just had to decide what it was."

"Well, you did a fine job," he patted me on the back. "Now, let's get to work. Call your mom and tell her we're in the office and we'll be answering the phone until about ten o'clock. After that, I'll have the calls for-warded to her. Mrs. Jordan is coming in at nine. She wants to talk to me about her daughter. Someone is stalking the girl."

"Wait a minute," I got in his face. "What about the case?"

"I'm getting ready to call the Carroltons right now."

"What are you going to tell them?"

"I'm going to up-date them on our progress. I will tell them about the purse and assure them that just because her purse has been found, it doesn't mean she's... well, you know. That's all we know for sure at the moment." He disappeared into his office and closed the door.

False hope were two words that came to mind.

In the meantime, I had called Mom and told her what Billy said. I filed paperwork that had been left in my basket, and went through the motions of being a secretary. I also fixed a fresh pot of coffee and sat at my desk drinking a cup, waiting for the outcome.

Twenty minutes later, Billy emerged from his office and said, "I talked to the Carroltons and told them we would keep them posted on any new developments. They were pretty upset. They wanted to pick up the purse, but I told them it would be held as evidence. They said they would wait to hear from us. What else can they do?"

"Ok," I said. "What are we going to do next?"

"Mrs. Jordan should be here any minute. After we talk to her, we are going for a little ride."

"Where are we going?"

Before answering my question, he stood there as if in a daze and then asked, "Think your mom would let us use your dad's little truck? Call her and ask," he insisted. "Seems to me she said one of the reasons your dad bought the truck was so he would have something he could drive through the woods. That's what we need to do... drive it through the woods. I don't want to take my truck through the brush, and I sure don't want you to take your new Jeep. I know the Mercury would have a hard time of it." He was rambling, as he left and walked back towards his office.

"Hold on, pal. What's going on?" I asked. He wasn't making any sense.

He stared at me. "We're going to follow up on your crazy suspicions and we need a tough, old rugged truck that can make it through the woods. So, get moving and call your mom."

I dialed the house and explained to Mom what we had in mind. She was more than glad to see someone get some use out Dad's truck. She said that he never really got to use it much. I told her we would be home to pick it up around noon.

"I'll have some lunch ready when you get here," she said.

I sat in and took notes while Mrs. Jordan explained to Billy about her problem. Her daughter, Angela, had been dating a college freshman at the university where she attended. When she decided to break it off, he didn't take it well. He started calling her all the time and kept leaving notes on the windshield of her car. He began following her everywhere she went.

"The police are doing all they can, but they said until they get some hard evidence of wrongdoing, their hands are tied," she continued. "He knows they are onto him, but he's smart and sneaky. They can't catch him at anything. It's been two months. My daughter is going out of her mind. She's scared to death. We need your help."

"I'll need to know everything about your daughter's habits: a list of her classes; where she eats; who her friends are; the whole nine yards. Any information about her lifestyle you can think of would be helpful. Don't worry, Mrs. Jordan," Billy said. "We'll take care of this guy."

Billy sounded like a hit man. All I did was sit there and take notes. It was not my job to judge. I'm sure Billy knew what he was doing.

"What was that all about?" I asked after she left. "You sounded like you were going to go out and hunt this guy down, and heaven forbid what would happen when you found him."

"That's about the size of it," he said. "You might want to change your clothes. Maybe dig something more comfortable out of the back of your Jeep. You know... dig something out of that Pandora's box you keep back there." He knew me all too well by now.

Billy and I were about to embark on another wild adventure. I could see it coming... jail was just a footstep away.

I changed clothes in the bathroom down the hall, while Billy waited impatiently by the front door. He was no longer dressed in his suit with the cowboy-stringed tie, but was clad in his familiar attire of jeans and a T-shirt.

"You sure are fast," I grunted.

Billy sat quietly in the passenger seat. I didn't have a whole lot to say either. The one thing that kept coming back to me was that Cole had done his job. He reported my statement to his superiors. Billy was right all along. Cole was an honorable man and would do what he had to do, regardless of the consequences. What I had to deal with was the fact that I would not be able to confide in him about certain aspects of my job. In other words I had to keep him at arm's length. This did not make for a good relationship.

"You're awfully quiet, Jesse," Billy spoke up. "What's on your mind?"

"I was just thinking about Cole."

"Yeah, I guess you know where the line is drawn now."

"Like my mother would say—live and learn."

It was eleven-thirty when we reached the house. Mom and Claire were just beginning to prepare lunch while the kids sat in front of the television watching cartoons. We had barely gotten in the front door when Jack and Dennis pulled into the driveway.

"It looks like the whole crew is here," I pointed to the window. "Jack just pulled in the driveway."

Mom stopped what she was doing and walked over to the wall phone. "I told Cole I would call him when y'all got here."

"What does he want?" I objected.

She turned to me with the phone in her hand and said, "He's having lunch with us. He said he wanted to talk to you before he goes on his four-to-twelve shift this afternoon."

"It will have to wait," I snapped. "Billy and I aren't staying for lunch. We're in a hurry. Can we have the keys to the Toyota, please?"

She hung up the phone and went over to the key rack hanging by the bar, removed the keys and handed them to me. The expression on her face said she knew something was going on, but was gracious enough not to bring it up in front of everybody.

"You might need to put gas in the truck," she said.

"Thanks, Mom." I gave her a quick peck on the cheek, and Billy and

I made a fast exit. I waved to Jack and Dennis as we entered the side door of the garage. I hit the door opener to raise the garage door.

"What was that all about?" Billy asked, as he tried to squeeze his large frame into the small truck.

"Nothing," I said, adjusting the seat up as close as I could so my feet would reach the clutch, and then turned on the ignition.

"Oh, this is going to be fun," he joked, pointing to his confined leg space. "Hey, I know you're pissed about something, but could you give me another notch for my legs? My knees are under my chin."

"Sorry," I said, as I adjusted the seat back a little.

The truck lurched and jerked as I tried to back it out of the garage, and then it stalled. It had been awhile since I had driven a stickshift. Billy threw his hands up on the dashboard and laughed at me.

"I'll get the hang of it in a minute," I said, restarting the truck. Billy rolled his eyes at me. I backed down the driveway and pulled up to my Jeep. After carefully loading his equipment into the back of the truck, we bucked and jerked our way down the driveway.

"Are you sure you don't want me to drive?" Billy asked, holding on for dear life. "You're giving me a whip-lash."

"See, I told you I would get the hang of it," I said, as we reached the end of South River Road.

"Yeah, but at what cost?" he asked. "My back will never be the same."

"WHINE... WHINE... WHINE," I joked, stopping at the stop sign. "Before we go any further, I want to know what we are doing. My last brush with the law was enough for one day."

"You're not quitting on me are you?"

"You know, I didn't sign up for this," I said, irritated.

"I know you didn't," he said, with a hurt look on his face. "If you want out, now is the time to tell me."

"No," I said. "I'm sorry. It's just that I'm mad at Cole and I'm taking it out on you."

"I figured that much," he whispered. "Do you want to tell me why?"

"I think you know. I don't want to talk about it right now."

"Whatever," he said, pointing to the road. "We're off to the cross-roads. Let's go 4-wheeling."

"This doesn't have four-wheel drive," I said, as I pulled onto Rt. 33 and headed to Zion Crossroads. We had made this trek so many times that by now the drive only took us forty minutes. We were cruising, listening to a radio station that Billy had picked out.

"What is this junk?" I motioned to the radio. "It sounds like somebody's dying. I feel like I should have a beer in my hand."

"It's country music," he stated. "Randy Travis is the best!"

"He makes my ears hurt."

"Listen to the words and you will wind up loving... hey, what the hell..." Billy said, as he turned and stared. Just ahead of us was a police roadblock closing off the road entrance to the Hudgins' house.

"Aren't we supposed to turn here?" I asked. "What do you want me to do? Speak fast!"

"Keep on going!" he demanded.

The police gave us a fleeting glance as we passed by. I tried not to draw attention to us by driving erratically, while Billy absorbed everything in sight.

"So, what did you see?" I asked.

"A couple of police cars, that's for sure. Keep on driving."

"Shall we have some lunch?" I asked Billy. We were fast approaching the Piney Mountain Grill, and I was hungry.

"Yeah!" he yelled. "That's a great idea. It'll give us a chance to see if anybody at the restaurant knows what is going on back there. You never know, we might get lucky."

"I just hope the food doesn't kill us."

I parked the truck in front of the grill and Billy and I got out. There were only two cars in the parking lot off to the side, and one of them was the Mustang. The other one was a beat up old Ford truck.

"Hey, isn't that Rose's car?" I asked. "I'm willing to bet the truck is Bubba's. I think you might be right, Billy. Maybe we will get lucky. The joint looks empty."

Inside, Rose was sitting on a barstool reading the paper, while someone in the back banged pots and pans. I assumed it was Bubba making that racket in the kitchen.

"Oh, it's you," she said, folding up the paper and staring at us. "Can I get you something to eat?" She slid off the stool and walked towards us. "As you can tell from the heat, the air conditioning is broken. So, if you can't stand the heat... well, you know the rest." She was not happy to see us.

Billy found a booth at the far end of the room away from the rays of the sun. "We'll sit over here," he replied. "Now, if you could just bring us a couple of ice teas and a menu, we would be grateful." He motioned for me to sit down.

I leaned over the table and whispered, "It's hot as hell in here, Billy." The restaurant had several ceiling fans and they were working overtime. Yet, they still couldn't alleviate the heat. "I will suffocate in here."

"Hang in there, kid," he said. "People sometimes act strange and say things they don't mean to when they get overheated. I want to see how hot I can get Rose."

"That's gross," I uttered. "Is this a sexual thing?"

"I hope you are kidding."

Rose returned with our drinks and said, "The special for today is fried chicken, mashed potatoes, and string beans." She handed us a menu. "We also have a hamburger boat for $2.95. It comes with fries, or potato chips. Just shout when you're ready to order." She walked away.

"I'm ready now," I called to her.

She came back to the table, pulled out her order pad and said, "What can I get you?"

"I'll take a cheeseburger boat, and maybe you can tell us what the police are doing at your house?"

She glared at me. "Why don't you ask them yourself?" She put her hands on her hips. "Or, maybe you already know. Why don't you tell me? They weren't there when I left this morning."

Billy butted in. "I'll take the cheeseburger boat, also."

"Two cheeseburger boats," she yelled at the top of her lungs and walked away. She acted cool, but I knew I had rattled her chain.

My ears were ringing from the noise. I stuck my finger in my ear and cried, "Give me a break!"

Billy scolded me. "This time, be quiet and let me do the talking. You're going about this all wrong. You're going to get her pissed."

"But, I thought that is what you wanted."

"I said I wanted to get her hot and make her sweat, not piss her off. There's a difference."

"I'll shut up," I sat back. "You talk to her, and I'll stay out of it."

The phone rang somewhere in the back and Bubba came out with a large pair of tongs in his hand. Rose had gone back to reading the newspaper in a feeble attempt on her part at ignoring us. He whispered something into her ear, and she jumped up and ran to the back.

"Ah, perhaps she didn't know the cops were at her house," I said to Billy, who by this time was engrossed in picking at his fingernails. "I bet that call is from someone at home. I thought she was a little too calm when we told her about the cops being there."

"I was just thinking the same thing myself," he replied. "We'll find out in a minute if she goes rushing out the door."

Two minutes later, she did exactly what Billy said. She ran out the door, purse in hand, with tears streaming down her face.

"I guess that answers our question," Billy said. He jumped up, pulled his wallet out and threw a five-dollar bill down on the table. "Come on, we are going to follow her."

"What about lunch?" I cried. "I'm starved."

"Forget lunch. We'll eat later," he insisted. We were just getting ready to walk out the door when Bubba walked up and blocked our exit. He stood poised and defiant, ready to react at a moment's notice.

"You folks don't want to leave without eating your meal first, now do you?" he stated, in a most demanding way.

"I left a five on the table," Billy pointed. "We have changed our minds. We are not hungry anymore."

"That's a load of crap," Bubba barked. "I know what you are doing. You're going after Rose." He raised a finger and poked it at Billy's chest. "I'm telling you right now, leave her alone!"

Billy's face turned red. Normally, he would never stand for anyone getting in his face like that, but Bubba's next move gave him pause.

Bubba took a step back, lowered his finger, and spoke in an octave quieter. "She's a good kid. She don't know nothing about that missing girl. Do us all a favor, and get off her back, please."

I just knew the situation was going to get out of hand. Billy is a big guy. He's six feet tall, and weighs close to two hundred pounds. He is strong as an ox. However, Bubba made Billy look like a kitten up against a mountain lion.

Billy's face faded back to its normal color. "We're not after Rose. All we're after is the truth," he said. Before Bubba could say anything, Billy continued. "As a matter of fact, we don't think she had anything to do with the missing girl. The problem is that the cops have evidence that was discovered on the Hudgins' property. They are all over it. They have cop cars blocking off the entrance to their road, search dogs in the woods, and helicopters flying overhead. It's a real circus."

"What evidence?" Bubba asked.

"I can't go into that," Billy said, acting like the hotshot investigator that he is. "It's classified and I can't give out that information. But I can tell you this, somebody had better get at the truth before Rose and her whole family winds up in jail."

Finally seeing the light, Bubba suggested, "Well, maybe somebody should check out that gas station guy, Tommy. He's Jay's best friend." He leaned in towards us and whispered, "They're both bad news. I can tell you that!" Then he stepped back to let us pass.

Billy and I made a quick exit, which was something we had been doing a lot of lately. We were constantly on the run.

"What kind of bull was that?" I asked, digging for my keys. "They've got helicopters? Search dogs? Did I miss something?"

"Just get in the truck," Billy commanded.

As usual, I did what he said. I got in the truck, cranked it up, and drove out of the parking lot.

"I didn't realize Helen's purse was found on the Hudgins' property," I stated. "I mean I knew it was close, but right on their property?"

"Well, it could have been."

"You are awful!" I admonished him, as I shifted gears. The truck made a loud, grinding, clanking noise. "Oops."

Rose's brake lights came into view as we rounded the curve and came up on her road. The two police cars were gone.

CHAPTER 23

"INTERESTING," Billy said. "Drive down the road a ways and make a U-turn. That will give her time to get home without seeing us behind her. We do not want to tip our hand."

I drove for about a mile until I found a place to turn around. Just before we reached her house, Billy motioned for me to keep going.

"Find a place to park where we can see them, but they can't see us."

"I thought this was a dead end," I replied. "There's a dead end street sign at the entrance to the road. But this sure doesn't look like a dead end to me. What's the deal?" As soon as the words were out of my mouth, the paved road came to an abrupt end, and a dirt path filled with ruts began.

"Shit!" I moaned, slamming on the brakes. I was unable to stop in time to avoid bouncing in and out of several potholes. Billy hit his head on the roof, and the truck stalled.

"You're the worst driver I have ever met," he said, rubbing his head.

"Don't yell at me. I'm doing the best I can."

"You're supposed to use the clutch, too... or did that slip your mind? You think you can turn this thing around without running into a ditch, or do I need to drive? I will if you want me to."

"I can handle it!" I smarted. I pushed in the clutch and restarted the truck. After several attempts at trying to get the truck turned around in such a small area, I backed into a huge pothole and the truck cut off once again. The rear bumper was now touching the ground.

Billy jumped out and slammed the door. "That's it!" he said. "I'm driving from now on!"

I started crying. I don't know if it was from stress or an inside desire to make him feel bad, but it didn't work.

"Stop whining, put it in neutral and steer, while I push," he instructed. "Hit the brakes as soon as you are out of the hole. There's a gully in front of you." I heard him mumble something under his breath.

My reaction time was very slow sometimes, and this was one of those times. I ended up with the front tires in the gully just like he said, and the bumper was now firmly planted on top of a big rock.

It was like something you'd see in a movie. Billy slapped his forehead and walked in circles, while I cried.

"*U-lv-no-ti-s-gi `ge ya!*" he yelled, walking from the rear of the truck to the front. "*Tla-i-`go-li-`ga.* Didn't you hear what I said?"

By now, he had lost all patience with me. I didn't know what to say and I hated it when he said stuff I didn't understand. All I could come up with was the two Indian words I had memorized, "*Da-qua-dov Tse-si*"— my name is Jesse.

That stopped him cold in his tracks and he burst out laughing. "You're nuts." He went back to the front of the truck, lifted it up off the rock and pushed it out of the gully. "Now, hit the brakes!" The truck came to rest in the middle of the road. "Pull the handbrake," he ordered, "and get out."

As usual, I did what he said. This was fast becoming a habit. He tells me what to do, and I do it.

Surveying the truck, he said, "Who taught you how to drive anyway? Athena?" Before I could get my two cents in, he got in the truck, read-justed the seat and pulled it off the road behind the trees.

"Hey, look at this Billy. There's a path over here with imprints of a bulldozer. It looks like someone took a bulldozer and plowed right through the woods," I said, as I walked towards the truck. "And you can see it goes all the way back there." I pointed in the direction of the tracks.

He got out of the truck and walked over to where I was standing.

"The tracks are old," he said. "See the mashed, dead leaves in the grass? That means whoever did this, did it some time ago."

"Maybe some time around Christmas?"

"The timing would be just about right," he said. "Let's see where the path leads. He walked over and locked up the truck doors and the camper shell. "Don't want anyone to steal my equipment."

"This must have been a road of some sort at one time," I guessed. "There are a few remnants of saplings, but no large trees."

The sun was high in the sky and blasting down on us with all its intensity. A slight breeze in between the trees hit my sweaty face and cooled me. I felt like I was going to fall out from the heat.

"I can tell summer is here," I said, wiping the moisture off my face with my shirttail. "Man, it is hot."

Billy looked at me, rolled his eyes and said,"This is not hot, baby. "

We scouted for what seemed like forever, when, dead ahead of us in the middle of the path, was the hill I had tried to explain to Billy. The top of the mound was about three feet tall and it was wide enough that if you dug a hole and put a car in it, it would be the perfect size. My deductive reasoning was working at maximum overdrive.

"See, I told you," I said, walking around the hill and pointing to its size. "He could have driven the bulldozer back to here," I pointed, "dug the hole and dumped the car in, and then covered the hole with dirt."

"Or, someone could have buried trash back here," Billy reasoned. "They could have buried a dead horse here. I think the whole thing about burying a car is a little far-fetched. Besides, if you didn't want to draw attention to it, you would have leveled the ground."

"I guess you would, unless you panicked. An adult would have more sense, but a kid... that's another story. Maybe he was in a hurry to cover his tracks. He wanted to..."

"Forget it, Jesse," Billy said. "You are stabbing in the dark."

The path ended with the hill. Trees and underbrush lined the background. A clump of ferns sprouted out of the mound.

I was losing wind. "You're probably right," I agreed. What did I know?

♪ "Maybe we should head back. I'm hungry as a horse. Oops, sorry. I wasn't trying to be smart." I looked down at the mound and then back to Billy.

"I'm hungry, too," he said. "We'll give it another half-hour, if you can hold out that long. After that, I will take you anywhere you want to go to eat. Is it a deal?"

I mumbled under my breath, as we turned and headed back down the path, "I guess I can hold out for a little while."

"I want to hang around and see if anything develops. Something might happen. Why else would the police have been here earlier?"

We got back to the truck ten minutes later. I got in the passenger's seat and dug out my purse, while Billy got in and rolled down the window.

"Want a piece of gum?" I offered, after pulling a stick out, breaking it in half , and shoving it into my mouth.

"Sure, why not? But I want a whole piece."

I immediately pulled out my pack of cigarettes and lit one.

"I see you have that old habit back."

"Yeah, and it's your fault!" I accused. "I have not had a cigarette in years, not until I hooked up with you. What does that tell you? You are one to talk, you smoke."

"Yeah, maybe two or three a day," he said. "That's different. I'm not... hey, it looks like we have company."

Behind the trees where we were parked, I could make out Rose and her father coming out of the house. He followed her to her car, pointing his finger at her the whole time while he threw his arms up in the air. She got into the car and sped off, leaving him standing in the empty parking space, eating dust. He spun around, looked in our direction, and ran to the house.

"Family feud," I grumbled, not paying much attention.

"I think he saw us. Let's get out of here."

We were flying down the road when the first shot rang out.

"He shot at us... that lunatic!" I screamed, looking through the back window. "Go faster, Billy. He's standing in the middle of the road with a gun. Oh my God..."

"I'm going as fast as I can! This is not a racecar. It only has a four cylinder..."

The next shot took out the rear windows of the camper shell, and then shattered the windshield. Glass flew everywhere. Billy didn't even stop at the end of the road. He turned onto Rt.15 and never slowed down. I looked over and he was covered with specks of blood.

I became hysterical. "Billy, you're bleeding! Pull over!" I never noticed the blood on me, just a stinging feeling I had on my face and arms.

He finally came to a stop when we reached a muddy pull-off area, a mile down the road. This was the same spot I remembered passing when I followed my parents on our move to the mountains. A cop car was sitting here at the time with a radar gun.

Billy stumbled out of the truck and made his way over to a shady spot under the trees. I was right behind him with a rag I had dug out from behind the seat, and my cell phone in my hand. I dialed 911. The emergency dispatch came on the line.

"911. State your emergency, please."

"Help us, please!" I screamed in her ears. "We need an ambulance. Someone shot at us. We need help!"

"Ma'am, can you give me your location?"

I looked around and tried to get my bearings. I didn't see a mile marker or a road sign of any kind. *Think, Jesse, think,* I told myself.

"We're on the north bound side of Rt. 15 on a pull-off. It's where the cops sit sometimes with radar. It's about three or four miles before you get to Zion Crossroads. We're in a black Toyota pick-up truck with a black camper shell. Please hurry!"

"Ok, Miss, just stay on the line."

I heard her barking out orders in the background and then heard her fingers clicking away on a computer. "Rescue One, we need an ambulance dispatched to look-out post number 4-5-0. Be advised... shots fired at moving vehicle/ with injuries... local law enforcement notified." She returned to me. "May I have your name, please?"

"Jesse Watson," I screamed. "My name is Jesse Watson. My friend, Billy Blackhawk needs help! He's bleeding!"

"Has he been shot, Miss Watson?"

"I don't think so. Let me check," I said to her. I looked down at Billy, who was now lying on the ground, soaked in blood. He had numerous, small rips in his shirt and pants, but I didn't see anything that looked like a bullet hole.

"Billy," I got down on my knees and got close to his face. "Have you been shot?"

"No, I'm ok," he replied. "I have cuts from the glass, but it is not bad. A stitch here and there and I'll be fine."

"He says he is not shot," I told the dispatcher, "He has cuts from the shattered windshield, and he's got a pretty bad gash on his arm. I'm tying a rag around it as we speak. He's going to need stitches."

"Are you hurt ma'am?"

When I looked at my arms and legs, I was shocked. My T-shirt was splattered with blood and I could feel the dampness.

"I'm covered in blood, too! Just like Billy!" I screamed.

"Are you shot, ma'am?"

"No, I don't think so," I answered, looking over my body. "But there's a gash above my knee." I heard sirens in the distance. "The ambulance is here! I can hear the sirens!"

"Ma'am, please stay on the line," she repeated herself.

The ambulance was the first to arrive. Seconds later, two state troopers pulled in, brakes squealing, lights flashing, and their sirens blaring. The paramedics worked diligently to fix us up so they could transport us to a hospital, while the two state troopers asked us questions and talked on their radios. A few minutes later, a tow truck arrived.

"Where are you taking my dad's truck?" I cried.

"Ma'am, your friend over there," he pointed to Billy, "told us to have it towed to Redman's Auto Center. Is that all right with you?"

"That's fine," I whispered. "But I need to lock it up first. Billy's got some expensive equipment in the back, and my purse is in the cab."

"We'll take care of it, Ma'am," the officer replied. "Don't worry."

"ANOTHER FINE MESS YOU'VE GOTTEN US INTO," I said to Billy, mocking a character from an old show I'd seen on TV many times, as we were being ushered through the emergency room. "I'd like to see how you are going to get us out of this one."

"Hey, we didn't do anything wrong," he said. "We're the good guys. But poor old Larry is not going to be so lucky. They are going to burn his butt on this one."

"He deserves it!" I snapped. "He tried to kill us!"

The emergency room crew put us on separate beds, pulled a curtain and began the process of tending to our injuries. It turned out not to be so bad: Billy took eleven stitches in his right, upper arm and I had seven stitches sewed into an area above my right knee.

"Are we done?" I asked the nurse. I was ready to get out of there.

"Not yet," she replied. "The doctor has some instructions for you first, and you will need to speak with the police before we can release you." She walked away.

Once alone, I got off the bed and went over to see Billy.

"I've been meaning to ask you, but I kept forgetting," I whispered. "What about Helen's purse? Won't the cops know it was dusted for prints before they got it?"

"My friend didn't dust for prints," he went on to explain in hushed tones. "She used an ultra-violet laser enhanced imaging scanner that scans for prints then feeds the data into a computer. You get fast results and no residue. It is pretty neat, huh?"

"Good, I was worried about the police finding out the evidence had been tampered with." I said, talking as fast as I could before the cops came in to question us. "Do you remember what Bubba said about Tom Dorey and Jay being best friends? Do you think it is true? Because if it is..."

"Why would he say it, if it wasn't true?"

"This puts a whole new slant on everything."

As if on cue, the doctor walked over to Billy's bed. Two troopers followed behind him.

"We are in for it now," I murmured, looking over at Billy.

"Just tell the truth," he whispered.

For the next half hour we told our story and answered enough questions to choke a goat.

"We contacted your mother like you asked," the officer said to me before we left. "She is in the waiting room."

By the time we walked out of the examination room to the emergency room admitting desk, we had been assured that Lawrence Hudgins would be arrested. The police would need a formal statement from us, but that could wait until tomorrow morning when we felt better.

I did not look forward to seeing my mother and having to explain myself again. I was burnt out on telling lies and trying to cover my ass.

"Jesse!" Mom cried out when she saw us. "Are you ok?"

"I'm fine, Mom," I said, walking up to her and giving her a hug. "We're both fine." I looked at Billy and gave him a weak smile. Then, I looked passed Mom and saw the whole gang standing in a huddle off to the side— Claire and both of the kids, Jack and Dennis... and Cole.

Every emotion in my body came surging forth. I broke down in tears as I ran into Cole's arms.

"I am so glad you came," I whispered in his ear. "I need you."

"That is why I am here," he wrapped his arms around me and replied. "I'm so glad you're ok. I was worried."

Mom took charge and led everybody out to the parking lot. That woman never ceases to amaze me sometimes. We were all gathered in a group beside Cole's police cruiser.

"Cole is going to take you and Billy home," she said to the two of us. "We'll meet you there." She physically pushed us in all directions. "The three of you have a few things you need to work out and now is the perfect time to do it, before things get any worse." She was determined. Claire and the kids got in the mini-van with her, as Jack and Dennis got into the Camaro. Nobody was happy.

"Ok, let's have it," Cole demanded, driving out of the parking lot with our gang in close pursuit. "How deep is the hole that you have gotten yourselves into now? Am I going to need an excavation crew for this one, or will a shovel suffice?"

I sat in the front seat with my mouth closed, while Billy sat in the back and spoke. "We didn't do anything. We were on routine surveillance when this guy comes out and starts shooting at us."

"Stop it right there, Billy," Cole said. "I know all about it, and what I don't know, I have pretty much figured out on my own. Let me tell you what I have and then you can try and lie your way out of it, ok?"

"Ok," we said in unison.

His unbridled analogy of actual events was astonishing. He knew about Jay shooting me, and guessed at Billy's parents' involvement in fixing me wounds. There was no record of me being treated at either one of the two local hospitals. The purse was a different matter. He knew Billy had some contact with it, but he didn't know that Billy took it to Caroline at the research lab, and neither one of us was going to tell him.

"And now this," he barked. "Don't you realize you both could have been killed? I blame you, Billy."

"Like I said—we are not the guilty parties here," Billy growled.

"Not entirely," Cole said. "Larry Hudgins will pay for what he did, but you can't go around harassing private citizens. It's against the law!"

"Yadda... yadda... yadda." Billy was antagonizing him. "All I care about is, have they arrested him?"

"They picked him up about an hour ago and brought him in for interrogation," Cole responded. "His lawyer was waiting for him downtown, screaming something about getting a restraining order against the two of you. Hudgins says that both of you belong in jail."

"If that's supposed to scare us," I was fast becoming belligerent. "It doesn't. Does it Billy?"

Billy shook his head and said, "Jesse, a court order is not a joke."

I couldn't believe what I was hearing. Billy was backing down.

"If we get caught anywhere near those people, we'll go to jail. It's time to throw in the towel."

"Has everyone in this car lost all perspective, except me?" I asked. "Who cares about Larry Hudgins? As far as I'm concerned, he's nothing but a butt fissure on the rear end of society. His son is an aggressive, angry, out-of-control, psychotic teenager who likes to torture small animals. Rita's a spoiled, pampered, brainless air head, and poor Rose is caught up right in the middle of all this. Barring all that, what about Helen? Isn't she the one who matters?"

Neither one of them had anything to say about that. Their silence indicated to me they were thinking it over. Hoping they would come to their senses and see that the most important thing was to find out what happened to Helen, I forged ahead. "If none of them had anything to do with her disappearance, then why are they getting so bent out of shape?"

"It might have something to do with the fact that you're harassing the hell out of them," Cole sneered. "You can't push people but so far."

"We're not getting anywhere," I hissed.

Cole parked his cruiser in Mom's driveway. None of us had spoken since my last statement, and frankly, I was getting a little tired of all the tension. Cole stepped out of the car and came over to my door.

"I will walk you inside, and then I am going to take Billy home," he said, helping me out of the car.

"That won't be necessary," I said. "I'll take him home." I opened the back door and held out my hand. "Need a lift, partner?"

"Why, thank you kindly, madam," he answered, taking hold of my hand. He turned to Cole. "I think we're done here, officer. Thanks for the ride." Together, we walked up the steps and waved good-bye. It was shitty, but it was the right thing to do. Cole had pushed us to our limit and now it was time for us to push back.

"Tell me one thing," I said to Billy, as we were walking inside. "Why was he driving his cop car when he picked us up at the hospital? He must have been on duty. Didn't you hear the radio squawking the whole time? What's he doing in Charlottesville? Isn't he out of his jurisdiction?"

"Welcome to the real world, honey," Billy replied, ushering me into the kitchen. "He's in law enforcement. They all work hand-in-hand. It's politics all the way. Somebody knows about his relationship with us and they used him to get to us."

"Do you think he went along with it?" I asked, heading straight for the refrigerator. "I am starved. Aren't you?"

Before Billy had a chance to reply, Mom and her lively crew overtook us. They piled into the house like a swarm of bees, buzzing around, searching for a new queen. Mom was the leader of the pack. They wanted to know every detail.

"I am so glad you are all right," Mom said. "We were so worried when we got the call. What happened?"

I took out some leftover fried chicken and Billy and I stood there eating it, explaining our latest fiasco.

"Weren't you scared?" Claire asked. She walked up to me and put her arms around my shoulder. "I know I would have been."

"Scared is an understatement. I was terrified," I replied, flinching from the pain in my shoulder I still had from my first encounter with one of the Hudgins' clan. "But I had confidence in Billy. I knew he would get us out safely, and he did."

"This time," Mom said. "Jesse..."

Oh, no, here it comes, another *I told you so*.

Seeing what was coming, everybody backed away leaving Billy and me to face her wrath.

CHAPTER 24

T HE LECTURE WENT ON AND ON, until she finally gave up. "Forget it. I can see neither one of you are going to listen to me. What do I know? I'm just an old, meddling mama. Don't pay any attention to me. I'm just trying to keep you two from getting killed, that's all."

"And we love you for it, Mama." I reached over and gave her a hug, motioning for Billy to follow me. Claire, Jack, and Dennis had fled the scene, keeping out of Mom's way. At least two of them knew what was coming. A hurricane was on its way and its name was Minnie.

From past experiences, I knew not to argue with her. It only made things worse. I wish I had known that when I was a kid, I thought. It would have saved me a lot of hassle. Now that I am an adult, I'm smarter than I was when I was a snot-nosed brat... and I was a brat. I was awful. Looking back, I am surprised that my parents didn't ship me off to some private school just to get rid of me. It really used to piss me off that Jack and Claire were so perfect. That thought brought a devious smile to my face. Yeah, right! I was the bad seed, but Claire's bibulous behavior and Jack's sexual preference made me look like a shining star. I don't drink... mostly... and I definitely want a man in my bed. So, take that!

"Mom," I yelled, walking to the front door, "I am taking Billy home and I will be back soon."

"Wait a minute," she came after me. "What about your dad's truck? What are we going to do about his truck?"

I looked at Billy. I had forgotten all about the truck.

"Everything has been arranged, Mom," Billy assured her. "I told the police to have it towed to Daniel's and to tell him to fix it. Whatever it cost, I'll take care of it. It'll be just like new when you get it back. So, don't worry. Ok?" He patted her hand and gave her a kiss on the cheek.

Billy followed me out onto the front porch where Claire, Jack and Dennis were sitting. Benny and Carrie were rolling around in the front yard, playing with Athena, and getting dirty. They were all smart enough to get out of Mom's way.

"You always know the right thing to say at just the right time," I turned to Billy. "I appreciate you being so thoughtful towards Mom. It means a lot to me that you treat her feelings with so much respect and not treat her like a silly old lady."

"Of course I wouldn't treat her like a silly old lady!" Billy retorted. "She's a good `ge ya. I love her just like I do my own mom."

"No!" I spat.

"What's the matter?"

"My purse is in the truck."

Claire jumped up and said, "Your purse is in the van. The police gave it to Mom when we got to the hospital." She made a funny face and added, "It's sitting on a piece of newspaper. It had blood on it. I think we got most of it off with some tissues Mom had." A tear came to her eye.

"Poor baby," I reached over and touched her cheek. "I'm sorry you had to be involved in all this. I've been so busy being concerned with myself that I forgot about the pain you must be going through with Carl." She began to cry. I felt like such a heel.

"I'm fine, but it has been really hard." She hiccupped between tears and pointed to the kids. "They don't have any idea about what has been happening. What am I going to tell them when they ask, 'Where's Daddy?' I don't know what to tell them."

"Claire, you are a good mother," I tried to reassure her. "Whatever you tell them, I know it will be in their best interest." I wiped a tear from her cheek. "I have confidence in you. I know you will do the right thing."

She dried her tears, straightened up and regained her composure. "You are right," she said. She looked out in the front yard and smiled at her children. "I will do what I think is best, screw Carl."

"That's my girl!" I said.

I looked at Jack and Dennis. Seeing Jack for the first time with a serene look on his face and a happy, contented attitude made me feel good. He no longer had that hidden something that always seem to keep him from completely being himself. Jack is the one I always worried about. I felt something lost within him, but I just never knew what it was, until now. Now that he has come to terms with his sexuality, he can go about being the person that he should be. I don't have to worry anymore.

"I love you, Jack," I said. "I am glad that you told us. I know it was hard. You deserve to be happy."

"Jesse, you are starting to get a little weird. You sound like you are giving a eulogy." He glanced at Billy and then at me. "You're not going to get in some more trouble are you? Do I need to follow you and keep you out of mischief?"

"You couldn't be talking about us," I smiled and poked Billy in the side. "I'm taking him home and then I will be right back. Besides, look at us. We look like refugees from a war zone." We were covered with what looked like tiny paper cuts on our face and arms. Both of us sported our own personal war wound. Billy had a terrible gash on his arm, and I had one on my leg. We still had on the same bloody clothes.

"Maybe I should change clothes first," I said, examining myself. "I will be right back."

I ran upstairs and changed clothes. By the time I got back outside, Dennis was helping Billy change into one of his T-shirts.

"It's probably not something you would usually wear." Dennis pointed to the front of the shirt that read—*It's my life and I'm proud of it.* "At least it fits and doesn't have blood on it."

Billy grumbled. "Man, you're going to get me killed! I can't wear this!

We're in the back hills. They don't cotton to this type of thing. "How 'bout I wear it inside out? That way I have on a clean shirt, and I won't get my butt kicked. I hope you don't mind."

Dennis laughed. "Sure, no problem," he said.

"I'm dressed and ready to go," I interrupted. This was fast becoming an embarrassing moment. I now know Jack's gay, but seeing it in print was a different story. I was not quite ready for that and I wasn't sure how Billy really felt. "Let me get my handbag."

We said our good-byes, promising not to get locked up or killed. I retrieved my purse from Mom's van, examined it and determined it was not wet and dripping with blood as I had anticipated. The leather was undamaged and devoid of any signs of its recent brush with what could have been devastating carnage.

I walked over and gave Benny and Carrie a kiss, patted Athena on the head, and then told Billy I was ready to go. I wanted to get back out on the road. We still had things to do, and people to see.

In the background, I heard Jack say to someone, "I have a bad feeling about this. I see jail time in their future."

I sank into the seat of my wonderful new automobile. It wasn't really new, only a couple of years old, but it felt new to me. It still had that new car smell of leather, and it had all the bells and whistles the car salesman tells you about, but you don't really appreciate until you use them. This was a step up from the usual loser cars I was used to owning. I added that to one of the plusses on my list of why I like living here.

"Are we going to go talk to Tommy Dorey?" I asked Billy, as soon as we got into the car and pulled out of the driveway,

"Haven't you had enough for one day, 'ge ya? I don't know about you but I'm fried. I hurt all over and I'm tired... not to mention how I look."

"You look fine," I told him. "It is still early. We have three or four more hours before it gets dark."

"No," he demanded. "We can do it tomorrow. The only thing I want to do is go home, fix a sandwich, take about ten pain pills and go to bed."

"Well, I'm wired," I tried to bait him. "I think I'll stop by and have a talk with him after I take you home."

"No you won't!" Billy commanded. "You go home and get some rest."

"You're the boss."

After I dropped Billy off at his place, made him a sandwich while he showered, and saw to it he didn't take too many pills, I headed to Zion Crossroads. I know I promised him I would go home, but all I wanted to do was have a little talk with the guy. What could that hurt?

⏵ I checked my handbag to make sure my gun was still there, wondering the whole time if the cops had seen it before they gave the bag to Mom at the hospital. Yep, it was there. I dug deeper, searching for my hand-held tape recorder as I approached the stoplight at the Ruckersville intersection. If I could get something on tape that would be worthwhile, maybe Billy wouldn't get mad at me for going against his orders. I found the recorder just as I was making the right turn at the light. The new cassette I had put in the other day was still there. Good. I was ready. All I wanted was for Tommy to be at work. I didn't want to go to his house alone.

I was astounded when I pulled into the gas station and saw Jay's Nova parked in the parking lot beside the dumpster. He was standing next to it, talking to Tommy, and smoking a cigarette.

Instead of pulling up to the pumps, I quickly parked on the opposite side of the building. I got out of the Jeep, clipped the recorder onto the waistband of my jeans, hit the record button, and headed towards the dumpster. When I got closer I realized it wasn't a cigarette they were smoking, it was pot. I would recognize that smell anywhere. When I was in my early twenties, I experimented with a few different illegal substances. Marijuana was the most pleasant, but it made me act ridiculous and my normal state of paranoia became so intense, I couldn't stand it. That was not for me. I had enough to deal with on a regular basis. I didn't need to have my phobias and anxieties jacked up another notch. And the one time I dropped a hit of acid, I thought I was going to die. I snorted cocaine two times before I realized anything that makes you feel that good, had to be really, really bad for you. That concludes my partaking of the evil weed and its associates. I've been there... done that... no thank you.

Nonetheless, I was determined to get into the middle of what they were doing if I had to, and get me some answers. It was the only thing to do that I could think of at the time. I walked up to them so fast they didn't know what hit them.

"Oh, man. I'd love to have a hit of that," I reached over and slowly took the marijuana cigarette out of Tommy's hand. "I haven't had a good buzz in a long time. You don't mind do you?" I took a deep drag, coughed a few times and then handed it to Jay.

At first they drew back, but once I took the drag from their joint, they relaxed. My limited use—and knowledge of pot and drugs, and my continued association with friends that still partied, gave me an advantage. I knew how to act and react.

"Oh, man, this is good stuff," I said, leaning back against the trash dumpster, making all kinds of silly faces. I knew that is how you would act if you were stoned. I intended to use every ploy I had to get their confidence and then get them to open up to me.

They stood there with me and smoked the entire joint, never suspecting I was preparing to move in for the kill. *Teenagers*, I thought to myself. *They have so much to learn.*

"Listen, guys," I said, trying to sound patronizing, "I'm sorry about what's been happening. It's not me. You see... I work for this guy and he has it in his head that you two are involved. He's not going to stop until he solves this case. Trust me, he will find out what happened to that girl. He's like a hound dog in heat. He will never back down. Let me help you. If you know anything, please tell me. I promise you, I'll do everything I can to keep you from spending the rest of your life in prison. If you were involved in her death, you will go to prison. You do know that, don't you? Prison is not a nice place."

Jay and Tommy glanced back and forth at each other. For just a second, I caught something in their demeanor that screamed evil. I should have paid more attention.

"Who said she was dead?" Jay asked. "I thought she was missing, not dead. You must be wrong."

"It's pretty obvious," I said, trying to act cool in a stoned-out kind of way. "The police found her purse about a mile from your house. It had blood and fingerprints on it. By tomorrow morning they'll know whose blood and whose prints they are. So, if you know anything, you had better start talking." Lying was fast becoming one of my better skills.

The few puffs of marijuana I had taken were starting to go to my head. I had tried to fake it and not inhale the stuff, but I must not have done a good job. I was getting light-headed.

"Whew, that was some strong stuff," I said, exaggerating my dizziness. "Personally, I don't think either one of you had anything to do with her death, but I think you know something. Having knowledge of a crime is considered just as guilty as doing the crime, in the eyes of the law. You'll still go to prison for it. When the truth comes out, and believe me it will now that the cops have this new evidence, the only thing that will save your butt is to come clean. I can help you now, but I don't know about later."

Jay's facade was slowly beginning to crumble. I could see from the look on his face, I had hit a nerve. He knew something. I had a feeling from the very beginning that he was the one who did it, but now I wasn't so sure. Maybe this young, troubled teenager who liked to hurt small animals, and judging from the cut marks on his arms and the way he pulled at his hair until he had strands of it wrapped around his fingers—would hurt himself, too. He might not be the killer after all, just a kid with problems.

"When's the last time that you were at home?"

"Not since I left this morning around ten o'clock," he answered. He pulled a pack of cigarettes out of his pocket, stuck one in his mouth, lit it, and then offered me one. I know I shouldn't have taken it, but that bad old devil was sitting on my shoulders, egging me on. I took one out of the pack, leaned over and let him light it for me.

"So, I guess you don't know they have your dad in custody?" I asked. I wasn't about to tell him the real truth about his father. I wanted him to think the worst, hoping I could scare something out of him.

"What for?" he asked, becoming obviously upset. His hands started to shake and he danced around like his pants were on fire.

"What do you think?" I spat. "They think he killed Helen Carrolton, and buried her on his property."

"Oh, shit!" he screamed, looking at Tommy, who had been standing there the whole time with his mouth shut. "They've arrested my dad, Tommy! We've got to do something! We've got to tell them what we know!"

"Shut up, you moron!" he yelled. "Don't you see she is playing you for a fool? They ain't got nothing, or they would be out here right now with a search warrant!"

That did it for me. Either I was in the company of killers, which was not a pleasant thought, or ensconced in the middle of a cover-up. One way or the other, I had hit paydirt.

"Here's what I know," I lied, taking a stab at the first thought that came to mind. "The cops arrested your dad because they think he killed Helen Carrolton. They haven't determined why he did it but that doesn't matter right now. Then, he buried her on his property with help from the two of you." I stopped and took a deep breath, letting it out slowly. They both began to squirm. "If that's true, you will both be in a world of hurt."

Tommy was the first one to speak up. "Listen, bitch. I ain't going to jail for nobody. I didn't kill the girl, and I ain't taking the rap for it. Talk to your man, here." He pointed to Jay. "Go ahead, Jay, tell her all about it. Tell her how your crazy old man likes to do the dirty with those young chicks. How he likes to pick them up, take them to some dark spot and do the nasty stuff he likes to do. That's it. I ain't covering for him no more. I don't care how much money he gives me! Look lady, I had nothing to do with that girl's death. All I did was watch him dig the hole."

This was worse than I could have ever imagined. Not only did the Dad kill the girl, but he also did it out of some deviate, sexual fantasy he liked to play out, and then he got his son to help him cover it up. All this time I thought the son was the bad guy. I should have known better. But what role did Tommy play in this? He had just confessed to his knowledge of the crime, so was he part of it, or did he just happen to be in the wrong place at the wrong time?

All this raced through my mind. Who cares? A girl was dead and somebody killed her. I wanted that somebody and I wanted the girl.

"Hey, let's keep it together here," I tried to calm them down. I had opened up a can of worms. "I want to help you," I murmured. "Just tell me what happened, and show me where she's buried." For the first time in our conversation, I really wanted to help these boys. I no longer thought they were the bad guys, but victims of a cruel killer.

It almost made me sick. Anyone who would use their own child to help them cover up their nasty misdeeds must be insane. Who would do that? Yet, Larry Hudgins was not the biological father of Jay Hudgins. He was the adoptive parent. It's not the same. No matter how you look at it... it's not the same. It can't be... or is it?

There was no doubt in my mine now. Helen Carrolton was dead and these two could lead me to her body. I was not going to give up, but I had to move fast. The day was quickly coming to an end and I was afraid it wouldn't be long before Larry Hudgins would be released from custody. According to Cole, his lawyer was in the process of getting a restraining order out on Billy and me. If that happened before we found Helen, we'd never get to the truth. We would be barred from getting anywhere near Jay or his family.

"My dad's a good man," Jay said. "I'm sure he didn't mean to hurt her. He said it was an accident." He was still crying and pacing back and forth. His big shot attitude was gone.

"I'm getting out of here," Tommy said. "It's time for me to go in and relieve that old bag." He gave me a creepy smile and nodded towards the store. "Now, that is someone I'd like to kill. She's about as big a nuisance as you are." Turning to Jay, he said, "If you think she's going to help you or your dad, you're in for a real surprise. Don't you see she doesn't care about you? She's using you to get what she wants and once she gets it, she'll hang us all out to dry." He spit on the ground, gave me a nasty look, and walked away. "Stay out of my way, bitch, while you still can."

Time was running out. I didn't know whom Tommy would call once he got inside, and I was not about to wait around and find out.

"Jay," I cried, "please tell me what happen to Helen. Did your father kill her? Did he make you help him get rid of the body?"

"If I tell you the truth, will you promise to give me immunity?"

This kid was not so dumb after all.

"Jay, I can't do that," I replied. "I'm not a cop. I do not have that authority. But I can promise you this, if you help me, I will go to my cop friend and get him to help you. But first, I need to know the truth."

"Ok, but not here." He looked around suspiciously, as if checking for someone that might be listening. "Meet me at the end of my road when it gets dark. I'll tell you the whole story then and show you where the girl is buried. Come alone, or it's no deal."

"It will be dark soon. Why don't we just go now?" I tried to convince him. I did not want to be alone with him after dark.

"No!" he shouted, walking away. "I don't want anyone to see you." He was in his car and gone before I had a chance to do anything.

I walked to my car, looking in the store window as I passed. My suspicions were correct. Tommy was on the phone to somebody and I knew that before long, somebody would be after me. I had to get out of there fast. I jumped into my Jeep, pulled out my recorder to check it, and then turned on the ignition. At first nothing happened. I began to panic as I pictured in my mind the awful things that could happen if I was still here when whoever was coming arrived. I scanned the dash, checking for any sign of life. I didn't understand it. The lights on the dash glowed, but the engine wouldn't start. Then I looked down at the console. The gear lever was still in drive. Maybe that's it. I had jumped out so fast, not only did I leave the keys in the car, but I also forgot to put it in park. No wonder the bells were still ringing when I got out. Shit. What to do? I put my foot on the brake, turned the key to the on position, and shoved the lever into park. It made a strange clank, but when I turned the key again it started.

"Hallelujah, Lord!" I screamed out loud, put the car in reverse and hauled ass. While heading in the same direction as Jay, I tried to decide what my next move would be. Should I just sneak up on the property alone, or should I go get Billy? I needed to think. First thing I will do is go to the grill. I can kill some time there while I figure this out, and also get something to eat. Yeah, that is what I will do.

Unlike the last few times I had been there, the grill was crowded with dinner folks. The six tables in the middle of the floor were overflowing with families eating supper. Large, boisterous mountain men having their before-dinner drinks occupied most of the booths. Pitchers of beer lined their tables. I chose the same booth where Billy and I had sat previously.

"What can I get you?" the waitress asked.

I looked up to see a heavy, middle-aged woman with burnt red hair, and a front tooth missing. Her make-up was so heavy, I felt weighted down just looking at her. She had a large mole over her right eyebrow. Any minute, I expected her to swing one of those huge arms at me and knock me out of the booth.

"Is Rose working tonight?" I asked.

"You don't see her, do you?" she hissed, swinging her arm out through the crowd and inviting me to look for myself. "What'll it be, Missy? I ain't got all night. I got other customers."

"I'll have the cheeseburger boat and a coke," I said, wanting her to leave.

She waddled off and within two minutes was back with my drink.

"Bubba wants to know if you're going to eat this time, or are you here to ask more questions? Cause, if you're here to..."

"No, I am just here to eat," I assured her.

"Then, your cheeseburger will be right up," she grunted. She turned and headed back to the kitchen.

It had just started to rain outside, pouring for a few minutes and then slowing to a drizzle. The rain cheered me up as I tried to put her ugly behavior out of my head.

The waitress returned with my food. She slammed the bill down on the table and said, "Enjoy your meal." She was not a very happy person. Maybe she needed a vacation, I thought... or a plastic surgeon.

The food was exceptional—as much as a hamburger could be, considering I wasn't eating filet mignon. I expected the meat to be greasy, the bun to be soggy, and the fries to be hard. Instead, I was pleasantly surprised. It was just as good as Mom's... and Mom is the best cook in the world.

By the time the sun had set into the trees, the rain had been long gone and I could see the steam radiating off the blacktop. I finished my meal and left the grill without incident. I didn't get to see Bubba, but I felt his presence. He probably had his eyes on me the whole time, wondering what I was up to. I got into my car and called Billy on my cell phone. It rang ten or fifteen times before I hit the off button. I tried his number again. Nope, I hadn't miss-dialed. I had the correct number, but he wasn't answering. Next, I tried his cell phone. No answer. I didn't know what to do. I explored all my options. If I take the time to go to Billy's house, I might miss out on meeting Jay. I had no idea whether or not he would still cooperate if I waited too long, and time was of the essence. I couldn't get Billy on the phone because he was most likely zonked out on pain pills, but yet, I didn't want to face Jay alone. I swallowed my fears, and drove down Rt.15 to meet him. I can handle this, I told myself. I have my gun, my cell phone, my tape recorder, and this car is designed to go anywhere and do almost anything. What else could I possibly need?

Perhaps a little bit more courage wouldn't hurt.

CHAPTER 25

I HAD NEVER NOTICED IT UNTIL NOW. There was a small, faded wooden plaque nailed to a tree that read—*The Hudgins' Farm*. Oh, yeah—it's a farm all right. I blasted the thought. It's a funny farm and I don't mean *ha-ha* funny, but funny like in strange. The family that lives on this road was definitely strange. They gave a whole new meaning to the phrase dysfunctional family. Mom is a whack-o, the kid is a screwed-up teenager, Dad is a killer, and poor Rose is just an innocent bystander—probably the only one in this group who doesn't have a clue.

I turned onto their road, and pulled off to the side. I dialed Billy's number again. When he didn't answer, I thought about calling Mom, but I didn't want her to worry. However, I'm nobody's fool. Someone needed to know where I was, just in case...

I punched in 411 for information and got the number for the Greene County Bed and Breakfast where Jack and Dennis were staying. *Please be there,* I said to myself.

"Hello," a lady answered, "Greene County Bed and Breakfast. Owned and operated by Ruby Pryce. May I help you?"

"Yes," I replied. "My brother, Jack Watson, is staying at your inn, I think. Could you connect me to his room?"

"Just a minute, please. I think he just came in."

The phone made a clicking noise, and then started ringing again. Jack answered after the second ring.

"Oh, I'm so glad you are there," I rambled. "This is Jesse. I need to tell you something, so listen closely..."

"Jesse, calm down," he said. "I'm here. What is the matter?"

"I need you to do something for me and I don't want Mom to know."

"Ok, what is it?"

"I want you to go to Billy's house and tell him something for me. He's all drugged-out from the pain pills and I can't reach him on the phone. I'm right in the middle of something really bad and I need his help. Tell him I have found Helen's killer. It's the dad. I'm meeting Jay at his place so he can show me where the body is. He will know what I'm talking about. Tell him to get here as fast as he can."

"Have you lost your mind? Don't do it Jesse. You don't know what you are getting into. Wait for help to arrive. I will go get Billy, if you promise to wait for him."

"Ok, but make it fast."

"How do I get to Billy's?" he asked.

I gave him the directions to Billy's place, and every pertinent phone number I knew. I warned him not to call me unless it was a matter of life and death. Deep down in the bottom of my gut, I knew this was going to be a delicate situation, maybe even dangerous, and I figured the less your opponent knows about you the better. A ringing telephone is a sure sign that you have outside communication with the world, and that is something the bad guys do not like. This I figured out on my own.

After ending my conversation with Jack, I called Billy one last time. I needed his 'I can kick their butt and break their neck' ability. I had no doubts he could, and right about now I wanted him here with me in case I needed him to do it. I knew my limitations, and what I was about to get into exceeded them. My unanswered calls made the pit of my stomach quiver. I was scared as hell.

"I guess I'm on my own," I said to myself, while I hit the off button on the phone, folded it up and stuffed it into my jeans' pocket. "But you better believe I am going to be ready for you, buster!" I stared down the end of the road. "When I leave here, somebody is going to be in jail and it isn't going to be me."

Swallowing a lump in my throat the size of a peach, I pulled back onto the road and drove slower. No matter how much I told myself I was doing the right thing, it still did not compensate for the intense fear that I felt. This was serious! People have died in situations less dangerous that what I was about to face. I know... I've seen it on television.

It was dark, and the only lights I had to go by were the ones on the dash and the small glare from my parking lights. I had my headlights turned off hoping nobody would see me. Slowly, I crept passed the Hudgins' house. Everything appeared quiet. Several lights were on, but the parking spaces in front were empty except for Jay's Camaro and the red sports car. It only seemed natural to me that the dad's car would be there because he was locked up in jail, and they don't allow you to bring your car. So, that meant Jay was the only one home. This was the way I hoped it would be.

I inched my way down to the end of the road, made a u-turn and parked my Jeep facing what was to be my get-a-way route. This time I had the power to get the hell out of here fast if I needed to, and I was going to be ready at a moment's notice. Not once did I get myself into a rut or a ditch like I did with the truck. I was probably too scared to screw up. It's amazing what you can do if you have to.

I sat there for a few minutes trying to get up my nerve. It was eerie outside and the sounds of summer pounded in my ears. Crickets, cicadas, and other foul creatures of the night blasted at me. The sound was horrendously scary, and I couldn't put aside the feeling that someone was watching me. I turned off the car, made sure to remove the key, and shoved it deep into my front jeans pocket. I had already decided not to lock up the car just in case a fast get-away was in order. Next, I put the cell phone in the other front pocket, and my tape recorder in my back left one. In the last pocket, I stuffed my gun. Now I was ready for anything... well almost. The palms of my hands were so sweaty they slipped off the door handle when I went to open the car door. When I finally managed to get myself out of the car, I just stood there and looked around. This was a spooky scenario I had gotten myself into. I was out here all alone and so scared I almost wet my pants. The darkness of the night had consumed everything, making it almost impossible for me to see.

Eventually, my eyes adjusted to the blackness, and I decided it was time to move my butt, or go home. I glanced towards the path Billy and I had once gone down and was ready to head that way, when I heard the start-up of a bulldozer in the opposite direction. This was not good. The vision of a grave being dug to put my car and me in raced through my head. What else could it be? Who in their right mind would be out here at night doing excavation work? But then again, who said any of these people were in their right mind?

Forcing my feet to move, I followed the sound of the bulldozer. It was an arduous journey creeping through the tangled mass of vines, trees, and rocks that seemed to be everywhere that I walked. One of the things I have learned about the mountains is you never have a shortage of rocks. They were everywhere you looked.

The decision not to bring a flashlight worked against me. I didn't want anyone to see the beam from it, but without one I couldn't see much. If I had to make a run for it, I would be in serious trouble.

Judging the distance the best I could, I realized I had gone too deep into the woods to make a fast get-away. I sat down on a huge rock beside a tree and tried to calm down. The air was hot, yet I had the shakes. My body shivered and my heart was pounding so hard, I had to put my hand over it to keep it from jumping out of my chest. I could see a full-blown panic attack heading my way.

Calm down, and breathe deeply, I told myself. I promised myself after this was over, I would follow my doctor's advice and go back on my medication.

In the distance, I saw a ray of light and heard the up and down roar of heavy equipment doing what it was designed to do—move earth. I crept slowly with my body crunched over like an animal stalking its prey. I had to be very careful. I had come to the conclusion that my life could depend on it. This was not a game.

This can't be real! Through the trees and underbrush, I saw Larry

Hudgins sitting on the seat of the bulldozer, shifting gears, and plowing through the ground digging a hole big enough... What was he doing here? He was supposed to be in jail!

A few minutes later, Jay walked into view, screaming above the noise, and making guiding hand gestures. Obviously, he was going to stand by his dad and do whatever it took to protect him. Reguardless of how hard I had tried, I could not break their bond. Jay had lied to me, and made me feel like a fool.I was dead meat. I had been used. This was not the way it was supposed to play out. Jay was supposed to meet me and show me where Helen's body was buried, but instead, he was here to assist in my demise. It was time for me to leave.

I moved through the woods faster than I had thought possible. I was scared, sweaty, and tired. I kept falling down, but managed to recover each time until I stumbled on a pile of rocks halfway to my car. I hit my head and felt the warm flow of blood run down my eyebrow to my cheek. At that exact moment, I decided this was not the life for me. The private detective business was out. Stick a fork in me... I was done. I couldn't handle the intensity of it all anymore. I wanted excitement in my life, but not this much. Just as I got almost to the edge of the woods, I tripped on a tree root, fell and hit my knee—the same one that had been stitched. I scrambled up and pressed my hand to my knee. It hurt like crazy and I could feel warm blood. I couldn't believe it. I had a new injury to add to the list, and before I could heal from the old ones, I went and tore one of those open. What else could possibly go wrong?

As of late, I assumed it was only going to get better. I was going to help catch the bad guy and everything was going to be fine. But now, all I cared about was getting out of here and never looking back. Forget these crazies. Let someone else worry about them. All I had to do was make it to my car! With a pounding headache, and limping by now, I made it to my Jeep, sat down on the rear bumper and hung my head between my legs. I felt sick to my stomach from the pain and was afraid that I was going to pass out. I silently thanked God for getting me out of this mess, and in return promised to change my lifestyle. No more smoking, no more cussing, and no more getting into situations like this! Sucking in my breath and mustering up all the energy I could, I forced myself to make it to the car door. I fished out my keys, and fell into the driver's seat, noticing only after I had sat down that the overhead interior lights had not come on. What the... Then I smelled it. A strong scent of Jasmine filled the air. I recognized it immediately. Jasmine has always been my favorite cologne. I wore it in the summer because it made me feel like a spring flower, but I had a feeling, after what was about to happen, I would never feel that way again. Instantly I knew I wasn't alone. I squeezed my eyelids together, trying to get my eyes focused, and when I opened them, I saw Rita Hudgins sitting in the passenger seat. She had what looked like a flashlight in her lap, but there was no mistaking the gun she shoved in my face.

"You know, Miss Watson, you have become a real pain," she spoke, as she stroked my face gently with her hand and leaned over so close I could smell the alcohol on her breath. Her hand brushed my breast as she pulled back. "As cute as I think you are, I'd hate to have to hurt you."

The way she touched me made me even sicker to my stomach than I already was. What was wrong with this woman? Why would she do that? Not only was I still reeling from what had happened in the last few hours, but now I also had this crazy woman sitting beside me with a gun stuck up against my head, and her hands exploring parts of my body she had no right to explore.

"We could have had so much fun together, but you had to go and ruin it." She reached over and ran her hand up and down my leg, stopping at my crotch.

This couldn't be true. I was not sitting here with Rita Hudgins' hand in my crotch. Is this really happening or am I dreaming? I had never experienced having a woman touch me in those places, and I sure as crap didn't know how to handle it. The worst part was... she was enjoying herself! She made groaning sounds and blew air kisses at me.

She must be jerking my chain, I thought. She's married and has a couple of kids. She's just trying to rattle me, and it was working!

Rita pulled back and relaxed in the seat, her gun still aimed at my head. "You've got it all wrong, you know." Her demeanor changed suddenly. "Why is it that everyone I have loved didn't love me back?"

I had no idea where she was going with this. She appeared to drift in and out of reality, not making any sense. But she was the one with the gun for now. I played along with her,

"I don't know what you're talking about," I tried to soothe her. "Who is it that doesn't love you back?" I could care less about what she had to say, but I had to do whatever it took to keep her from going off the deep end and pulling the trigger. At first my words seem to calm her, but then she became agitated again.

"Them! All of them!" she cried. "I loved them all and they turned their backs on me. At first, they denied their true feelings, but I knew it was there. First it was Lisa. She told me I was sick right up until the end. Then Sandy used me to get my money. I should have killed her sooner. And that little girl in the red car was so sweet to begin with, then she turned into the same crybaby slut as the rest of them. She didn't want me to touch her, and she said I was crazy," Rita whimpered. "But I showed her just like I showed the rest of them. I am not crazy!" Her hands shook, as her momentum built. "It was her fault... you know... she's the one who offered me a ride that day at the grill. My car wouldn't start and she said she would give me a ride home. It was snowing pretty hard.

I used that moment of weakness on her part to jump out of the car. I didn't even take the time to slam the car door before I took off into the woods. My mind was flying a mile a minute as I shot through the underbrush, my aches and pains totally forgotten. I ran until I felt like I couldn't run anymore. My leg was bleeding badly by now and the cut on my forehead gushed with every beat of my heart.

I was sure I was going to die out here in these woods and nobody was going to know. *"I'll be just another missing person's face on a milk carton,"* I said out loud. Then I stopped long enough to think about Helen Carrolton. Has her face made it to one of those cartons, yet? Do they only put your face on one after you've been missing for a long time, or do they do it right away? I sure as hell didn't want to know. I wanted to go home and forget this all happened. But I couldn't. I was stuck right in the middle of hell, with no way out. There were too many of them and too few of me. Rita blocked the way to my only means of escape, and her two guys were waiting somewhere in the background. Eventually, they would overcome me, and my life would soon be over.

Where the hell was Billy?

Once deep into the woods, I sank down and tried to rest. Rita had not followed me like I had expected, but I knew she was out there somewhere. They would re-group and come after me. It was only a matter of time before they found me and I knew it. They would surround me and drag me off to be buried in the hole they had been digging just for me. My life would be over.

I laid there for what seem like an eternity. The air had become hot and humid from the late afternoon rain. My knee was throbbing and the cut on my forehead was still bleeding. I held my breath as I crouched down, hiding in the damp leaves and the tangled mass of underbrush. Coming here alone was a stupid mistake... possibly the last one I would ever make. There was a killer on the loose in the woods, and he was after me.

Then I heard a twig snap...

"Oh, no, they have found me..."

CHAPTER 26

B UT THE KILLER WASN'T A HE—it was a she. Or was it? I was confused and couldn't make heads or tails of what was going on here. At first I was sure Jay was the one then he led me to believe his dad was the guilty party, and now Rita Hudgins has confessed... or at least hinted at it. Were they all guilty? What if... no, I don't want to think about it. It's too sick. I tried to put it out of my mind, but everything kept coming back to one thing. Helen Carrolton was dead, the killer was here and it wasn't me!

I heard the sound of cracking branches under someone's feet getting closer. The faint whisper of my name echoed through the air. Was this friend or foe? I didn't recognize the voice and until I did, I wasn't about to answer. I sat and waited, quietly reaching into my back pocket for my gun. What the h...? Where is my gun? This was unreal! This was just too unreal! I've seen better plots than this in one of those stupid B-movies where the dumb, screaming girl runs, falls down, and just can't seem to get up in time to save her self. Her arm instantly flies up to protect her face, while she pleads for her life. I always wondered why she didn't have a gun in her pantyhose. Now I know it would not have mattered because she probably would have lost it just like I did! I couldn't believe I could be so stupid. I had turned into one of those girls I always wanted to slap in the face.

Closer, my name was again whispered. This time I recognized the voice. It was Rose. I felt a momentary sense of relief. I truly believed she had nothing to do with Helen Carrolton's death. My relief was short lived and replaced with fear. If she had nothing to do with Helen's death, why was she out here searching for me? Was she going to help me or try to capture me?

"Jesse, where are you?" her voice low and begging. "I had nothing to do with this. I had no idea until just now. Please, I want to help. They are going to kill you. You've got to get out of here."

She was going to help me. I pulled myself up off the ground, favoring my good leg, and leaned against a tree. I was wet from head to toe with blood and the dampness of the woods, and I hurt all over. My ponytail was filled with debris and the few strands of hair that had fallen down in my face were now stuck to it and matted with dried blood. The dried blood was covered by fresh blood. I must look like a wreck, I thought... then regained my senses. Who cares what I look like?

"I'm over here," I whispered. "I'm hurt. I need help."

Rose appeared. Even through the darkness I could tell her usual demure personality had been replaced with savage obedience. It was the look in her eyes that gave her away. Whatever she might or might not have known about this situation, she was not here to help me. She was here to help her family cover up yet another ugly truth. One of them was a killer!

She grabbed me from behind, locking my arms together and twisting them back until I thought they were going to break. She shrilled in my ear, "You must be stupid if you think I'd help you after all the crap you've put my family through."

"You lied to me," I murmured. "All this time, I thought you were an innocent by-stander, but you're not. You're just as sick as the rest of your demented family. You'll never get away with it. You might kill me, but Billy Blackhawk will not rest until he gets you and your whole crazy crew. Your only chance to get out of this unscathed is to help me bring an end to it. You've got to let me go." I did my best to confuse her. If I could convince her to listen to me, maybe I could save myself. It was now, or never.

I took a stab in the dark. "The police know about your mom. They know about Lisa and Sunny... and her last indiscretion—the girl in the red car. They're just trying to figure out where the rest of you fit in before they come out here and throw all of you in jail. But let me assure you, I only had a slight jump on them. I'm surprised they're not here already."

Suddenly, we both heard sirens in the background. They seemed far away, but I wasn't going to let that stop me. I had lied about the police and figured the sirens were probably just a state trooper pulling somebody over for speeding. However, the sirens were working in my favor and this was my chance to bullshit her.

"See," I reassured her. "They're on their way. They'll be here any minute. Let me help you. I know you're innocent. You're just doing what you think is right. You want to help them, but it's too late now. You have to save yourself."

She released her grip on me and sank down, sitting on an enormous rock. My ploy had worked.

"I really didn't know anything until a little while ago," she began. "When I got home, I parked my car behind the barn and attended to the horses like I usually do. Then my mom pulled up. She was hysterical. She said Dad had been arrested and she didn't know what to do. I'd never seen her in such a state. She kept mumbling something about how nobody loved her and she was sick and tired of living a lie. I thought she was flipping out, so I took her to the house and made her lay down. She was out of it, and I didn't know what to do. Finally, Dad came home. He had just been released from jail and was in a frenzy. He ran through the house scream-ing something about Mom. His exact words were, *'She's a stupid retard. The jig is up. This is the last time!'* I stopped him in the middle of his screaming fit. *'Dad, what's going on?'* I asked him. He gave me a weird look and said, *'Mom is sick, honey. She killed that girl, and we covered it up.'* Of course, I freaked out. When he told me all the sordid details, I cried. I couldn't believe this could happen to us."

"I know it's hard to believe," I took her hand in mine and tried to comfort her. "Sometimes, bad things happen to the best of us. Come on, let's get out of here."

She stood, saddened from all that was happening around us, and we helped each other find our way out of the woods. We reached the clearing to my car and found Jay standing beside it holding a shotgun.

"I see you found her," he said to his sister. "Bring her over here."

"Wait a minute Jay," she said to him. "We need to talk."

"What is there to talk about? You know what the old man said," he was getting upset. "He told us to find her and take her to the pit. Now get the lead out!" He handed her the shotgun. "Hold this while I tie her up." He grabbed me by my T-shirt, slammed me up against the car and forced my arms behind my back. I heard the jingling of metal and then felt the cool steel as he put handcuffs on my wrists. I tried to fight him, but it was useless. He was strong for his size and determined to get the job done. He grabbed me in the bend of my elbow and jerked me off the car.

"Where's your car keys?" he screamed at me.

"I don't know," I lied. "I think I dropped them somewhere in the woods. I fell down a couple of times."

"Jay, we have got to stop right now before this goes any further," Rose begged, backing up and raising the shotgun. "Jay, please. I can't let you do this. The police know everything. It's only a matter of time before they get here. Please don't make matters worse."

"Shut up!" he yelled. He lunged at her bringing the full force of his fist to her face. She stumbled backwards and fell to the ground, dropping the shotgun. Blood oozed from her lip.

"I won't be a part of this," she cried, wiping the blood from her mouth.

"The hell you won't!" He picked up the gun and pushed me back up against the car. Pointing it at me, he screamed to her, "Now get up and search her pockets for the keys. We ain't got all day."

She got up and walked over to me. "I'm sorry," she whispered, as she went through my pockets, retrieved the keys and reluctantly handed them to him. "If I don't do what he says he will hurt me."

"It's ok," I whispered.

It wasn't ok, but I couldn't help but feel sorry for her. She had no control over the situation and would probably end up like I was going to if she went against any of them. These people were capable of anything and it wouldn't surprise me if they decided to bury her right along side me to shut her up. One of them was responsible for one death already and possibly two others—if what Rita said had any meaning. What's to stop them from adding another one to the list? How far would they go to save them-selves? Would they kill their own flesh and blood? I had no doubts about the answer to that question.

Jay opened the door and shoved me into the back seat.

"Please, Jay," I begged. "Let me go. I promised you I'd help you out and I will. Just let me go."

He drew back and hit me in the head with the butt of his gun. I felt the blood cover my face just before I fell over and blacked out.

When I came to, I was still in the back seat of the car. My eyesight was blurred and my head felt like it was going to explode. Through the flashing white spots and pulsating visions of the melting background, I saw Rose slumped over the steering wheel with blood running down her face from an ugly, open wound to the side of her head. Her right wrist was cuffed to the gearshift.

"Damn!" I panicked. "Rose! Rose! Wake up!" I bumped the back of her seat with my shoulder. Pain shot through me like a sledgehammer. This was the same shoulder that had suffered the original attack from that maniac and up until now was just about healed.

She didn't stir. She was dead, killed by the hands of her own family.

Reality finally sunk in. I was going to die in this dark and god-for-saken place. I would never get to experience the joy of having kids and the love of a fine man... something I was so close to having. What about Mom, Claire, and Jack? They needed me! Billy, my newfound friend, where was he? Why hasn't he come to save me?

Breathing was becoming more difficult. *Not now,* I thought to myself. A panic attack is the last thing I needed! I soon found out I wasn't having a panic attack, but instead, the air in the car was getting thin. That's when I realized we were buried in the hole, our graves sealed with dirt.

I looked at the dash. The lights were on, but everything else was shrouded in darkness. The keys were still in the ignition!

My mind took a bouncing leap forward. If I could just get to the keys and start the car I could save us. I'd plow through the tightly packed dirt and come zooming out in a flying blaze of glory. I don't think so. Where had my mind gone? First of all, I could never get the car to start. The exhaust pipe was probably packed full of dirt by now and a car won't start without a means of releasing its ... what... *breath*? I don't remember too many of the things my father tried to teach me about cars, but I do remember him telling me that if the exhaust was blocked off the car wouldn't run, or something like that.

Rose groaned, and tried to straighten herself up in the seat.

"Rose!" I cried. "You're alive! Thank heavens! I thought you were dead." I was so glad she was still alive I would have reached over and given her a big hug if I could.

"I feel dead," she moaned. "Where are we? What happened?"

"I'm not sure. What's the last thing you remember?"

"Well," she seemed to be thinking. "I was driving. We had just come up to where the path crosses the stream, and I couldn't get the car into 4-wheel drive. Jay got angry and called me stupid. Then he hit me in the head with his gun."

"Then what happened?" I urged her. Even if we were in a no-win situation, I now had the satisfaction of knowing the car might still be in 4-wheel drive. That alone, would give us one advantage. If worse came to worse, somehow I would get this damn car started and at least make a last desperate attempt at saving our lives.

"That's it. That's the last thing I remember until now."

We sat silently for a moment. We both knew we were in a bad way and it was going to take a miracle to get us out of this mess.

A thought came to me. My cell phone! Was it still in my pocket? Yes. I felt the bulge of it. Would it work here?

"Rose," I said. "My cell phone is in my pocket. If you could just reach over and get it with your free hand, we could call for help." I scooted up to the console.

Turning sideways, she reached over with her left hand and dug into my pocket.

"I've got it!" she rejoiced. A second later she screamed, "I've got a dial tone! What now?"

"Hit the number three. That is my mom's number. Someone will be there, I'm sure."

She hit the button and waited for a response. "There's no one there," she replied. "I'm getting a lot of static in the background."

"Hang up and try hitting one."

"It's still ring... Hello, yes... we need help!" she cried into the phone.

"Stick it up to my ear!" I demanded.

She put the phone to my ear and I could barely make out Billy's voice over the static.

"Billy, shut up and listen. Rose and I are buried," I tried to say. The line went dead before I could finish my sentence.

"Dial it again," I shouted to Rose. "I lost the connection."

She tried it several times and in desperation turned back to me. "I'm sorry. I can't get anything, not even static... it's a goner. What'll we do now?"

"I don't know, Rose." I sighed. Depression was over-taking me and the future was looking dim. Could I dare hope that Billy heard my cries, or did the static drown me out?

"Wait a minute," Rose said. "The handcuffs..."

"What about the handcuffs?"

"I have the key in my pocket!" she shrilled. "Dad was real big on enforcing the safety of our home. Everybody had a gun of their own and was taught how to use it, and we all were given keys we had to keep on our key chain at all times. *It's your life line to freedom,* he would say. He was right!"

She shook with laughter. "I'm free!" she exclaimed, as she reached into the back seat and unlocked my handcuffs.

"Move over," I demanded of Rose, as I climbed into the front seat. "I'm going to get us out of here, or we're going to die trying!" What a cliché! It didn't matter. It worked for me. I was full of piss and vinegar and ready to take on the world. I wasn't going to die like this!

"Hold on," Rose said, reaching over to stop my hand from turning on the ignition. "Let's think about this before we do anything rash."

"Rose, I think rash is the only option we have left. We're running out of air." I knew the chances of us getting out of here were slim, but I refused to give up hope, and the longer I waited, the worse our chances got. I had to do something, and I had to do it fast.

I heard the sound of a muffled roar, and then felt the earth vibrate.

"What's that?" I asked, looking over at Rose. "Is that the bulldozer?"

"It is a backhoe, not a bulldozer," she said. With the glow from the dash lights, I could see her eyes were filled fear.

"Bulldozer... backhoe... who cares? What's going on up there?"

"Well, they're either packing the dirt down on top of us, or someone's here to save us. What's your guess on which one it is?"

"I'd say the chance of someone making it to our rescue in the nick of time is probably zero. We're got to save ourselves if we want to get out of here."

"Ok, then... let me think... " She put her head in her hands, and started to massage her temples. "I remember now." But she didn't say anything. She just sat there like she was in a trance.

"What, Rose?" I screamed at her. "What do you remember?"

"Don't yell at me," she cried. "I'm trying to think."

My patience was wearing thin. I wanted to grab her by the hair and shake her senseless. Didn't she realize we didn't have time for a casual chat? I was just about ready to pounce on her when she raised her head and looked up at me.

"I remember him hitting me because I couldn't get the gear right. It hurt like hell. I started seeing stars. I thought I was going to pass out, but I didn't. He kept yelling and yelling." She gasped for air. "He made me back the car down in the hole. He said he wanted to be able to pull it out with a winch, in case he ever had to move it. I was so scared. Then he raised the butt of the gun and hit me again. That's the last thing I remember."

"Whoa! Wait a minute," I said. "You're telling me you backed this car down an incline? We weren't just dropped into a hole?" My spirits lifted one hundred percent, as I thought about the prospects of us actually making it out of this death trap alive.

I leaned over and took Rose's hand in mine. "I know you're scared. So am I. But you're going to have to trust me on this one." I wanted her last thoughts to be comforting. If we were going to die in the next few minutes I wanted her to know that I didn't blame her. "I don't blame you for this. I want you to know that."

A tear slid down her face and mixed in with the blood. She smiled a faint smile and said, "Don't you think we should buckle up? I got a feeling this is going to be a bumpy ride."

❦ I had to laugh. Here we were at the footsteps of death's door and she wanted to buckle her seatbelt.

"Sure, why not?" I replied.

This could almost be funny if it wasn't so sad. Here we were, two young women in the prime of their lives—well, maybe one not so young— battered and beaten, strapped into seatbelts and buried in a car covered with dirt. This was going to take a miracle.

I believe in God, but I'm not a religious person. I hate to admit it, but the only time I seem to talk to him is when I need him. I don't go to church unless I have too. So, I try not to ask him for much. I know it might be a sin in everybody's eyes, but I have always felt that if you live your life honestly and try to be the best person you can be, that's all he asks of you. And I do my best.

I gave Rose's hand one last squeeze. "Get ready! We're getting out of here!" I let go of her hand and reached over to the ignition. "I'm going to turn the car on, slam it in gear, and then floor the gas. Got any questions?"

The backhoe overhead was coming to life. The roar of it, compiled with the scrubbing sounds I heard boosted me into action. Whether someone was packing us down or digging us out was no longer a consideration. I grabbed the key, and turned on the ignition. The Jeep fired up and sprang to life like the fine automobile it was intended to be. I put the car in gear and stomped down on the gas pedal. A vibration shook us.

"We're moving!" Rose shouted. "We're moving!"

I felt the dirt slowly give way as I rammed my foot on the gas and held the steering wheel tight. The inside of the car began to fill with an unpleasant odor, but the Jeep kept running and I kept on pushing it.

The pressure of a car trudging through dirt was like shoving your hand through a bangle bracelet that is two sizes too small. You knew if you twisted and forced it hard enough, it might fit. I kept on forcing.

We both coughed and hacked from the fumes and the dust floating into what little air we had left. My eyes burned and my throat felt raw. But I was determined not to give up. I looked over at Rose one last time. She was laid back in the seat, her eyes closed and her head hung down. She had stopped coughing. In that instant, I knew that these were our last few seconds of life.

Something came crashing down on the back of the Jeep, causing the front end to lift up. Glass from the hatchback shattered as something heavy scrubbed the roof. I could hear the dirt rushing in. But, the force of the backhoe had given us just the boost and lift we needed to free ourselves. When the pressure let up, the Jeep took off. We had made it through the gates of hell! The Jeep was still at full throttle.

A second later, the Jeep sputtered, slowed down... and died. The dirt had cleared the windshield enough for me to make out a huge pine tree within inches of the car's front end. My foot was still pressed to the floor with the gas pedal mashed down underneath. I was frozen and couldn't let up on it. I tried to catch my breath as my fingers found the controls on the door. I pressed the buttons down. The automatic windows hissed and a rush of fresh air came pouring in.

When the dust cleared, I looked at Rose. "Please don't be dead!" I cried, reaching over to shake her. When she didn't stir, I shook her harder. "Wake up Rose!" I demanded, tears flowing down my cheeks.

Her voice crackled under the coughs, as she gasped for air. "Did we... make... it?"

"Yes we did!" I said proudly. "We're alive!"

The excitement immediately died when the realization hit us. We sat staring at each other. Had we made it out of the jaws of death, only to return to the hands of our captors?

The backhoe had been silenced. Voices echoed in the distance and the sky was lit up with flashing blue lights. The familiar sound of a van door sliding open, and the bark of a dog brought me to my senses.

"Athena!" I wailed, forcing my tired and broken body out of the car. "Is that you?"

CHAPTER 27

A THENA CAME RUNNING up to me at full speed, charging like a raging bull. She was all over me, licking and digging her paws into my flesh. Her size overtook me and we both went tumbling to the ground. Her feet managed not to miss a sore spot on my body, as her excitement became frenzied.

I grabbed her head in my hands and nuzzled her face, kissing her wet nose and getting dog yuck all over my face. Normally, I wouldn't let a dog lick my face. They lick their butts with those tongues. But this was different. This time I relished the thought. I was alive and I was safe.

The commotion that ensued next was mind-boggling. The police and paramedics surrounded the car. Rose was helped out and put on a stretcher, while two paramedics squatted beside me and tried to help me push Athena away. I heard the command of Mom's voice a short distance away.

"Athena! Come here!" she ordered. Instantly, Athena stepped back, turned and ran in her direction, leaving me sitting on the ground with my mouth hung open.

"What is this, dissention in the ranks?" I joked.

I was barely coherent by the time they strapped me down onto the gurney. Questions filled my ears from all different directions. The police wanted to know all the details of what had happened here. I heard Mom and Billy in the background asking me if I was all right.

"Not now," said one of the guys who was carrying me to the ambulance. "You can talk to her after we're done."

Seeing they were at a stalemate, the police relented and went about trying to keep everybody else back, doing their duties in crowd control—and there was definitely a crowd forming. Mom, with her hand holding Athena's collar, stood to one side, while Jack and Dennis stood next to her with comforting expressions on their faces. Cole and Billy approached the back of the ambulance. In the background, amongst a field of police cars, I saw Jay. He was sitting in the back of one with the interior lights on, while an officer in the front seat wrote on a clipboard. A few cop cars down, sat Rita and her husband. They all leaned forward as if they had on handcuffs.

"It serves you right!" I hissed. "I hope you all rot in jail!"

They hoisted me up into the ambulance, and prepared to leave. The driver was in the front seat, pushing buttons and talking into a box on the dash, while another guy started to close the back doors.

"Ok," he yelled. "We got room for one more person."

I heard Billy say to Cole, "You go ahead. I'll follow you in my truck."

"No," Cole whispered. "You be with her now, because from now on, she will be mine."

"I don't think so," Billy said.

"Shut up both of you!" I screamed, raising my head up just enough to see them. "Would one of you please get into the ambulance and let's get out of here! You bunch of cry-babies!"

Billy jumped up inside and helped the paramedic close the door. Sirens blasted as we sped down the road. The paramedic bandaged the wound on my head and then went to the one above my knee.

"The cut on your head isn't so bad Miss, but the one on your knee looks like it might leave a healthy scar. I'm going to cover it for now," he said.

"The one on my forehead isn't real bad?" I asked, trying to talk through the oxygen mask. "I thought for sure it was bad because it's been steadily bleeding."

"Head wounds usually bleed heavily and appear a lot worse than they are sometimes," he reassured me. "You might need a couple of stitches."

Once the paramedic gave the ok and backed out of the way, Billy leaned over into my face and grabbed my hand. "Two things," he demanded. "First, I'm going to seriously kick your butt when this is over, and two, as much as I hate to admit it, I think Cole really does love you."

"So, where is he now?" I mumbled. "Why isn't he here with me instead of you?"

"Because he knows how to let go," Billy said. "He knows if he gives you what you need now—your family and your friends—when all is said and done, you will come back to him in the end."

"Is that what he told you?" I asked.

"Those weren't his exact words," he went on. "But when you get right down to it, he is right. You do love him don't you? When this is all over, where is the first place you are going to run?" He was testing me and I fell into his trap.

"I don't know, where?"

"You will run right back into his arms."

"Maybe," I said. "I'm still thinking that one over."

Changing the subject, Billy asked, "What possessed you to pull such a stupid stunt like this? Don't you know you could have died back there? You promised me you were going straight home!"

"I know, Billy."

"If it had not been for my great wisdom and expertise as a great Cherokee hunter," he stuck his chest out and bragged. "You would probably be dead by now. You are lucky to have me as a friend."

"So, you are the one who found me?"

"Well, I can't take all the credit. I had a little help, but that is another story. I will add this one to my list of great tales."

"I can't wait to hear it," I replied. "I just don't want to hear it now. I've got this whole thing figured out. I know where Helen's body is buried!"

"Save it," he demanded. "As a matter of fact, don't answer any questions when we get to the hospital until Jack is by your side."

"What? Why?" I was confused.

"Because, if this plays out the way I think it's going to, the police are going to charge you with obstruction of justice. You interfered with an ongoing investigation, and got caught. The cops don't take kindly to people getting in their way, and boy did you ever get in their way."

"But I solved the case!" I cried.

"I hate to tell you this, but the cops already had it figured out. Once they had Helen's purse that was all they needed."

"But do they know where the body is buried?" I asked.

"Oh, they'll find the answer soon enough," he replied. "After what happened to you, by tomorrow morning, they will have their guys out there digging up every inch of ground. It's just a matter of time now."

"I can take them right to it, and save them some time," I offered.

"No way!" he objected. "You tell me where she is and I'll tell them."

"That is not going to happen! After all I've been through, I deserve to be there. I earned that right."

"You are one stubborn `ge ya," he hissed. "You can barely walk, yet you want to go back to the place where you almost died?"

"I want to see for myself if I was right."

"You mean you're not sure? Nobody told you her exact location? What kind of private eye are you?"

"We didn't get around to in-depth details," I cried. "They were too busy trying to bump me off."

THE AMBULANCE PULLED UP to the emergency room entrance. I was whisked into an examining room, leaving the waiting area filled with police. Billy was by my side.

"You will have to wait outside," the intern told Billy.

"No!" I screamed, removing my oxygen mask. "He stays, or I'm getting up from here and walking out!"

"I'm afraid that's not going to be possible, Ms. Watson," the intern replied. "They've posted an officer outside the door to make sure that you don't leave. They want to question you first."

I looked over at Billy and asked, "Can they do that?"

"I'm afraid they can," the intern answered before Billy had a chance to reply. He looked at Billy. "Are you a relative, sir?"

"He's my boyfriend," I butted in.

The intern grabbed the curtain to close it and looked at Billy then back at me. Smiling and shaking his head, he said, "Who am I to judge? I'll be back in a minute."

"What is that supposed to mean?" I screamed after him. "That guy has some nerve! Who does he think he is?"

Billy laughed. "Don't get your panties in a bunch! He's got a point, you know. I'm almost twice your age."

"Sixteen years, that's all!" I corrected him. "Besides, who knows, maybe I like old men."

"Thanks a lot!" Billy said, acting insulted.

"You know what I mean..."

A few minutes later, the curtain was pulled back and people dressed in green hospital scrubs surrounded my bed. A tiny, young woman removed the bandage from my head and began washing up my wound, while an even younger looking guy took a pair of scissors and cut the leg of my jeans. A tall, slender, blond-haired girl—I guessed her age to be around sixteen—took down information on a clipboard.

"Don't you have any grown-ups working in this hospital?" I cried.

"Jesse!" Billy admonished me. "Don't pay any attention to her. She's delirious," he said to the group around me, trying to apologize for my rude behavior. "She's been through a lot today. You have no idea."

"It's ok, sir," the young man replied. "We realize people say and do things they don't mean when they're in a place like this. Hospitals are intimidating. They're in pain, and pain does weird things to people's manners." He smiled, as he scrubbed, poked and prodded.

"Go to hell!" I spat. "I was already in pain and now you're making it worse. What the hell... Ouch... that hurts! I want some morphine!"

He motioned to the blond and spoke under his breath as he continued to torture me. "Miss Jensen's going to get the doctor."

"You mean you guys aren't doctors? What are you then, Candy Stripers?" I continued to lash out at him. I hurt all over, and my disposition was quickly turning ugly. I had suffered enough for one day.

Billy was in the process of trying to calm me down and assure me everything was going to be fine when the doctor walked in, followed by a whole new team of hospital personnel. The tall blond handed him her clipboard and the first group left, so the real doctors could take over.

"I'm so glad you could make it, doctor!" I spewed forth my venom. "I just told that little boy I needed something for the pain if he was going to continue his ritual act of human torture."

The doctor scanned the chart and then looked up at Billy and said, "She's going to be fine."

"Don't talk to him!" I became hysterical. "Talk to me!" Everything that had happened to me in the last twelve hours came crashing down. I had been shot at... again... beat up, buried in a hole, and left to die. The police were sure to hound me until they could come up with a reason to lock me away for the rest of my life. These were just some of the things that had happened to me *since I moved to the mountains*. The list was quickly becoming a long one.

I felt the prick of a needle. "This will help ease the pain," a soft voice said. I turned my head to the side and looked into the nurse's bright blue eyes. "You should start to feel better in a moment," she promised.

"Are you kidding? Now that the doctor's here, I feel better all ready."

Two hours later, my wounds repaired, I was bedded down for the night. Rose was in the room across the hall, according to Billy. It was decided that because of our inhalation of a toxic substance, we should be monitored overnight for possible side effects of said poison. With the two of us so close to each other, the police would have easy access. They could question me, and then run next door and question Rose.

"I'm nobody's fool," I whispered to Billy. "I know what they're doing."

"It doesn't matter," he said. "Tomorrow, they're going to have to release you, assuming you don't go into a coma and die tonight. By then, we will have had plenty of time to fix this mess."

"What do you mean?"

"Well, right now, they're only letting the family in to see you. Procedures, you know. But as soon as the family has seen you, the cops will be turned loose. They will swarm in here like bees on honey."

Mom entered the room, followed by Jack and Dennis.

"Well, where's Athena?" I asked. "Your little posse isn't complete without her."

"Don't be cute," Mom retorted. "She's outside on a leash. Cole's taking care of her. You don't think I would leave her locked up in the van on a warm night like this, do you?"

"She's on a leash? How did you manage that?"

"It is not important. We need to be concerned with what is happening here, and what are we going to do about it. We have been given fifteen minutes, and then the police are coming in to question you. We need to get our stories straight."

Jack walked up to my bed. "Listen carefully," he began. "When the police start to question you, don't say anything until I give you the go-ahead. You have a right to have an attorney present during questioning."

"But I though you handled real estate. What do you know about criminal law? How can you help me?"

"Jesse, where have you been?" Jack was stunned. "My first case was real estate. I've come a long way since those days. Criminal law is my field of expertise now. So, trust me, I'm not going to let anything happen to you. So, let's get right down to the nitty-gritty. Tell me everything."

I spent the next fifteen minutes allotted to me, telling them everything I could think of, beginning with the moment I left Billy, until my escape to freedom.

"So, as you can see," I said at the end of my statement, "I know where the body is buried."

"You think Rose had nothing to do with it?" Billy asked.

"No, she didn't," I replied. "She had no idea what was going on until the last minute. But by then it was too late. She was in their grips just like me. You saw what happened to her. They tried to kill her and she was their flesh and blood. Can you imagine that?"

"Well, actually," Cole said, as he walked into the room smiling that intoxicating smile of his. "Rose Hudgins just so happens to be the biological daughter of Chase Teale—the father of Rita Hudgins. The story gets even more ugly. Rita's brother, Perry Teale—who was supposed to have killed his wife and taken his own life... was Jay's father. Jay was adopted.

There was a lot of bad blood there. But for right now, all I want to know is how you're doing?" He walked over and planted a kiss on my forehead.

"I could be better, but at least I am still living thanks to my family." I scanned the room and saw their proud, smiling faces. They had come through for me!

"Well, actually..." Billy started to say, when the police walked in.

Detective Hargrove introduced himself and the two detectives that came in behind him, to the group in my room. Two uniformed officers accompanied them.

"If you are up to it now, Ms. Watson, we would like to ask you some questions," he said. "If the rest of you would please wait in the hall, this won't take long."

Everyone left the room, except Jack. "I'm Jesse's brother, Jack Watson." He reached out his hand to the detective. "I'm also her attorney."

"Nice to meet you," responded the detective, as her shook Jack's hand. Then he got right down to business. Turning to me he said, "Before we get started, Officer Downey is going to read you your rights."

"I think we have a neighbor named Downey. Maybe you're related," I said. Why did I say that? This was not the time for chitchat. It didn't matter because Officer Downey was not interested.

"... Do you understand these rights that I have just read to you?" the officer asked, and then stepped back.

"Yes, I do."

"Ms. Watson," Detective Hargrove asked, "Were you aware there was a restraining order on you when you trespassed on the Hudgins' property?"

"Don't answer that," Jack ordered.

"It's ok, I want to," I replied. "I wasn't trespassing, I was invited."

"Who invited you?"

"Jay Hudgins."

The detectives looked back and forth at each other, and then Detective Hargrove spoke again. "Why don't you tell us your side of the story?" Officer Downey walked closer to my bed and began taking notes.

Jack leaned over and whispered in my ear, "Be very careful what you say. I'll be right here to stop you if you get into dangerous territory."

I smiled at Jack and nodded my head in acknowledgment. I told them my story. "I went to talk to Tom Dorey at the gas station where he works, and Jay was there with him. I talked to both boys and tried to convince them to come clean. Jay got scared. He led me to believe his father had killed Helen Carrolton and that he'd show me where she was buried, if I'd help him out of this mess. I agreed to do what I could. He told me to meet him at the end of his road after it got dark, and to come alone. I did, but he wasn't there like he promised. Then I heard the bulldozer start up. I sneaked through the woods and found them digging a hole. I knew exactly what they had planned for me, so I took off running back to my car."

"Is that when you sustained your injuries?" one of them asked.

"Most of them," I continued. "When I got into my car, Rita was sitting in the front seat waiting for me. She had a gun. She confessed to killing Helen Carrolton, and said something about a girl named Sunny, and one named Lisa. I managed to get away from her and fled back into the woods. Then Rose found me. After I told her what I knew, she tried to help me get away. When we got back to my car, Jay was there. The next thing I knew, I came to and Rose and I were in my car, buried in the ground."

"That's a pretty amazing story," Detective Hargrove said.

"It's the truth, every last word," I responded. "Just ask Rose!"

He ignored my demand. "Did either one of them tell you where Helen Carrolton was buried?"

"Not in so many words," I answered. "But I know."

"Where might that be?" another officer asked, speaking for the first time since he had walked into the room.

"I'm not too good with directions, but I can show you."

"Just try to explain to us the best you can, and we will take it from there," Officer Downey stated.

Not on your life, I thought to myself. I did the work and I wanted to be there when she was found. I needed closure, and that was the only way I was going to get it.

Fortunately, the doctor walked in and said, "I'm sorry, but your time is up. My patient needs her rest if we are going to be able to release her in the morning. I'm sure your questions can wait until then."

After a mumbled discussion with his men, Detective Hargrove turned to me and said, "We will return in the morning. We will post a couple of officers outside your door. Officially, you're under arrest for trespassing."

"What about the Hudgins? Have they been arrested?" I asked before they had a chance to leave.

"No formal charges have been filed yet, but we have them in custody. They are being interrogated at the moment."

The doctor ushered them out and then came over to me. "Everything seems to be normal with your tests, so you should be able to leave in the morning. But for now, I want you to get some rest."

Finally, everyone left except Billy. He was determined to stay and make sure that I was not going to die.

"Billy, why don't you go home and get some rest," I asked. "You look like you could use it."

"I'm fine," he replied. "Besides, we still have a few things to discuss."

"Forget it, I know what you want, and I'm not going to tell you until you promise to let me go with you."

Billy refused to make me the promise I demanded. Instead, we talked about everything else until I finally dozed off. When I woke up the next morning, I expected him to be gone, but instead he was sitting in a chair next to my bed, drinking coffee. It was eight o'clock. I tried to sit up, but the pain in my head only got worse when I did. I slumped back onto my pillow.

"Rough night?" he asked.

"More like rough life," I said through a haze. "Yuck, my mouth tastes like garbage. I need a mint."

"Want some coffee?" Billy offered me his cup.

I took a sip, and spat. "Gross, it has sugar in it! You know I don't like sugar in my coffee!"

"Oh, that's right, I forgot. I'll go get you a fresh cup with just cream, right?" He left the room, passing the nurse that entered.

A few questions later, she handed me two pages of instructions on how to take care of my wounds. Finally, she said the doctor had signed my release form. I could leave anytime.

"What about Rose Hudgins?" I asked. "Has she been released, too?"

"I'm not sure, but I can check for you if you want."

"Please do," I said.

She left the room as Billy walked back in carrying a cup of coffee.

"Have you been sprung yet?" he asked, handing me the coffee.

Seconds later, Mom walked in with a small duffel bag in her hand and said, "I thought you might need some fresh clothes." She leaned over and gave me a kiss and then looked at Billy. "I tried to call you last night when we got home, but there was no answer. So, I figured you stayed here."

"Somebody had to make sure she stayed in bed," he laughed. He gave Mom a hug. "I will wait out in the hall while you help Jesse get dressed. I think she's going to need it."

I was dressed and ready to go when the nurse came back in. "Miss Hudgins was released ten minutes ago. Her grandfather took her home."

I didn't say anything. It was no longer any of my business. Yet, I couldn't help but feel sorry for the girl. She would have a long road ahead of her, if she were to recover from the emotional trauma she had suffered at the hands of her family.

I walked out into the hall to find all the familiar faces staring back at me—Billy, Cole, Jack and Dennis and the police detectives from last night. Detective Hargrove came up to me first.

"We have arrested Rita Hudgins for the murder of Helen Carrolton and we are looking into the deaths of her brother and his wife, Sunny. Lisa Wilson was the Lisa you told us about."

"Is she dead, too?" I asked.

"No," he replied. "She's been institutionalized for the last fifteen years in a place called Shady Retreat in Charleston, South Carolina. We've got two detectives on their way there now." He stopped long enough to catch his breath. "We got a confession out of Rita, but she says she doesn't know where Helen is buried, and we can't get anything out of Jay and his father. They refuse to talk, and without a confession we will have to let them go. I have a search warrant to search the property, but it would go faster if I could get your help."

"What do you mean?" I yelled. "They tried to kill me and Rose, and you are going to let them go free?"

"They're claiming Rita did it," Detective Willis spoke up. "They both say they didn't know anything about the attempt on your life."

"That's a lie!" I screamed. "Jay was the one who hit me in the head with the shotgun, and I doubt very seriously Rita has the ability to operate a backhoe. They're lying! Rose can back me up."

"Rose Hudgins has already confirmed what she could of your story. Now, if we can find the body, forensics will be able to piece it all together," replied Detective Hargrove. "I'm sure they left some kind of evidence. You can't dispose of a car and a body without leaving something. Plus, if it is buried on their land, you can bet the bank on a guilty verdict. I can assure you they won't get out of this."

"What about me?" I asked him.

"Immunity from prosecution," Jack stepped forward, "of any and all charges concerning this case."

The detective called his men to the side. After a brief conversation, and a little head-scratching, he returned. Two of his detectives stood to each side of him.

"Immunity it is," he replied. "We're even willing to forego the charge of withholding evidence in the matter of the girl's purse, if you can lead us to the body." He winked at me and smiled at Billy. "See, we're not as dumb as you might think."

"If she can't lead you to the body," Jack jumped in. "What then?"

"I'm afraid..." he started to respond.

Cole was next to step forward. "May I have a word with you, Detective Hargrove?" They turned and walked over to the nurse's station. Cole kept poking his finger in the detective's chest while they talked.

"What do you think is going on?" I whispered in Billy's ear.

Jack slid over to us and said, "They're working out a deal. It appears the detective is being hard to get along with, but from the way it looks to me, Cole has the upper hand. There's something going on they're not telling us."

"Like what?" I lowered my voice.

"It doesn't matter," Billy spoke in hushed tones.

Jack agreed, "As long as the two of you aren't held accountable for anything, who cares about the rest?"

"You have a point," I said, glancing at Billy. "The only thing I care about is saving our butts."

After what seem like a long, argumentative battle, Cole and the detective walked back over to us.

"Complete immunity," Detective Hargrove stated. "But I want to warn both of you," he pointed his finger at Billy and me, making a twisted, distorted face. "From now on, until the two of you get a badge pinned to your chest, I want you to remember one thing. You're not one of us. I don't want to ever hear about any of your improprieties again. If you want to be detectives, you had better obey the law. Do I make myself clear?"

Billy and I were like two cats that had just pissed up against the living room furniture. We swore it wasn't us... and we didn't do anything wrong.

"Sure," the detective growled.

"Ok, let's go!" I shouted.

CHAPTER 28

MOM HELPED ME OUT of the hospital room to the front entrance, while the men brought the cars around. The nurses insisted I be wheel-chaired out, but the minute we hit the front door I jumped up and left the wheel chair behind.

"After all the obstacles I've faced in the last few days, I'll be damned If I am not going to walk out of here on my own!" I said.

"You're absolutely right!" Mom replied. She looked at me and smiled.

The caravan of automobiles pulled out of the hospital lot. A state trooper led the way, with the white Buick carrying the three detectives, following behind. Cole was next in his Jeep. Billy and I rode together, and Mom, Jack and Dennis brought up the rear. I probably should have ridden with Cole when he asked me to, but I felt like I needed to be with Billy. We had been through so much, and now that a major milestone had been crossed—we had solved our first really big case together—I wanted to be with him.

Billy didn't say a whole lot to me until we reached the turn off in Ruckersville. He had been so quiet that I did not know what to expect.

"You know, you really have to get over this obsession you have with me," he joked. "You just broke that poor man's heart. I've seen the way you've been giving him the brush-off."

"What are you talking about?" I shook my head and threw up my arm. "I don't want to go there. Forget it! I want to talk about you and me."

"What do you mean, you and me?"

"I mean, if I'm going to get shot at all the time and someone's always going to try and kill me, I want more money!"

"No problem," he murmured. "I think we can work something out. You have earned a raise."

The two of us were a fine pair. I don't know which one was physically mangled up the most, but I knew both of us suffered from a mental collapse that could only be rebuilt by what was to be a saddened outcome. We would get our closure, but at what cost?

"I hope you know what you are doing," Billy said. "If you come up empty-handed things could get a little sticky."

"Don't you worry about me, pal," I hissed. "I've got my ducks in a row!" Or, at least, I sure hoped I did.

When we turned onto the road that led to the Hudgins' house, I shivered. Coming back to the place of my *almost* death made me feel eerie. I could have died right here not more than a few hours ago... never to be seen, or heard from again. I broke down and cried.

Billy broke the chain of cars and pulled over to the side.

"It's ok, Jesse, go ahead and cry. You've been through an ordeal. It's only natural that you would be upset."

"It's just that I can't seem to get beyond that feeling that someone's after me. It is such a creepy feeling."

"It will pass in time," he said. "You have been hunted, and the hunted never sleep. Eventually, you will get over it."

"There you go again sounding like my mother."

He gave me time to cry out my tears and then pulled back out into the road. The rest of the group had pulled over earlier and were sitting in their cars, waiting on us. Maybe they knew I was having a mental breakdown.

"Where is my Jeep?" I cried, as we passed the Hudgins' house. I kept remembering about my poor, beautiful car that I once loved so much. Now, I didn't know if I could ever get in it again.

"I called Daniel and he had somebody come out here and tow it away.

He said between you and me, we were going to keep him in business forever. He just got your dad's truck fixed when your car was hauled in. He said we were his best customers."

"Billy, you and I both know we're going to find the body of Helen Carrolton, don't you? This is the first time I have ever come face to face with someone that has been murdered. I've heard about it, but I've never been involved like this. Even when that crazy woman killed her husband for cheating on her with another man, I wasn't there. I wasn't in the middle. I'm right in the middle of it now."

"It'll be ok. Trust me," he said. "You can handle it. I'm sure of it!"

Billy and I was now the lead car. By the time we reached the end of the road, Billy looked at me and said, "I guess this is the right place, huh?"

"You knew all along didn't you?"

"Well, I was pretty sure," he replied.

"Why didn't you go ahead and tell the police of your suspicions?"

"What, and deprive you of your chance to see if your *feelings* had any merit?" he asked. "I could not do that to you."

Billy parked his truck and we got out, waiting for everybody else to do the same. Detective Hargrove and his men walked up to us, and once Mom, Jack and Dennis joined the group, the detective signaled for me to show them the way.

"The forensic team should be here any minute, and the medical examiner is waiting for our call," Detective Hargrove stated. "The department should have some of our guys out here soon. I just got off the radio with my captain and he said to wait for him, they were on their way." No sooner had he spoke, the road filled with cop cars and blaring sirens.

A tall, slender man with a head full of brown, curly hair and a scar across his right eye was introduced to us as Captain John Waverly of the CPD. He appeared to be around forty or forty-five, and in good physical shape. Surprisingly, he pulled out a pack of cigarettes, offered us all one, and then lit up. Although he seemed pleasant, he was all business-like as he motioned for his men to follow him.

By the time I had led them down the path Billy and I had traveled before, I noticed several more official looking men had joined the group, which now consisted of about twenty-five people. At least ten of the men were in uniform and some were taking notes, while others talked on walkie-talkies. Several of the officers carried shovels and duffel bags.

Once we reached the site, officers began putting up yellow crime scene tape, as several others dressed themselves in disposable jumpsuits and facial masks. They picked up their shovels, ready to start their task. We were asked to stay behind the yellow tape so the men could do their job. I wanted to help, but Captain Waverly assured me his men could handle it.

"It might be best if you go back and wait by your cars," he walked up to us and said. "If we find the body, I can send someone to inform you. This could be pretty ugly."

"I'm not going anywhere," I said, digging in my heels. "I almost got killed over this girl. I think I'm entitled to be here."

He glanced around at us and shook his head. "You know I could have my guys remove you from the scene?"

"You could," I replied, but firmly stood my ground.

"Ok, I'll let you stay for now," he said. "But if you get in my way, I will have you removed."

We all backed up as if to let him know we would stay out of his way, but we were not going to leave unless we were forced to. I was tired, my body ached, and I needed to sit down. I found a pile of rocks off to the side, walked over and sat down. Mom, Jack and Dennis followed while Billy and Cole had their heads together with the two detectives.

"What do you think they're talking about?" Mom leaned over to me and asked.

"I don't have the slightest idea," I answered. I looked passed her to Jack and said, "I never did thank you for going to get Billy. If you guys hadn't showed up things might not have turned out the way they did."

He glanced at me with a surprised look on his face. "Didn't he tell you? We couldn't find him."

"How did you know where to come looking for me if you didn't get up with him?"

"Well, there is a simple explanation," Mom joined in. "When we got to Billy's we couldn't get him to come to the door. We rang the buzzer to the office and even walked to the side door and banged on it. We banged on the garage door. Finally, I used my keys and let us in through the front door. I had a heck of a time trying to remember the code to the alarm because I was so frantic and thought for sure we were all going to get arrested. Fortunately, I finally remembered the code, punched in the numbers, and then we went about searching for him. We checked downstairs and then went up to his apartment, but he was not there."

"Athena was the one who led us into his office," Jack added. "She jumped up and started knocking things off his desk and that's when we found the file on Helen Carrolton. Mom said that was the case you were working on, so we looked through it and found the Hudgins' address. It was the one name that Mom had remembered hearing you and Billy talk so much about. So, we took a chance. We were almost to their road when we noticed Billy's truck in front of us. Cole was with him. That's when we knew we were on the right path so to speak."

"Then what happened?"

"We followed them to the end of the road and got out," Mom replied. "That's when we heard the bulldozer."

"Billy yelled for us to follow him and that's what we did," Dennis finally spoke.

"We turned around and headed back towards the highway. When we passed the house, Billy turned off onto a dirt road," Mom explained. "We followed him for a good long ways until we came to a stream."

"You should have seen your mom handle that van of hers," Dennis chuckled. "I was sure we would never make it across that stream, but she was one determined lady."

"My poor van will probably never be the same for it," she sighed.

"Billy and Cole pulled right up to the bulldozer, jumped out and ran up to Larry Hudgins as he was climbing down." Jack went on, "Larry Hudgins took off running and Cole tackled him to the ground. Next thing we knew, Billy was up on the bulldozer, while Cole handcuffed the man to the truck door and took off after the kid. By the time Cole got the kid cuffed, Mom had already called the police."

"That's right, I forgot to tell you. Billy bought me a cell phone," she giggled. "I am sure glad he did."

"Where was Rita Hudgins?" I asked.

"They found her sitting by a tree, babbling to her self," Dennis said. "That woman is crazy."

"By the time Billy got the bulldozer started and began moving the dirt, the police arrived. I wet my pants when I saw that red Jeep of yours come flying up out of the ground," Mom said.

"She sure did."

Before Jack could finish what he was saying, everybody around us started yelling and running towards where the men had been digging. Instantly, Mom and the rest of us jumped up and ran over to the yellow tape, getting as close as we could. Billy came up to me and put his arms around my neck as the red roof became visible.

One of the men in the hole yelled, "We got a body in here—or what's left of one."

I sank to the ground on my knees and cried. Billy had his arms wrapped around me as I rocked back and forth, my body racked with uncontrollable sobs. I leaned over and puked up the contents of my stomach. My insides were shaking as I gladly took the handkerchief Billy had fished out of his pocket.

I looked up at him, my breath smelling awful, and said, "What would I do without you?"

"Not to worry," he planted a kiss on my cheek. "I'm not going anywhere. Besides, you would never make it without me to keep you straight."

Just about the time Billy kissed me on the cheek, Cole walked over, bent down and mumbled something in his ear. Billy told me he would be right back and he got Mom to come sit with me.

"You know, I'm still trying to figure out which one of them loves you the most," Mom whispered.

"Don't be silly," I objected.

"I think it's great," she went on. "First, you can't get a decent man and now you have two of them fighting over you. I just knew one day you'd have someone, but I never thought you'd have two."

"You're being ridiculous," I said.

If I live to be a hundred, I don't think I will ever be able to explain how I felt when I finally stood up and looked down into that hole and saw the little red car. I should have been glad that I was right all along, but the overwhelming feeling of sadness took that away from me. I felt like a little piece of me had died with Helen Carrolton and I knew I would never be the same. I had a knot in my stomach as a cold dread swept over me. Who would tell her parents?

With tears in my eyes, I walked over to Billy and collapsed in his arms. "It's her, isn't it?" I already knew the answer, but I still had to ask.

"Yes it is," he sadly whispered.

When they used the winch on the back of Billy's truck to pull her car out of the ground, I had to walk away. It was so sad I couldn't stand to watch any longer. I knew what it was like to lose a loved one.

As I was growing up, my contact with death was very limited. However, as I got older I had experienced it first hand. A close girlfriend of mine died at the age of thirty from breast cancer, and one of the guys that I worked with at a department store, committed suicide. The death of my grandparents was another sad memory. Those were hard, but they didn't compare to the two recent deaths that would squeeze the life out of my heart every day. I mourned for my father, and ten months before Dad died, my cousin Danielle was killed in a car accident. She was only eighteen years old. I still cry sometimes when I think about her and had sad it was that her life had been cut short.

Danielle was the youngest of Uncle Bill and Aunt Edie's three girls. She always seemed to manage to keep them on their toes with her wild, teenage shenanigans, while Anita—the middle daughter—dealt with her own demons, eventually recovering and making a life for herself. The oldest, Belinda was married to a wonderful guy named Will, and along with their two kids in tow, traveled all over the United States as professional storytellers. They seemed to be the all-American family... until Danielle died. Nothing was ever the same after that. Now this brought it all back. All the hurt and pain flooded my soul.

"Billy," I barely got out. "Please take me home."

He ran his hand across my face and whispered, "Come on, baby girl, let's go home. You don't need to be here."

Much of what happened next was a blur. All I remembered was the ride back to Stanardsville in Billy's truck. The whole way he tried to get me to talk. He said he was worried about me and I didn't look so good.

I hissed at him. "How do you expect me to look? I've been through the mill. I almost died. A poor young girl has lost her life to a bunch of loony tunes, not to mention the fact that her parents will probably never get over it... and you're worried about how I look?"

"I'm just saying that I think this has been a little too much for you. You have not been exposed to the underworld of death and destruction like I have. It's hard to get used to it."

"I know the pain of death. This is just a different form of it," I moaned. "Who tells the parents? Can you imagine what they are going to go through?" I started to cry again. "I remember when my cousin, Danielle died. She was so young..."

"I'm taking you home," he replied as he rubbed my arm and drove his truck through the green traffic light in Ruckersville. "Captain Waverly agreed with me that it would be better if someone went in person to tell the Carroltons about their daughter's death. I convinced him to let me."

"I'm going with you," I declared.

Mom, Jack, and Dennis were in Mom's van behind us, with Cole fast on their rear end. I looked into Billy's rear view mirror and saw his green Jeep. I caught Billy looking at me.

"So, what do you think?" he interrogated me. "What is it going to be?"

"I don't have the slightest idea of what you mean."

"You know what I'm talking about," he shouted. "What's the deal? You gave this man the boot like you were throwing out yesterday's trash."

"He betrayed me."

"Get over it," Billy demanded. "You have no idea what this man has been through for you."

"Well, why don't you tell me?" I said, with the strange feeling that I didn't want to hear what he had to say. "Since when did you become his best friend, again? I thought you two had become mortal enemies," I dug at him. "Remember? You said he only cared about himself, and no matter what, in the end he would do what he had to do? Well, I see that now. He turned us in. It was from his report that they learned about the purse and our involvement. I can't trust him anymore."

"There are things you don't know about," Billy came back.

"Yeah, like what?"

"*Like...* he's the one who called me yesterday after you left. Those pain pills I took were making me groggy. I was just getting ready to crawl into bed and go to sleep when the phone rang. It was Cole and he was acting crazy. He was nuts. He kept going off about a file he had just gotten. He said Larry Hudgins was a sex pervert. His wife had lesbian tendencies and the teenage son was an extremely troubled youth—and then proceeded to go down the list of the boy's priors. To top that all off, he said the Charleston Police Department suspected the mama was involved with the death of her brother-in-law and his wife, but never could get anything on her."

"Are we going someplace with this story?" I sneered. "Or are you going to string me along until I choke on my own rope? Get to the point!" I was getting tired of listening to him go on with what was obviously to be the last minute heroics of the boyfriend that had betrayed me. I guess I'm just not a forgiving person, but to me, when someone betrays you, it is over. Cole could have been *the one*, but he betrayed me. That's something I just couldn't tolerate.

"The point I'm trying to make is..." He looked at me with his eyebrows curled in, like he does when he's trying to be serious. "He said he called you when he found all this out and your Mom told him you hadn't come back from taking me home. He hurried over to my house and hustled me out of bed. I knew you were up to something when he told me you weren't home. We put two and two together and came looking for you."

"So, what you're saying is... if Cole hadn't come to your house, I might still be buried in the ground?"

He looked at me skeptically. "That's a strong possibility."

"You think I should give him another chance?"

"I think you should do what your heart tells you."

This gave me something to think about. If Billy was eager for me to forgive Cole then maybe I should listen to him and try to put Cole's past betrayal behind us. Everybody is entitled to one mistake... right? My problem is—I'm just not as forgiving as Billy.

"Like I said, I'll give it some thought."

We pulled into the driveway and by the time we got out of the truck, Claire came rushing out of the house.

"Thank God, you're all right," she screamed, as she ran up to me and gave me a hug. "I was worried to death about you! Don't you ever pull a stunt like this again, do you hear me?"

I mumbled a couple of responses, agreeing with everything she said, while we walked up to the porch. There was no arguing with her when she got like this. She would go into one of her lectures and never let up. I didn't need that now. I had other things on my mind.

Billy and Cole were standing by the truck having a deep conversation, while Mom and my other rescuers went inside. I wanted to know what they were talking about, so I convinced Claire I was fine and got her to go in the house with the promise that I would be right in. I swallowed the lump in my throat and walked up to them. Their conversation stopped immediately.

"Ah, you must have been talking about me," I joked.

"As a matter of fact, we were," Cole looked at me. "We were just discussing what to do next."

"Yes," Billy added, looking at his watch. "We've got until the six o'clock news broadcast to get to the Carrolton's or they're going to find out about Helen on the television. Captain Waverly said he couldn't keep a lid on it passed then. So, we've decided that Cole and I would be the ones to do it. You're staying home."

"I most certainly am not! I'm going with you."

Billy and Cole exchanged glances.

"We already discussed it once and decided I was going—and I am going," I said, determined to get my way. Nobody was going to stop me from seeing this to the end.

"I told you she would say that," Billy grunted. "Let's go to work."

Twenty minutes later, after Mom had fed us and given us one of her long-winded lectures, the three of us got into Billy's truck and headed for Poquoson. It was a good feeling to be alive, even though we had a nasty job ahead of us. I dreaded having to tell the Carroltons their daughter was dead, but I also knew it had to be done. I hoped that someday, down the road, they might recover and go on with the rest of their lives.

That's what you have to do, isn't it?

EPILOGUE

T HE 4TH OF JULY WEEKEND turned out to be beautiful. The weath-
erman had forecast thunderstorms for both days and as usual he was
only half right. Each day was sunny and nice all day long with a light
rain both nights. We had long since passed the glory of witnessing the
blooming of the Dogwood and the Redbud trees, but were now enjoying the full bloom of summer. Flowers of different varieties and blooming bushes lined just about every house and filled their flowerbeds.
When I first moved to the mountains, the woods and the greenery were
just starting to come to life, but now the trees were full of leaves and
the vegetation was at full throttle. There was not a bare spot between
the trees anywhere.

Sunday morning, everybody gathered at our house to prepare for the
big bash at the *Blackhawk Meeting Grounds* as Billy so aptly put it. He
promised the mood to be festive and the food to be abundant. He swore it
would be an event we would never forget. He guaranteed nobody would
leave hungry and when they did leave they would go with just a little bit
more appreciation of the Cherokee way of life.

He had a semi-captive audience. Dennis and Jack sat on the sofa listening intensely, while Aunt Edie, who had arrived two days earlier with

Uncle Bill for their promised visit—threw in a few words. Uncle Bill was asleep in the recliner as usual and Claire was upstairs doing whatever it is that mothers do with their children.

"Enough is enough!" I yelled across the room to him, as he was just about to entertain the group some more. "Come on over here and help me with these eggs, please."

Billy said something about a wife before he joined me in the kitchen.

"I heard that!" I hissed. "If you were talking about me, you can forget it. I can't even cook."

"You two stop it!" Mom fussed, standing at the counter behind us frying up chicken in one of those big, electric deep fry-things. "Just boil the eggs for the potato salad, and try to behave yourselves or get out of my kitchen!"

"See," Billy leaned over and whispered. "You've done gone and ruffled her feathers."

"Just shut up and help me," I groaned. "How do you fix boiled eggs? I know you have to do it just right or they turn out gross."

He reached down into the cabinet by my legs and pulled out a pot, filled it with water from the sink faucet in front of us, then sat it on the stove.

"Just turn on the gas," he instructed. "You do know how to do that, don't you?"

I looked at him and then looked at the stove. Then I looked back at him. I couldn't let him know how bad my cooking skills were, so I reached over and turned one of the knobs. A flame ignited on the front left burner under the pot, and I breathed a sigh of relief.

"You got lucky," Billy laughed. "I can tell you're lost in the kitchen."

"I do all right!" I boasted, as I picked up the first egg, cracked it open on the corner of the pot and then let the contents drop in the water. I laid down the shell, picked up another egg and started to do it again when I noticed Billy and Mom were standing behind me, laughing their fool brains out. They thought I was hilarious.

I turned around, still holding the egg in my hand, and said, "Do we have a problem here?"

"No, of course not," Mom replied. "But I think it might be better if you left the egg in the shell, honey. That is what I would do."

This brought the house down. Even Uncle Bill woke up.

I regained my composure and said, "For your information, this is the way the rich boil eggs. I saw them do it on TV."

Billy threw his hands up in the air. "Well, what does that tell you folks?"

He shooed me aside and started all over, explaining the process as he went along. He refilled the pot with water, put the eggs in and waited for the water to come to a boil. He let them boil for exactly three minutes and then tuned off the burner.

"Now, we will let them sit for fifteen minutes, and then they will be ready to peel." He looked at me and grinned. He pulled a colander out of another cabinet and sat it in the sink. While the eggs were *resting*, he went to the refrigerator and removed the mustard, mayonnaise, pickle relish and a bottle of vinegar. He took the pot of potatoes Mom had boiling on the stove and poured them in the colander. Twenty minutes later he had a bowl of potato salad sitting on the counter ready to take to the party.

"Where did you learn how to do that?" I asked. I was impressed with his cooking ability, and thought he would make someone a fine husband.

"In our tribe all the children were taught how to cook," he replied. "We were taught to hunt, fish, and prepare your own meals. It was a lesson in survival we all had to learn."

"Well, fortunately," I smiled, "I grew up with a mother who did all that for me."

"And look at you now," he said, as he turned to Mom. "No offense Mom, but your daughter would be in a world of hurt if she had to eat her own cooking for a week. She would starve to death."

Everyone thought that was just hilarious. Aunt Edie got up off the sofa and came into the kitchen and put her arm around my shoulder. "But she has so many other good qualities," she smiled at me. "Not everybody has to be a good cook, do they Jesse?" Bless her heart. Aunt Edie was always the first one to rally to the aid of the under dog.

"That's right," I agreed.

"This fall when I take my week off to go hunting, I'm taking you with me," Billy said. "We'll camp in the woods for a week, kill our own food, and I'll teach you how to cook. You will love it. Trust me. It will be fun."

"I live for the moment," I sarcastically replied. I hated to tell Billy, but this was just not going to happen.

COLE ARRIVED AT NOON, and by then the food Mom wanted to take had been prepared and we were ready to go to the party. Claire loaded the kids into the van while we helped Mom carry the food. Jack and Dennis talked Uncle Bill and Aunt Edie into riding with them in the Camaro—which wasn't hard because Uncle Bill had a fondness for high perfor-mance cars. Dad's truck and my Jeep had been repaired and returned a few days before, but I still couldn't bring myself to get in either one. I rode in Billy's truck with him and Cole.

Once Billy pulled out of the driveway and was heading down South River Road, he reached down under his seat and came up with a box wrapped in newspaper from the comics section and tied with a red ribbon.

"What's this?" I asked, as he handed it to me. "What did I do to de-serve a present?"

"After the trip to Poquoson, Cole and I had a long talk," Billy began.

"Wait a minute," I butted in. "I know I missed work this past week, but that doesn't mean I'm not coming back. So, if this is a retirement present, you can just keep it. You can't get rid of me that easy."

"Chill out," Billy demanded. "Like I was going to say, after your or-deal in the woods and the way you handled yourself with the Carroltons... well, that took a lot of guts. You're a strong `ge ya, and we know it."

"Billy, get to the point!" I yelled.

Cole leaned over and said, "We came to the conclusion that if you could survive this ordeal you wouldn't let anything stop you now. You've had a taste of blood and now you're hooked. You've got that look in your eyes. Doesn't she, Billy?"

"What look?" I asked.

"The look of someone that has been exposed to the evils of the world and now you want to do something about it," Billy answered.

"Unless we're wrong," Cole added. "If you're going to continue doing this kind of work, you have to learn how to do it right. The best way to do that is through training. There are classes at the college you can take and when you finish you can apply for your private investigator's license. There's a one day class you have to take to be able to get a concealed weapons permit, so I won't have to haul you off to jail for carrying that gun in your purse."

"For your information," I said. "I don't have a gun in my purse."

"Yeah," Billy whispered. "We went back and found your pea-shooter."

"Excuse me, it is not a pea-shooter. It's a great gun. I want it back. Who has it?"

"It's at my house," Billy said. "You can pick it up when you get back to work. Get it, take it home and clean it, and then store it some place safe. You need a real gun if you're going to do battle with the criminal elements that are out there now. I want you to..."

"Can I open my present now, or do the two of you have more plans for my future I need to hear first?"

"Go ahead," Cole answered. "Billy and I went in half on your present, and we're both going to help you practice using it."

My curiosity peaked as I tore open the present. Inside the case was a Glock 9MM. I recognized the handgun immediately. Billy and Cole both had one exactly the same.

"It's beautiful!" I exclaimed, turning it over in my hands and then looking down the barrel. "Wow! This is so cool!"

Cole reached under the seat and came up with another present. "This is for you just in case you'd rather wear it instead of carrying it in your purse." The package contained a holster that was threaded through a leather belt, and it was just my size!

"You guys are too much," I cried, leaning over to give both of them a kiss on the cheek. "So, when is my first lesson?"

"Today," Billy said. "One of the activities planned is target shooting."

"I told you," Cole said. "When his family throws a party, they really throw a party. They will have games for the kids, dancing, horseback riding, and much, much more. At the end of the day we will sit around the camp-fire and smoke the peace pipe."

"Is he joking about the peace pipe?" I asked Billy, as he laughed and shook his head. "Forget it, I have had enough of the evil weed."

Cole looked at me skeptically. "I think this falls under the category of... *things I do not need to know*."

BILLY'S PARENTS owned a large, sprawling ranch on a hundred acres of land south of Charlottesville. He explained that his great grandparents bought the land when there wasn't much in the county but a couple of farms. Charlottesville was the size of Stanardsville.

"They lived off the land and eventually were buried in the family graveyard, like the rest of us will be when we die."

He said his folks had divided out sections for their children. But so far, Daniel, Robert, and Jonathan were the only ones that still lived on the property.

"Ruth and I built our house when we first got married, but now the only ones who ever use it are the boys when they come for the weekend."

"You mean to tell me you have a home on this beautiful land and you don't even live there? It just sits empty?"

"Maybe when I decide to retire I'll move back," he sadly proclaimed.

We followed the long graveled road deep into the woods until we came to a clearing filled with cars. In the background sat a house the size of a shopping mall. I had never seen a house this big in real life, and couldn't wait to go inside and have a look around.

"Oh, wow!" I shouted with glee. "This is magnificent, Billy. I've never seen anything quite like it. It's so... so... big."

"Well, it's been added onto a few times," he explained, as he parked the truck behind one of the cars. "Chief Standing Deer always insisted on having plenty room for the whole family."

"I would say so," I replied, as I crawled out of the truck and took a deep breath. "The air smells so good. I love the mountains. There's something special about living here that no one can appreciate until they do."

"You're absolutely right," Mom said, as she walked up to us. "Like your dad said when we first moved here... *this is God's country*."

She pulled Billy aside and I heard her ask him, "Did you give her the present, yet?"

"Yes, he did," I said. "I take a few days off from work and everybody treats me like I'm a china doll. I won't break, and I'm not going to sit up against a wall just because life got a little rough."

"Of course you're not," Aunt Edie came to my rescue. "You're one hell of a tough guy but even tough guys have mothers that worry about them. Trust me... I know." She gave me a wink and locked her arm in mine.

"I guess you do," I murmured. "You have more courage than I could ever hope to have." We both knew what I was talking about.

Uncle Bill was the last one to walk up as we gathered together for our assault on the party.

"I'm hungry," he said, rubbing his eyes. "When is this big ho-down going to start?"

"Uncle Bill," I slapped him on the back, "You've got to stop sleeping so much or you're going to miss out on a lot of stuff."

"Ignore him," Aunt Edie whispered in my ear. "He can't help it. It's those pills he has to take. They make him fall asleep at the drop of a hat."

We descended on the party that was already in full force in the back yard of the house. A line of tables set up under a canopy of open tents were loaded with food. Kids were playing all over the place while the adults milled around in circles. The men in our group were given the chore of carrying the food to the tables. The rest of us huddled together, laughing and carrying Claire's kids. As usual, Aunt Edie always had a joke or some wild story to tell us. Even in her own time of personal tragedy she could still make us feel good.

"Jesse," she whispered to me. "Your mom tells me you've got both these guys falling all over you. Which one are you going to marry? She told me you would be getting married soon, and I was just wondering which one was the lucky guy."

"Mom, you're at it again!" I screamed. I looked back at Aunt Edie. "Mom is crazy. Marriage is the last thing on my mind."

"Not from what I heard," Claire chimed in. "Mom told us all about it."

"Excuse me," I stated. "I need to talk to my mother." I gave Mom the evil eye and pulled her off to the side. I was going to get her straight if it was the last thing I did.

"Mom, you've got to stop telling everybody I'm getting married," I whispered to her. "It's not true and it's embarrassing."

"Honey," she sighed. "I'm telling everybody what I've been told."

"What are you talking about?" I asked her.

Just as she was about to speak, Billy walked up with his parents.

"Mom and Dad," he said to his parents, "I want you to meet my other mom—Minnie Watson. You know Jesse and Cole." He motioned to us, as he made introductions. "And this is Claire—Jesse's sister—and Claire's two kids—Benny and Carrie. This is Jesse's brother Jack, and his partner, Dennis." He pointed to them. "Over here we have Jesse's Aunt Edie and Uncle Bill." With the introductions made, he proudly turned to his parents and said, "These are my parents, Chief Standing Deer and his wife, Sarah Blackhawk."

Chief Standing Deer was dressed like one of the tribal chiefs I had seen on television many times. He had a massive animal fur slung over his shoulders even though it was seventy degrees outside. The outlandish feathered headdress he wore enhanced his tanned and wrinkled face. The feathers started at the top of his head and extended down to the his heels. He wore tan suede pants with fringed strings down the side and his shirt was muslin cotton. His chest was covered with the proud beads and feathers interwoven in a pattern that only an Indian would understand.

Sarah Blackhawk was dressed in a simple, yellow sundress. She was the wife of an Indian chief, yet she still dressed and acted like the person she was—a white woman. She was the mother of this clan and proud of it. Even if she was a little bit different it was obvious she was not going to let anybody try to change that, or her position in this family.

Mom tipped her head, as if to bow before the chief, then stepped forward, gave Sarah a hug and said, "I'm glad to finally meet both of you. Why, I feel like we're family already!"

"I am so glad to hear it and so glad you could come to our home," Sarah broke the embrace but still had her arm around Mom's shoulders as they walked away. She turned back to the rest of us and said, "Please...

everybody have some food and enjoy the festivities." She looked directly at Claire. "Over by the picnic tables we have a group of ladies in charge of taking care of the children if you'd like some time for yourself."

I HEARD MOM SAY, as the two of them walked off, "We have so much to talk about. Aren't our kids wonderful?"

She's at it again. By the time this party is over, Mom will have Billy and me, or Cole and me at the altar, ready to say wedding vows. I had to do something fast.

"Hey, Billy," I motioned to him. "Go get my mom before she does something crazy."

"She's fine. Don't worry," he said. "She is having a good time."

"No, she's not!" I demanded. "She's been talking about all kinds of weird crap all morning and if you don't go get her away from your mother, she'll have your mom helping her pick out baby names for our kids by the end of the day. If you know what I mean."

"Oh, Jesse," he grinned and put his arm around my shoulder. "Let her have some fun. I'm not worried. Are you afraid she will embarrass you?"

"Yes, I am," I mumbled under my breath. "You don't know my mom."

Being with Billy's family was like being at home only it was a little different. If we were at home, for our 4th of July celebration we would cookout and socialize, dressed in shorts and spraying bug spray everywhere, and at night we'd set off a few fireworks. But we were dealing with a whole different culture of people. We saw a side of life we had never seen... and we loved it. Almost everyone was dressed in feathers and buckskin, or some other form of Indian clothing, except a few others and us. They played games, ran races, rode horses, and did almost anything you could think of to have fun. Not once did I see a fight, or a wife and husband off to the side arguing. The warmth of these people and the love they shared for each other was astounding. They were proud of their heritage and weren't afraid to express their feelings. By the end of the day we all rallied around the campfire to pray and give thanks, while watching an enormous display of fireworks.

For the first time in a long while, I felt relaxed and at ease with my-self. I was happy with my life. As I sat by the campfire, I couldn't help but think about everything that had happened to me. I grew up in a good home and lived a fairly normal life—however drab it had seemed at times. I've had my share of trials and tribulations, but in the end it was those experi-ences that put me on the road to a new life. I had my family, my new friends, and a boss I adored. What more could you ask? Maybe one day Cole will get his head out of his ass and I'll be able to trust him again.

Still holding my hand, Billy leaned over and whispered to me, "We've got a big day ahead of us come Tuesday. I've been working on this stalk-ing case all by myself. Are you going to be ready?"

"You can bet the bank on it!" I answered, my thoughts drifting. "I was just thinking about the Hudgins family. What do you think will happen to Rose now that her mom's been arrested for Helen's murder? What about Jay and his dad? You think they'll get much jail time for trying to cover it up and for what they did to me and Rose?"

"Forget about it for now, Jesse," Billy whispered. "You'll have plenty of time to think about it when they go to trial. As far as Rose is concerned she's a big girl. With some good therapy she will recover."

"So, you can put it out of your mind just like that?"

"You have to," he replied. "Or you'll go crazy. Not to change the subject, but did your Mom get around to telling you that Claire and the kids are going to move here?"

I looked over at Claire who was ensconced in a conversation with Chief Standing Deer. It was strange seeing her sitting on the ground with her legs crossed, swaying to the beat of the drums being played by one of the Blackhawk boys. She seemed so much happier now that she was back with us.

"Where's she going to live?" I asked, wondering if she was going to move in with us.

"We've discussed the possibility of her renting my house," he replied. "I just hate to see the house sit empty and I'm not planning on moving back in any time soon."

I leaned over and kissed him on the cheek. "Billy, you're a good man."

Cole grunted. "What about me? I'm pretty wonderful, too!"

"Yes, you are," I kissed his cheek. I had decided to forgive his trespasses and give our relationship another go at it, if he was still interested. I leaned over and whispered in his ear, "How about later on, you and I try to get this romance off to a new start?"

He wrapped his arms around me and gave me a deep, passionate kiss right in front of everybody.

He smiled that big, beautiful smile of his and said, "Does that answer your question?"

To be continued...

ACKNOWLEDGMENTS

I WOULD LIKE TO EXTEND A SPECIAL THANKS to Diane Reid for her help, honesty, and encouragement while writing this book. You were always there with a kind word and a pat on the back just when I needed it. Warm blessings go to my daughter and dearest friend, Wendy Kantsios, for giving me the courage to fulfill my life-long dream of writing a novel without worrying about what others thought. Applause to my son, Tommy Mullen, for not going crazy as he relentlessly taught me how to get started using computer software. It took a lot of repeat instructions. Thanks and love to my husband of twenty-five years, Tom, for putting up with the temperamental rantings of a writer.

I would like to acknowledge Larry Mayhem (Private Investigator, Stanardsville, Va.) and Bill Kerr (NYPD, New York) for taking the time to answer my questions about the law. Thank you.

A warm thanks and much love to Vanessa Rose Holder (Volunteer Office Assistant and friend). I will never forget the day we spent writing poetry (I'm a joke, but you have real talent), and laughing until we cried. I still have it all on tape.

When funds were low (because I did not have a *real* job), I reached out to family and friends for help. It was through their generosity that I was able to keep my writing afloat. A heart-felt thanks to Keith & Barbara Wynn (Stanardsville, Va.); Tommy & Brandy Garrow (Suwanee, Georgia); Wendy & George Kantsios (Carrollton, Va.); Dolores & Fred Lamn (Williamsburg, Va.); Jan Nesbitt (Williamsburg, Va.); and last, but not least, my mother, Minnie Crumpler (Newport News, Va.)—Three hours away, but always in my heart.

I couldn't have done it without you!

ORDER THIS BOOK FOR A FRIEND

AFTON RIDGE PUBLISHING
P.O. Box 162
Stanardsville, Virginia 22973

Price: $24.95
Sales Tax @ 4.5% (for VA residents only): $1.12
S&H: $3.95

Total: $30.02

TALK TO THE AUTHOR:

E-mail address: AftonRidge@aol.com

LOOK FOR ANN MULLEN'S NEXT BOOK:

South River Incident

A JESSE WATSON MYSTERY